COVER UP

OTHER TITLES BY
CLAIR M. POULSON:

I'll Find You

Relentless

Lost and Found

Conflict of Interest

Runaway

Mirror Image

Blind Side

Evidence

Don't Cry Wolf

COVER UP

a novel

CLAIR M. POULSON

Covenant Communications, Inc.

Covenant

In memory of my good friend and colleague Judge Floyd Nielsen. His sudden and unexpected passing impacted my life in ways I could not have imagined. I feel a deep personal loss and will continue to for years to come. Judge Nielsen was a kind and gentle man who was sincerely loved and respected by the people he served.

PROLOGUE

The Island of Kauai
The First Day of January

The man speaking was grossly overweight, with sagging jowls, small dark eyes, and prematurely gray hair. Fleming Parker, at forty-one, was a powerful man within the corporation he was bleeding dry. His eyes darted around the room, stopping only momentarily on each of the co-conspirators.

"About the next few days, here is what we need to get done. Royce, get those contracts signed, and don't, whatever you do, let Lauren know how you've changed them," he instructed. "Since she both wrote and negotiated them, she'd notice the changes immediately."

"It'll be done," Royce Cantrell said. "She's finished her work on them. She has no reason to ever look at them again."

"Good." Fleming then spoke to each of the remaining people in the room, reminding them of exactly what they needed to accomplish before they could finalize their plans and make ready for their flight from justice to lives of luxury awaiting them in foreign lands.

Finally, he looked around the room, and even though the blinds were drawn, he acted nervous. When he spoke again, his voice was so low the others almost had to strain to hear him. "Let me make this perfectly clear. We are in this together, and if any of you get cold feet at this point or in any way jeopardize the success of this operation, intentionally or otherwise, you will pay the ultimate price."

There was a murmur throughout the group. Heads nodded in assent. Only one person spoke after the chilling warning.

"We all agreed to that up front," Royce reminded Fleming with a nervous laugh. "No one is going to take any chances."

There was a murmur of assent.

Fleming nodded his head, and his great jowls shook with the effort. "I have only one worry, really," he began blandly. "Some of you hold a certain fondness for some of our colleagues." All the heads nodded like puppets on strings. "I believe we have been sufficiently careful that in the few weeks it will take to finish our work, our secret will remain just that—a secret." He paused for effect. "We have been *very* careful, and I'm quite certain that no one will figure out what we've done until we're gone. But if by some stroke of genius or dumb luck someone does figure it out, there can be no squeamish stomachs on the part of any of you as to the fate of such an unlucky and foolish person."

More nodding. More murmuring. Fleming smiled—never a pretty sight—and on this lovely day in one of the most beautiful parts of the globe, his smile was particularly unsightly and out of place. But it had the effect of solidifying the support of the small group of people in the room who had pledged themselves in support of the cunning plan.

"All right. Tomorrow we'll all be back at our desks as usual. And please, try to act normal," Fleming stressed. "Don't give anyone a reason to suspect anything. And leave the way you came, one at a time. I don't want any two of you on the same flight back to Honolulu. And of course, this meeting never happened."

CHAPTER 1

She might have missed it on a normal working day. She almost wished she had. If she hadn't decided to sacrifice part of this gorgeous January Saturday to get caught up on some work she'd left unfinished the day before, she probably would have never stumbled onto what was happening. Lauren's stomach churned, and she wondered if what she had just discovered was going to make her physically ill. It was more horrible than she could have ever imagined.

Lauren Olcott loved the company she worked for, and she enjoyed the people she worked with. Paradise Pharmaceuticals had grown into a fairly large company, and it was now doing business outside of Hawaii. Based right in sunny Honolulu, it had exceeded all expectations. Already several new drugs developed by the company had been approved by the Food and Drug Administration, and sales were soaring throughout the country. Some lucrative distribution contracts were already in place, and more were pending as final testing was now taking place on additional drugs that had been developed by their brilliant team of scientists. And research at the company was moving steadily forward. In addition to medicine, the company had even begun to produce a line of cosmetics developed from plants that grew locally in tropical Hawaii. Branches of the company were to be established worldwide over the next five years, with one in Los Angeles already in the planning stages.

Though Lauren was only twenty-six, she was rising fast through the ranks and had been given both heavy responsibilities and a great deal of trust. She had looked forward to a long and fulfilling career at Paradise Pharmaceuticals.

Until an hour ago.

When she'd arrived at the office, her computer had booted up normally—at first. But as soon as she'd opened the contract template she'd created, everything froze. She'd tried to restart the computer, but in less than a minute it had shut itself off completely.

"Fine," she had muttered. "Now what am I supposed to do?"

The template was on her hard drive, so she couldn't access it anywhere else. She had made a backup file, of course, but she'd loaned the disc to someone else in the department, and he had said the disc was bad. Unfortunately, she'd forgotten to make a new copy. Knowing a tech specialist couldn't look at it until Monday, Lauren briefly considered leaving her work undone. But a thought dawned on her. *Of course! Royce has copies of the contracts on his computer. I'll just pull those up and use them to create the new contract. He won't mind if I do a little breaking and entering. After all, he's the one who needs this by Monday morning.*

Lauren closed up her office, then located Royce's key. He'd told her about his hiding place many months ago when he'd taken a sick day and had needed her to access something that was filed in his cabinet. Now she entered his office and made herself comfortable at his massive desk, enjoying the luxury of the setting.

But when she tracked down an old contract on Royce's hard drive, she wished she'd never even come to the office that day.

Lauren now sat holding her head in her hands. The cool breeze of the air conditioning blew gently across her back, but it failed to cool the fever burning in her head. She couldn't hold back the tears. They were from both shock and sadness. Then from bitterness and anger.

She pulled a Kleenex from a box and wiped her eyes. After wadding it up and throwing it in the wastebasket, she again studied the computer screen in front of her. Then she examined the printed pages on the desk, hoping beyond hope that by some miracle she wouldn't see what she'd found earlier. But there was to be no miracle this morning. Large sums of money had been cleverly drained from the company, and contracts that had held promise of great wealth for Paradise Pharmaceuticals had been compromised. Unless the dark secrets were exposed very soon, Paradise Pharmaceuticals would find itself bankrupt, destroyed by the unholy greed of a few people in the company. She sat still for a few minutes and listened to the creaking and groaning of the large building, hoping that none of those greedy people, whoever they were, would show up here before she finished and could get out of the building. She had a terrible feeling that those who were behind the crimes would go to any length to protect their guilty secret.

Fearful and alert, Lauren studied the contracts for several more minutes, then began to work rapidly, her anger driving her on. She would never have believed that her own boss, Royce Cantrell, a senior vice president, and his good friend Fleming Parker, the chief financial officer, would have committed the crimes she'd just discovered. But the revolting evidence lay in front of her. She was especially appalled that Royce could be involved in such a scheme. She'd worked closely with him for the past six months, and she had found him to be quite pleasant. She'd written many contracts under his supervision and negotiated the terms contained in them personally. Even though she'd always believed Royce had the future of the company at heart, the subtle changes that she'd discovered in recent contracts were fatal. Quite by accident she had learned the horrible truth about a man she had both liked and trusted.

She'd been able to identify Royce Cantrell and Fleming Parker as principal parties to the scam, but she knew there were others. It would take more time than she had right now to dig deeper into Royce's records to discover their identities, if that could even be done. She felt terrible as names and faces passed suspiciously through her mind. *Who can I trust to share this awful knowledge with?* she asked herself. Who among her friends and associates were helping those two as they bled Paradise Pharmaceuticals of its profits, and at the same time, were attempting to cover up the deceit so that others would have no idea what was happening until it was too late? She wasn't sure she wanted to know.

It was a misspelled word that had tipped her off. Lauren took great pride in her work, so she always spell-checked it and had an assistant look it over. Yet the document she had accessed on Royce's computer contained a blatant typo, and its presence in the contract had caused her to read the entire thing more carefully. Then she'd reviewed other contracts and found more subtle but equally alarming alterations in them. In each instance, she'd personally gone over every word of each contract with representatives from the companies they pertained to, with both parties' lawyers present. But the final documents had been delivered for signatures to Royce and Fleming, who personally attended to the signing of every contract. As Lauren could now see, the final contracts contained language that minutely changed the payment terms so that money could be skillfully funneled off and sent to places unknown.

It was all more than Lauren could stand, and she had to suppress the urge to scream. But she forced herself to concentrate, to locate relevant documents on the computer and save them to a couple of backup discs. She worked quickly, and her nerves were so keyed up that every sound in the large, empty office building was beginning to make her jump. Again she wondered what would happen if someone found her here looking at this information. She didn't want to find out.

Lauren soon was accessing the company financials. She was suddenly grateful for the corporate finance and accounting classes she'd been required to take in college so she could make sense of all the information. She was also grateful that Royce, apparently wanting to show off his technological prowess, had once shown her how to bypass Paradise's computer security systems. That had been shortly after she was made director of marketing, probably before this scam had even been conceived. Now Lauren had solid evidence against Fleming Parker, one person in the company she'd never liked, although he'd never given her reason not to trust him. As the chief financial officer, Fleming controlled the money and the entire accounting system in the company, and putting all her information together, Lauren could see that he'd carefully moved large amounts of money to offshore accounts. *Flat out stolen it, is what he's done,* Lauren thought grimly as she examined the various documents. She copied the records of his theft and then searched in Royce Cantrell's filing cabinets for signed copies of the altered contracts. It only took her a few minutes to confirm that the documents were in fact the ones that had been signed by unsuspecting senior officials of trusting companies Paradise Pharmaceuticals was doing business with. She made hard copies as well as scanned copies of all of them and returned the originals to where she'd found them.

A sound pricked Lauren's ears, and she jumped with fright. She was certain that a door had just been closed somewhere on this floor, and her heart raced. *Who else would be coming here today?* she wondered as she gathered up the files and discs and stuffed them into her briefcase. Another door closed. She could tell that it was not too far up the hallway from Royce's office. Swiftly she shut down the computer and looked for a place to hide in case someone came in. There was a small closet near the door that contained only a few cleaning supplies. It would be terribly uncomfortable, but it was her only choice. She shut off the lights, squeezed into the cramped space with her briefcase, and waited, her heart in her throat and perspiration stinging her eyes.

Footsteps in the hallway drew near. Two people were approaching, and they were talking softly. Only when they stopped outside the office door could she identify the voices, both men from the company whom she knew well. One was Mr. Cantrell, and the other was one of Fleming's assistants, a young accountant by the name of Leroy Provost. She'd dated Leroy for quite some time before her current serious boyfriend, Dexter Drake, had entered her life. Leroy had an intense personality, and his possessiveness had eventually led Lauren to break up with him. But she still liked Leroy and hoped that his presence here with Royce was not an indication that he was involved in the scam.

Though she recognized the voices, she could only make out a word here and there. Leroy sounded agitated, while Royce seemed to be trying to soothe him. She was quite certain at one point that Leroy said something about a lot of money. And Royce, answering calmly, had included the words *caught* and *suspicious*. The door to the office opened, and she held her breath. The light switch clicked, and slivers of light seeped through the cracks around the door to her cramped hiding place.

"Are you sure Lauren's car was in the parking lot?" she distinctly heard Royce ask.

"It was there," Leroy said with conviction. "But she's clearly not in the building. I suppose that Dexter Drake picked her up here and that they went somewhere together for the weekend."

There was jealousy in his voice, but that didn't surprise her. He'd asked her out again just a couple of weeks ago, and she'd firmly but politely informed him that she was only dating Dexter now. He'd been crestfallen and had said, "If things don't work out, I'll still be here."

"Well, let's go," Royce said, a touch of anger in his voice. "I actually expected Lauren to be here. She was supposed to have finished a contract I will need Monday, but it was unfinished when she left last evening, and it's not on my desk now. I really thought she'd come in and finish it today."

"Maybe she'll do it tomorrow," Leroy said, and the slivers of light disappeared from Royce's closet. A moment later the office door closed.

Lauren eased herself from the closet and attempted to stretch the painful kinks from her back and legs. Then she waited while sounds of walking, talking, and gently closing doors continued for several minutes. Even after she was convinced that the men had left, she waited another fifteen minutes before leaving Royce's office, briefcase in hand, and heading for the elevator. She couldn't quit thinking about Leroy, becoming more certain every minute that he, as hard as it was to believe, was one of the thieves. And she felt more ill than ever, for Leroy was basically a nice guy, or so she'd thought, but now he frightened her, as did Royce.

Even when she was behind the wheel of her car a few minutes later she didn't feel safe. She felt like unseen but prying eyes were watching her every movement. She attempted to console herself with the fact that she had the evidence of what she'd found locked in the trunk of her car. What she didn't know was what she was going to do about it. That would come later, she decided, after the shock had worn off and she could think more clearly.

Lauren didn't drive directly home. Instead she drove toward a beach. She'd put on her swimsuit under her clothes that morning in hopes she would have some time to enjoy the ocean. Now she doubted she'd enjoy herself as much as she had planned. Retrieving an umbrella and a beach mat from her trunk, Lauren headed across the warm, dry sand to an area that was less crowded, hoping she'd be able to think more clearly there. In spite of the stress of her situation, she was already feeling less tense as she listened to the constant rushing of the ocean waves. Settling herself comfortably, she closed her eyes and tried to clear her mind for a moment.

Her thoughts wandered to her past. She had been doing that increasingly, it seemed, and now more than ever she really wished she could talk to her mother. She was sure her mother would have advice for her. Somehow even the thought of her was comforting, but Lauren really wanted to just pick up the phone and call her. *Too bad I ruined that chance years ago,* she thought. *I thought I didn't need my family, but . . . oh, I do miss them.* She shook her head slightly. *Today is not the day for that. Now, focus on the task at hand.*

When she had made all those copies at the office, she hadn't known exactly what she was going to do with them. She still didn't. But she knew she had to do something. As much as feeling an ethical responsibility to uncover the fraud occurring at Paradise, Lauren also felt a personal need to do so. Though she had only worked at the company for three years, she felt that it was now an integral part of her life. Joining the company in its infancy, when Lauren herself was fresh out of college, she had worked hard and proven her abilities time and again. She had both paralegal training and a bachelor's degree in marketing; it was an unusual combination, but one that was valued in the young but growing corporation. Everyone agreed she deserved the director of marketing position awarded her just six months ago. Part of the reason was undoubtedly her suggestion to branch away from pharmaceuticals into the cosmetics and skin-care areas.

When she had heard of the remarkable skin-smoothing properties of certain herbal products that the research team had happened on accidentally the previous year, Lauren had seen the potential for tremendous growth at Paradise. To expand their market so rapidly, especially given how young the company was, was risky. And aggressively promoting the idea to her superiors had been gutsy. But the president of the company had quickly latched onto the idea, and Lauren was given full credit. Lauren realized now that it was this very expansion that gave Fleming, Royce, and the other conspirators an opportunity to implement their crime. With so much going on, it had to be easier to slip a few things past company officers and internal auditors. Clearly some people had let their greed get the best of them.

Even in the warm sun, she shivered, considering how much the company stood to lose if the scheme went through as apparently planned. The biggest contract Paradise had yet to see was just a few weeks away. It was a cosmetics contract, one that would give a company in L.A. an opportunity to license Paradise's special formulas. It was worth millions of dollars in instant revenue alone. The private correspondence Lauren had uncovered, in combination with her own reasoning, suggested this was to be the final contract Royce and Fleming doctored before silently disappearing.

Lauren decided to swim for a while, feeling a need to do something—anything. Never straying too far out, she tried several different strokes, then eventually just sat near the water in the wet sand, letting the smallest waves splash up against her.

Somehow, Royce and Fleming, and probably Leroy, had to be exposed. The documents she found implied there might be other conspirators. They had to be identified as well. And yet, even if that happened, it was clearly too late to save the company from suffering serious damage, although it might still be saved from total collapse. *But how should I do it?* she wondered. She certainly didn't want to draw attention and peril to herself.

Her first impulse was to share the desperate secrets she'd discovered with her boyfriend, Dexter. But she wasn't sure she wanted to do that; it might put him at risk. If Royce and Fleming were villainous enough to divert the hard work and profits of so many other people to their own selfish use, who knew what they might do to anyone who exposed them. Dexter was a junior partner in a prestigious Honolulu law firm, and he did a lot of work for Paradise Pharmaceuticals. She knew he would be as sick over what she'd discovered as she was. No, she didn't want to tell him, at least not yet. If she could keep him from being involved in the whistle-blowing that had to occur, it would be so much the better.

Finally she decided she had better inform the president and CEO of the company, Milo Thurman. She was certain he wouldn't be a part of the scandal himself. He was in his early sixties, was in excellent health, and was a man of vision who never looked back. His background included a master's degree in business as well as a doctorate in pharmacy, followed by years of hard work—first as a pharmacist, then for a major pharmaceutical company, then as the founder of this company. Milo spoke of Paradise in such glowing, enthusiastic terms, there was no way he'd do anything to hurt it! He would be devastated when he learned what two of his most trusted men were doing. She hated to be the one to break it to him. But he had to know.

By the time she finally made her way back to her car, she had a plan. It could work. It had to work. It would avoid putting herself at risk, for as much as she loved her job and the company she worked for, she loved her life more. She could pretend to be as surprised as everyone else when the corruption was brought to light and the perpetrators exposed.

After driving to a public library across the city, Lauren entered, clutching tightly the briefcase containing the incriminating evidence. She quickly invented a name and used it to check in and reserve a computer. Then she sat down and began to work. She began by creating an e-mail address, using still another invented name. Then she typed a short but detailed message, outlining what she'd learned that day about the fraud and how to locate that information. Next she attached the incriminating files to an e-mail and, after drawing a deep breath, sent it to two people whose e-mail addresses she knew by heart. The first was her friend Billie Maio, the personal secretary to the president, Milo Thurman. She wanted to send it to Milo directly, but couldn't recall his e-mail address. She trusted that Billie would get it to him. She also sent it to Ken Fujimoto, the senior partner in the law firm Dexter worked for. Fortunately his address was easy to remember. With any luck, both messages would be opened first thing Monday morning, someone else could find the evidence she now possessed, and she could stay out of the turmoil it was bound to cause.

Lauren spent several minutes deleting her newly invented e-mail address and cleaning the computer she was working on of any evidence that she'd used it. That done, she went home, taking pains to hide the incriminating file beneath some clothes in her dresser. On Monday she'd leave work early and get it to a safety-deposit box. She had earlier wondered if she should just destroy it, but for some reason that didn't seem like a good idea, even though she hoped that others would now find the evidence for themselves and she'd never need to use her copies.

That evening, Lauren went out with a few girlfriends, wishing she could be with Dexter, but knowing he was busy all weekend. Maybe that was just as well, she decided, for she didn't want to be tempted to tell him what she'd learned and what she'd done. She had to stay anonymous. She had to stay alive!

CHAPTER 2

Maybe it was just her imagination, but Lauren thought she sensed a growing tension at work as the week progressed. It might be that it was only she who was worried; certainly by Friday her gut was in a constant uncomfortable stir. Not a word had been spoken about the fraud that she knew existed and that others by now should know about. But there was no evidence that it was known by anyone, not even among the hierarchy. Even her friend Billie Maio, secretary to the CEO, had appeared to be unaffected, and yet Lauren couldn't imagine that she hadn't read the e-mail. That caused her to worry more. She wondered now if Billie was a party to the crime and had withheld the information from Milo. She hated herself for even thinking that. Then she had an even worse thought. What if she had passed it on, but Milo himself was stealing from his own company? He was the one person who seemed unusually tense this week. She had been sure of his innocence, but by now she couldn't help wondering. She even wondered if both Milo and Billie were involved in Fleming and Royce's plan.

Both times Lauren had talked to Dexter he hadn't mentioned a word about any fraud or even an impending scandal. So no one had mentioned it to him. Of course, it was likely that the senior partner in the firm was keeping the information close to his chest while a quiet investigation was proceeding. She hoped that was the case. Lauren knew that she was probably far more paranoid than she needed to be, but she let the thought slip in that Dexter's boss, Ken Fujimoto, might also be part of the conspiracy.

Her immediate boss, Royce Cantrell, seemed to be his usual self, and that surprised her the most. He couldn't possibly know that his dark secret was out, she decided, and not display some sort of emotion that she could pick up on. Fleming Parker was certainly acting no different than usual. Of course, she reasoned, whoever Ken and Milo might have assigned the investigation to, if one was even proceeding, they wouldn't let Royce or Fleming know until they were ready to have them arrested.

The evidence she'd collected now lay safely tucked away in a bank vault. Every day, at the close of work, she felt drawn to that bank, tempted to pull the evidence out and present it to someone who would do something. Maybe she should tell the police, she'd thought on several occasions. But fear for her safety prevented her from making any further disclosures.

Friday night, Lauren had a date with Dexter. After a movie, they ate a leisurely and late dinner. Dexter seemed especially affectionate. He held her hand whenever he had the chance, pulled her head against his shoulder, and stroked her long, wavy, dark brown hair. It was wonderfully relaxing after the tension she'd felt all week. She turned her head upward, gazed into his gunmetal eyes, and wondered when he'd ask her to marry him. They hadn't been dating long, but Dexter was the type of guy who saw something he wanted, pursued it, and got it. He'd already told her he loved her. It seemed so inevitable.

Those eyes, dark and full of mystery, were only one of the things that attracted Lauren to Dexter. He was a bright and very handsome man. A dark, swarthy complexion, broad shoulders, narrow hips, and full, black hair were all part of what made Dexter turn the ladies' heads. He was, at thirty-four, eight years older than Lauren, but that difference meant nothing. He seemed to take pride in pampering her, but he never smothered her. He always respected her desire for a certain amount of space and independence. He was fast becoming the man of her life.

As they gazed across the candlelit table, Lauren wondered, as she had so often before, what exactly had happened to end his marriage three or four years earlier. All that he'd say was that he and his wife had "wanted different things." He didn't talk much about his ex-wife, which suited Lauren fine. He did talk about his two young sons. He was fond of them, and every other weekend he spent time with them.

She'd met them several times and was becoming very fond of them herself. She wouldn't mind at all having them be a permanent part of her life.

But that night, as they prepared to part company, Lauren felt the nagging doubts that occasionally bothered her when she was with Dexter. It was all about religion. She'd been raised by devout Mormon parents, but had started drifting from the Church before she ever graduated from high school. Dexter was not affiliated with any religion. In fact, he claimed no belief in God. That was where the nagging doubts arose. Though she didn't go to church anymore, there was still ingrained in her a faint but recognizable belief in both God and the Church. And many times in the past year, she had actually thought about searching out a chapel and slipping in to attend a sacrament meeting. As much as she loved her job, she still felt that her life wasn't as meaningful as it could be. There was in her a sense of loss, and if someone were to invite her to go, she told herself she'd do so. But to go back alone seemed too hard.

Considering her recent spiritual stirrings, perhaps she shouldn't even contemplate marriage outside of the beliefs that had never quite left her, despite her youthful rebellion. But as usual, she was able to brush such concerns aside, telling herself that if she did decide to go back to church, a good man like Dexter would allow her to go, and then eventually go with her. That bit of rationalization always made it more comfortable to engage in romantic conversation.

After a few minutes, their talk turned to work. Lauren was surprised when Dexter asked, "Have I mentioned my latest assignment?" He spoke with a mysterious smile, and she felt a tingle race through her, hoping for an exotic venue or a famous new client.

"No," she answered slowly.

"It's for Paradise Pharmaceuticals," he revealed.

The tingle vanished; apprehension took its place. "Really? Doing what?" she asked, wondering if he was involved in investigating the company. Maybe he was about to be the first to mention the fraud.

Her concern made her totally unprepared for what he had to say next. "I've been asked to go to Los Angeles and begin the legal work for Paradise to set up a branch there."

Though Lauren tried, she was unable to completely suppress her surprise. "Another office, now?" she asked shakily.

Dexter frowned. "Yes, now. You know expansion is coming, Lauren, and you know L.A. is first on the list. You work for a growing company," he stressed. "I can't believe you're surprised."

"Of course, you're right," she said, wondering as she had for the past few days what was happening as a result of her e-mail warnings. She wanted to tell Dexter right then about what she'd discovered, but once more, the urge to protect him as well as herself was stronger than her motivation to take further steps to expose the fraud. So she smiled and masked her feelings by kissing him gently and saying, "Congratulations. They picked the right man for the job."

"There's only one drawback," he said with a sadness to his voice.

"Oh?" Lauren coaxed.

"You won't be there. I'll be gone for several weeks, and I know you won't be part of the Paradise team they're sending."

"Oh, Dexter," Lauren said. "I thought you'd only have to be gone for a few days. I really wish I . . ." She paused, not sure what to say with the mix of emotions that was running through her. Finally, she said lamely, "I don't think this is such a good idea."

What if the scandal comes to light while he's gone? she thought to herself. *I don't want him to be gone when it becomes known, and surely it can't be much longer.*

"I'll miss you," he said. "I'll call you every day or two," he added. "And we can e-mail regularly."

Lauren wrapped her arms around his back and laid her head against his chest. He held her and ran his fingers through her hair for several minutes. Finally, she spoke again. "Maybe Royce would let me go with you. It wouldn't hurt to ask. I have a couple of weeks of vacation coming." She couldn't imagine that Royce would object, for he obviously didn't care about what happened to the company.

"That would be great," he said. "Why don't you ask him?"

"I'll talk to him on Monday. If need be, I could do some work while we're there and just e-mail it to Royce." As she spoke, she was thinking that once she and Dexter were away, then she could tell Dexter what was happening and he'd know what to do to stop it.

"When do you leave?" she asked.

"Next week. They don't know what day yet," he said.

"Oh, Royce has just got to let me go," she said hopefully.

Later, after Dexter had gone, Lauren sat in front of her mirror, removing her makeup. Her mind was in a turmoil. Dexter was being sent on what she knew could turn out to be a meaningless assignment, but if she could go with him, it wouldn't matter as much. And maybe they could somehow save the company that meant so much to her.

She moved to the sink to wash her face. Her skin was clear and sun-browned, not an unusual thing here in the islands. She was naturally a little on the dark side, but nothing like the real natives of Hawaii. She envied their dark brown, glowing skin. She patted her face dry and began to brush her long, wavy brown hair. She had no need to curl her hair—Mother Nature had done that for her at birth. At times, she wished it was straight, but as she watched her reflection in the mirror, she admitted that she had beautiful hair. And she'd always liked her almond-shaped eyes. The smoky gray coloring which was so unusual—but according to Dexter, so pretty—was easy to distinguish beneath her long eyelashes.

Lauren turned away. Worry surfaced again. If she was able to go with Dexter, she'd finally be able to make sure the truth about Royce and Fleming came out. *But would it be too late?* she wondered. And for a moment, she felt a touch of guilt, for she had the power to bring it out right now. What she didn't have was the courage.

She reminded herself that Milo and Ken were probably already working feverishly to save the company and that she was worrying over nothing. Then again, they could both be involved. It was all so agonizing to think about.

* * *

As Lauren sought the sanctuary of sleep, Royce, Fleming, and some other employees of Paradise Pharmaceuticals were having a serious, late-night discussion over a round of beers in a very private setting. "Lauren suspects something," Fleming was saying. "We've got to deal with her."

Fleming folded his thick hands over his ponderous stomach and brooded for a moment. Then he took a sip of his beer, frowned, and said to Royce: "So what do you think we should do about her?"

Royce wiped away the beads of perspiration that had popped out on his forehead and said, "We don't know she's figured it out. We better not do anything yet."

"Somebody knows something," Fleming said. "We have evidence of that."

"It's probably not her," Royce argued.

"But again, it might be. Who knows the contracts better than Lauren? Who would recognize that they've been changed quicker than her?" Fleming persisted.

"But we still don't know. We can't do anything to her at this point."

"And risk everything we've worked for if she is the one?" Fleming asked. "That's not an option."

"If she knows, she may have tried to tell someone else. If so, we need to know who," one of the others said.

"Then we can make her tell us and then do what has to be done with her," Fleming suggested.

"But if she's told anyone, someone might be protecting her. We can't do anything obvious to her," said another.

There was another suggestion made. It was discussed. Tempers flared. Distrust mounted. No final decision was made. A few minutes later Fleming adjourned the clandestine meeting.

CHAPTER 3

Winter held the beautiful Ashley Valley in its icy grip. It had been long and cold, beginning with an early, heavy snowfall in October. It hadn't let up since. And now, with deep snow on the ground, thick fog had descended over northeastern Utah and it was refusing to lift. The trees, bushes, and power lines were coated with close to an inch of pure white frost. It was pretty in a way, but Donovan Deru had endured about all the winter he could stand. His hopes for a January thaw had been dashed when this latest snow fell. Then came the fog, and he wondered if he'd ever get his fishing pole out again, or if he'd just have to endure the cold, gray mist forever.

He was standing at the front bedroom window of his new house in Maeser, just outside of Vernal, buttoning his crisp white shirt. He'd hoped to find the fog gone this morning, the same as he'd hoped every other morning for days. He turned and walked back across the room. It was large but undecorated. His only purchase for the room had been a king-size bed. It was much larger than he needed, but he thought it would help fill the space. He had added a few pieces of hand-me-down bedroom furniture, but they were more practical than attractive. His entire home was mostly bare, obviously a bachelor's house, and he knew that Kaelyn was right. He needed to add some more furniture, hang a few paintings, even buy some artificial plants. He had selected the house before even meeting Kaelyn, but he had made sure to buy something that was family friendly. It was a house he could "grow into," as his dad had commented when he saw it.

He frowned as he thought of Kaelyn—short, petite, beautiful. Thoughts of her pixie-cut blond hair accenting her angelic round face and misty blue eyes usually cheered him up. But lately, she'd become a little difficult, and he couldn't quite put his finger on it. After only a few weeks of courtship, he'd asked her to marry him. She'd accepted but was resistant about setting a date for the wedding, and now—weeks after their engagement—he was wondering if he'd made a mistake. Maybe the age difference was bothering her; he was six years older. Maybe she simply didn't want to marry him and didn't know how to tell him.

Whatever it was, he had no intention of breaking up with her unless she initiated it. He was committed to making their relationship work. They were obviously perfect for each other; they shared many of the same interests and found one another attractive. He frankly was tired of the dating game and was ready to settle down. Even his house cried out in its emptiness for a woman to fill it with the things that make a home. The Vernal Temple was just a few short miles away, and it would be there that they'd go when they finally decided when to get married. Well, when *she* finally decided.

On that negative note, the phone rang, and he picked it up, irrationally checking himself in the mirror, as if the person calling would see him. Appearance was important to Donovan. He was slightly under six feet, but he filled a suit out nicely, and that was important when facing a new client or a jury.

"Good morning, Donovan," the high, lilting voice of his fiancée greeted him over the line.

"Hi, Kaelyn," he returned, trying to cheer himself up over her call. "What's up this morning?"

"The sun, but I can't see it," she said. "It's depressing, so I thought I'd call you just to cheer me up."

"And me," he said with a forced chuckle as he turned and gazed at the large picture of Kaelyn that sat on his nightstand. Her cute, cupid face smiled up at him, and he felt the fog lifting from his heart even as it settled in heavier outside the house. "I was just thinking about you," he told her.

"Sure you were," she teased. "I know you. You're standing in front of the mirror, combing your lovely light brown hair—even if it's too short to comb—and wishing it wasn't getting a little thin on top."

That finally made him grin. "That's not quite true," he retorted. "I was *just getting ready* to comb it when the phone rang, and it's not all *that* thin." For some reason she was in one of her better moods, and he was grateful. He really did love her when she was happy. *This* was the Kaelyn he had proposed to.

As her laughter came through the phone, he turned back to the mirror. He propped the phone against his muscular shoulder with his head and gave the comb a few quick flicks through his hair. "And you already have your contacts in those gorgeous tawny eyes of yours," she said with a chuckle.

He did indeed. And for a moment, as she rattled cheerfully on, he examined his eyes. He'd never cared for the yellowish-brown color Mother Nature had painted them. They worked against him with judges and juries, he always thought, because they made him look sort of wolfish. But for some reason, the girls had always fussed about them.

For the next few minutes Donovan and Kaelyn made small talk, light and wonderfully cheerful, then Kaelyn said, "I was just thinking last night that we should talk about setting a date for the wedding."

Donovan's heart skipped a beat. "Great," he said, suppressing his surprise and wondering what had made her finally come to this point. Maybe it would all work out after all.

"I just thought maybe we could talk about it tonight," she added.

"Sure," he said. Then he remembered that this was going to be a difficult day and it might run late for him. He hated to do anything to dampen her good mood, but there was nothing he could do about his schedule. "Oh, Kaelyn, that might not work. Remember, I have a jury trial today, and the judge made it clear that he wants it over in one day. That means it could be a very late evening."

"How late?" she asked, the disappointment in her voice creeping over the line.

"I don't know," he answered, his deep, resonant voice perhaps a little too strong for the phone. He tried to tone it down a notch. "You know how juries are. It could go to midnight, although I hope not. How about tomorrow night? We could talk over dinner, a long and relaxing dinner."

"What if I change my mind by then?" she asked. The sudden petulance in her tone dampened his own spirits again, and he forced himself to take a deep breath before he answered her.

"Please don't," he said as lightly as he could muster. "This big house of mine is closing in on me. It needs someone pretty and vivacious to make it into a home."

"Okay, I'll be patient," she said impatiently. "I gotta run now. I'm going to the gym for an hour before I get ready for work."

"I've got to go too," he agreed as he picked up a dark blue tie to go with his conservative suit. Then as an afterthought he said, "I'll call you if we happen to get out early this evening."

"Okay," she said, but her voice lacked enthusiasm. He guessed she knew that wasn't likely. "I'll be home . . . unless I go to a movie with my roommate or something," she added with a noticeable bite to her words.

"I'm sorry, Kaelyn," he said. He could tell that she'd built herself up to this, and now his work had caused him to hurt her. He felt terrible, but he did have his job, and the trial was important. His client, unlike most he represented, was actually innocent, and Donovan owed him his best effort today in order to convince the jury. He couldn't worry about Kaelyn. She'd just have to understand. *If she doesn't understand now, before we're married, then what will it be like afterward?* he wondered, wishing that thought hadn't inserted itself, but knowing it was something he had to get resolved in his mind—and in his heart.

* * *

When Donovan walked into his office a few minutes later, his secretary, Barbara Olsen, was already there. She greeted him as she always did with a motherly smile followed by quick, short instructions about what he had to do that day. This morning it was especially short. "You have to be at the courthouse in ten minutes, Donovan. Your client will be waiting."

"Thanks, Barbara," he said as she handed him a thick file. "What would I do without you?"

She blushed and then said, "I'll take care of the mail. If there's anything terribly pressing, I'll run over and catch you in a recess."

She was efficient, kind, a little fussy, thirty-five years his senior, and yet much more of a friend than an employee. From the time that he'd been forced to take over the well-established practice when his partner of less than a year had died of a sudden heart attack, she'd taken him under her wing. Without her, he knew that the practice would have suffered, but she kept things going, having worked with the man who had generously given Donovan a job shortly after he'd passed the bar exam. Now, just twenty-eight and practicing alone, he was making very good money, and he was very generous with Barbara. He was quite certain she was the highest-paid legal secretary in Vernal. But she deserved it, he always told himself. And he secretly hoped she'd work until she was eighty.

Donovan started for the door, but she stopped him with, "Kaelyn called a few moments ago. She said to tell you she wouldn't be home tonight, that something had come up, so not to try to call her if you finished early. I told her that I was certain that wouldn't be a problem, that your trial would probably go late."

Donovan said, "Thanks," and stepped out into the dismal gray fog, his mood suddenly a strong match for the weather. He honestly wasn't sure where he stood with Kaelyn. Darkly he wondered if he was destined to live alone in his big, empty house for the rest of his life.

Despite his personal concerns, Donovan was in superb courtroom form that day, and the jury finished their deliberations in almost record time. He won his case for a grateful client. He tried calling Kaelyn from the courthouse, but as she'd told Barbara, she wasn't in. He went home grumpy, despite his victory in court, and decided he didn't care if it was still foggy the next morning.

CHAPTER 4

It was not foggy on the warm, green island of Oahu. In fact, a light breeze blew in from the beaches, carrying the pleasant, salty scent of the ocean. Low, scattered clouds hugged the mountain tops, their white painting a stark contrast to the dark green that crept to the highest points. Hawaii knew no winter, and flowers bloomed across the island even in January. Clear, fresh water cascaded over craggy cliffs and entered slowly moving rivers that flowed smoothly between banks thick with trees and shrubs, some bright with scented blossoms. The fresh water met the salty ocean and became part of it. Tourists streamed across the island, enjoying the sun and the fun. Residents who didn't have to work poured outside to enjoy the beauty and serenity of their sanctuary.

Lauren Olcott missed all the beauty and wonder of her surroundings. After worrying all weekend about the embezzlement, and knowing that every day was leading the company closer to collapse, Lauren felt near the point of collapse herself when she entered the office on Monday morning. She had never felt such stress in her life. Surely, she told herself, something would happen today that would indicate that something was being done about Royce, Fleming, and whoever else was involved in the embezzlement. But the only thing out of the ordinary was the absence of Billie Maio, the CEO's secretary. At her desk was a woman from the typing pool on the fourth floor. That was quite normal, since whenever Billie had a day off someone from there would fill in for her. And yet because of the message that Lauren had sent anonymously to her, Billie's absence today made her stomach churn. She popped a Rolaids in her mouth.

Lauren was also stressed about asking Royce for some time off to go with Dexter to L.A. She had worked herself into such a state of hope over the weekend that she was afraid to hear Royce tell her no. She put off asking him, worrying about Billie and not daring to hear his answer. After working quietly in her office for an hour, Lauren decided to introduce herself to the woman at Billie's desk. Maybe she would learn something about Billie's absence that would put her mind at rest. What she learned only raised her concerns. Tammy, the sub for the day, told her that Billie had called Mr. Thurman on Sunday morning and said that she wouldn't be back to work again.

"But she wouldn't just quit," Lauren protested in poorly disguised alarm.

"But she did," Tammy said with a shrug.

Lauren felt like she'd been punched, for she and Billie were friends, and surely she'd have said something if she'd been planning to leave the company. "Did she tell him why she was quitting?" Lauren asked.

"Said she was going to move to Arizona," Tammy said. "That's all I know."

It made no sense, and Lauren felt compelled to learn more. She remembered wondering briefly if Billie could be part of the group destroying the company, even though it seemed completely out of character for Billie. Now she further wondered if Billie had already received a large amount of money and taken flight. Despising herself for even thinking such a thing about a friend and hoping to dispel her concerns, Lauren asked Tammy to tell Milo that she wanted to speak to him.

Tammy nodded and buzzed the president's office. She made the inquiry, then said, "Go on in."

"What can I do for you this morning?" Mr. Thurman asked as soon as Lauren had shut the door behind herself. "If you're here to see about getting Billie's job, I can tell you right now that you're overqualified." He grinned when he said that, and Lauren felt herself relax ever so slightly. "You look worried," he added seriously. "Are you wondering what happened to Billie?"

"Yes," she said. "I can't believe she'd just quit like this."

"I was very surprised myself," the president admitted. "When she called and told me she was moving to Arizona, I asked her why."

"And what did she say?" Lauren asked.

"She said she has a boyfriend there, and he wanted her to be closer to him. She made it sound like a wedding was in the works."

"I see," Lauren said. But she didn't see at all. Billie did not have a boyfriend anywhere. She'd recently broken up with the fellow she'd been dating for almost a year. And if there had been someone new in her life, surely she would have mentioned it to Lauren, and she hadn't.

"I'm going to miss her. I'm sorry she's gone," Lauren said courteously and turned to leave.

"I'm sorry too," Milo said. "She won't be easy to replace."

Lauren was thoroughly rattled as she left the CEO's office. There was no way that Billie Maio went to Arizona to get married, or even to be near some mysterious boyfriend. Either Milo was lying very smoothly to Lauren, or Billie had lied to Milo, and from what Lauren thought she knew of Billie, she doubted that. Lauren was frightened for Billie—as frightened as she'd ever been for anyone in her entire life. She walked thoughtfully to the break area and put a dollar in the juice machine. A can of apple juice came out, and she opened it and took a sip.

"Hi, Lauren," a cheerful voice said, and she spun around.

"Oh, hi, Jim," she responded. Jim Roderick was from the sales department and was one of the nicest guys in the company. But he always made Lauren feel a little uneasy. He was an active Latter-day Saint and had served a mission in Hawaii almost a decade before. She'd known him then and had been surprised to see him at Paradise. Talking to him, she'd learned that he'd graduated from BYU in Provo, Utah. He'd married a girl he met there who was from Maui. They both wanted to come back to the islands and eventually did just that. Now Jim and Sally had two kids and seemed very happy and content with life. Jim's presence reminded Lauren of how much she'd given up when she'd fallen from activity in the Church.

But he often reminded her of more than that. She hoped he wouldn't this time. She had too much on her mind already. But he did. "My old companion asked about you yesterday," Jim said.

"Oh, where did you see him?" she asked, trying to show no emotion at all.

Jim grinned. Lauren knew that he'd never forgotten the fact that Lauren, as a teenage girl, had fallen head over heels for his companion.

She remembered only too vividly herself. "I didn't actually see him. We spoke on the phone. Donovan's on a committee to organize our mission reunion in April, and he's been trying to locate some of the missionaries whose addresses we've lost. He called me about a fellow that used to be in our zone."

"Oh," Lauren said as she thought about Donovan Deru, someone she'd known only as Elder Deru. She'd had a crush on him that wouldn't quit, but he'd been a totally devoted missionary that refused to even step near the line when it came to the mission rules. The only attention he'd given her was what she still thought of as a call to repentance. She'd been skipping church to go surfing, and her folks kept inviting the missionaries over for dinner in hopes that it might help. And Elder Deru had, on several occasions, encouraged her to attend her church meetings. He'd even preached to her about how she needed God in her life, the importance of prayer, and on and on.

She'd refused to follow his advice, and yet she'd loved the sound of his deep, strong voice, and she couldn't shake the feeling she'd had whenever she'd looked into his eyes. They were an unusual color, but were not in any way unattractive. Just the opposite. When his eyes fell on her, even accompanied by a mild rebuke, she'd always experienced the thrill of a rapidly beating heart. Even after nine years, she still felt a tiny bit of girlish twitterpation at the thought of him.

"I told him you were doing well, and he said to tell you he's fine too," Jim said.

"Thanks," she responded with a forced smile. Lauren knew that Donovan was an attorney somewhere in Utah. He'd even e-mailed her a couple of times since Jim had moved here. And the first time, she even e-mailed him back. All she did was tell him a little about her work, but she'd kept his address on her computer. She recently considered telling him that she was thinking about going to church, but she refrained, thinking that would only bring a preachy message from him, and she didn't want that.

Jim's next words struck her in a way that caused a twinge of disappointment, even though she knew there was no reason that it should. "Donovan's finally found him a girl. He's engaged."

She must have looked crestfallen, because Jim looked at her with inquiry in his eyes. She struggled to regain her composure, did not answer the questioning look she was receiving, and simply said, "I hope she's a nice girl."

"I'm sure she is," Jim said. Then he added, "Donovan asked me to do him a favor."

"Oh," she said.

"Actually, it's something I've been meaning to do anyway. Sally and I would like to invite you to come to church with us on Sunday."

"I don't think so," she answered, feeling guilty. An invitation was the very thing she'd promised herself would lead her back to attending meetings. But for some reason, just because it had come from Donovan Deru, a man whose influence she couldn't shake no matter how hard she tried, her pride stepped in the way. But she did force herself to add, "Maybe sometime, though. Thanks for inviting me."

Jim grinned, the inquiry still in his eyes, and said, "Sure, some-time." Then he suddenly asked, "Hey, did you hear about Billie?"

Lauren was rocked again. Jim's reminder of Donovan had driven the worry of Billie's strange departure from her mind. Now he brought it back, and the emotion of it almost overwhelmed her. She didn't say a word.

Jim said, "It's not like her to just leave like this. I hope she's okay."

"I'm sure she is," Lauren said tightly, knowing that something might have happened to Billie because of the e-mail she'd sent warning of the embezzlement.

Jim looked at Lauren for just another moment. He looked worried now too. Then he asked, "Are you all right, Lauren?"

"Yes, I'm fine," she said quickly, anxious to get away from him, to retreat to the privacy of her office, where she could sort out her feelings and gain control of her emotions. "I'm just worried about Billie. But I better get moving. I've got a lot of work to do," she added apologetically. After finishing her juice and throwing the can into the recycling bin, she abruptly turned and hurried away.

Lauren's heart jumped to her throat when she approached her office. Leroy Provost was standing beside her door talking with Royce and holding a box of chocolates. Even though she had previously dated Leroy, she was now very suspicious of him. She certainly didn't want to talk to him.

So she tried to slide past the two of them, but Leroy wasn't about to let that happen. He reached out and grabbed her arm. "Hey, I've got something for you," he said. "I know how much you like cherry chocolates, and I came down here just to give you one."

He opened the box, looked carefully at the assorted contents for a moment, then said, "This is the only one left in here, and I saved it just for you." He picked it out of the box and handed it to her.

"Thanks," she said as she put it in her mouth. She really did like cherry chocolates.

"Sure," Leroy said with a grin. "See you around."

As he walked away, Royce said, "So how are you today, Lauren?"

"I'm fine," she lied, knowing that if she was going to ask about going to L.A., now was as good a time as any. "Royce, Dexter said he would be going to L.A. this week to work for a while. I have some vacation coming, and I really would like to go with him. I could work on my laptop over there if you needed me to. That way we wouldn't get behind."

"Gee, Lauren, we're awfully busy," he began. She braced herself for his negative answer as he seemed to be thinking the request over in his mind. Finally he said, "You know, you've earned it, Lauren. Of course you can go, but you better hustle today. Milo says he may be sending the team as soon as tomorrow."

The relief Lauren felt was almost overwhelming. "Thanks, Royce. I can't wait to tell Dexter. And I'll work all night if I have to."

"That won't be necessary," Royce said, "but I better let you get back to work now."

Back in her office a moment later, Lauren took a deep breath and slowly let it out. She was so relieved he'd given her permission to go. *But it had been almost too easy. And why was that?* she wondered, before scolding herself for her extreme paranoia. She was just glad it worked out. She picked up the phone and called Dexter's office. To her delight, he was in. When she gave him the news he said, "Wow, that's great. I'm sure glad. We'll have a wonderful time. By the way, Milo tells me I'll be leaving tomorrow—*we'll* be leaving tomorrow. I'll call you tonight and we can make plans. I'll see to the airline tickets right now."

They talked for a couple of minutes, and when she finally hung up, Lauren found herself wishing she could go home and start packing right then. She wanted to get away from here, share her dark secret with Dexter, and then wait for Royce and Fleming to be arrested.

* * *

Donovan checked his e-mail when he got back from the courthouse a little after twelve. He was surprised to see one so soon from Jim Roderick, an old mission companion. He'd asked Jim to track down an elder and hadn't thought it would be an easy task. But Donovan was surprised to find that the message was not about a missionary at all, but about a teenage girl he'd known in the mission field. She'd had a bit of a rebellious streak, and he remembered how hard he had tried to convince her to get close to the Lord.

He'd pretty much forgotten about her until a year or so ago when Jim had written and told him she was working for the company he'd just been employed by. He'd thought of her a few times since then and had even e-mailed her twice. However, she'd only responded to the first one, and when she did, she made no reference to the Church. Later Jim had told him that she was not active but that she seemed like a really decent and hardworking person. Jim had even suggested that Donovan come over to the islands to visit, and said that if he would, he would see if he could set him up with Lauren. "I know she doesn't smoke or drink," Jim had said. "I think she's just waiting for some encouragement. I'm sure she'd go out with you."

Donovan had, of course, brushed that off, even though he and Kaelyn weren't even dating at that point. But when Jim had mentioned her again on the phone the day before, Donovan had suggested that Jim and his wife might try to get her to attend church. The message he'd just received indicated that Jim had made the attempt. It had been refused, Jim had admitted, but he also wrote that she'd left the door open for sometime in the future. The rest of Jim's message had left Donovan feeling a little unsettled. He'd written that Lauren had seemed upset over something, suggesting that it could have to do with the sudden resignation of another employee of the company, a friend of hers. However, Jim had portrayed the feeling that her reaction seemed odd, as if there was some other problem bothering her. And finally, Jim had written that when he told Lauren about Donovan's engagement, she'd acted disappointed. "I don't think she's ever gotten over the teenage crush she had on you. Are you sure about this girl you're engaged to?" he'd jokingly concluded.

Donovan shook his head slowly as he thought about the message. No, he admitted to himself, he wasn't all that confident about Kaelyn, but he was sure it would all work out. He'd made a commitment to her by giving her a ring, and she'd made one by accepting it.

* * *

Lauren left the building just after noon to find some lunch. She was having a difficult time getting much done, for she couldn't get Billie's sudden departure off her mind. And the more she thought about it, the more she worried that her e-mail had somehow caused Billie a great deal of trouble. As she walked out the door, she nearly bumped into the elderly groundskeeper, Ned Haraguchi, one of her favorite people. "You have the grounds here looking beautiful," she said to him, bringing a smile to his wrinkled face. "I just don't know how you do it in so few hours a day."

Ned had retired years ago, only to go back to work part-time after his wife died. "Thank you," he said with a grin. "When I tend the flowers, I have only to speak to them and tell them to watch for you each morning and evening. 'If you'll just try to look as good as Lauren,' I tell them, 'you will be the most beautiful flowers in all of Hawaii.' And I believe they must take me at my word."

Lauren grinned affectionately at the old man. He was always telling her how pretty she was. She suspected he told the other women that as well, but she was flattered anyway. Suddenly, she wanted company, someone she knew was above deceit, just to spend a little time with. "I'm just going to get some lunch. I'd be honored if the most handsome man at Paradise would let me buy him some as well," she said, offering him her arm.

Ned's grin spread across his wrinkled face, and his dark eyes shined as he said, "I was just finishing up here for the day. I'd be most honored to accept your invitation." And with that he took her arm, and they walked together up the walk, past the old man's flourishing work of living art. Ned was a small man—the top of his perfectly white hair only reached about the bottom of Lauren's ears—but they walked in companionable silence, impervious to the stares that others threw their way.

They entered a Japanese restaurant five minutes later. "Ah, you know how to treat your elders," Ned said. "You know I love the food of my grandfather's native land."

She did know that and had chosen the place to please him. As they ate, she asked him about his neighbor, Vivian Likio, a former home-care nurse who assisted in the research department and watched over the company's sickroom as needed. Lauren had spoken at length with Vivian one day when Lauren visited the sickroom with a migraine, and she knew Vivian was fond of the old man. "She's a grand woman," he said, sitting a little straighter in his chair. "A man couldn't ask for a better neighbor or a more faithful friend." He smiled and added, "And you are a good friend too. It is an honor for an old man like me to have one so young and beautiful take the time to brighten my day."

"Actually, you are the one who brightens my day," Lauren said sincerely, for he had done much these past few minutes to lift her drooping spirits.

"I'm glad. Today, for some reason," he said, peering deeply into her eyes, "you seem to need cheering up. Something is bothering you, isn't it?"

"I'll be okay. I'm just worried about a friend," she said. *And a lot more,* she thought.

Ned nodded, then, putting his fork aside, he leaned forward and said quietly, "If there is something I can help with, you have but to ask."

Suddenly, Lauren had the urge to tell Ned everything she knew about the terrible crimes that were occurring within the company they both loved. But she restrained herself, regretting that she might have placed Billie in danger. She was determined not to do the same to him.

The wise old man seemed to read her mind as he continued to look steadily into her eyes. "Miss Olcott," he said, suddenly becoming more formal, "there is more than a friend's problems upsetting you. Are you sure I can't be of help? I am a good listener if nothing else. Sometimes it brings relief from worry when one just talks to another about things. I give you my word that I will repeat nothing of what you tell me."

Oh, how Lauren would have liked to share some of her burdens with this kind old man, but she couldn't bring herself to do it. But she did say, "You're right. There is something troubling me, but I can't speak of it."

"And why not?" Ned asked softly.

"Because I like you, Ned, and it could be dangerous to tell you," she blurted. "Oh! I'm sorry. I've said too much already. Please, forget that I said anything."

He continued to watch her face closely, his dark eyes filled with concern, until finally she looked away. "If you change your mind, you can come to me anytime," he said. "I will always listen, and maybe I might even be able to draw on my many years of life to give you a little advice."

"Thank you, Ned. You're an awesome friend."

When she got back to her office, Leroy was again by her door with the box of chocolates in his hand. "I was wrong," he said. "I found another cherry one. Thought you should have it. I've eaten too many today."

She accepted it. He grinned at her. "I'll be going then," he said as once more he strode away.

How odd, she thought as she slipped the chocolate into her mouth. *Still, it was a sweet thing to do.*

Only moments after Lauren had sat back down at her desk, she was surprised by Dr. Wilda Mitsui, the head of the research department, who entered her office. Lauren stood up as she greeted her visitor. Dr. Mitsui, a psychiatrist in her early sixties, had practiced for many years at her chosen profession before joining Paradise Pharmaceuticals to do research. Even though she still saw a few patients, she'd soon risen to the prestigious position as head of the research department. It was well known that her main interest was in the development of new drugs to help control behavior. She was well respected in the community as well as in her profession, and had been instrumental in helping the company to make the great strides it had experienced the past couple of years.

"Can I help you?" Lauren asked in greeting.

"I hope so," the doctor said, her face serious as it usually was. "Do you have a few minutes to come down to my office? I need to run an idea by you. I'm making excellent progress on a new drug to help restore memory to victims of blunt-force trauma, and I was told you might be able to give me an idea as to who might be interested in such a product because of the contact you've had with the companies we do business with."

"I'd be glad to help if I can," Lauren said. She'd always been a little intimidated by the highly intelligent Dr. Mitsui. She gave the impression to Lauren that she thought she was much better than others in the company. And yet, she admired the doctor for all the good she'd accomplished.

A half hour later, after having listened as patiently as she could to a more detailed explanation of the new drug and what Dr. Mitsui hoped it would accomplish, Lauren named two companies she thought might be interested in being briefed.

"Excellent," Dr. Mitsui said. "I knew you could help me. Thank you so much. Do you have names and phone numbers of ones it would be best for me to contact?"

"In my office, I do," Lauren said. "I'll find them and give you a call."

"Better yet, bring the names and phone numbers back down here. Perhaps you wouldn't mind making the calls yourself and introducing me," the doctor suggested.

"Sure. Give me just a minute," Lauren said. As she rode the elevator up to the third floor, she thought about the head of the research department. She didn't have the most pleasant personality, but Lauren couldn't help but place her low on the list of people who might be involved with Royce and Fleming. The woman's life was about helping others.

When she returned with the names and phone numbers in hand, Dr. Mitsui was drinking a Pepsi. Dr. Rhoades, who was Dr. Mitsui's assistant, and Milo Thurman were also in her spacious office, and they were each having a Coke. Lauren scarcely knew Dr. Rhoades. He was a quiet man, although reputed to be brilliant. He moved about the company almost like a mouse. At times, people hardly knew he was there.

"I'm sorry. I didn't realize you were busy," Lauren said.

"I was just telling Mr. Thurman and Dr. Rhoades how helpful you've been."

"Let me get you a drink," Dr. Rhoades offered in his quiet, unobtrusive voice. After hearing her request, he pulled a can out of a small fridge, popped the tab, then turned back and pushed a cold, open can of Diet Coke across the table.

"Now, let's look at those names and see if you can reach them for us."

Lauren glanced at Milo, still wondering if she was intruding. But he said, "Go ahead, Lauren. I'm very interested in this new drug, and I'd like to hear the preliminary reactions of the contacts you have there."

After drinking deeply of her pop to calm her nerves, Lauren looked at her short list and dialed the number for the first name she'd written. The call was put on speakerphone, and even Milo and Dr. Rhoades participated in the conversation. It went very well, and there was clearly a high level of interest and excitement over the newly developed drug. An appointment was made for a meeting at a later date, and the second person was called.

By the time they'd finished three calls, Lauren wasn't feeling well. She wondered if something she and Ned had eaten for lunch was disagreeing with her.

Dr. Mitsui asked, "Are you feeling okay, Lauren? You don't look like you feel well."

"I don't, I'm afraid. It must have been something I ate for lunch," Lauren said. "There's still one more name here. Let's call and—"

Dr. Mitsui waved her off and said, "The three of us will take care of it. Let me call the nurse." She immediately began to dial. A moment later she said, "Vivian Likio will be right down. You look very pale, my girl."

Milo spoke up then. "She's worried about why Billie Maio suddenly quit. Could that be it?" he asked with concern in his voice.

Lauren shook her head as Dr. Mitsui asked, "Your personal secretary quit? But she's so good! That worries me too. And yes, such a worry could make someone not feel well."

"She quit over a man," Milo said. "Next time I'll not hire someone as pretty as Billie, then maybe she'll stay," he joked.

"Yes, it's always so hard to have to train someone new," Dr. Rhoades commented. Then turning to Lauren, he said, "Here, finish your Coke. It might help settle your stomach."

Lauren did as she was told, wishing she could get out of there and be sick in private. She'd blamed her lunch, but it occurred to her that all the worry and turmoil might actually be causing it. After a few moments, Vivian bustled in. She was in her sixties, round and solid. She took one look at Lauren and said, "Let's get you up to the sickroom where you can lie down."

Lauren started to get up, and Vivian took hold of her arm, steadying her.

"The poor thing looks worse by the minute," Dr. Mitsui said, concern softening her usually stern expression. "Ms. Likio, why don't you take her to her apartment and help her get settled there. If you wouldn't mind staying with her, maybe I could check in later and make sure she's okay. We can manage the sickroom for a few hours."

"That sounds like a fine plan," the nurse said, and she gently helped Lauren from the office.

Lauren hadn't been home long when she began to feel very dizzy and drowsy. In fact, she was so sleepy that she couldn't think clearly, and without steadying herself she knew she'd fall. A touch of panic ran through her. She went to the phone, intent on calling Dexter to tell him that she'd be okay by tomorrow. She had to be. But she couldn't remember his office number, she was so drowsy. Vivian insisted that she go right to bed, and she helplessly complied. She was soon in bed but didn't hear the phone ringing insistently a few minutes later, nor did she hear Vivian tell Dexter that she'd suddenly taken ill.

Vivian Likio spent the next hour gently sponging Lauren's head with a cool, damp cloth. "Do we need to get her to a hospital?" she asked Dr. Mitsui after the doctor's arrival a few hours later.

"Not if you could stay here with her. I talked to Royce Cantrell. He insists that we care for her personally. She's very valuable to Paradise, you know. He said that she's been working very hard lately and that he's been concerned that she was pushing herself toward a breakdown. And my professional opinion is that a breakdown is what we have here. I think the fact that her friend Billie Maio suddenly quit was what finally pushed her over the edge," the doctor explained. "She needs rest."

"Oh, the poor girl," Vivian said. "I'd be glad to stay with her. I'll just need to run and get a few things and then I can stay as long as I need to."

"That would be lovely," Dr. Mitsui said. "I'll wait here with Lauren while you're gone and give her a thorough exam. But don't be too long; I have a meeting later."

"I'll hurry. I'll just need to ask my neighbor to take care of my cat. Then I'll get some clothes and a little something to eat and hurry right back," Vivian said. "Oh, her boyfriend, Dexter Drake, called. He was quite concerned and will be over to see her in a little while."

"Yes, I know Dexter. He does a little legal work for us as I recall. Seems like a fine man. I'll let him know what's going on if he comes before you return. In fact, he might be able to shed some light on why she's been reacting the way she has lately to the pressure of her job. Maybe he knows of something in her personal life that could be a contributing factor."

CHAPTER 5

Ned was working in his front yard when Vivian drove into her carport. Tommy, Vivian's big yellow cat, had been with him since he came outside an hour ago to tinker in his garden. The cat scampered to greet his mistress. Vivian knelt down and petted him for a moment, then called out a greeting across the fence to Ned. After hurriedly packing a bag and throwing it in her car, she walked over to talk to him. "I'm going to be gone tonight," she began. "A girl from work became very ill this afternoon, and Dr. Mitsui had me take her home. She's with her now, but I'll need to spend the night with her, and maybe longer. Tommy will—"

"I'll watch the cat," Ned interrupted with a smile. "He's been helping me for the past hour or so anyway."

Vivian thanked him and took a moment to give some specific directions as to the cat's food and water. Then she said, "I better hurry. I'm really worried about Lauren."

Ned had leaned down to pluck a fading blossom from a shrub. He jerked upright and turned toward Vivian with alarm. "Lauren Olcott?" he asked urgently.

"Yes, why?" Vivian responded, surprised at the urgency in her elderly neighbor's voice and the alarm in his kind eyes.

"Vivian, this may be nothing, but I've been worrying about her all afternoon," Ned revealed. "I had lunch with her today, and she wasn't herself at all."

"Dr. Mitsui says she's afraid it's a breakdown, that she appears to be suffering from stress. She was apparently very concerned that Mr. Thurman's secretary suddenly quit. But that shouldn't have caused her to be so ill. I can't imagine; she's such a pleasant girl, and I've never noticed her to be—"

Ned broke in again. "Vivian, there's something else," he said as worry lines grew deeper on his furrowed brow. But then he failed to say more and stood there staring thoughtfully at the pounding surf on the far side of the highway.

"What?" Vivian pressed. "If you know something, please tell me. It might be helpful to Dr. Mitsui."

Ned shook his head gently, and he turned his eyes to meet Vivian's. "I asked her if something was wrong, if there was something she wanted to talk about. Not that I could help, but I'd be willing to listen to her is what I told her. Then she admitted that something was troubling her, but she said she couldn't say anything to me about it because it might put me in danger."

Vivian felt a sharp prick in her chest. Then she said, "I can't imagine how she could tell you anything that would be dangerous to you."

"Well, she apparently thought so," Ned affirmed. "But then she told me to forget it, that she shouldn't have said anything. The look of panic in her eyes about broke my old heart. I couldn't get her to say another word about it after that."

"That worries me," Vivian said. "I better get back to her apartment."

"You be careful," Ned said.

Vivian looked at him and shook her head. "We're both overreacting," she concluded. "The poor girl's just suffered a breakdown like Dr. Mitsui said."

When Vivian got back to Lauren's apartment, Dr. Mitsui was pacing the floor impatiently.

She gave the nurse a bottle of pills that looked very similar to aspirin. "Give her one of these when she wakes up," the doctor instructed. "And give her another one in the morning. It's a sedative and will help calm her down. Then maybe we can get her feeling better."

Vivian nodded and said, "I'll take good care of her."

"You do that, and call me if anything unusual occurs. You have my cellular phone number, don't you?" Vivian nodded, and then the doctor added, "Mr. Drake came by with a dozen roses for Lauren. I put them in a vase in her room. He's very worried about her and even offered to stay with her, but I assured him that that wasn't necessary, that it would be better to have someone like yourself with her, someone with medical training. He seemed very upset. She was planning to go to L.A. with him tomorrow. He wants to see if he can get the trip delayed. He stayed about fifteen minutes and left. He asked that we be sure and tell Lauren he came by."

After Dr. Mitsui was gone, Vivian hurried to Lauren's bedroom to check on her patient. Lauren was still sleeping soundly, so she didn't disturb her. It was after eight that night before Lauren stirred. Vivian, who was sitting beside the young woman's bed, put her hand on Lauren's. Lauren turned her head and slowly opened her eyes, trying to focus them.

Vivian turned on a lamp, causing Lauren to squint. But before long her eyes adjusted to the light, and she again attempted to focus on Vivian's face. The nurse noted, as she had before, how pretty Lauren's eyes were. They were such an amazing color. Smoky was the best way she could describe them. But they seemed empty now, devoid of any emotion, and the nurse felt tears sting her own eyes.

"Where am I?" Lauren asked, her voice weak.

"You're at home, my dear," Vivian answered. "I'll be with you now. You have become very sick, but you will be better soon. Would you like a little something to eat?"

Lauren didn't answer, like she hadn't understood the question, so Vivian said, "I'll get you something. A piece of toast perhaps?"

Again there was no response, and Lauren's eyes closed. Vivian patted her hand and went to the kitchen. After preparing the toast, she also poured a glass of orange juice and removed a pill from the bottle Dr. Mitsui had left. She carried it back into the bedroom. Lauren's eyes were open again, and she was looking around the room as though she were frightened.

"Who are you?" she asked as the nurse placed the small plate of toast on the nightstand.

"I'm Vivian Likio. You know me, Lauren. I work at the same place you do. I take care of the sickroom."

As she spoke, Vivian offered the juice to Lauren, holding the glass to her lips. Lauren took a sip and then pushed it away. "You need to drink some," Vivian insisted. "And you also need to swallow this pill." She held it up for a moment, then put it to Lauren's mouth. Lauren obediently let Vivian place it on her tongue, and with another little bit of juice, it was washed down. After that, she ate a half dozen small bites of toast, drank a little more juice, then drifted off to sleep.

* * *

There was some dissension in the small group that had again assembled at their secret house on the island of Kauai. Fleming Parker spoke angrily to those who were assembled there. "We can't wait any longer for our other partner to arrive, so we'll begin. First, let me remind each of you that we are in this together. And let me also make it clear that I don't like what happened to Billie either, but it was an accident. The drug she took was experimental, as you all know. We had no idea it would kill her. Dr. Mitsui, when I asked her about that drug, said it was designed to attack muscle strength. It is supposed to make a person physically weak. It's being developed to help control violent criminals. She said it had only been used on mice and dogs so far and seemed to work well, but it was too early to predict exactly how it might affect a human. I suppose it might have been a reaction of some kind with Billie that might not occur with anyone else. At any rate, it was a risk we had to take."

Royce Cantrell spoke up next. "Well, let's hope we don't have to give it to anyone else! I'm not at all happy with the way things are going. Death wasn't part of the deal!"

Fleming shook his massive head in disapproval of Royce's statement and then made another of his own. "We will do whatever we have to." The others in the room looked at each other, attempting to mask their own feelings. Fleming went on. "We need that final contract signed. That could mean millions more to each of us. But it might take as much as a week or two to finalize it. When that's done, and payment has been received, we'll take the money and go. Until then, no one can be allowed to interfere with our plans. Is that clear?"

The others nodded as there came a knock on the door. Fleming went alone to answer it, leaving his colleagues in the darkened room at the back of the house. "I don't like this," Royce growled as soon as

Fleming was out of earshot. "No one was supposed to die."

"I don't like it either, but what's done is done," another said. "We have got to forge ahead. We definitely can't afford to get caught now."

Royce nodded in reluctant agreement. "There shouldn't be a need for anyone else to get hurt."

"We hope not, but there is the matter of Lauren," he was reminded.

At that point, the final member of the illicit group came in with Fleming, apologizing for being late, blaming the airlines. "I heard mention of Miss Olcott," Fleming said. "She'll be given a lighter dose than Billie. She'll live, but she'll be unable to get out of her bed. She won't be a problem. I can assure you of that."

"We don't even know that she knows anything," Royce objected.

The newly arrived party said simply, "She knows something, Royce. I can assure you of that. And she must not be allowed to speak of it."

"The rest of you can quit worrying about Miss Olcott. You take care of your assignments. We'll see that Lauren doesn't move until we're gone," he said, nodding toward the latecomer.

When the meeting broke up a few minutes later, Fleming again reminded everyone to be cautious as they returned to Honolulu. "We don't want to give anyone else a reason to be suspicious. That's the only way I can assure you that no one else will die."

* * *

"I'm sorry," Vivian told Dexter when he called around ten. "Lauren's a very ill girl."

"I know that. I saw her earlier. I just want to know how she's doing now."

"She's sleeping. Dr. Mitsui has assured me that she needs rest right now, and I'll make sure she gets it, I can promise you that. And I'll let her know the roses are from you when she is able to understand."

"Thank you. I'm awfully worried. It's not like her to get sick like this," Dexter said.

"I'm sure she'll be fine in time," the nurse replied.

"I need her to be well tomorrow," he said faintly. "We were going to L.A. together. I'm not sure I can get it delayed, but you'll make sure she comes to meet me when she is strong enough, won't you?"

"I'd be glad to do that," Vivian said with a smile. "And I'm sure that's what she'll want."

Late that night, Vivian, who had been sleeping in the guest bedroom, awoke when she heard the sound of someone moving around the house. She found Lauren stumbling absently about, moaning softly and crying off and on. She helped the young woman back to her bed and sat beside her for the next hour until she'd finally drifted into an uneasy sleep. Concerned, she pulled a sleek recliner from the living room and through the double doors of the master bedroom.

Vivian soon fell asleep and did not hear the front door open, nor did she hear the soft footsteps that trod across the floor. She didn't even see the tiny flashlight that threw quick darts of light around the room. And most importantly, she didn't see someone pick up the bottle of pills that Dr. Mitsui had left with her. The bottle was placed back on the table a minute later, but the pills that had filled it were now in the intruder's pocket, and similar-looking pills were now in the bottle. The silent intruder, undetected by the soundly sleeping nurse and her patient, left with as quiet an exit as the entrance had been.

* * *

Lauren awoke shortly after the sun rose. Her head was pounding, her mouth was dry, and her eyes were slightly blurred. Her mind was operating in a sort of fog. A large, gray-haired woman was asleep in a recliner by her bed. She closed her eyes tightly and rubbed at them with her fists. When she opened them, the woman was still there. She rubbed her eyes again and, with a great deal of effort, swung her legs slowly over the edge of the bed. Her head pounded. The room swayed. She thought for a moment that she was going to throw up. But after sitting there for a few moments, the feeling passed.

She stared at the gray-haired woman. She looked like many native women of the island, but Lauren thought she'd seen her before. However, she couldn't place her. She wondered, no matter who it was, what she was doing here in her bedroom. She pressed her fingers against her temples and forced herself to think, willed her mind to clear. She vaguely remembered having begun to feel dizzy while helping Dr. Mitsui, but she couldn't imagine what she would have been helping her with. She even had flashes of memory of someone helping her from the office building, but everything was blank after that. She backed her mind up and tried again to remember why she would have been in Dr. Mitsui's office, if she even was.

Her eyes strayed to her alarm clock. She studied it diligently for a moment. She felt a touch of panic wash over her. If she was reading the clock right, she was late for work. She forced herself to stand, but that was a mistake. She knew it even before she began to fall. She hit the floor so hard that pain shot through her body. She tried to move, but it hurt too much. Then a soothing voice was speaking to her. "It's all right, Lauren. I'm here. I'll help you," the woman from the chair said.

Lauren felt the woman checking her arms and legs and lifting her eyelids. "Nothing broken," the woman said, more to herself than to Lauren. Then she began to sit Lauren up. Lauren tried to help herself. She managed a little. In a minute, she was again stretched out on the bed. It felt like the room was moving. The woman smiled and said, "I'll get a cold cloth, my dear. That'll make you feel better."

She disappeared, and Lauren closed her eyes. Time moved slowly. She wanted to remember what had happened after she'd begun feeling ill. For that matter, she wanted to remember what had been happening prior to her getting sick. But no more details would come back. It seemed like an eternity before the gentle voice of her visitor spoke again. "This will feel good," the woman said as something cool and moist fell across Lauren's forehead. It did feel good, and gradually the dizziness passed.

Lauren had no sense of time, but she was sure that the cool cloth was changed several times. As the woman removed it for the third or fourth time, Lauren opened her eyes. The face peering down at her was friendly, smiling, and seeming more familiar than ever. "Hello, Lauren. You know me. I'm Vivian Likio. I work at Paradise Pharmaceuticals. I'll be attending you until you feel better. Is there anything I can get you?"

"I'm thirsty," Lauren said softly, surprised at what an effort it was to speak. Her tongue felt thick and her jaw stiff.

"Oh my goodness, of course you're thirsty," Vivian said. "And we are a little late with your medication. Dr. Mitsui said I needed to get it to you right on time. She called this morning to check on you. She's concerned but confident that you'll be right as rain in no time at all." Vivian smiled reassuringly. "I'll be right back."

As the nurse hurried from the room, Lauren struggled with her memory, and gradually things began to fall into place. She remembered now who Vivian Likio was. That triggered a connection that brought Ned Haraguchi back to her mind. Vivian was Ned's neighbor. But the return of that memory brought a feeling of terror and urgency that she tried to bring into focus.

When Vivian returned, she carried a glass of water in one hand and held a white pill, one about the size of an aspirin, between the thumb and forefinger of the other hand. At that moment, Lauren finally remembered the terrible secret she held, and with that memory her mind began to clear rapidly. She could be in danger. Her friend Billie was gone. Bad things were happening at Paradise Pharmaceuticals. She didn't know who all of her enemies were. *Am I really sick, or have I been somehow made to be sick?* she wondered desperately.

One thing became very clear in her mind: she didn't want to take any medicines, even from someone as nice as Vivian Likio. She didn't know who she could trust, so she would trust nobody. "Here, you've got to sit up," she was told, "so you can drink this water and swallow your medicine."

Vivian placed the glass and the pill on the small nightstand beside Lauren's bed and helped her until she was propped up against the headboard. She stuffed brightly colored pillows around Lauren, then she said, as she retrieved the water and the pill, "Okay, now you can have a drink. But first put this pill in your mouth."

Lauren accepted the pill, but as she lifted the cold glass to her lips she tucked the pill beneath her tongue. She drank deeply. When the water was gone, she said, "Would you please get me another glass?"

"Of course," her nurse said helpfully, and taking the glass from Lauren's trembling hand, she again left the room.

Lauren reached for a Kleenex from the box on her nightstand. Then she spit the pill into it. Much of it had dissolved, and even as she tried to spit more out, she felt herself involuntarily swallow, and she knew that some of the drug had gone down her throat.

She leaned into the pillows, wadding the Kleenex tightly in her hand, hoping that whatever she'd swallowed wouldn't make her more ill. She could hear her nurse returning, and she stuffed the Kleenex under her covers. She'd have to get it to a wastebasket later, she told herself as Ms. Likio reentered the room with another glass of water, which Lauren drank.

Ms. Likio was very solicitous. She offered to cook Lauren a bowl of oatmeal. While she was gone from the room fixing it, Lauren managed to drop the Kleenex containing the remains of her pill into the nearby wastebasket. She did it without falling out of bed, although it was an effort. Later, after eating some of the oatmeal, Lauren was given a sponge bath. She didn't enjoy it at all, but she felt like she was losing the strength in her arms and legs and realized that she could have never managed a shower or even a bath.

As Vivian worked, she made sure Lauren saw the roses Dexter had brought. "He's very devoted to you," she said. "He came last night and again before dawn this morning. I tried to wake you so you could talk to him, but you were still in a deep sleep. But he was here, and that's what's important. You're lucky to have a man like him in your life."

So Dexter had been there the evening before and again early this morning, and she'd been asleep both times, Lauren thought in dismay. If she could only have spoken to him. Maybe he'd be back soon.

But Vivian dashed her hopes of that when she said, "Dexter said to tell you that Mr. Thurman insisted that he needed to leave for California this morning. But he said that you will be allowed to fly over and join him as soon as you're feeling up to it."

"I hope that will be soon," Lauren murmured as depression seemed to overpower her.

Lunch consisted of a toasted tuna sandwich, of which she ate a few bites with Vivian's help. She was alarmed that she could hardly hold her own hands up. She also didn't want to fall asleep again, for she felt that she needed to get out of bed and get away, but despite her resolve she drifted off after a feeble effort to get up. It was late afternoon before she awoke again. Once more, she was somewhat disoriented, but not so badly that she couldn't remember that she'd swallowed part of a pill that she didn't want. Vivian stayed at her side and spoke softly to her from time to time. Gradually, Lauren again recalled the events of the past few days, and the feeling of danger returned. Vivian chatted at her and seemed to want her to speak, but Lauren's thoughts were not something she dared speak of to anyone except Dexter, and she couldn't do that until he came again. So she remained silent.

As the afternoon turned to evening, Lauren was very much aware of Vivian sitting in the chair beside her bed, but she was also aware of her own physical weakness, and it was worrisome. The woman dozed from time to time, and Lauren wondered if she could somehow muster the strength to get away if Vivian fell soundly asleep. But she answered her own question when she tried to pull herself up. She was dizzy again, but not seriously. The most frightening problem was in her arms and legs. They felt like jelly. Reluctantly, she settled back in her bed and waited, hoping she'd soon become stronger. When Vivian brought her some stew for dinner that night, she was encouraged that she was able to sit up with only a little help, and she forced herself to eat, for she knew she could not regain her strength without food.

After the meal, Ms. Likio brought another white pill. Once again, panic set in. "I'm feeling a little better. I don't need more medicine," Lauren protested feebly.

But Vivian grew very stern. "You must take it," she said. "Dr. Mitsui would be very unhappy with both of us if you didn't take your medicine."

Lauren actually thought about physically resisting, but the strength wasn't there, so she did the only thing she could; once again, Lauren tucked the pill beneath her tongue. But as before, she knew that much of it was being swallowed, despite her best efforts to avoid that. After Vivian finally left the room, Lauren spit what was left of the pill into another Kleenex. Within an hour she was again feeling the effects of the drug, and she fought hard to keep her mind alert as her body grew ever weaker.

She eventually drifted to sleep, but awoke when the doorbell rang. She could hear a man talking to Vivian in the living room and recognized the voice as belonging to her boss, and that sent a chill through her body. What she heard him saying was very alarming and did nothing to calm her pounding heart.

"Is she going to be all right?" Royce asked.

"I think so, Mr. Cantrell. The medication seems to have her pretty well out of it," Vivian responded. "But she did eat some stew earlier."

"Good," Royce said. "Does she remember anything about her work? Has she said anything to you?"

"She isn't saying much of anything," Vivian said. "And I get the feeling that her illness has frightened her a great deal."

"I see. Unfortunately, Dr. Mitsui is certain that she's suffered a very severe breakdown, and I suppose that is frightening. I feel just terrible about it. She was going to take some time off and go with her boyfriend to L.A., but it doesn't look like that will happen now. But there is some work we need done. It could have been done in California and e-mailed to us, but we need her to do it in any case. It is essential that she recover from this breakdown as soon as possible."

Breakdown.

The word pounded in Lauren's mind. *Have I actually let the stress of what I've learned about Royce and Fleming get me down?* she wondered. *Or did someone help to bring about the breakdown? And is Billie suffering somewhere right now like I am? Or . . .* she didn't want to think further about Billie. It was just too frightening. *If only I could get up from this bed and get out of here.*

Royce's voice was coming closer as he spoke to Vivian. "I'd like to see her," he was saying. "I want to see for myself that she's getting better."

"I'll check and see if she's awake," Vivian said.

"I want to see her regardless," Royce snapped, and that made the alarm Lauren was experiencing accelerate. Royce was usually more mild mannered than this. Did he suspect she knew something? She didn't have the strength to get up and flee, let alone fight. If only Dexter hadn't had to go to California. He would fight for her. He would help her. But he wasn't here. And since she couldn't flee or fight, she must be mentally on guard.

Royce entered the room, and she felt her body stiffen at his presence. She fought to remain calm as he said, "Lauren, it's me, Royce. I know you've been very ill, but they tell me you're feeling a little better."

She held her eyes tightly closed. She didn't want him to see her fear, and she was afraid her eyes would disclose it. She said nothing, and he asked, "Can you hear me, Lauren?"

She could hear him, but she pretended not to.

"Lauren," he said again, "please let me know if you can hear me."

She didn't allow a muscle to move. She felt she had to make him think she was deeply drugged. He spoke again to her, then turned to the nurse. "You are seeing to it that she gets her medication, aren't you?"

"Of course," Vivian answered defensively. "And I really did think she was doing a little better, even though she doesn't appear to be now."

"That's okay," Royce assured her. "Unfortunately, Dr. Mitsui doesn't expect her recovery to be very fast. Let me know if there's any change."

"Of course," Vivian said.

"And don't let her miss any doses of medicine," he emphasized.

"I know my job," Vivian answered, her voice tightly controlled.

"I'm sure you do," Royce agreed, "but I can't help that I'm concerned about your patient. She's very valuable to me, and a good friend as well. I want her to get better."

He left the room, and Vivian trailed after him. Lauren's eyes popped open. If Royce wanted her to take the medicine so badly, then it was crucial that she avoid it at all cost. But until she had the strength to get away, she had to make them think she was taking it and she had to act like she was drugged.

The phone rang shortly after Royce left. Vivian answered it. Lauren could hear her speaking to someone, her voice filled with concern. "She's very much out of it," she told the caller. It was silent for a moment. "Yes, I'll let her know you called when she's alert enough to recognize that she's being told something," Vivian said a moment later. "Of course I told her it was you who brought the roses, although I'm not sure she understood. But I'll make sure she knows you've been here twice and why you can't come again."

Dexter! It had to be Dexter on the phone. There was another period of silence; then Vivian said, "Yes, that's what I just said. I'll let her know you had to go on to Los Angeles without her and that she is to join you as soon as she can. Now you try not to worry. Dr. Mitsui is a good doctor, and your sweetheart will get better soon."

Oh, how Lauren wished she could be with Dexter right now in Los Angeles! As soon as she could get away, she'd see if she could join him there. But she also needed desperately to talk to him right now. She almost called out, but then she heard the phone being hung up. Her eyes filled, and sobs shook her body. If only Dexter could have delayed his trip. He was the one person she could trust.

Much later, after having fallen asleep, Lauren again woke up. She was still weak, but her mind was quite clear. She must not have gotten too much of the drug, she concluded. She had to make sure she didn't get any of it in the future. Royce and Fleming were out to do her harm—she was almost certain of it. And she couldn't help but wonder if Dr. Mitsui was involved in the plot against her. She had never particularly liked the woman, and if she was involved, danger was imminent. Somehow, she had to get word of her plight to Dexter. Even though he was so far away now, he would know what to do. She wished now she'd told him before. Then maybe she wouldn't be in this terrible situation.

It was dark in the apartment, and only a little artificial light from the streetlights outside was able to steal in past the edges of the drawn blinds. But it was enough that she could see the nurse, Vivian Likio, sleeping in the recliner near her bed. Lauren slowly, quietly, rolled onto her stomach and mustered the strength to slip from the bed. To avoid another fall, she dropped to her knees and crawled ungracefully from the room. She continued to crawl across the living room until she was in her home office. She silently shut the door.

The effort had been so exhausting that she had to rest right there on the floor for several minutes. She shuddered to think what condition she'd be in if she'd taken the full doses of her medication. Finally, she forced herself to her knees and reached for the light. After turning it on, she crawled to her desk and eventually managed to pull herself onto her chair. She picked up the phone and dialed Dexter's cellular phone number, but it appeared that it was out of service. She hung up and dropped her head into her hands and sobbed. She didn't know who else to turn to. In desperation, she even thought about her parents, but they had recently moved again and she had misplaced their new number. Then an idea slowly formed. Dexter would never leave town without his laptop, and she knew that he checked his e-mail several times a day, so she turned on her computer. Because of the effort it had taken her to get this far, she was quickly losing what little strength she had, and her mind was working more slowly by the minute. But she knew what she had to do with what little energy she had left.

After accessing her own e-mail, she clicked on her contacts list. She was getting very dizzy and her eyes were blurry, but she scanned down through the contacts and finally clicked a check mark. She had to rub her eyes several times as she worked but was pleased as the address appeared on her screen. She was feeling terrible and knew she needed to get back to bed, but not until she got a message typed to Dexter. She worked slowly. She tried to tell him she was being drugged and needed help. She hadn't written much when she realized she had to send the message before she collapsed. She couldn't let that happen, for Vivian would find her here and see the message and then—well, she didn't know what then, nor did she want to find out. So she simply typed her name at the end of the message and sent it. Then she shut off the computer, lowered herself to the floor, crawled to the door, and reached for the doorknob and pulled. As it opened, light flooded the adjoining living room.

"Lauren, dear!" Vivian's voice rang out. "You must get back in bed at once. You might hurt yourself."

Ms. Likio was moving swiftly across the living room as she spoke. Lauren felt her knees giving way, and she collapsed onto the soft carpet. Over the next few minutes, Vivian helped her back to her bed, mumbling about how disoriented she must be. Lauren didn't make any response, but it was a relief when she was finally able to lay her head on her soft pillow. She must leave it up to Dexter now—she had to sleep.

When Lauren awoke the next morning, her head had cleared considerably, but the effort during the night had taken a terrible toll on her physical strength. She could hear the nurse bustling about in the kitchen, and she could smell the pleasant odor of frying bacon. She was hungry, and a good breakfast was a pleasant prospect, not so much because it would taste good but because it would help restore her strength. But only if she could avoid taking the white pill again.

* * *

Nurse Likio was worried. She knew that when a doctor prescribed medicine for a patient, it was important that the patient take it exactly as instructed. She again examined the crumpled Kleenex in her hand. Over half of a white pill was in it. After putting some bacon on to fry, she had gone to Lauren's room and taken her wastebasket into the kitchen. There she'd been emptying the waste it contained into a larger garbage bag when a Kleenex had fallen to the floor. As she'd picked it up, a pill had rolled out. Now she was examining another Kleenex, and the discovery of a second partially dissolved pill had caused her to panic.

Both Dr. Mitsui and Mr. Cantrell had emphasized the importance of the patient's medicine, and she had assured Mr. Cantrell that it had been given properly. She couldn't afford to let this happen again. For some reason, Miss Olcott was not swallowing her pills, an unfounded and unreasonable fear, she supposed. She'd never get well if she didn't take her medicine. Vivian resolved to be more careful next time. She couldn't let the sweet girl go without her medication. Then she had an idea how to accomplish that.

Vivian Likio congratulated herself on her ingenuity as she patiently dissolved Lauren's next white pill in a small glass of orange juice. Her patient might not swallow her pill, but she would get her medicine anyway—when she got her breakfast. And she would get well.

Vivian had thought a lot about what Ned had told her, but she couldn't imagine that the girl was really in any danger. She was just very ill. And she would make sure she got better.

Knowing that a double dose could be as serious as no medicine at all, Vivian took only an aspirin to Lauren a few minutes later. She didn't have to worry whether she swallowed it or not. It wouldn't matter if she didn't swallow the aspirin; Lauren would get the medicine she needed in her orange juice. And when she took her the juice a few minutes later, Vivian was relieved that her patient drank every last drop.

* * *

Lauren was sure she'd swallowed only a tiny amount of the pill, and yet, within a few minutes after drinking her juice and eating a light breakfast, she began to feel its effects and she realized too late that she'd somehow been duped. While Ms. Likio cleaned up the kitchen, Lauren struggled from her bed and crawled to her bathroom, where she threw up in the toilet as quietly as she could. She didn't know how she'd taken the drug, and she feared that it was too late to get rid of most of it. She was very frightened when she crawled back into her bed. She cried herself to sleep.

CHAPTER 6

The fog persisted. It was so heavy this morning that Donovan had to drive at an annoyingly slow pace to the office. He wondered if Mrs. Olsen would be late as well, but as usual, she was there ahead of him. He greeted her as he entered, and she began immediately to give him a quick outline of his day. He listened impatiently, thanked her when she'd finished, and entered his private office.

Donovan was not in a good mood this morning. He hadn't heard from Kaelyn. They still hadn't set a date for the wedding, and he felt like she was punishing him for the trial that had messed up her plans. She could be immature at times, he admitted to himself, and again, as so often lately, he wondered if he was making a mistake. But he brushed that thought aside. He needed and wanted to talk to her. He reached for the phone, looked at it thoughtfully for a moment, then changed his mind. Maybe it would be best to let her call him.

He turned on his computer, and while it booted up he thumbed through the mail Mrs. Olsen had placed on his desk. There was nothing terribly pressing there, so he turned back to the computer, ignoring the stack of files on his desk, and entered his password to get into his e-mail then waited again.

There was quite a number of new items awaiting him. One caught his attention. It was from someone named Lauren. And it said *Help me* in the subject area. The only Lauren he knew was in Hawaii, and he couldn't imagine that it could be from her.

But it could genuinely be from someone needing his help. After all, he was a lawyer. What he did for a living was help people. He'd never had a request for his services come in this fashion, but he supposed it could happen. So after checking several other e-mails, discarding some, answering others, and talking on the phone a half-dozen times, he finally opened the one calling for help.

As he scanned through it, something about the message held his attention. He started over and read more carefully a second time.

> *Help me. I'm being doped. I don't trust anyone, not even this nurse who is in my apartment. I'm scared. Please help me.*

Donovan read the message a third time, and then he paid closer attention to the address of the sender. It looked familiar, and he began to wonder if the Lauren he knew was in trouble. He clicked open his own contacts list and scanned down through the names listed there. Sure enough, it was from Lauren Olcott, the girl he'd known on his mission.

He read Lauren's message again. *If this is real,* he thought, *she must really be scared and desperate to e-mail me.* He moved the cursor to Reply, clicked, and began to type.

> *Lauren, I need more information. Please provide more details about the situation and I'll see if there's something I can do to help.*
> *Donovan Deru*

He looked over the brief message, clicked on Save Reply, and then sent it on its way into the vast reaches of cyberspace, wondering if he'd heard the last of it.

A moment later Mrs. Olsen informed him that he'd received a call from the clerk of the district court and that he now had a new client. "He's in jail, and the judge wondered if you'd take the case."

"Wondered as in *do it or else*," Donovan murmured.

"That's right. You've been appointed. He'd like you to run over there now and speak to the guy."

"What else is there to do?" he said grumpily as he stood and retrieved his jacket.

"Actually, there's a lot," Mrs. Olsen reminded him in a kind voice. "You need to spend some time on the Smith case. And you have a couple of matters you need to brush up on for juvenile court tomorrow. Those files are all on your desk. And—"

Donovan cut her off with a wave of his hand. There was a lot to do, as the stack of files on his desk attested, and he needed to get on it, but he wasn't feeling much like it this morning. He knew it was because of Kaelyn and the fog, but there was nothing he could do about the fog, and he'd already decided that the next move was Kaelyn's. So he committed himself to paying better attention to all that he had to do in the office. "I know. I'm sorry I'm behind," he told Mrs. Olsen. "It's this horrible fog. It's getting to me. I'll go see this character in jail, and then I'll come back and get to work."

The defendant at the jail was not an easy case; he had a lot to say, and it was a little after noon before Donovan got back to the office with several pages of notes on a legal pad. Mrs. Olsen had left him a note telling him that she was at lunch and that Kaelyn had called. She wanted him to call her back at work when he got in.

That cheered him up a little, and he hurried to the phone in his office. "Sorry I wasn't in when you called," he said as soon as she answered. "The district court gave me a defendant who is in jail and wanted me to see him right away."

"That's okay," Kaelyn said, sounding bright and cheerful. "Have time for lunch? The teacher I'm subbing for has a prep period after lunch, so I get a nice long break."

Donovan had planned to skip lunch and start to work on the stack of files on his desk. But this was more important. "Pick you up in five minutes," he said. "You decide where to eat."

It was barely over three minutes later when he pulled up outside of the school where she was substituting, and she ran out, jumped in the car, and slid over beside him. She planted a warm kiss on his cheek and said, "Golden Corral."

Enjoying their shrimp and salad, the couple talked about mutual friends, a touring Broadway play they wanted to see in Salt Lake, and the pros and cons of the public school system. Donovan was having a great time and didn't regret his choice to go to lunch, even though he knew he'd have to make up the lost work time later. Over brownies and cherry cobbler Kaelyn said, "We still haven't set that date. But there's not time to really talk about it now. Do you have plans for tomorrow night?"

Donovan grinned. "I do now," he said. "Dinner at seven? We'll talk at my place after."

Kaelyn smiled and reached across the table and squeezed his hand. "You're okay, Mr. Attorney," she said.

Donovan didn't notice how the fog had become a little thicker when they left the Golden Corral, hand in hand, a little after one. He was already looking forward to the next evening with Kaelyn. She had just brightened his day. He felt sure they could make it work between them.

* * *

Lauren awoke late that night to a murmur of voices from her living room. Her mind was quite clear, but she was still very weak. It had been a long and difficult day. She'd eaten, as usual, in bed and had waited to drink her milk until Vivian had gone out of the room. Then she'd used every ounce of energy she could muster and crawled to her bathroom, grateful it was only a few feet from her bed, and poured the milk down the drain. When the white pill appeared a little later, it seemed to her that Vivian was confident that she'd gotten her medication with the milk, for she didn't even watch to see if she took it, which she didn't. Lauren wasn't sure what the medication had done to her, but she was certain that it had at least contributed to her weakened condition. She suspected that she was still suffering some effect from the earlier doses, and she clung to the hope that she'd get her strength back soon and be able to get away and get help, if Dexter wasn't able to help her first.

The murmur came nearer, and with a sinking heart she recognized Royce's and Fleming's voices as well as Vivian's. "We'll stay here for a little while so you can go get some groceries if you need to," Fleming was saying solicitously.

And leave me here alone with those two! Lauren thought with horror.

"If you don't mind, that would be very helpful," Vivian said. "Whatever caused Lauren's breakdown has left her very weak. She can't even sit up by herself for very long, and she can't get to the bathroom without me pretty much carrying her."

Lauren had at least fooled her on that point. Apparently Vivian thought she was even weaker than she really was.

Vivian went on. "If you fellows are worried about her wandering away and getting herself hurt or something, there's no need. She couldn't leave without help if the place were burning down."

"I'm so sorry to hear that," Fleming responded. "She's such a valuable employee and such a good person. We just feel terrible about all this."

Lauren could hear Royce making sympathetic noises, and she knew they were both so terribly phony she wanted to scream out in protest. But of course she didn't make a sound.

"I'll be back in a few minutes then," Vivian said. "I do appreciate the two of you sitting here with her while I'm gone."

"Take your time. We'll take care of Lauren," Fleming said. His tone was kind enough, but Lauren read a sinister meaning into his words, and panic flooded over her. There was no way she could ever defend herself. If they were here to hurt her, she was at their mercy, she realized. Lauren found herself resorting to the habit she'd once had as a young girl, and she began pleading with God to protect her.

She could hear the door to her apartment close as Vivian presumably left to run her errands. Almost immediately, Royce and Fleming entered her unlit bedroom.

"Lauren, if you're awake we need to talk to you," Fleming said.

She didn't want to talk to them, so she feigned sleep.

"Lauren, we need to talk to you," Fleming said a little louder.

"Are you sure she's not drugged out of her mind?" Royce asked. "I don't think she can talk to us."

"She's just asleep," Fleming said in a much softer tone. "The drug she's taking should have very little effect on her mind. On the mice it did exactly what it's supposed to do; it rendered their muscles so weak they couldn't move. And from the way Vivian spoke, it sounds like it's having the same effect on Lauren."

"Maybe it was that first drug she was given on Monday, the one in the—" Royce began.

"Could be, I suppose," Fleming interrupted with a wave of the hand.

Lauren tried to remember what she'd been given and by whom, but Monday afternoon was still a little fuzzy.

"Fleming, she's not moving," Royce said, and to Lauren it sounded like there was a note of alarm in his voice. "Are you sure she isn't getting too much? One death is too many. We can't let her wind up like Billie."

Lauren felt like she'd been kicked in the head. Her worst fears had just been confirmed. Something terrible had happened to Billie, and it was probably her fault, since she'd sent the e-mail that somehow Royce and Fleming must have found out about. She began praying harder than she'd ever prayed in her life. She found herself, in her terror, promising God that she'd start going to church again if she could just be delivered from these two terrible men.

"She won't die," Fleming growled. "Unless of course she does know something and chooses to talk about it. Then there'll be no choice, as you well know and better not forget."

From the tone of Fleming's voice just now, Lauren was certain that Royce's own life would be in danger if he did anything to cross Fleming. Royce confirmed that when he said, "I know, we're in this together. Quit worrying. I just don't want there to be any more deaths if it can be prevented."

Lauren's heart sank even lower. Billie was almost certainly dead, she thought, and she fought back the tears.

"Lauren, are you listening to this?" Fleming suddenly asked in a normal tone.

She made no move, hoping that she would seem very much asleep.

"She appears to be in awfully bad shape to me. Are you sure—"

"She's not dead!" Fleming said. "Turn on the light, then you'll be able to see she's breathing."

The light came on, but Lauren tried not to make any reaction. "There, see, she's breathing. I can see her blanket moving slightly," Fleming said.

"Oh, good," Royce responded. "Well, let's let her sleep then."

She didn't feel quite as much in danger now as she had, because it appeared that Royce didn't want her to die, and despite all the evil he was involved in, she felt grateful to him.

"I need to wake her up," Fleming said. A moment later, the fat man's hand had grasped her shoulder and begun to shake her almost violently. "Lauren, wake up," he ordered.

Lauren was determined to play out this scene properly. She decided to pretend to wake up, and so she groaned and opened her eyes, immediately shutting them again against the brightness of the light.

Once more, Fleming shook her, not quite as hard this time, although it was not out of kindness on his part, she was quite sure. She opened her eyes again but squinted while they grew accustomed to the light. "What . . . who . . ." she stammered, hoping she sounded like she was just waking from a deep sleep.

"Lauren, it's me, Royce," her boss said. "Fleming and I came by to see how you're feeling."

"Royce?" she said in the form of a question.

"Yes, and Fleming."

"Oh," she said with a moan and turned her head toward them. "Why are you here?"

"We are worried about you," Fleming said in a sweet, sickening tone. "You're one of our most valuable people. We need for you to get well soon."

Liar, she thought venomously to herself. With an extreme effort she made herself say, "I'm sorry I'm sick. I'm just so tired." She closed her eyes.

"It's not your fault," Royce said. "Sometimes people just get sick."

And sometimes they are made sick, she thought bitterly.

"I understand you're very weak," Fleming said.

"Yes," Lauren agreed. "I can't move. Am I going to die?" Tears spilled from her eyes, the ones she'd been suppressing after learning of Billie's death.

"Of course not. Dr. Mitsui has assured us that she'll make sure you get well. And if she needs to consult other doctors, we've told her to be sure and do that," Fleming told her.

Lauren pretended not to hear, trying to convince them that she'd fallen asleep again.

"We miss you at the office," Royce said, but it sounded lame to Lauren when he said it.

He went on. "Fleming, we better go and let her rest. I thinks she's asleep again anyway."

They left, shutting off the light as they did. And immediately, the urgency of her plight struck her. They'd committed one murder, and despite what Royce had said, she knew they'd do it again if they felt they needed to. And she could be next! She had to get stronger and had to get away. *If only Dexter were here,* she thought as tears again began to flow.

Lauren could hear the men's voices, but she could no longer tell what they were saying. And she was surprised when shortly she heard the front door open and close. Surely Vivian couldn't be back already. She strained to hear any sound that might be coming from the other room. The voices were gone, and there was no sound like there would be if Vivian were putting groceries away.

She lay very still, and when there was still no sound she decided to make another attempt to get to her computer. Maybe there was a message from Dexter. She slowly got out of her bed, more falling to the floor than anything. With another determined effort, one driven by fear and desperation, she crawled to her home office. She didn't know how much time she had before Vivian returned, so she pushed herself to the limit.

When she'd finally dragged herself onto her chair and turned on her computer, she waited impatiently, then at last she had her e-mails in front of her. She scanned through them, and gasped in relief when she saw a reply to the one she'd sent entitled *Help me*. She quickly opened it, only to gasp again. Her hands began to shake terribly. She broke into a heavy sweat. She rubbed her eyes in an attempt to clear them. She steadied herself to keep from falling from her chair. Then she read the reply she'd received a second time.

This message wasn't from Dexter, it was from Donovan Deru! What was he doing answering Dexter's message? She wondered if it could be a trick of some sort that Royce or Fleming had devised—a trap of some kind. She sat for a full minute wondering about it. Then it finally occurred to her that she must have sent Dexter's message to the wrong man. She opened her contact list to make sure. It only took a glance to convince her that she'd hit Donovan's address instead of Dexter's. Dexter's followed Donovan's on her list, and the addresses were even similar in appearance. She'd simply clicked on the wrong one. Tears stung her eyes. Dexter still didn't know the danger she was in.

She hung her head for a moment, thinking of Donovan as her tears dried. He was a nice guy and a good man. He'd recently asked Jim Roderick about her and had even cared enough to ask Jim to invite her to church. Maybe there was something he could do, she decided. He at least deserved an explanation. So she drafted a short message.

I meant to e-mail my boyfriend that last message, not you. But I really do need help. My life is in danger, and I haven't been able to contact my boyfriend, Dexter Drake, who's out of town. Certain people are stealing money, and now they think I know about it and want to kill me. They are drugging me until I can hardly move. I'm so weak that I can't get away. I even had to crawl to my computer because I can't stand up. Please, help me, Elder Deru. I don't know what to do.

She sent the message, cleared it from her computer, and prepared to send one to Dexter. But just then she heard the front door open. Frantically, she shut down her computer and crawled back onto the floor. There she lay in fear, wondering how she would explain to Vivian what she was doing. She couldn't think of anything, so there was nothing she could do now but wait for Vivian to find her.

"Lauren," Vivian called out frantically. "Where are you? You shouldn't be out of bed." Lauren waited, not bothering to call out. Then Vivian called to her again, and both the words she spoke and the tone in which she spoke them gave Lauren some hope. "Please be here, Lauren," she pleaded. "I shouldn't have ever left you with those two. Oh, why did I trust them?"

"I'm in here," Lauren called out. "I'm too weak to move."

A moment later Ms. Likio entered the room and dropped onto her knees beside Lauren. "Oh, Lauren, I was so afraid they'd taken you away from here. I guess that's silly, but when I came back and found them gone, it made me angry, and it still does. They could at least have had the decency to stay until I could get back with the groceries. Then when I found your bed empty, I got this terrible feeling and I was afraid for you." She touched Lauren lightly on the forehead, then stroked her hair softly. "I'll help you get back to bed, and I'll help you get better, Lauren. I promise I will."

Vivian Likio didn't seem like a dangerous person. Maybe she could trust her, Lauren thought. Maybe she wasn't part of the conspiracy. But she couldn't be sure. Anyway, she was so very tired. The efforts of the past few minutes had drained her.

Then Vivian asked, "What are you doing in here? Why did you leave your bed?"

"I was afraid," she said lamely. "I was alone."

"Oh, those men!" Vivian exclaimed again. "They should have known better. They know the condition you're in."

Finally back in bed a few minutes later, Lauren uttered a silent prayer of thanks to God. She was certain that she'd received help, and she thought about the promise she'd made to go back to church if Heavenly Father would keep Royce and Fleming from hurting her. She intended to do that, once this nightmare was over . . . if she survived it. Finally, despite her worries over Billie being killed and her own danger, she fell asleep.

The following morning she felt a little stronger but she didn't let Vivian know. She was even able to get out of bed more easily to get rid of her orange juice, which she was certain was laced with the drug that killed Billie. And later, she began to think about how she could get back to her computer again. She had to contact Dexter, and she wanted to know if there was a reply from her latest e-mail. She also wondered how long it would be before she had enough strength to get away from Vivian. She even devised a plan. By continuing to fake a total weakness of her muscles, she might be able to talk Vivian into running to the store to get her something when she felt up to walking to the door and down the stairs and away.

CHAPTER 7

Lauren lay wide awake that afternoon thinking about Donovan Deru. There was no denying she'd had a crush on the elder when she was seventeen. She'd first been attracted to his unusual golden eyes. She felt a stirring deep within her as she remembered them now. She also recalled how he'd made her angry one day when he and his companion had been at her house for dinner. Those were the days when she began spending more time with her surfing friends and spending many of her Sundays in the surf instead of in church and with her family. Shortly after the meal, she and her little brother had had their picture taken with the two missionaries. It was then that Elder Deru lectured her about staying close to the Church and to God. "You can surf on Saturdays," he said. And she'd wondered who he thought he was, telling her how to live. He was only two years older than she was, and she'd wondered what made him such an expert. She tried to hate him after that, but she never really did, she admitted now. In fact, she'd never really even come close to hating him. She felt herself flush with shame as she remembered the awful things she'd said to him that day.

"I don't need you to tell me what to do, and I don't need the Church," she'd stormed. "My friends are good kids and we don't get in any kind of trouble. We're smart too. I'm not even the only one who graduated from high school a year early. We just prefer surfing to going to church. Maybe you don't know about this, but between school and work I have almost no free time. I need a chance to relax, not some stuffy church meetings."

And he'd responded with, "We all need the Church, Lauren. And we all need God. Someday you'll realize how true that is. It may not be until you are in some sort of serious trouble, but it'll happen."

Now Lauren suddenly began to sob uncontrollably. Thinking of him and what he'd said cut her to the core. He'd been right, and she'd started to realize that before her current trouble. But never had she known that she needed God like she did now. And perhaps it was what he'd said as much as what her parents had taught her that was causing her to yearn for her spiritual roots in this desperate time.

She'd never given up her belief in God, but she had been living her life without Him. She sobbed and regretted the path she'd taken and resolved again to do better if she got out of this mess alive. And maybe someday she could actually help Dexter to believe in God and join her in Church activity.

She found herself yearning for her parents. They'd left the islands about a year after she graduated from high school. She stayed behind, living with the family of a friend. Her parents had tried so hard to get her to come with them, but at that time the local college, her friends, and her love of the surf had won out over them. She gradually quit communicating with them, except for an occasional card, for they always managed to remind her that she was missing out on an important part of her life. And she resented that—largely, she realized now, because she knew they were right and her pride wouldn't let her admit that to them. She wasn't even sure what she'd done with their address. They'd recently moved again and sent her a note telling her about it, but she hadn't written it down in her address book at the time, and then she couldn't find the letter when she looked for it later. They had mentioned that her little brother was dating a girl seriously and that a wedding might be on the horizon. She couldn't help wishing she could be more involved in their lives.

As Lauren lay there she contemplated how impermanent things like money and careers were. But families were forever. How foolish she'd been! She missed them now in a way she hadn't missed them before and she longed to make contact with them. If she survived this situation she was in, she resolved to find them and make amends.

Lauren closed her eyes tightly, and once again she offered an awkward prayer, expressing to God her feelings the best she could and once again asking for help. She felt better after the short prayer. And she fell asleep thinking of Elder Deru and of how he'd told her that someday, when she was in trouble, she'd need God again. How right he'd been.

Lauren could hear the doorbell ringing. She listened as Vivian answered, hoping that Royce and Fleming weren't there again. She was surprised when Vivian came in and said, "You have a visitor." A moment later, as she stepped back, Leroy Provost entered the room. In one hand he held six red roses. In the other was a small box of cherry chocolates.

"I heard you were sick," he said. "I wondered if you could use a little company."

* * *

This was going to be a good day. A stiff wind had come up during the night, and the fog was gone by morning. It was cold but clear when Donovan stepped outside of his house. The sun was shining brightly to the east, and he couldn't help but laugh out loud with the sheer joy of it. This was great! And on top of that, he and Kaelyn would be setting a marriage date that night. Nothing could darken this day—absolutely nothing.

The judge had unexpectedly moved one of Donovan's cases up to the top of the schedule that morning, and that necessitated his making some fast preparations, but he wasn't angry. When he got back to his office a little before eleven, there was a note from Mrs. Olsen that she'd received a call from a daughter who had an emergency and needed her to hurry over and watch the kids. She might or might not get back before the day was over. That was okay. She'd laid things out for him that morning. He knew what had to be done and he'd get along just fine.

He took off his jacket, rolled up his sleeves, and tackled the morning's mail which he'd had to leave earlier. That done, he finally got around to checking his e-mail. The day had been so pretty that he hadn't entertained a negative thought all morning, at least not any big ones. And he also hadn't thought about the disturbing call for help he'd responded to, so he was surprised and worried when there was another e-mail message from Lauren Olcott.

Donovan opened the message and read it. Then he sat back in his chair, staring at the message on the screen, trying to picture the young lady as he'd last seen her. Anger had flashed from those gorgeous, smoky eyes, and she'd tossed her long, wavy hair with a haughty wave of her head as she'd risen from her chair and stormed from the room. Her brother, a few years younger than Lauren, had apologized on her behalf. Donovan still remembered what the boy had said next. "She has a huge crush on you, Elder Deru. I think you just broke her heart." Then he'd grinned and added, "But maybe it'll help her."

It apparently hadn't, and yet now, a good nine years later, she was reaching out to him for help. He wondered if she was overreacting to whatever was happening to her. Maybe she'd become mentally ill. Those and a dozen other questions raced through Donovan's mind. An even bigger question inserted itself: how could he help her? She was thousands of miles away.

Then he thought of his former companion, Jim Roderick. Surely he'd know what was going on; he worked for the same company as she did. He wanted to call Jim right then, but Jim's number was at home. Looking at his watch, and calculating the three-hour time difference between there and Hawaii, he thought that if he hurried he might be able to reach Jim before he left for work. And if not, he could get Jim's number from his wife and call him at his office. Donovan saved the message from Lauren, threw on his jacket, and left the office, locking it behind him. He drove home, so deep in thought that he didn't even notice how the fog was settling back into the valley. He parked in his garage and hurried into the house.

He found his address book in the nightstand beside his bed. He looked up Jim's number and dialed. Sally answered and told him that Jim had just left twenty or twenty-five minutes ago. "It takes him almost a half hour to get to the office," she said. "If you give him ten minutes and call there, you should be able to reach him."

Donovan wrote down the number, looked at his watch, and decided to spend his lunch break at the house. While waiting for his friend to get to work, he impulsively went down into his basement in search of his missionary journals. He readily found the box they were in and carried it upstairs. It only took a moment to find the journals and his missionary photo album. It took him a couple of minutes to find the entry he remembered writing about Lauren. He'd begun with a caveat, writing, *Missionaries aren't supposed to think about girls. But this girl is different. I've thought a lot about her, not because I'm interested romantically but because she seems like someone special who is throwing everything away. She's both beautiful and intelligent. It tears me up, just like it tears up her family, to see her dropping activity in the Church just to be with her surfing friends.* Then he'd gone on to describe the conversation he and his companion had carried on that afternoon in the Olcott living room with Lauren and her brother Larry, and how angry she'd been.

Donovan checked his watch and decided to wait a couple more minutes before trying to call Jim. He laid down the journal and picked up the photo album that his sister had put together for him after his mission and began to idly thumb through it. Suddenly, Lauren Olcott's smiling face was looking up at him along with his own, his companion's, and her brother's. His sister had written next to it, *Prettiest girl in Hawaii.* He felt a stab of pain in his chest. He'd forgotten how beautiful she was. He wondered what she looked like now. Jim had mentioned that she was very attractive, but he wondered if she was also hard and worldly.

He laid the album beside him on the sofa, with the page open to Lauren's picture, and picked up the phone from the end table. A minute later he had Jim on the line.

"Hey, buddy," his friend said cheerfully. "To what do I owe the honor of another call from you so soon? If it's about Elder Jordan, I haven't found out where he is yet."

"It's not about him," Donovan said. And he went on to describe the e-mails from Lauren. Then he asked, "Is she okay, or has something happened to her?"

Jim was quiet for a moment, then he said, "No, she's not okay, but I don't think that she's in any danger. For some reason, she seems to have been under a great deal of stress lately, and she had a severe breakdown."

"A breakdown?" Donovan asked.

"Yes, a mental breakdown, according to the scuttlebutt around the office. And it's made her physically ill as well."

"So, she's in the hospital then? How could she be getting access to a computer from the hospital?" Donovan asked.

"Well, actually, she's at home. The head of our research department here is a psychiatrist who has a practice on the side. She's top-notch from what I hear. And I understand she has a staff nurse who is really good. The two of them are taking care of Lauren. Dr. Mitsui says the prognosis is good and that she's quite certain Lauren will be back to work in a couple of weeks."

Donovan was thoughtful for a moment, then he said, "You told me you talked to her about going to church and that she seemed worried about something. Is that right?"

"Yes, like I told you before, I saw her on Monday morning. She had her breakdown later that day. And she did seem awfully stressed. You're right, you know. She needs the Church. Sally and I will invite her again when she feels better."

"Great," Donovan said. "But I really am worried about her. Those messages she sent me were a bit scary. You said she seemed stressed and that she was particularly worried about a friend that hadn't come to work. Is that right?"

"Yes, she was worried about Billie Maio, the secretary to the CEO of our company. She didn't show up to work on Monday and had apparently called Mr. Thurman to tell him she was quitting and moving to Arizona. She and Lauren were friends, and Lauren seemed to think that she wouldn't do something like that. I know she was worried about Billie. Other than that, I can't imagine what might have been stressing her, unless it was her work."

"Does she do something that would create a lot of stress?"

"She helps write contracts with distributors and other companies that are using our products or services, and apparently she does a lot of the negotiation on the terms of those contracts. Some of them are worth millions, which has got to be stressful," Jim said. "At any rate, she's definitely ill now, but I'm sure Dr. Mitsui will have her feeling better soon. Like I say, she has a tremendous reputation in her field. I think Lauren's lucky to have her."

"Did she say anything to you to make you think she might be in danger?"

"No, not really."

"Okay, I appreciate your help. If you hear anything about Lauren's progress, let me know, will you?"

The fog that had now returned as thick as ever was not lost on Donovan as he backed from his garage. He remembered, just a few hours earlier, feeling like nothing could dampen this day. But something had. For some reason this young woman from his past had reached out to him. Perhaps it was in fact a mental illness and she was delusional; that was certainly what Jim believed. *But is there something more that drove her to such a collapse?* he wondered. *And if so, what could it be?*

He couldn't stop thinking about Lauren and her troubles while he and a client conferred shortly after his return to the office. Fortunately, it was not a complicated matter they were discussing, and no harm was done when he failed to give it his full attention. The client didn't seem to even notice. After he left, Donovan placed another call to Jim. "I'm sorry to bother you at work again, but just to put my mind at ease, would you mind stopping by Lauren's place and checking on her?" he asked.

"I'll swing by after work," Jim promised, "and I'll give you a call after I've seen her."

When Donovan came out of his office, Mrs. Olsen, who had returned, said, "Tough case, Donovan? You seem really worried."

"I'm worried, but not about that client."

"Another one?"

"No, not exactly, Barbara. I've gotten a couple of e-mail messages from a woman in Honolulu asking for my help."

"Honolulu?" Mrs. Olsen asked, a little taken aback. "Didn't you serve your mission there?" He nodded, and she asked, "And is this woman someone you knew back then?"

"She is. And I just spoke with a former companion of mine who works for the same company she does, and he seems to think she's getting all the help she needs from a psychiatrist there. I suppose he's right. Do I have anyone else coming in the next few minutes?"

"No," Barbara replied.

"Good, then maybe I'll just send a note back to this girl. It'll only take a few minutes."

"Girl?" Barbara asked with a raised eyebrow.

"Young woman. She was seventeen when I knew her on my mission. I guess that would make her twenty-six now."

"I see," Barbara answered with a questioning look. "Well, you better get to it then."

Donovan sat for the next few minutes and fashioned a reply to the troubled woman in Hawaii. He said he was grateful she'd asked him for help and that he would do whatever he could if she could tell him a little more specifically what was happening. He thought about telling her that Jim would be coming by, but he decided it might be better for that visit to be a surprise. He then told her that he hoped she was feeling better soon.

He sent the e-mail flying away at the speed of light somewhere out into the Internet, where it would wait until she opened her e-mail—*if she can still do so,* he thought with sudden and considerable concern. *Is her condition deteriorating to the point where she is totally irrational?* he wondered. *Or is there a chance that she really is in some kind of physical danger?* He could only wait to hear from Jim again. Maybe then he could quit worrying so much and let the doctor over there deal with Lauren.

CHAPTER 8

Lauren lay in bed worrying. The woman who had come to the door was Dr. Mitsui. She hoped the doctor wouldn't come in to see her. If she did, Lauren wasn't sure she could fool her the way she'd managed to fool the nurse and her bosses. She became increasingly concerned as the minutes dragged on and the two women continued talking. Finally, she heard them get up from their chairs and come to her door. It opened, and she forced herself to keep her eyes shut.

Dr. Mitsui spoke to her directly. Lauren didn't respond. Then the doctor gently shook her shoulder. "Lauren, can you hear me?" she asked.

When Lauren didn't answer this time, Vivian said, "Sometimes she's like this. She doesn't always respond or wake up easily. And yet I've found her out of bed, crawling on the floor. When that happens she's so weak she can hardly assist me in getting her back in her bed."

Lauren felt the touch of the doctor's hand on her forehead. "Temperature feels about right. The sedative we're giving her shouldn't have her out like this unless her condition is a lot worse than I thought at first. And the physical weakness isn't right either. Just because someone has suffered a mental breakdown doesn't mean they will lose all their physical strength."

Lauren lay there confused. If the medications were prescribed by Dr. Mitsui, then she should know what the result would be. If she knew that Lauren was quite alert mentally, the doctor would probably really wonder what was going on. Lauren lay silently, trying to breathe evenly while her temperature, blood pressure, and heart rate were checked.

The doctor and nurse continued to talk. "Her blood pressure is high, but that's to be expected with the breakdown she's had," the doctor said.

"Temperature is only very slightly up," the nurse commented.

"And her heart's good, too," the doctor confirmed. "Something's going on here that's not at all what I would have expected at this point. Let me look at that medication, Vivian."

The nurse left, but Dr. Mitsui again put a hand on Lauren's forehead. Lauren wondered if it was time to trust the doctor, for she seemed so concerned for her well-being. But the fear that had been instilled into her by Royce and Fleming was overpowering, and she dared not speak. She only hoped she could get away soon and join Dexter in California.

Lauren heard Vivian return and listened in horror as the doctor said in anger, "This is not the medication that was in this bottle when I gave it to you!"

Vivian's voice quivered as she responded, "It has to be."

"I'm telling you, these pills are not the sedative I gave her!" the doctor thundered.

"I've just given her what was in that bottle," Vivian said defensively.

"Well, someone has switched them. I'd have to run a test to be sure, but I believe this is an experimental drug that I've been working on that weakens muscles. Its intended purpose is to make it easier to control people who are violent. That would explain why she's so weak. In fact, if she's gotten a full dose twice a day, she shouldn't even be able to move her head, let alone her arms and legs."

Lauren wanted to scream in horror, but she restrained herself as the doctor said, "I'll take these and bring back something to counteract the effect. In the meantime, you stay right with her and keep the doors locked while I'm gone."

"Why do I need the doors locked?" Vivian asked, her voice breaking. "Lauren clearly can't leave, if that's what you're worried about."

"That's not what I'm worried about!" Dr. Mitsui yelled. "I'm worried about someone getting in."

"What? I don't understand. Why would that . . ." Vivian began. Then she said, "Oh, no. Did someone sneak in and change the pills in that bottle?"

"Unless someone switched them in my office. And I can't imagine that," Dr. Mitsui said in a strained voice. "Either way, I've got to know."

Vivian groaned. "Shouldn't we move her to a hospital?" she asked.

"And try to explain why she's been receiving experimental drugs?" Dr. Mitsui asked. "I don't think we'd better do that until we can explain how this happened. It could bring about the forced closure of the entire business while we were all investigated. That would be devastating to the future of Paradise Pharmaceuticals, not to say what it would do to my career. For now, I'm going back to the lab to make sure that I'm right about the drug, and if I am, then I know what will be most likely to bring her back to normal. We just can't afford to let anyone know that this has happened."

The emotions running through Lauren were wild and frightening. At least, she reasoned as she attempted to calm herself, she wouldn't be getting any more of whatever it was she'd been given. But she wasn't at all sure she wanted any other drugs from Dr. Mitsui.

The last instruction the doctor gave Nurse Likio before she left the bedroom was, "Don't forget to lock the door behind me, and check her vital signs every few minutes. If things change dramatically before I get back, call me. And don't let anyone in here while I'm gone. No one!"

Vivian agreed, and the two of them left the room. A minute later, she heard the door open and then close. She even heard the click of the dead bolt. Then the nurse reentered her bedroom. "I wish you'd wake up," Vivian said gently to Lauren. "I'm so afraid for you."

Lauren wanted to tell her that she was very much awake and scared to death, but she didn't quite dare. So she again tried to lie quietly, trying to calm herself while Vivian checked her vital signs. She clearly failed to slow her racing heart, for when Vivian felt her pulse, she gasped. "Your heart is racing," she said in alarm. "I better call the doctor right now."

Again she left the room, and when she came back she was mumbling to herself. "She must have forgotten to turn it on," Lauren thought she heard her say. Lauren assumed she meant the doctor's cell phone, and the thought passed through the frightened young woman's mind that maybe the doctor didn't want to be reached. That maybe she had no intention of coming back. That maybe she, Lauren, was being left to die!

Again Lauren debated with herself. Maybe she should risk trusting the nurse. She might be dead before Dexter could ever get help to her if she didn't. Tears welled up in her eyes, and despite her best effort to control them, they spilled out and wet her cheeks. The nurse mopped them gently up with tissue, mumbling to herself some more, something about her being a poor, poor, dear girl. Just then the phone rang, and Vivian left the room to answer it. A moment later, she came back in and stood near Lauren's door as she spoke.

She was surprised when Vivian said, "Oh, Ned, you dear man, I'm glad you called. I am so worried about this girl."

There was silence while he presumably asked Vivian why she was worried about Lauren. Then she spoke again. "I'm afraid you were right, Ned. She might be in terrible danger."

Silence again. Then Vivian spent a couple of minutes explaining what Dr. Mitsui had just discovered. After the next pause, Vivian said, "I'm not sure if I trust Dr. Mitsui or not. I'm just all shook up right now, and the poor girl is deathly ill. She would at least wake up before. Now I can't get her to respond at all. Tell me what to do, Ned. Please help me to help this dear girl."

She was walking away from the bedroom and her voice grew more quiet. Lauren couldn't tell what else Vivian was saying, but found herself wanting to trust her, for she did trust Ned. Lauren turned again to the God she had turned her back on years ago and offered a short but fervent prayer. "Please help me to know if I can trust Vivian," she pleaded silently. "Or else send someone else to help me." Then she closed her prayer and opened her eyes, looking around the room. She could see the two bouquets of roses, one from Dexter and one from Leroy. She also spotted the box of cherry chocolates, and her mouth began to water. She slowly moved her hand toward the box on her nightstand. She took off the lid and fumbled with one of the chocolates.

The doorbell rang. *Could it be someone coming to help me?* she wondered as she pulled the candy from the box. *Could the Lord really be answering my prayer so quickly?*

She strained to listen, holding the chocolate in her hand. She heard Vivian moving silently to the door. She expected to hear it open at any moment. But there was not a sound from the living room, and she remembered Dr. Mitsui's instructions to Vivian to not allow anyone in. Lauren became so intent on listening that she absently dropped the chocolate onto the nightstand and forced herself to the edge of the bed. As she swung her legs over, someone knocked on the door. And as she eased herself to the floor, the doorbell rang again.

When she crawled to the bedroom doorway and looked through, Vivian was standing silently at the front door, one eye peering through the peephole. Lauren couldn't stand the suspense anymore. "Who is it?" she called out weakly.

Vivian let out a muffled scream and spun around. "Oh, Lauren, you frightened me, dear girl!" she exclaimed. "I didn't know you'd woken up. You must get right back in bed."

"Who's at the door?" Lauren insisted.

"No one. He left."

"Who left?"

"A man from the sales department. I can't recall his last name, but I think his first name is Jim," Vivian revealed.

Lauren let out a cry of anguish. "Jim Roderick," she said. *The one person I might have trusted.*

It was as if Vivian read her thoughts. "We can't trust anyone," Vivian said. "Ned and I and Dr. Mitsui think you're in danger."

Suddenly, even though one possible answer to her prayer had just left, a feeling of peace came over her, and Lauren felt she could trust Vivian Likio. "Yes, I'm in danger," she agreed, her voice suddenly fading from exhaustion. "Please help me."

It was a half hour before Lauren was back in bed and had recovered enough to talk. Vivian insisted that she tell her what kind of danger she was in. "I don't want to put you at risk too," Lauren told her. "Just help me get away from here. Dexter can help me after that. It would be better if you didn't know what was going on."

"I'll take that chance," Vivian insisted.

"But I won't," Lauren countered firmly.

"At least tell me who we should be worried about," Vivian said.

"Royce and Fleming," Lauren said. "Other than the two of them, I don't know for sure."

"I'm not surprised about them. They were acting awfully strange when they were here. When Dr. Mitsui gets back, we'll have her help us."

"No!" Lauren said in alarm. "I'm not sure about her either."

"But she's trying to help you," Vivian insisted. "And we need to let her do so."

"But we can't," Lauren insisted, pleading, sobbing with worry.

Vivian's face grew soft, and she patted Lauren's arm. "Very well. But you'll have to do your sleeping act again."

"I can't take any more drugs," Lauren said. "I don't dare."

"But she might have something to counteract—" Vivian began.

Lauren interrupted. "I'm getting stronger. I didn't take much of the—"

It was Vivian's turn to break in. "The pills I gave you were just aspirin. I gave the others to you in your orange juice and your milk."

"And I threw them up or poured them down the drain," Lauren revealed.

There was a surge of relief on Vivian's face, and she said, "You're a smart girl. Okay, I'm not sure how, but I'll make sure you don't get any more medicine."

"I'll help," Lauren said. "But we've got to get away from here soon. I'm getting stronger. I've got to hide somewhere. And we should make it look like you didn't help, like I forced you to let me go."

Vivian shook her head. "No, my dear girl. I'll help you, and that's all there is to it."

"But others can help. Dexter can help," Lauren insisted.

"He's in Los Angeles, hoping you'll soon be able to go there."

"Yes, that's it," Lauren said brightly. "I can fly to L.A. They can't find me there."

* * *

"I went to her apartment," Jim was telling Donovan on the phone. "I knocked and rang the bell. I even tried the door. It was locked. I'm thinking that she must be in the hospital now."

"Will you check around, Jim? I know it's a lot of trouble, but I'm honestly getting worried. I'd just be relieved to know she's getting help in a hospital," Donovan said. "Then I could probably forget about the whole thing."

"I'll let you know what I find out," Jim promised.

Donovan slowly put the phone down. "Was that your friend in Hawaii?" Mrs. Olsen asked.

"Yes."

"Is the young woman all right?"

"I don't know. He can't find her. She was apparently not in her apartment. At least the door was locked and no one answered the door," he said. "I'm getting a bad feeling about all this."

"I'm sure she'll be fine," Barbara said comfortingly. "You've done all you can for now."

* * *

Dr. Mitsui's visit was short. Lauren faked sleep again, and the doctor made it easy for them. "I'll just leave these pills with you, and you can give them to her when she wakes up again," she told Vivian. "I'll be back first thing in the morning. But call me if she doesn't wake up, and I'll fix something we can give her in a syringe. I wish I'd thought of that before."

Vivian had told her that Lauren had woken up briefly, eaten a little, and then gone back into a deep sleep again. She assured Dr. Mitsui that Lauren would wake up again soon and she'd get her started on the medication, but promised to call if she didn't wake up shortly. Once again, Vivian was told to let no one in.

A half hour later, feeling stronger, Lauren was able to go to her computer with the help of Vivian. On her way, Lauren picked up one of the cherry chocolates on her nightstand and popped it into her mouth, thinking that it would give her energy.

To Lauren's delight, there was an e-mail from Dexter. She opened it and read:

> *I'm so sorry you're not feeling well. I'm really busy here.*
> *Let me know how you're doing. And please, darling, come*
> *as soon as you can. I'm missing you.*
> *Love, Dexter*

"I'll answer it in a minute," Lauren told Vivian as she opened an e-mail from Donovan Deru. She read it slowly. Then she typed a response. She told him a little about Dexter Drake. She also gave him a condensed version of her problems, up to and including Dr. Mitsui's recent visit. She admitted that the woman's visit had scared her, even though she seemed very concerned about her. Then she explained that she'd learned that she could trust her nurse, Vivian Likio, and that as soon as she was strong enough to make it down the stairs, they'd be leaving. She also explained her plan to fly to Los Angeles as soon as she was feeling better. She was quite confident that it would be the next day. She thanked him for his help and told him she would probably be okay as soon as she could get away. She ended by typing, *Thank you for your concern. Oh, and I've started praying again. You were right. I need God in my life.*

Lauren had no sooner sent the message than a sudden tremor shook her body and the room began to spin. She would have fallen from her chair had Ms. Likio not been standing right beside her. "What's the matter?" she asked with concern as she steadied Lauren.

"I suddenly don't feel well," Lauren said, wondering with unwelcome suspicion if Vivian wasn't really a friend after all. *Did Vivian give me something in the sandwich or milk I had shortly before the doctor's return?* she wondered.

Then she remembered the cherry chocolate, and she was filled with horror. "It was L . . . L . . ." she mumbled as consciousness faded and she slipped to the floor.

* * *

A beautiful day in the Ashley Valley had turned into a day full of concern for Donovan. He worked late to catch up on the work he'd neglected when he'd gone home to call Jim and look at his missionary journals. When he finally finished, he was running late. He arrived at Kaelyn's apartment fifteen minutes late—she was already grumpy. That didn't bode well for the evening ahead. He apologized, explaining that he'd had an emergency and hadn't been able to complete his work in time.

"Well, what's done is done," she said. "I was afraid you'd forgotten."

"Forgotten!" Donovan said with a grin as he kissed her cheek. "How could I forget to pick up a beautiful woman like you?"

That brought a little smile to her lips, and she said, "I'm glad you came, even if your work always makes you late."

Donovan let that remark pass and said, "I don't know about you, but I'm hungry. Should we go?"

Donovan was solicitous of her during dinner, and her mood gradually lifted. It was a little after eight when they entered his house. It wasn't until they stepped into his living room and he saw the cardboard box beside his sofa and the open photo album beside it that he remembered he hadn't taken the time to put them away before rushing back to the office.

Kaelyn let Donovan help her with her coat. As he hung it beside his coat in the coat closet, she stepped over to his sofa and reached for the open photo album. "Who's this?" she asked when he joined her. She was pointing to the photo of Lauren where she was standing with her brother and the two missionaries. Both the tone of her voice and the stiffness of her posture were accusatory, not curious. Donovan suppressed a moan.

"It's a mission photo," Donovan said. "I got these pictures out on a whim after this girl recently contacted me, asking me for assistance."

"This is someone you knew on your mission," Kaelyn stated flatly.

"That's right. These two kids standing with my companion and me were members of the Church. The boy was as solid as could be, but the girl was drifting from the Church. She liked to spend her Sundays surfing. My companion and I tried to help her see how important the Church was and how much she needed the Lord. She wouldn't listen."

"She's gorgeous," Kaelyn said. "You wrote beside the picture that she was the prettiest girl in Hawaii." She looked concerned.

"She was seventeen," Donovan countered. "And my sister wrote that. She put that album together for me. She knew I'd never get it done myself."

Kaelyn set the album down, a frown on her face, then said, "She's, what, twenty-six now?"

"Yeah, that sounds about right," Donovan agreed. "Here, let me put this stuff away. I didn't have time earlier since I had to get back to the office."

Kaelyn picked up the album again and said, "She's gorgeous."

"You said that already," Donovan remarked evenly. He couldn't understand why she was acting so jealous when he hardly knew the girl. He was trying to be very patient, not to raise his voice or show even a hint of anger, yet he was becoming irritated.

"She need a lawyer?" Kaelyn asked.

"I'm not sure at this point, but I think maybe her problem will be solved soon. My companion is over there and works for the same company she does. I called him and he's working on it. I'm sure everything will work out for her. Anyway, this is our time right now—you know, Kaelyn and Donovan time." He reached for the album. She slammed it shut and handed it to him with a scowl. He placed it in the box and put the lid on. "I'll stick this box in the bedroom for now," he said. "Then I'll get us each a dish of ice cream."

"The bedroom, huh?" she asked. "Where you can get it out again?"

Donovan ignored her questions and the nastiness in her voice as he continued to the bedroom, where he placed the box of missionary memorabilia on the floor and returned to the living room. Somehow Kaelyn had gotten the wrong idea over this thing, even though she knew nothing about it. He wished she could see that Lauren was just another person asking for his help.

Kaelyn was slouched against the sofa when he came out of the bedroom. She had that little pout on her pixie face that he wished she'd lose. He smiled and reached out and pulled her into her arms. "Hey, my love," he said tenderly, "let's not worry about my work right now. We have important things to do. We have a big decision to make."

She resisted and he pulled a little harder, and she finally melted into his arms. He kissed her lightly on the lips, then pushed her gently back and looked at her. "You're beautiful," he said. "Have I mentioned that before?"

Finally, the smile he sought crept across her face. "Yes," she said.

"It's true," he told her. "Now, what kind of ice cream would you like? I have three choices." All of which he knew she liked. He only cared for two of the flavors, but he kept one on hand just for her.

"Do you have mint chocolate chip?" she asked.

That was the one he didn't like. "You know I do," he said. "I keep it just for you."

Donovan pulled a couple of bowls from his sparsely stocked cupboard, set them on the counter, and stepped toward the refrigerator. The phone rang. He didn't want to answer it, to take a chance of putting Kaelyn into a sour mood again, but he also didn't want to miss the call if it was important. He wondered, as he headed for the phone, if she'd be jealous when they got married. He didn't like that thought, but he knew it was one he had to deal with if she was to be his wife.

"Hello," he said into the phone, smiling at Kaelyn as he did so.

"Donovan, this is Jim. I've checked with every hospital on the island. She's not in any of them, at least not under her name."

"Thanks for calling me back, Jim," he said even as a cloud fell across Kaelyn's face.

"I tried to call Lauren's apartment just minutes ago, but the phone had been disconnected. I'm really worried now."

"What about hospitals in Maui or one of the other islands?" Donovan asked, trying not to say anything to give Kaelyn any reason to be more angry.

"I can try that, but the best hospitals should be in Honolulu," Jim reasoned, and Donovan knew he was right.

"I would appreciate it if you'd just check," Donovan said.

"I'll call if I get anything," Jim promised. "I'm getting worried now too. Maybe I should call the police."

"It wouldn't hurt," Donovan said. "Maybe they'd check at Lauren's apartment too."

"I'll do that," Jim promised before the call was disconnected.

"Lauren is the name of the girl in the picture?" Kaelyn asked.

"Yes, Lauren Olcott."

"You said her problems were solved."

"I thought they were. Jim's going to call the police. They can take it from here," he said.

"So will they be calling you?" She looked at her watch. "It's getting late, you know. It would be nice if we weren't interrupted again."

"Good grief, Kaelyn! Will you get off it?" Donovan said sharply. "I hope we won't either, but it's part of my job. Now, if it's okay, I'll dish up the ice cream."

He started to do that, but then Kaelyn asked, "So is Lauren a criminal or what?"

Donovan took a deep breath, then slowly released it before saying, "I don't think so, but there may be some mental issues." He knew that was possibly true, although he was beginning to think more and more that she really was in danger.

"So you think she's mental?" Kaelyn asked.

Donovan wanted to scream but maintained an even voice. "I don't know, Kaelyn. I'm not sure what's going on. Now can we forget it? I'll work on this problem later if I need to. But for now, let's forget it, please."

"Why did she call you for help?" Kaelyn persisted.

Donovan tensed all over. Then he clamped his jaws closed for a moment and dropped a scoop of mint ice cream into a bowl for Kaelyn. When he spoke again, he was once more in control. "She didn't call me, she sent an e-mail. And she said she was in trouble."

"But you don't think she's a criminal," Kaelyn pointed out.

"I know that. She didn't mean that kind of trouble."

"When was the last time you heard from her? People don't just know everybody's e-mail addresses. You've obviously been in touch with her. Why haven't you ever mentioned her to me before? I thought you'd told me who all your old girlfriends were," Kaelyn said stubbornly.

"I haven't seen her since that picture you were looking at was taken. I've heard from her once, after my old companion went to work for the same company she works for. That was before you and I started dating, and anyway, my only concern was whether she's finding the Church again," he stressed. Donovan finished scooping the ice cream and carried the boxes back to his freezer. Then he dropped spoons in both bowls and handed one of the bowls to Kaelyn. "Let's sit down and eat this before it melts," he said.

Kaelyn sat across the table from Donovan and took a bite of ice cream. She savored it, then swallowed. He took a bite of his and nearly choked on it when she said, "There's something wrong here,

Donovan. The prettiest girl in Hawaii sends you an e-mail when there's got to be a ton of lawyers in Hawaii. But she chooses to ask you for help instead of one of them. Is that what you're telling me?"

Donovan was about to explain that the e-mail had been sent accidentally but realized that wouldn't make this conversation any easier. The situation did seem pretty ludicrous already, he had to admit. "That about sums it up," Donovan said dryly. "Except she probably isn't the prettiest girl in Hawaii."

"Oh, so who is?"

"Kaelyn! Will you drop this? You have nothing to be jealous about."

"Why shouldn't I be?" she snapped. "You bring me here to your house to set a date for our wedding. Instead, we end up talking all night about an old girlfriend."

Donovan paced himself as he said, "I'm glad you like me enough to be jealous over me, but Lauren is not an old girlfriend. I was a missionary when I knew her, and I kept the rules. I barely knew her, and anyway, she has a boyfriend who is a lawyer. He's in California on business, and she's apparently having a hard time getting ahold of him. But when she does, I'm sure he'll be able to help her."

"May I see her e-mails to you?"

"Good grief! Why would you want to?"

"Just to see what she said to you," Kaelyn said with fake sweetness.

"Fine, I'll turn on my computer." He did just that, and while he waited for it to boot up, Kaelyn nibbled at her ice cream. Donovan sat at the computer fifteen feet from her and let his ice cream get soft.

When he opened his e-mail account, there was a new one from Lauren. Despite himself, he wanted to open it right then and see what she had to say in response to the one he'd sent her. But Kaelyn was standing beside him now. She pointed. "There are three of them from Lauren. This one is new. You haven't even opened it."

"Yeah, so I see," he agreed. "I'll have to read it when I get to the office tomorrow."

"Open the first one," she ordered. He really didn't like her tone of voice, but rather than argue, he did as she asked.

Kaelyn read it—maybe twice, Donovan guessed from how long it took her. Finally she said, "She sounds like a mental case to me. Let's look at the next one. I assume it was in response to one you sent her."

"You should have been a detective," Donovan said half under his breath as he opened the second message from Lauren.

Kaelyn read it, then she said, "So she didn't even mean to e-mail you. Is Dexter her lawyer boyfriend?"

"Yes," he answered shortly. He could see Kaelyn was more relaxed now, so he relaxed a little himself.

"Let's look at the new one now. You don't have to wait until morning."

The couple read the third message from Lauren together. Donovan relaxed even more. He was worrying for nothing, it appeared. She had help now. Probably the reason she couldn't be located was that she and this nurse of hers were hiding until she could catch a plane to California.

There was one especially positive note in the message, he reflected as he waited for Kaelyn to finish reading it for the second or third time. It appeared that Lauren was actually making an attempt at finding God in her life again. He prayed that she would be successful.

"Donovan," Kaelyn said as she finally straightened up from the computer. "I'm sorry about how I reacted to all this. It looks like she's probably going to be taken care of now and that you won't have to worry about her anymore."

"Looks that way," Donovan agreed.

"Will you forgive me?" she asked.

For an answer, he stood and took her tenderly in his arms and pressed his lips to hers. Later, they set May first as their wedding day.

CHAPTER 9

Royce and Fleming looked at each other with concern, then back at the computer screen. "The drug is not working exactly the way that Dr. Mitsui claims it's supposed to," Fleming said. "Somehow Lauren is managing to send e-mails. I told the phone company to shut the phone off yesterday, but they apparently didn't get it done."

"It's disconnected now," Royce said. "They must have just done it this evening, because when I tried to call to check on Lauren just before you got here, it wasn't working. So we don't have to worry about her sending any more messages."

"That may be true, but the damage is done, and what's to say she won't find some other way, like the nurse. It sounds like she's talking to the nurse," Fleming said.

"So what do we do now?" Royce asked.

"What we should have done all along. We get rid of her and the nurse."

Royce's face went white. "But we agreed that no one else would have to die."

"Only if no one got in our way. It looks like we're going to have to get rid of several interfering people. We've gone too far to quit now, Royce. It's them or us. Don't you agree?"

Royce reluctantly nodded his head.

* * *

Lauren regained consciousness at about ten that night. She was confused and disoriented at first, and it took her a minute to remember where she was and why she was there. It took even longer to place Vivian and recall why she was in her apartment. After about a half hour, she was able to speak coherently with Vivian, who asked, "What happened, Lauren? Do you think we better give you the medication Dr. Mitsui brought?"

"No!" Lauren protested strongly.

"But it might be that the drug you've been taking has side effects the doctor understands, and the pills she brought might work as an antidote," the nurse reasoned. "Something is wrong. You seemed to be doing fairly well before you suddenly got sick and passed out."

"I'm . . . I'm trying to remember," Lauren said. "I know that I was sending an e-mail to . . ." She paused and then wailed, "I never answered Dexter's message, just Donovan's. You've got to help me get back to the computer. I've got to—"

"Not yet," Vivian said in a soothing tone. "You seem very sick. Maybe I should call Dr. Mitsui."

"No, please don't," Lauren pleaded. "I can't trust her. It was something else." She looked around, saw the roses on her dresser, one bouquet from Dexter and one from Leroy. She let out a gasp and turned her head sharply so she could see her nightstand. There she saw the box of cherry chocolates Leroy had brought, and she remembered that she had eaten one.

"Lauren, my dear, you're pale. What is it?" Vivian asked. "What is upsetting you so?"

"These chocolates. Leroy brought them," she said. "I ate one just before you helped me to the computer room."

"Yes, that's right. But what does that have to do with your illness?"

Lauren struggled to sit up and Vivian helped her. "Maybe nothing," she said after she was comfortable and a small wave of dizziness had passed. "And maybe everything."

"I guess I don't understand. Leroy seems like a nice, bright young man," Vivian said. "He is so concerned about you."

"And jealous," Lauren added. "I dated him for quite some time before Dexter and I began going out. He acts nice to me, but I know he's jealous of Dexter."

"But what could that possibly have to do with your sickness? Surely he wouldn't try to harm you."

"When I got sick on Monday," Lauren began as she pulled her thoughts together, "I was in Dr. Mitsui's office."

"Yes, that's where I picked you up before I brought you here," Vivian agreed.

"Well, just before I went down to her office to help her, I met Leroy outside my office door. He knows that cherry chocolates are my absolute favorite. He gave me one then, and I ate it!"

"And shortly after that you got sick," Vivian said. "Yes, I can see now why you're afraid of him. It seems very unlikely that he would actually try to poison you just because he's jealous, but under the circumstances, we can't afford to take any chances. In fact, I'll just move this box out of here right now. I'd like to throw them out, but I guess we need them for evidence. Are you sure they aren't related to this other business?"

"There is something else," Lauren said. "The day I discovered that Fleming and Royce had been embezzling was a Saturday. I was alone in the office building when I came across the information. But others came in the building—Royce and Leroy. They didn't know I was there, because I hid in a closet. But Leroy was with Royce, and I can't help but wonder if he's involved with him and Fleming."

"Lauren, we've got to get you away from here tonight. Who knows what could happen next?" Vivian said. "Are you feeling any stronger?"

"I think so," Lauren said. "If you'll help me, I'm sure we can get out of here, but first I've got to send a message to Dexter."

"Okay, but you must hurry."

"It won't take long. I'm sure I didn't turn the computer off. In fact, the Internet is probably still connected."

Despite a wave of dizziness, Lauren managed to make it to the computer without falling. Vivian helped her sit down and she said, "Okay, now all I have to do is write him a note and send it." She looked at the computer, puzzled. "The Internet isn't connected. Did I shut it off?" she asked Vivian.

"No, and neither did I. It must have done it somehow on its own," Vivian said.

But when Lauren tried to connect again, she got no response. "Vivian, it won't dial," she said. "Surely the phone isn't dead."

"I called Ned earlier," Vivian reminded her.

"And I used the Internet," Lauren added.

"I'll grab the phone and see if there's a dial tone. Will you be all right for a minute if I leave you?" Vivian asked.

"I'll hold onto the desk. I'll be fine," Lauren assured her.

When Vivian returned seconds later, she was shaking her head. "The phone is dead," she announced.

For some reason that confirmation frightened Lauren, and she said, "We've got to get out of here now. With your help I can make it."

Vivian said, "Let's get you back into the bedroom so you can get dressed. Then we'll pack a few things into my car and get away. What will you need to take?"

"My laptop for sure. I've got to be able to communicate with Dexter," Lauren said.

"Where is it?"

"In my car."

"Where are your keys?"

"In my purse, which was in my office when . . . Oh no! It was in my office and—"

Mrs. Likio cut her off gently. "I brought it. It's in the kitchen. I had to have your keys to get in here when I brought you home on Monday."

Lauren was relieved. "Oh, thank goodness." She was already moving slowly toward the bedroom. When they got there, Lauren sat on the edge of her bed. "If you'll get me some clothes, I think I can dress while you're packing a bag for me," she suggested to Vivian. "And would you just make sure my cell phone is in my purse? The charger is plugged in on the kitchen counter. At least it was."

"We can be away from here in ten minutes," Vivian said. "If you can get your clothes on that fast."

* * *

"Arrangements are made," Fleming announced. "If that Deru guy shows up at Lauren's place in the next couple of days, he'll be taken care of, and it won't look like we had anything to do with it."

Royce nodded morosely. Being rich had appealed to him, and even leaving his wife, after the way things had been going between them lately, didn't bother him. But taking people's lives was not something he'd even considered when he entered into the pact with Fleming and the others. Now things had spiraled out of control. One person was dead, others were going to die, and he was powerless to prevent it.

"Come on, we've got to get over to Lauren's. I've got the syringe in my pocket. We'll just send the nurse out like we did last time. And we'll make it look like it was her that gave the shot. Then we'll make Ms. Likio disappear."

"I'm not going," Royce said. "I won't try to stop you, but I can't help you do this to Lauren."

Fleming turned and glared at him for several seconds before he spoke. "Fine, but your cut of the profits just got smaller," Fleming finally said angrily. Then he stormed out to his car and drove off with tires squealing.

* * *

Lauren had barely finished dressing when she heard the door open. She nearly fainted when she heard Fleming's voice. "You two thought you could just drive away from here, did you?" he was asking.

Vivian was sobbing, barely able to talk, and Lauren couldn't make out what she said in response.

"Let's see how Lauren's doing, should we? She must be better if you two were planning to fly the coop."

"You leave that girl alone," Vivian managed to say.

"I'm the one with the gun," Fleming said. "Now move! And I'll let you give her a shot. She really needs some medicine to calm her down," he added with a sadistic smile.

Lauren stood and walked as quickly as she could to the dresser, where she grabbed the vase that held the roses from Dexter. She pulled out the dozen roses and dropped them behind the dresser, then slipped clumsily behind the door and steadied herself against the wall. Vivian was the first to walk in, and Lauren prayed that she would know what to do.

Her prayer was answered when Vivian said, "She's in the bathroom. We'll have to wait for her to come out."

"I'm in a hurry. Give her the shot in there," Fleming ordered. "If you don't, I'll be forced to shoot the pair of you, and that would be messy."

Vivian stepped obediently to the bathroom and reached for the door handle. Fleming stepped into the room. Lauren brought the vase down on his head. The big man stumbled forward, the pistol in his hand waving wildly. Vivian dropped to the floor. The gun discharged, the bullet going through the wall only inches above Vivian's head. Lauren struck him again, and this time Fleming fell. Vivian leaped to her feet, stepped over Fleming, and caught Lauren as she began to collapse.

Lauren did not lose consciousness, but she had no strength left. She had to lie on the bed while Vivian took the gun away from Fleming, who was unconscious and bleeding from the back of his head. "Lauren, what can we tie him up with?" she asked.

"I have some duct tape below the sink in the kitchen," she said.

"That'll work," Vivian agreed and hurried from the room.

When she got back a minute later, Fleming was beginning to stir. She struggled to pull his fat hands around behind his back, but she only had one of them before he regained consciousness and began to thrash at her. Vivian jumped back, grabbed the gun from the nightstand where she'd laid it only moments before, and pointed it at him. By that time he was to his knees.

"I'll shoot if you move any more," she threatened.

"What makes you think it's loaded?" he asked in a mocking voice.

"You try to get to your feet and we'll see," Vivian threatened.

Lauren was stirring again, and the adrenalin was flowing. Fleming was at the foot of her bed. She still grasped the vase in her hand. With all the strength she could muster, she slid from the bed and struck at Fleming one more time. He roared as the vase glanced from his shoulder, and he spun toward her with amazing speed for such an obese man. She swung again and this time she caught him on the wrist. It slowed his attack, but Lauren expected the gun in Vivian's hand to fire. But instead, the nurse grabbed the second vase of roses, dumped the flowers out, and joined in the attack.

The two women kept swinging while Fleming spun on the floor like a giant slug. Lauren gave out again, but Vivian kept at it until she had him subdued, then taped his wrists and his mouth. She had to tape his wrists in front of him, because his arms were so fat that she couldn't get them to come together behind his back.

Vivian picked up the syringe that had fallen to the floor and thought briefly about injecting its contents into Fleming's arm. But the thought was only that, a thought. Even though she knew that Fleming had intended to do harm with the contents of that syringe, she would not—in fact, could not—stoop to his level. She rolled the syringe around in her fingers for a moment, then dropped it on the floor beside him. "Let's get out of here," she said to Lauren.

Vivian laid the gun on the nightstand. The two women then began the laborious process of escaping from the apartment. It was all Lauren could do, even with Vivian's help, to get down the stairs and to the car. She finally collapsed into the front passenger seat, and Vivian helped her lay it back. Fifteen minutes after the fight, Vivian was across town, searching for a hotel where she and Lauren could safely spend the rest of the night.

* * *

Not all of Fleming Parker was useless, ugly fat. Beneath the thick rolls of fat was muscle, and when coupled with the massive weight of his arms, it provided him with physical power that most would never suspect he possessed. That strength enabled him, over the next hour, to free himself from the duct tape with which he'd been bound.

As the last of the tape was thrown on the carpet, he heard steps on the stairs leading to Lauren's front door. He rubbed blood from his eyes with his sleeve. The only light in the apartment seeped through the blinds from the streetlights outside, but that was enough to enable him to steer his way from the bedroom and through the apartment to the front door. There he waited while a key was fitted in the lock. When the door opened, a woman entered. He didn't even wait to see who it was before he threw a massive arm around her neck and clamped a huge, bloody hand over her mouth to muffle the scream that followed.

* * *

Vernal was clear again the next morning. Despite that, Donovan wasn't feeling upbeat. Yes, he and Kaelyn had managed to salvage the previous evening. But after he'd taken her home, he'd returned and studied the e-mails from Lauren and thought about the call from Jim. Donovan felt distinctly uncomfortable about Lauren's situation. The thing that worried him the most was the fact that he'd received a plea for help that she had meant to send to someone else.

Was it just a chance error on Lauren's part? he'd asked himself. *Or was it divine intervention?* And if it was divine intervention, then he couldn't just assume she was okay now and forget about her. He didn't feel right about leaving it all up to her boyfriend, who was currently in California. Finally, after worrying for over an hour, Donovan had dropped to his knees.

And he had received a strong impression, an answer to his plea. He just wasn't sure he wanted to do what he felt he should, for it would seem like a radical move on his part to outside observers—especially to Kaelyn. So now he was torn between his fiancée's feelings and the prompting to help someone he barely knew, someone whose last communication had been for him not to worry anymore. He drove to the office, still stubbornly debating if he should follow his impressions or not. When he arrived, Mrs. Olsen had his day outlined. "Is any of this pressing?" he asked.

"It's important, but if you're asking if I could reschedule some things so you can do something that's clearly eating at you this morning, then the answer is yes," she said intuitively. She favored him with one of her motherly smiles. "Is that what you'd like me to do?" she asked.

"Maybe," he said slowly, thinking as he talked. He looked at his watch. It was only six o'clock in Hawaii. Perhaps he should wait until he could talk to Jim again. If he still felt the same, then he'd do what he felt impressed needed to be done. "No," he said. "I'll let you know by noon though."

Donovan entered his office, turned on his computer, and began going through the mail Mrs. Olsen had already laid on his desk while he waited for the computer to boot up. When it was running, he accessed the Internet to check his e-mail. He was surprised to see a message from Lauren. *Maybe she's just writing to make sure I know she doesn't need my help anymore,* he thought. *Then I really can forget about her problem.* The impression he'd felt didn't mesh with that thought, though, and his hands were slightly unsteady as he opened her message.

He read it through, rubbed his eyes, and then read it again. It said:

> *Donovan,*
> *It's the middle of the night here. I'm frightened and need help again. I'm sorry to bother you, but I don't know what to do. Vivian and I got away after a man tried to kill us. We left him in my apartment, bleeding and bound with tape. We were in such a hurry when we left that we forgot to take some important evidence, so it's still there. Vivian left me at this motel and went back after it. She hasn't come back. I'm frightened. I don't know what to do. It may sound dumb, but I haven't taken anything to the police because I don't want to be the whistle-blower. I haven't heard back from Dexter, although I'm sure I soon will. But please, just tell me what to do. Thank you, Donovan.*
> *Lauren*

Donovan read through it a third time, then picked up his phone. He was afraid he might wake Jim up because it was still early morning in Hawaii. He did, but Jim didn't complain. Donovan read Lauren's message to him and then asked, "What do you think, Jim?"

"I think something's got to be done," Jim answered. "I called the police last night. They checked her place and said it was dark there and locked up. They didn't feel like they had enough to go on to break in, so they didn't. And Sally and I checked with every hospital we could find listed on all the islands. She's either not in any of them or they aren't saying."

"Jim, I have a bad feeling about this thing," Donovan said as he again looked at Lauren's desperate, pleading message.

"I'll help if I can. What would you like me to do?" Jim offered.

"Call the police again. I'll forward this message to you, and you can print it and show it to them. Try to get someone with rank to look at it. Then see if they'll go back to the apartment. Maybe this e-mail will give them enough probable cause to go inside."

"I'll do it," Jim promised. "And I'll keep in touch."

After hanging up, Donovan stepped out of his office. He was terribly worried. Something very bad was happening in Hawaii. Lauren was surrounded with something of evil origin that threatened her life. He was certain of it.

"Donovan, what's going on?" Barbara asked when she looked at his face. "Is there something I can do?"

"Would you mind getting on the phone and seeing how soon you could schedule me a flight to Honolulu?" he asked. "I just got a desperate message from the woman in Hawaii. I need to send an e-mail to her and then get home and throw something in an overnight bag."

"I'll get right on it, Mr. Deru. Do I need your credit card?"

"Probably, if you can arrange a flight for me," he replied.

He sent a message to Lauren. It was short but direct. He told her not to let anyone know where she was except Dexter, that he was coming and would have his cell phone with him. He gave her his number and told her that if she had a phone, she wasn't to answer it unless she was absolutely sure of the caller. He then reminded her to keep praying. And in her behalf, he offered a prayer himself.

An hour later, Donovan was boarding a SkyWest Airlines plane at the Vernal Airport. Mrs. Olsen had miraculously succeeded in getting him on a series of flights that would get him to Los Angeles by early afternoon and to Honolulu by late evening, Hawaii time. The last thing she'd said as he headed for the door was, "I'll get your Monday work covered. But I'm not sure I can do anything about Tuesday. You have court that morning."

"Thanks. I'll be back," he'd told her. And he fully intended to be.

Now, as he settled into a seat, he pulled out his cell phone and started to dial Kaelyn, then shut it off as he caught a dirty look from one of the flight attendants. He'd call Kaelyn from Salt Lake, where he had a short layover. He didn't look forward to that call. He knew she'd somehow read into his sudden trip something that wasn't there.

CHAPTER 10

After knocking and ringing the bell several times and receiving no answer, Dexter Drake tried the door. It was unlocked, so he pushed it open and stepped inside. "Lauren," he called. "Are you here? I've been worried, so I came back."

The apartment was still as death and quite dark, even though the sun had just risen. A quick glance told him that every blind in both the kitchen and living room was closed. He flipped on the switch beside the door and immediately noticed an open box of cherry chocolates on the table. If there was one thing that he and Lauren totally agreed on, it was cherry chocolates. He grabbed three of them from the box, popped one in his mouth, and moved slowly in the direction of Lauren's bedroom. He paused at the closed door and once again called out: "Lauren, are you in there?"

Nervously, he touched the doorknob, turned it, and slowly eased the door open. There was someone in the bed. He turned on the light and let out an involuntary gasp. Dexter had never seen death except in a casket. Yet he knew he was seeing it now. The face was turned away from him, and his first impulse was to flee, but he had to know who it was. So he stepped closer and leaned over the bed. He recognized her from the work he'd done at Paradise Pharmaceuticals. He was shaking as he straightened up and looked around the room. It was a mess, and he realized with a jolt that there was blood on the carpet and on the bed coverings as well as on the body.

Red roses were scattered on the floor and two empty vases lay against the wall. On the nightstand was an empty syringe. He used a Kleenex to pick it up, examine it, and set it back down, then backed from the room, totally rattled at what he'd found. All he wanted now was to get away.

Dexter shut the bedroom door behind him, crossed to the front door, and left. At the bottom of the stairs he realized he was still clutching two cherry chocolates. Instinctively, he popped one of the slightly melted candies in his mouth and crossed the street to where he'd left his car. He jumped in, ate the last chocolate, and then wiped his now-gooey hand with a wet wipe. Finally he drove off, dazed and frightened, worried about Lauren, and feeling a little light-headed. By the time he got to his huge home on the beach, he was feeling sick. He stumbled into his bedroom and fell across his bed fully clothed.

* * *

Lauren awoke to the sound of a parrot outside the window of the small motel. She'd cried herself to sleep after Vivian failed to return from going back for the cherry chocolates. She remembered pleading with her not to go, but Vivian had insisted, saying, "We might need them for evidence. I'll hurry, and maybe I'll bring us a few groceries from your apartment, too. I'm sure Fleming won't be a threat. He's probably out cold for the night. I won't be long. You're safe here. Don't you worry."

But Lauren had worried when Vivian left, and now she was sick with concern. She was positive that something had happened to Vivian or she would have been back hours ago. She felt more alone than she ever had in her life. *If only Dexter were here,* she cried to herself.

The only positive thing she could think of was the strength that had returned to her muscles. She sat up in bed fairly easily. The dizziness she experienced was only minor. She had a headache, but it was nothing to worry about. She climbed out of bed, still very tired but not wanting to sleep. Though quite weak, she was able to walk without having to hold onto anything. She checked the door to make sure it was locked. Then she stepped over to the small table beside the shuttered window where her laptop was. She turned it on, and as soon as it was booted up, she dialed into the Internet. In her panic the night before she had e-mailed both Dexter and Donovan. She hoped someone would respond to her pleas.

She cried out in relief when she saw that there was finally a message from Dexter. She noticed one from Donovan as well, but she ignored it and opened Dexter's. A sense of security washed over her. He told her he was worried and was flying back at his own expense to check on her. He told her that he didn't know what time he'd be there but that he would come as soon as he could get a flight.

Lauren was learning the power of prayer, and she dropped to her knees and offered a short one to thank the Lord for sending Dexter back to help her. Then she grabbed her cell phone, thinking she'd call him right then. If he was back, she could let him know where she was and pour her burdens out on him.

Her phone battery was dead. She'd failed to plug it in after arriving at the motel. She reached for the room phone and dialed it instead. Dexter's phone rang four or five times before his voice mail came on.

Discouraged but still grateful to know he was at least coming to help, she left a message and told him to call her cell phone when he could. Then she began to dig through the things Vivian had packed to find the phone battery charger. When she finally located it, she plugged it in and the phone began to charge.

Only then did she remember that she also had a message from Donovan waiting for her on the computer. She sat down and opened up the message and read. Tears stung her eyes. This man she really didn't even know and had accidentally contacted cared enough to fly here to help her. She could hardly believe it. She dropped to her knees, and for the second time, she offered a short prayer. She thanked God for listening to her, and asked Him to help both Dexter and Donovan make it there soon. When she finished, she got up, wrote down Donovan's cell phone number, deleted the message, and shut down her computer.

* * *

"Are you Jim Roderick?"

"I am."

"I'm Captain Ray Hafoko," the tall, rather imposing officer said as he reached out his hand. "What can I do for you?"

Jim explained quickly, and the captain said, "Oh yes, we had officers there last night, and they were quite certain there was no one at home. The lights were out and the door was locked. I'm not sure we can do more without something concrete to go on."

"Will this help?" Jim asked as he held out the copy of the e-mail he'd printed earlier. "This was sent during the night to Donovan Deru. He's an attorney from Utah who's had several messages from this woman saying she's in danger."

Captain Hafoko read it over and then said, "Yes, this might help, although I need to authenticate it if I can by talking to Mr. Deru."

"He's on his way here now, so he may be on a plane. However, we could always call his office and talk to his secretary."

Captain Hafoko tried the cell phone but it was out of service, so he also tried Donovan's office number. He spoke for a moment with Mrs. Olsen. When he hung up he said, "Do you know Miss Olcott personally?"

"Yes, I know her reasonably well," Jim said. "We work at the same place."

"Is there any chance she's making this up?"

"None. She'd never do that."

"But you did say she'd been sick, that she had a breakdown of some sort."

"Yes, but at this point I don't know what I believe about that. Something is wrong, and I honestly think she may be in danger."

The captain took a deep breath, reread the e-mail message that now lay on his desk, then said, "I'll send a couple of officers over. If the place is open, I'll have them look in. If it's not, we'll have to contact a judge."

"Thanks," Jim said. "Is it okay if I wait around for a few minutes? I don't have to be to work for a while yet."

"Suit yourself," the captain said as he picked up his phone.

Jim waited nervously outside the captain's office for twenty minutes. Suddenly, Captain Hafoko's door burst open. "Mr. Roderick, could you go with me for a few minutes?"

"Sure, what's happening? Is Lauren okay?"

"It doesn't look like it," the captain said without emotion. "Hurry, we've got to get over to her apartment right away. I'll have you ride in my car so we can make better time."

They were in Captain Hafoko's car before Jim learned anything else about Lauren. Then, as they hurried through traffic, the captain said, "It looks like your friend is dead. At least there's a woman lying on her bed who is dead. We'll need you to tell us if it's her or not."

Jim felt like he'd had the wind knocked out of him. "But, it can't be Lauren," he said. "She said in the e-mail that she'd gotten away from her apartment."

"I understand that, but I've learned over the years that you believe what you see, Mr. Roderick. If it isn't her, then she certainly will have a lot of explaining to do, because there is a deceased woman in her bed and there's blood all over the place."

They rode in silence for a few minutes. Jim's cell phone buzzed in his pocket, and he pulled it out and looked at the number, then answered. "Donovan," he said. "I tried to call you a few minutes ago."

"I'm sorry," Donovan said. "I must have been in the air. I just landed and thought I'd call and see if you learned anything."

"I'm afraid so," Jim said soberly.

"What?" Donovan asked. "Has something happened to Lauren?"

"Possibly. I'm with Captain Hafoko of the Honolulu Police Department right now and we're on our way over there. I don't know quite how to say this . . ."

"Just spit it out," Donovan said urgently.

"Well, a couple of officers went over there after Captain Hafoko read the e-mail Lauren sent you. Someone is in Lauren's bed and she's dead—"

"Lauren's dead?" Donovan shouted into the phone, his deep voice so strong that Captain Hafoko looked over at Jim.

"We don't know if it's her or not. That's why they asked me to go, so I could identify her. Maybe it's somebody else, Donovan," he said.

"I can't believe this," Donovan roared over the phone. "I should have come sooner and maybe I could have prevented something."

"It's not your fault, Donovan. And maybe it's not even her."

"Yeah, and if it's not, then who is it and what . . ." He stopped for a moment and Jim didn't say anything. "Oh, no. Lauren said in the e-mail that her nurse was going back to get something. It must be the nurse."

"I don't know, but if it's not Lauren who's dead, then she might have to explain who killed whoever is dead," Jim said, passing on the thought the captain had given him earlier.

"Call me back as soon as you know something," Donovan said. "Of course you can't if I'm in the air again, because they won't let us keep our phones on in the plane. And the plane I'm on doesn't have phones at the seats like the bigger ones do. So I guess I'll just have to call you from LAX when I land there if I don't hear from you first."

"Okay, then I'll talk to you later," Jim said and snapped his phone shut. It was several more minutes before they pulled up in front of a small apartment complex.

Jim was impressed with how nice it was. The yards were beautiful. The palm trees were perfectly manicured, and the grass was kept neat and even. Carefully trimmed shrubs bloomed along the sidewalk they walked up, and the building itself was attractive and fairly new. It was not the kind of setting where one expected to confront death, especially violent, bloody death.

Police cars lined the streets, and an officer stood at the foot of the stairs. Curious neighbors watched from as close as the police would let them get. "Morning, officer," Captain Hafoko said. "This fellow is with me."

"Very well, Captain," he said, and they passed him and climbed the stairs.

Jim was feeling woozy at the very thought of what lay ahead. He prayed that it wasn't Lauren in there, and yet he couldn't help but think that it was. He followed the captain through the door and stopped when he did. "She's in there," another officer said, pointing to the bedroom.

"I presume nothing has been touched," the captain said sternly. He stood a good six inches taller than the young uniformed officer and Jim.

"Oh, no sir. We haven't touched a thing except her neck, and that was just to make sure she was dead, although it was pretty obvious."

"Very well. The lab folks will be along shortly. This is Jim Roderick. He's a friend of the woman who lives here. He's going to take a look and tell us if the deceased is in fact Miss Olcott."

The officer looked at Jim with pity in his eyes. "I'm sorry," he said and turned away.

"Well, we may as well get it over with," Captain Hafoko said as he led the way to Lauren's bedroom.

Jim's heart was in his throat, and it almost stopped when he saw the bloody clothes and bedding. But looking closer, he felt a little relief. The body was too short for Lauren. It must not be her.

"Walk around the other side of the bed. Then you can see her face better," the captain said as they both noticed that her head was turned that way.

Jim did as he was asked and walked around the bed. He stared for a moment and felt bitter, burning bile rise from his stomach. "It's not Lauren," he said, feeling both relief and revulsion.

"You're sure?" Captain Hafoko asked.

"Positive," Jim responded. "Can we leave now?" He was thinking how embarrassing it would be to faint or even throw up.

He didn't stop until he was clear out of the apartment, where he took several deep breaths of the fragrant, moist air. The captain had followed him. "Jim," he said, "if it isn't Miss Olcott in there, do you happen to know who it is?"

Jim's throat was burning. His words were hoarse when he forced them out. "Yes," he said. "She works at Paradise Pharmaceuticals."

He couldn't say more, for he had to rush down the stairs so he could lose his breakfast in the sweet-smelling shrubs beside the sidewalk.

* * *

Lauren was starved and there was nothing in the room to eat. She was feeling much better physically despite the hunger, but emotionally she was a wreck. She'd tried Dexter's phone at least twenty times, and Donovan's six or seven. She'd left messages at both numbers. She tried to watch TV, but she couldn't concentrate. She just sat and flipped the channels. At noon, she forced herself to find a news program. She didn't know what might have happened to Vivian. She prayed that she was alive somewhere, but she also had to know if something terrible had occurred.

Then a story came on that caught her full attention. It was sketchy, and the police weren't releasing much information, but what the newscaster said was enough to nearly send Lauren into shock. He said the body of a woman had been found in an apartment, and they showed the front of the building Lauren lived in! She could see police officers keeping the crowd at bay. She recognized several of her neighbors among the onlookers. Then, as she listened to the newscaster explain that the woman's identity was not yet being released, she saw a man walk across in front of the camera.

Leroy! What was he doing there? she wondered.

They switched to another story about a car that had crashed in the middle of the night, and Lauren shut off the TV. She couldn't stand any more. Vivian was dead. It was almost beyond comprehension. Regret flooded over her. If only she'd insisted that Vivian not go back there, she thought. But she *had* insisted. Vivian just hadn't listened. So then she blamed herself for not confiding in Vivian earlier and getting away before Fleming came with his pistol full of bullets and his syringe full of something that was probably just as deadly.

For a long time, Lauren sat and did nothing. Then she finally picked up her phone and tried once more to call Dexter. That didn't work, so she tried Donovan. That was also futile. Finally, knowing it would be hard to talk to Ned, Vivian's kind old neighbor, she looked him up in the phone book and dialed his number anyway. It rang several times before she gave up and put the phone down.

She told herself she'd try later. Then as she thought about what had happened to Vivian, she decided she wouldn't. It was her fault Vivian was dead. It was her fault Billie was dead. She couldn't live with herself if she involved Ned and he met the same terrible fate.

CHAPTER 11

As the day wore on, Lauren became more restless and worried. She grieved over the death of Vivian, but she finally began to think ahead, to plan again for her own survival. Suddenly, a terrible thought occurred to her. What if Vivian had been forced to speak before she died? What if Fleming knew where she was staying?

That thought brought action, and ten minutes later, Lauren was climbing into a taxi. She didn't have a clue where she should go, only that it had to be somewhere besides this little motel. She didn't even bother to check out. She'd just called for a taxi, grabbed her things, and left. "Where to?" the cab driver asked, looking back over his shoulder at Lauren.

"I . . . I . . ." she stammered.

"You do know where you're going, don't you?" he insisted impatiently.

The thought occurred to her that it was easy to get lost in a crowd. And the most crowded place she could think of was Waikiki, with all its high-rise hotels and endless mob of tourists. So she told him to take her to any hotel on Waikiki and that would be fine. Lauren was lucky, for after she was out of the cab, she very quickly found a hotel with a vacancy. After checking in under the first name that came to her mind, she lugged her purse, suitcase, and laptop into the elevator and punched the button for the thirtieth floor.

Feeling much more secure but weak with hunger and fatigue, she called room service and ordered a meal as soon as she'd settled into room 3012. Then she plopped down on the bed to wait. She was startled at the loud knocking on the door and realized she'd fallen asleep.

"Just a moment," she called out as she stumbled to her feet, fought off a wave of dizziness, and crossed the room to the door.

She almost opened the door before it occurred to her that just about anyone could be on the other side. She leaned against the wall weakly, trembling with fright and hunger. There was another knock. Finally, she forced herself to look through the little peephole and felt a soothing relief wash over her. She opened the door, had the room-service waiter place her meal on the table, and shut and locked the door behind him as he left.

She couldn't eat much, for her stomach had shrunk during her induced illness, but what little she did eat sent strength surging through her body. She shoved the meal aside and dialed Dexter's home again. There was still no answer, so she tried his cell phone with the same result. Then she dialed Donovan's. When she received the message that his phone was out of service, she fought down rising panic and moved to look out the window. Below her, on the sun-drenched beach, the masses moved about in seeming unconcern, and she yearned to be there with them, relaxing without a worry in the world.

She nibbled at her lunch again, then once more left it and stretched out on her bed. Almost instantly she was asleep.

* * *

The yellow tomcat prowled Ned's living room restlessly. "I know," Ned said. "I'm not much of a substitute for Vivian. And I don't have any idea how much longer she'll be. Right now, Miss Olcott needs her worse than you do, though. So you've just got to be content with me for a while."

He looked at his watch and groaned when he saw that it was one o'clock in the afternoon. "My company plants need me," he said unhappily to the cat, who didn't even have the courtesy to bend an ear in his direction. He always referred to the plants at work as his company plants. "I haven't been to work yet today, and I need to go. I was hoping Vivian would call by now."

He ate a sandwich, then left for work, intending to spend only a couple of hours there. He missed seeing Lauren's face, as he had all week. She was always so friendly to him, more so than anyone else except Vivian. To most of the employees, Ned felt like he was invisible. *Perhaps that's a good thing,* he thought as two men walked past. He glanced up and recognized Royce Cantrell, Lauren's boss, and Leroy Provost, the young man she used to date. Neither of them even looked his way. "Did you say she's dead?" Leroy was asking.

Ned nearly fell over at those words. His first thought was that it was Lauren they were talking about, and he remembered how she'd told him she couldn't say anything to him or he too would be in danger.

"That's exactly what I said," Royce answered angrily.

"And she was in Lauren's apartment, on Lauren's bed?"

That question was worded funny, Ned thought. *If Lauren was dead, Leroy would have asked it differently. Maybe he'd have asked, And she was in her apartment on her bed?*

That thought was still being processed by Ned's mind when Royce said in disgust, "Yes, that's the word going around the office."

The two men walked on past, and the only other thing Ned heard was Leroy asking, "Are the cops saying who they're looking for?"

Ned couldn't hear Royce's answer, but both men seemed especially nervous. And that didn't make sense, for they were both men that Lauren had always expressed a liking for.

Perhaps it wasn't Lauren they were talking about, he concluded. Then a thought so terrible came to him that he literally sank to his knees in agony, crushing some of his favorite flowers.

Vivian!

She had been with Lauren in Lauren's apartment. He couldn't imagine that the men could have been talking about anyone else. He couldn't do another thing. Grief filled his gentle soul, grief akin to that he'd suffered when his wife died. Vivian had become more than a neighbor to Ned, even more than a friend. Although he'd never told her this and hadn't planned to, he loved her dearly. If not for the difference in their ages, he'd have asked her to marry him long ago.

Ned stumbled to his car, fumbled for his keys, and drove home. When Vivian's cat met him at the door, he fell to his knees, scooped Tommy into his arms, and unashamedly sobbed into his thick, yellow fur.

* * *

Donovan hadn't heard from Jim before leaving Los Angeles for the last leg of his journey. So he used the air phone on the plane and called him as he winged his way across the wide expanse of the Pacific Ocean. What Jim had to say was both a relief and a cause for concern to Donovan. "The dead woman wasn't Lauren," he said. "But the police are looking for her. When I last spoke with Captain Hafoko, who's heading the investigation, they didn't have any clue where she might be."

"So they do know she's in trouble then?" Donovan asked.

"Actually, they think Lauren might have murdered the woman in her bed," Jim said. "And that's simply stupid. She's not capable of that."

No, surely not, Donovan thought. Yet even as he thought it, a tiny trickle of doubt edged its way into his mind. His thoughts turned to the victim. *Poor Vivian. She sounded like a good woman. I hope she didn't suffer long.* He felt he had to ask, "So what was the cause of death?" He wasn't sure he wanted to hear the answer.

"I actually don't know how she died," Jim said. "It's good I didn't decide to be a doctor. The whole thing with death and blood all over the place made me sick. I had to leave after I told them who it was. But there was an empty syringe and a gun beside the bed. That's all I can tell you. I suppose the cops know, but if so, they aren't saying yet."

Donovan hung the phone on back of the seat in front of him. He wondered what kind of a mess he might be getting himself into. He was so worried about Lauren's situation that it didn't occur to him to try calling Kaelyn from the phone he'd just used.

* * *

Lauren again tried phoning Dexter late that evening. She was starting to worry about him now. He'd told her he was on his way back, and he should have been here a long time ago. She checked her e-mail just in case he'd sent her a message, but again she was disappointed. Finally, she dialed Donovan's phone again. It had only rung a couple of times when a deep, rich, booming voice said, "Hello, this is Donovan."

"Donovan," Lauren fairly cried. "This is Lauren Olcott. Oh, thank goodness you finally answered."

"Lauren, are you all right?" he asked.

"Sort of, but I'm scared to death. They've murdered Vivian, and I can't get ahold of Dexter even though he e-mailed me to tell me he was coming," she said, fighting to keep control of her emotions. She didn't want to break down and cry at the sound of the voice of this man who was more stranger than friend.

"Oh, Lauren, I'm so sorry. Are you sure you're safe?" he asked.

"Yes, I'm sure. Where are you?" she asked.

"I'm at the airport in Honolulu," he said. "Where are you?"

The relief Lauren felt was almost overwhelming. Even though she barely knew Donovan, and hadn't seen him since he was a missionary, she felt confident that he would help her, and already just the sound of his voice, knowing he was close by, was a comfort to her.

She gave him the name of the hotel and its address, and he said he'd be there as soon as he could rent a car. She thanked him and then said, "Will you keep your phone on? I'm really scared, Donovan."

"Of course I'll keep it on," he said.

There was something about the sound of his voice that instilled confidence in Lauren. "Thank you, and please hurry," she said.

"I will, and you keep the door locked until I get there."

* * *

Donovan had only brought one bag and his laptop computer on the trip, and he'd carried them on the plane with him, so he was able to go directly to the Hertz location and pick up the car Mrs. Olsen had so efficiently arranged for him. He kept thinking about Lauren's call. *If she'd killed someone, she wouldn't be calling me,* he thought. But then again, who knew what she might have to tell him when he got to her hotel.

Donovan suddenly remembered that he hadn't talked to Kaelyn yet, even though he'd tried calling at each airport he was in. So he forced himself to make the call, dreading how it would go if he was able to reach her. He was almost certain that she'd be angry when he told her where he was, but he had to do it. He felt that one of the worst things he could do in going into a marriage was to not be totally honest with his fiancée.

"Where have you been?" he asked when he finally heard her voice on the phone.

"The question is, *where are you?*" she fired back with such venom that he involuntarily jerked the phone from his ear for a moment.

"I had to leave the state for a day or two," he said defensively. "I've been trying to call you."

"I know, and I haven't been answering," she said with snide firmness.

"Kaelyn, please don't be angry," he pleaded. "Let me at least explain." Even though he'd known that she wouldn't be happy with him for going to Hawaii, he couldn't imagine that she already knew that's what he'd done.

"Angry is a mild term for how I feel," she said. "Why didn't you tell me you had to go somewhere?"

"It came up very suddenly," he answered as he recalled the prompting he'd so clearly received after his earnest prayer and that last desperate message from Lauren. "I called to let you know, but like you said, you didn't answer."

"I didn't want to talk to you then. Ellen and I saw you turn into the airport. Later, I drove by again and saw your car parked there. I can't believe you didn't say anything *before* you left. And now you're already over there. I'm guessing you're in Hawaii."

"What makes you think that?" he asked defensively. "I could be anywhere."

"Donovan, I would really think you'd be more thoughtful of me," she complained. "Suddenly chasing off after *the prettiest girl in Hawaii* is not exactly being thoughtful of your fiancée, you know."

"Kaelyn, I am not chasing off after anyone. I'm just trying to help someone in need, to be of service. I'm trying to think of someone other than myself." He was very irritated now, and he let it show. "Maybe you could try a little of that yourself."

"Ooh, I can't believe you said that!" she shouted into the phone. And before he could try to repair the damage he'd caused, she hung up. He was angry with her for jumping to conclusions and for not trusting him, but he was equally angry at himself for not giving her the courtesy of a phone call before he left.

He considered ringing her back, but knowing she wouldn't answer, he put the phone in his pocket, got in the rental car, and drove out of the airport and onto the familiar roads of Honolulu. A rush of memories flooded his mind. He'd loved this place on his mission, and he'd always wanted to return. In fact, he'd been seriously considering bringing Kaelyn here for their honeymoon. He'd certainly never expected to come here under these circumstances. He rolled down his window and breathed deeply of the sweetly scented air and felt in a way like he'd come home.

It took a little while, but he eventually located the hotel Lauren had called from. As he walked past a fragrant African tulip and beneath a row of king palms to the front doors, he braced himself. He really didn't know what he was letting himself in for—there could be a seriously disturbed woman in there, a real mental case, even a killer, although he doubted all of that. Or there could be someone who was in a lot of trouble not of her making who needed help. There could be someone whose life was in imminent danger. All he knew was that if he could help, no matter what he found inside, he'd do so, and then he'd get on his way back to Kaelyn, hoping he could somehow smooth over her hurt feelings.

After riding the elevator to the thirtieth floor, Donovan quickly located room 3012. He knocked on the door and stood waiting. A moment later it opened. And standing there, an attempt at a smile on her face, was a slightly older version of the pretty girl from his photo album. She was clearly in a terrible state of emotion, and those smoky gray eyes he so clearly remembered were full of pain and fear. They looked past him into the hallway, as if afraid of what might be there.

"Aloha," the woman said in a voice that matched the look in her eyes. "Thanks for coming. I'm sorry I'm such a bother, Elder Deru."

He stepped past her, and she closed the door behind him after one more quick glance into the empty hallway. "I just hope I can help," he said, offering his hand for a handshake. "And I'm just Donovan now."

"I appreciate your coming all this way," she said, clasping his hand briefly. "It's been a long time."

"It has," he agreed. "Now, I wish we could enjoy some small talk, but we'd better get right into this. Tell me everything that's happened, and maybe we can find a way to clear this thing up."

"Would you like to sit down?" she said, waving distractedly at a hard-backed chair.

"Yes, thanks," he said.

Lauren pulled up a chair for herself, and the two of them sat facing each other across a small, round table in awkward silence. Finally, Donovan said, "Why don't we start from the beginning? I'll just make a few notes if that's all right." He'd brought in his laptop computer in its bag that doubled as a briefcase. He pulled a yellow legal pad from it and jotted down the day and time. Then he looked up, and she again tried to smile. He realized that if she were happy, it would be a very attractive smile, but for now it looked quite pitiful.

"Oh, maybe before you begin, you'd like to try calling your boyfriend one more time. Maybe he's just gotten in," Donovan said, feeling that it would be nice to have another lawyer sitting here while she told her story. "They won't let us keep our cell phones on while we're in flight," he added lamely, thinking of the air phones and wondering why Dexter wouldn't have used one of those if he'd been delayed or something.

Lauren shook her head sadly. "He should have been back many hours ago," she said. But she did as he asked and again tried calling Dexter. "Something must have come up," she said when there was still no answer. "He must still be in L.A. He'd been sent there to lay the legal groundwork for an expansion of our company over there, an expansion that can never happen after what Royce and Fleming and whoever they have helping them have done."

"Okay," Donovan responded. "Well, let's take it from the beginning then."

Lauren did just that, and as she recited how she'd stumbled across the evidence of fraud, Donovan listened carefully to her story while also trying to analyze her mental state. Although she was clearly under a great deal of stress, she didn't appear to him to be suffering from any kind of breakdown. He found her believable and her story was consistent as it went along. Lauren seemed to be not only mentally sound, but highly intelligent.

She recited her story in some detail while he took notes. She repeatedly apologized for the periods of time she couldn't recall, explaining that she now realized she'd been drugged sometime after learning about Billie's failure to come to work on Monday. At times her memory was a little fuzzy, but if she was telling him the truth about drugs being administered to her both before and after being taken to her apartment, Donovan could certainly understand why.

When she'd finished her tale almost an hour later, she sighed. "It's such a relief to be able to tell someone all of this," she said. "Thank you for listening."

Donovan nodded. "I'm glad I could. I do have a few questions though, just for clarification."

She smiled and said, "I'll answer the best I can. Part of the time is very fuzzy."

"I recognize that," he told her. "Just let me ask what I need to, and you answer the best you can.

"First, Lauren, do you have any idea who besides Royce and Fleming are part of the conspiracy to defraud the company?" Donovan asked, wiping his brow. The humidity was drenching him, even in this air-conditioned room. The temperature had been near zero when he left Vernal. It was quite an adjustment.

"Probably Leroy," she said. "I'm almost certain there was some kind of drug in the cherry chocolates he gave me. And I've wondered even about Dr. Mitsui. I suppose that she could have put something in the Coke her assistant gave me in her office. And yet, she was so kind to me later and seemed sincerely upset about her pills being switched. She seemed to think I was in danger. I don't know what to think. I even suspect that poor Billie might have been involved, although it certainly doesn't seem like her at all. But it also doesn't seem like Leroy."

Lauren stopped and an especially pained look crossed her face. "If Billie wasn't involved, then I'm responsible for her death because of the e-mail I sent," she said. "Honestly, Donovan, I've been thinking about this a lot. And I don't dare trust anyone, except Ned and Vivian." Upon mentioning Vivian's name, Lauren finally broke down, stammering though her sobs, "I'm responsible for Vivian's death too. If only I'd trusted her sooner."

Awkwardly, Donovan reached over and patted Lauren's hand. "Hey, don't go trying to absorb blame that isn't yours," he said tenderly. "You didn't create this situation. Those who did bear full responsibility, and I'm sure there'll be a way to bring them to justice."

"I hope so," she said as she dabbed at her eyes and slowly regained her composure.

Donovan waited for a few moments then asked, "Can you still access the information you found? They claim you had a breakdown, according to Jim Roderick. We've got to prove them wrong. If you have the proof to back up your allegations of fraud and embezzlement at Paradise Pharmaceuticals and can get access to it right away, then we can prove you're telling the truth and the authorities can get to the bottom of this whole thing and make some arrests." What he didn't add was that it would also help diffuse the suspicion the police had that she had committed murder. It had occurred to him that she had no idea they might be thinking such a thing, and he didn't want to worry her with that right now.

"I have the proof you're asking about," she said. "It's all in a safety-deposit box at my bank. It consists of several pages of printed material and a disc with everything backed up on it. Would you like to see it?"

"I would," he said. "After I've had a chance to evaluate it, we can contact the police and let them take it from there."

"They'll be watching for me, Royce and Fleming will," she said as a shadow crossed her face. "We'll have to be really careful. I'd feel terrible if you got hurt after going to so much trouble to help me. Already two others—"

Donovan lifted a hand and shook his head. "Don't say that anymore," he warned. "You have no reason to be putting blame on yourself. And I'll be okay." But even as he said that, he had to admit to himself that there was undoubtedly a large element of danger involved, and it was far worse than he'd realized when he'd made the decision to fly here.

Donovan asked several more questions, which Lauren answered quickly and thoroughly. Then he asked, "You and Vivian left Fleming Parker bound with tape in your apartment?"

"Yes," she said. "But like I already told you, he must've gotten himself loose, or else someone else did. Royce, maybe, or Leroy might have gone there and helped him get loose. I don't know if Vivian locked the door when we left—we were just anxious to leave. I suppose they could easily have gotten in." Again her eyes welled up and she said, "If only Vivian hadn't gone back, she'd still be alive."

They talked awhile longer, then Donovan had her again try to call Dexter. He still wasn't answering his phones. "What do we do now?" she asked.

"I guess I need to get a room. I hope there's one available in this hotel. Given the time, I don't think there's anything we can do tonight," he said. "But tomorrow, we'll go to the bank and get your evidence and take it to the police."

There was not only a room available, but there was one on the same floor, just a few doors down from Lauren. Donovan wished there was something he could be doing now, but he needed sleep, and then in the morning, perhaps he could get the thing wrapped up to the point where Lauren would be safe, freed from suspicion. Then he could go home and try to make amends with his fiancée.

CHAPTER 12

A woman in her sixties lay on her back, bandages covering her head, squinting at the light that was blinding her eyes. For a moment, she didn't remember who she was, much less where she was. Only when her eyes had become accustomed to the light and a nurse came in did she begin to remember. Even then, it only came in little snatches, and she had a hard time piecing those bits of memory together to make a comprehensible whole.

"Good morning," the nurse said in a light, cheerful manner. "I see you're awake. Is there anything I can get you?"

"Where am I?" she asked.

"In a hospital. You got a nasty bump on the head. You've got a few other bumps and bruises, but nothing's broken. Would you like a sip of water?"

"Yes, please," she said, concentrating more on the bits of memory that were floating around in her mind like ducks on a pond. They just wouldn't stop long enough for her to put any of them together.

"What happened to me?" she asked at last as the nurse pushed a button that gently lifted the head of her bed. She remembered who she was, but other than that she was lost.

The nurse told her, and she shook her head in disbelief. She sipped a little water through the straw that she was offered. Then she pushed the cup away. "I'm tired," she said. "Maybe if I sleep a little, then I'll remember better."

"I'm sure you will," the nurse said as she lowered the head of the bed. "If you need anything at all, you just push this button."

But the patient was not paying attention. Her eyes were closed and she was remembering more bits of information, which, if she could just connect them, would probably make a lot of sense.

* * *

Donovan awoke shortly after dawn Friday morning, and stepped out on his balcony to check the weather. The sun shone brilliantly across the blue-green water and the almost deserted beach. He laughed at himself for even wondering about the weather. *Warm and humid, of course,* he thought. Then he sighed, wishing he were here under better circumstances. Donovan went back inside, showered and shaved, and then called Lauren's room. She was up and also showered and was just running a brush through her hair. "Have you eaten?" Donovan had asked.

She hadn't, so he ordered breakfast, which they ate in her room. When they were finished, Lauren said, after trying Dexter's phones again to no avail, "You have a rental car, right?"

"Yep."

"Would you mind if we drove to Dexter's house before we go to the bank? We have loads of time before the bank opens," she said. "And nobody would recognize us, since they don't know you and we wouldn't be in my car."

"Okay, we can do that," Donovan said. "Maybe with some luck he'll be home by the time we get there and he could go with us."

"I sure hope so," Lauren said.

As they ventured into the heavy morning traffic, Lauren kept glancing nervously about. She admitted to Donovan that she was very frightened, but she also insisted that she knew they were safe in the rental car.

"Nice house," Donovan said when they finally reached Dexter's large beachfront home. "And beautiful grounds."

"Dexter makes a good living," Lauren agreed. "He takes pride in his home and does a lot of entertaining here. I think you'll like him. He's a good man."

"He must be or he couldn't have attracted such a nice person as you," Donovan said.

He opened the car door for Lauren. She stepped out, and he shut the door behind her. "The view of the ocean is spectacular from here," he said as they started up the long walk.

"Better from the back. You can only see bits of it from here," Lauren said. They reached the front door and she rang the bell. There was no answer. "His housekeeper only comes in twice a week." She rang it again. Donovan could hear it reverberating through the house. "He must still be in L.A.," Lauren said. "I can't imagine why he hasn't contacted me to say so, though. I wish I knew for sure that he's okay."

"He hasn't come back yet, Miss Lauren," a soft, cultured voice said.

Donovan jumped. He hadn't seen the little Chinese man come around the corner of the house. "Hello, Mr. Soo," Lauren said brightly. "I didn't see you. Donovan, this is Mr. Soo; he's Dexter's gardener. He's the one that keeps things looking so perfect around here. Mr. Soo, this is a friend of mine from Utah, Mr. Donovan Deru."

Mr. Soo bowed and said, "It's a pleasure, Mr. Deru."

"The same here, I'm sure," Donovan responded.

"Mr. Soo, did you just say that Dexter was still in Los Angeles?" Lauren asked.

"Oh, no, miss. He came home very early yesterday morning, but I haven't seen him since. I'd just barely come to work when he drove into his garage. I don't think he even saw me."

"But you didn't see him leave again?" Donovan asked.

"No, but I'm sure he did. I had to take my wife to the doctor so I was gone much of the day. That was why I'd come so early to work yesterday," Mr. Soo told them. "I was surprised to see him, because he'd told me a few days ago that his work in California would take quite a while. Maybe he went back to Los Angeles." Mr. Soo looked puzzled and then asked, "Surely he talked to you, Miss Lauren?"

She shook her head, and Donovan could see that she was both worried and very puzzled. She turned to Donovan. "I know where he keeps a key hidden. I know he wouldn't care if I went in. I could at least see if his suitcase is gone."

Mr. Soo spoke up quickly. "I'm sure Mr. Drake would be happy for you to go in, Miss Lauren. I'll get the key for you."

"I'll wait out in back of the house and watch the surf," Donovan said.

"Oh, no, I'm sure it's okay if you come in," Lauren coaxed.

"No, I'll just stroll down toward the beach. Shout at me when you're ready to go."

It wasn't long before Lauren shouted much more quickly and with more urgency than Donovan had expected. In fact, her voice was so full of anguish that he sprinted to the door. Mr. Soo also came running from the front. "Lauren, what is it?" Donovan asked when she met him at the door, tears in her eyes.

"It's Dexter. He's here but . . ."

When she couldn't go on, Donovan rushed past her into the house and asked over his shoulder, "Where is he?" He expected the worst.

Lauren directed him to a large, sparkling kitchen. Dexter lay on the floor, halfway between an oak breakfast table and the sink. Mr. Soo had followed Donovan in, and he began to moan and rock back and forth on his feet. "One of you call 9-1-1," Donovan instructed as he knelt and pressed a trembling finger to Dexter's neck.

* * *

The little morsels of memory were coming more frequently now to the patient, and she began to piece them together. She recalled the screeching of brakes and a scream, maybe her own. That was followed by the face of a beautiful, young woman pleading with her not to go. *But not to go where?* she wondered.

Then she remembered a gun and a syringe, and it made her tremble with fear that felt far too familiar. She pictured roses strewn on carpet. She was sure there was a connection between those two things, but she couldn't figure out what it was. Finally, just as a nurse entered the room again, she had the strangest sensation of something soft vibrating beneath her fingers. She looked at them, puzzled, turning her hands over.

"Are you feeling better?" the nurse asked. "Your doctor will be right down."

But the patient didn't hear a word she said, for she had suddenly identified the strange vibration. It was the purring of a cat. A large, yellow tomcat. "Tommy!" she suddenly cried in anguish. "Was Tommy hurt too?" she asked the nurse.

"Tommy? No, there was no one else in the accident. Just you."

"Tommy wasn't with me?" she asked. "You didn't see a yellow cat?"

"I wasn't at the scene of your accident, but no one's mentioned anything about a cat. Now you just lie back again and rest. The doctor will be along shortly."

"I've got to go. I've got to check on Tommy. He needs me. He's alone if . . ." The patient paused as the face of an old, white-haired man swam into her mind. "Ned?" she asked. "Have you seen Ned?"

"Ned who?" the nurse asked. "Is Ned a friend? Is he someone we could call to come see you?"

"Oh, yes, please call him for me," the patient cried as the fragments of memory slowly came together, fitting neatly like a finished puzzle. "Yes, I must talk to him," she insisted urgently.

"Okay, Ms. Likio, just be calm. Can you remember Ned's phone number?"

Vivian couldn't remember that well yet, but she said, "He's my neighbor, and he has my cat. His name is Ned Haraguchi. Please, find his number. Call him."

The nurse rang for help, and when another nurse came running into the room, she said, "Stay with Ms. Likio while I find a phone number. She remembers a neighbor's name. I need to call him at once."

Before she got out of the room, Vivian cried out in anguish, "Lauren! Oh, my poor Lauren. They may have found her. She needs me. She must be so very frightened."

The two nurses looked at each other, shook their heads, and then the first one left the room to find a phone book.

* * *

The night had passed, and Ned guessed he must have slept some, but it couldn't have been much. The loss of his dear Vivian was almost more than he could bear. Tommy, he was quite certain, could sense the loss as well, for he was more subdued than normal, and he followed Ned around the house like he was afraid to be left alone.

When the phone rang, Ned considered not answering it. *It's probably just a salesperson,* he thought to himself. He couldn't imagine who else would be calling. His children on the mainland never called on any day but Sunday. However, after the fifth ring, he went ahead and picked up the phone.

"Mr. Haraguchi?" a pleasant voice asked.

"I'm Ned Haraguchi," he said, his voice breaking from the strain of a sleepless night and the loss of his best friend.

"Oh, good. Mr. Haraguchi, there's someone here who wants to talk to you."

Before he could ask who, a voice came on the line that shocked him so badly he had to find a chair to keep from keeling over. "Ned, this is Vivian. I need your help."

"Oh, Vivian! Are you sure it's you?" he asked.

"Of course it's me, you dotty old man," she said affectionately.

"But I thought you were dead. I heard Royce and—"

"I'm not dead," she broke in. "I can't imagine why you'd think such a silly thing, but I'm terribly worried about Lauren. She's alone at a motel. She must be scared to death and is probably starving."

Ned was at a total loss. He felt he was hearing the voice of someone who had returned from the dead. He trembled with gratitude over the very sound of her lovely voice, but he couldn't imagine where she was. The mention of Lauren made him worry now in a different way. He must have misunderstood the conversation he'd overheard between Leroy and Royce. It must be Lauren that had died. That thought brought anger, and anger brought him to his full senses.

"Vivian," he said urgently, "someone died in Lauren's apartment. It must have been—"

She cut him off again. "Lauren isn't there. I took her away myself. I need for you to go check on her at once. I'd come, but they tell me I was in a car wreck and my head got a nasty bump. I'm in the hospital and the doctor says I can't leave yet."

Ned was very much in control now. Two women he was very fond of were in need of his help. He'd do whatever needed to be done and he'd do it now. If Vivian said she got Lauren away from the apartment, then he believed it. They were both alive! He'd go find Lauren, then he'd visit Vivian.

* * *

Donovan and Lauren were both on their knees with Dexter when a pair of paramedics burst in. Dexter was groaning, and Lauren was gently stroking his hair. She was relieved that he was even alive. She'd been certain he was dead when she saw him on the kitchen floor, so when Donovan had announced that there was a strong pulse, she'd screamed and flung herself to the floor beside him and pulled his head onto her lap.

They both gave way to the paramedics, who started an examination, firing questions at Donovan, Mr. Soo, and Lauren as they worked. Finally, satisfied that Dexter could be moved safely, they loaded him onto a gurney and wheeled him out the door. "I'm going with him," Lauren announced to Donovan.

"There's nothing you can do for him right now," Donovan said reasonably. "He'll get good care. You've got to think about yourself for a minute here. You need to get that evidence you have in your bank. And the sooner we get that to the police, the better off we'll all be. Whatever has happened to Dexter may not have been an accident. If so, whoever did this to him may be after you next."

Considerably sobered by Donovan's reasoning, Lauren said, "You're right. Thanks for keeping me straight. It's just that I'm so worried about Dexter." She looked at her watch. "The bank's open— let's go there right now."

Though Donovan knew they should wait for the police, he felt an increasing sense of urgency to get Lauren's files. They hurried to the rental car and left. A police car passed them just a block from Dexter's house. "I'm glad we missed the cops," Lauren said. "But I hope they can figure out what happened. Somebody might have tried to kill Dexter. And if so, I bet Royce and Fleming know something about it."

"Probably," Donovan agreed. "And when we take that stuff you have at the bank to the police, I'm sure they'll be able to see that."

Lauren noticed that Donovan kept glancing at his rearview mirror. She turned in the seat and looked back.

"That car, the blue Ford, do you recognize it?" he asked.

"No, never seen it before," she said as a new worry began to gnaw at her.

"I'm sure that car was parked across the street from Dexter's house when we left. They may be following us," he said. "Hang on." He suddenly turned right, tires screeching on the hot pavement. The Ford followed. He sped up. The Ford sped up. He turned left. The Ford turned left.

"They're after us, aren't they?" Lauren asked, fear clutching at her throat.

Donovan sped up more, and so did the old Ford. He made another turn, and they pulled away from the Ford for a minute. But it kept coming, traveling at an insane speed. There were no side streets for a while, and Lauren's heart began beating wildly.

The blue car pulled up beside them. Lauren screamed, "Look out!" as a gun was raised and pointed at Donovan.

Donovan slammed on the brakes. The old Ford flew past them. The sharp crack of a pistol made Lauren scream. But the bullet flew by harmlessly. Donovan cranked the wheel, and his car slid into a dangerous turn. Then he was facing the other direction and jamming the accelerator to the floor. "Lauren, get down and stay down," Donovan shouted as the car accelerated perilously.

"They shot at us," she said with a trembling voice as she bent over, her head against Donovan's leg.

"Okay," he said a moment later. "They're still coming, but we've got a little lead on them. Hang on, because I'm going to try to lose them now."

They took a turn so sharp that for a moment, Lauren thought the car was going to roll, but Donovan kept control even though they fishtailed wildly as he attempted to straighten out. Lauren couldn't stand the suspense and peeked over the back of the seat a few seconds later. "They're still coming," she cried. "They're gaining on us!"

Lauren looked ahead for just a moment, seeing a huge palm tree on the left edge of the road at the crest of a small rise. Then Donovan shouted, "Stay down. They could start shooting again."

She ducked. She hated not being able to see, but she knew Donovan was only watching out for her safety, so she curled up on the seat, rested her head against Donovan's leg, and prayed.

Suddenly she could hear the roar of an engine again, and when Donovan hit the brakes, she rolled off the seat. There was a loud crash, then Donovan gunned his car over the hill's crest. They were airborne for a few seconds, and when the car again hit the pavement, a tire blew. But Donovan kept driving, the car bumping along in protest. As she scrambled back onto the seat, he said, "I think they hit a tree."

She looked back. The old Ford was on its top at the very crest of the hill, sliding across the street, spinning like a top in slow motion. Donovan turned a corner so they were just out of sight.

"I stayed in the middle of the road," Donovan said as he pulled the car to the side. "When they came up beside me, they were too far over and watching me. The passenger had that gun up again, but when I hit the brakes, they must have bounced off the tree and rolled. Thank goodness there were no other cars on the road. I'm sorry about the bumpy ride. Are you okay?"

"I guess so, but I'm more frightened than ever."

"With good cause," Donovan said. Lauren had moved close to him, and he instinctively put a protective arm around her shoulder and felt her trembling. "We'll be okay now."

He dug his cell phone out of his pocket and began to dial. "Who are you calling?" she asked.

"9-1-1," he said. "Those guys back there are probably hurt, and anyway, they tried to kill us. As for us, I'd love to keep on going to the bank, but we've already left one potential crime scene today, and I'd like to break the habit."

CHAPTER 13

Ned tapped on the door to the motel room and waited. Nothing. He knocked harder. When there was still no response, he walked to the office and rang the bell. When the attendant came, she said in a gravelly voice, "Can I help you, sir?"

"I was looking for the ladies in number 10. They haven't checked out have they?"

The attendant scowled. "No, they didn't. But they left and I have a bill that needs paid."

"When did they leave?" Ned asked, concerned about where Lauren might be now, hoping she was safe somewhere.

"Look, old man," the woman said rudely, "if I knew when they was leaving I'da made 'em pay. Now they're gone, and I got no money and the owner will make me cough up for them."

Ned pulled out his checkbook. "How much do they owe? I'll settle the bill for them."

She gave him a figure which sounded rather high, but he didn't have time to argue, so he wrote a check and left. A few minutes later, he was gazing with affection at Vivian in her white hospital gown and bandaged head. He didn't know if he'd ever seen a prettier sight in his life.

* * *

"Donovan would be happy to see that there isn't a single bit of fog and that the sun is actually melting the snow today," Kaelyn said absently as she stood staring through her window.

Her roommate, Ellen Randall, said from her spot on the sofa, "Thought you weren't going to think about him until he came home."

Kaelyn turned and smiled sadly at her friend. "I can't help it. You know that."

"Yes, I certainly do," Ellen agreed. Then she added softly, "Kaelyn, you've got to trust him. He's a good man. He's only trying to help someone who's in trouble."

"I want to trust him," Kaelyn said. "But having him in my life still seems like a dream, and I keep thinking I'll wake up one morning and he won't be part of it anymore. He's such a smart guy, so nice, and so cute. I'm afraid of losing him."

Ellen stood and put an arm around her. "You are who he wants. Don't let yourself think otherwise."

"I try not to, but every time I talk to my mother, she says something like, 'Kaelyn, don't let Donovan get away. You'll never find anybody that makes that kind of money again.'"

Ellen bristled. "Your mother has no right to say that to you. This engagement of yours is not about money."

"To Mom it is. And it's sort of true. I'll never have to work after I marry Donovan. If I lose him, then I'll always be comparing every man I date to Donovan. And I'll be an old maid before I know it, and I won't have a penny to my name."

"Quit it! You're not losing him. If you do, it'll be your fault because you drive him off with your jealousy. I said it before and I'll say it again. Trust him, Kaelyn. That girl he went over there to help is no threat to you."

Kaelyn shrugged free of Ellen's arm and turned back to the window. She stared out for a long time, not seeing the beautiful sunshine the way she had just moments before. All she could see was the picture of the girl Donovan's sister had called the prettiest girl in Hawaii. Finally, she said quietly, "You haven't seen her picture, Ellen. And I wish I hadn't either. With him over there with her, he probably doesn't even think of me."

Ellen shook her head. "Hey, you haven't lost him," she said. "I have an idea. Instead of sitting here worrying yourself sick, just call him. Tell him you miss him. Tell him you're sorry you got mad. Don't pout, don't ask about what's-her-name. Just make sure he has you on his mind. And keep calling every few hours if you need to."

Kaelyn brightened up. "Good idea," she said as she headed for the phone.

* * *

Donovan and Lauren were ushered into the office of Captain Ray Hafoko of the Honolulu Police Department. Lauren was listening in horror to the police account of the death of Dr. Mitsui. Her joy at hearing the dead woman was not Vivian had been dampened by the soberness of the situation. She couldn't believe the doctor had been found in her bed and that there was no sign of Fleming Parker. And yet she'd last seen him bound on the floor at the foot of her bed just moments before she and Vivian left. Lauren kept glancing at Donovan, and he was hoping that she would remember his advice not to volunteer any information. So far, she was doing well and she hadn't mentioned Fleming.

As the captain spoke, Donovan's cell phone rang. He answered it quietly, surprised when he heard Kaelyn's voice. "Is something wrong?" he asked.

"No, I was just thinking about you and missing you. I'm sorry I've been such a jerk," she said. "I just wanted to call and tell you that."

"Thanks, Kaelyn. I haven't been as nice as I could be either," he said, glancing at Lauren, whose face was pale over the news of what had happened in her apartment after she and Vivian had left.

"You'd love the weather today," she went on. "There's no fog and the snow is melting."

"Great," he said. "It's about time. Maybe we'll be able to do a little fishing in a few weeks."

He knew that Kaelyn didn't like fishing, but he was pleased when she said, "I'd love that. I'd love doing anything with you right now."

"Well, you hang in there, and I'll be seeing you soon. Can I call you back in a little while? There's something going on right now, and I need to be involved here." Donovan hated to brush Kaelyn off, but he could see the look in Lauren's eyes, not a look that was caused by this phone call, but one that was caused by what Captain Hafoko was saying. Donovan could tell that she was just realizing that she was being considered a suspect in the doctor's death, along with Dexter and Vivian.

"Oh, Donovan, I hoped we could talk for a little while," Kaelyn said.

Donovan was listening to her, but impatiently now, for he was also trying to listen to Captain Hafoko, who was saying, "We'll need a complete statement from you as to your activities for the past few days. There is an awful lot here that doesn't add up, with you, with your boyfriend, and with Vivian Likio."

"Where is Vivian?" Lauren asked. "Have you arrested her already?"

"We don't know where she is. But we'd like to know," the captain said firmly. "We were hoping you could lead us to her."

Kaelyn had said something that Donovan didn't catch. But he had to intervene in Lauren's behalf right now. "Just a second," he said into the phone to Kaelyn, cutting her off from whatever she was trying to tell him. Then he said to Lauren, "Don't say any more, Lauren. We need to find a local attorney to help us."

She looked sharply at Donovan, then nodded her head. The captain gave him a look that he'd received in many a police interrogation of his clients.

Kaelyn spoke again. "You're with Lauren right now, aren't you?" He could hear the pouting in her voice.

As she was speaking, he heard Ellen Randall's voice in the background saying, "No, Kaelyn. Don't pout."

Clearly Ellen was trying to keep Kaelyn from getting mad again, and he was grateful. But he had to get off the phone right now, so he said, "I'll call you back in a little while."

"Okay," was all that Kaelyn said.

Donovan realized he hadn't answered her question about Lauren. He'd wanted to tell her that he was in fact with Lauren and that she was in trouble and needed his help right now, but the way Lauren's face was crumbling, that would have only made the situation worse. So he simply said good-bye, hoping that Kaelyn could be mature enough to understand.

As he shoved the phone back in his pocket, Donovan said, "Captain, I'm sorry, but I don't think it's in Lauren's best interest to talk to you anymore at this time. I'd like to find a local attorney for her and see what we can learn before we go any further here."

Lauren was on the verge of tears. "Donovan," she said, "maybe the cops don't believe me, but how can they not believe you?" Then she again faced the captain, and despite a protest by Donovan, she said, "He's only here because I accidentally asked him to come. He came all the way from Utah to help someone he didn't really even know. And why did he do it? I'll tell you why. Because he has a big heart and is a good man. That's why. So why don't you believe him?"

The captain just shook his head. "We are investigating. We are not bringing any charges at this point. And nobody is saying your friend here is not a good man, but he doesn't have firsthand knowledge of most of what's gone on here. We are just being thorough."

"Thanks, Lauren," Donovan said. "But we don't have any more to say to the police. They need to go do their job, and when they do, they'll learn the truth." But even as he spoke, he was wondering if they would investigate the way they should. He had his doubts.

"You two wait here. I'll be right back," Captain Hafoko said. He got up from behind his desk and walked to the door. Left alone with Donovan after learning that her life had taken a dramatic turn for the worse, Lauren said emphatically, "I didn't kill Dr. Mitsui, Donovan. You've got to believe me. And neither did Vivian or Dexter. The police saw Dexter at the hospital and said that he's just now starting to come around. What are they thinking? He's a victim, just like I am."

"I believe you," Donovan said sincerely. "But we've got to prove it now. First, we need to get the documents you have in your safety-deposit box and prove that there is a major fraud being perpetrated against Paradise Pharmaceuticals," he said. "We've also got to find Vivian Likio and get a statement from her."

"But she's a suspect just like I am. And worse, Fleming and his people probably want to kill her too. What if they have already? They probably think I told her everything. Where could she be?" Lauren asked with a shudder. "This is all so horrible. I wish I'd never tried to do anything to stop Royce and Fleming and whoever is helping them. I felt I had an ethical responsibility, and besides, I was worried about my career. Now somebody wants to kill me. And someone did kill Dr. Mitsui and Billie. Oh, Donovan, I can always find another job. I can't come back from the dead."

"Stop it, Lauren," Donovan said fiercely. "I realize that you've been through a lot, but you've got to be strong. We can beat them, but not if you aren't willing to fight."

She looked at him, then her eyes fell. "I'm sorry, Donovan. None of this is your problem. And I'm probably causing you problems at home. I wouldn't blame you if you just went home and left me to figure this all out by myself."

"Is that what you want?"

"Of course not. But I almost got you shot over something that you don't even have a stake in, and you have a life to live."

"Those things are my worries," he said. "I can handle them. Right now you need my help, and I'm ready to give it to you in the best way I can."

"Why?" she asked. "You have so much to lose."

He thought about her question for a moment. *Yes, why?* he asked himself. And he knew the answer. "Because I believe you," he said. *And because I believe God wants me to.*

There was silence for a moment. "I'll change," she said suddenly. "I promise I will. You were right all those years ago, and I'll do everything I can to become a better person."

He gave her arm a quick squeeze. "I know you will. And I can't think of anything that will make you—or your family—happier."

"Okay, maybe I could get you two to help me a little here," Captain Hafoko said as he walked back into his office.

"I thought I made it clear," Donovan said crisply. "She has nothing more to say right now. However, if you'll allow us, we will get some documents that will shed a lot of light on this matter. If fact, when you see them, you'll realize that she's both innocent and in danger."

"Just hold on. Sit down for a few minutes," the imposing captain said, waving his hand at the chairs they'd just vacated. "We'll talk. I won't ask any questions, if that's what you want. And anyway, I'm now convinced that it is dangerous out there for you two."

"I'm glad you understand that. Speaking of dangerous, you did bring in those men who were shooting at us, didn't you? Or are they at the hospital?" he asked as he thought about how lucky he'd felt that a couple of police units had been only a block away when he'd called 9-1-1. "Your men brought us here before we even had a chance to see if they were hurt badly."

"There was no one in the wrecked car," the captain told them. "The men who shot at you must not have been hurt too badly, because they fled the scene. Which is one of the reasons it might not be safe for the two of you to be out there."

Donovan looked at Lauren. "He's got a point. We'll stay for a minute more, but don't say anything unless I say so. Okay?"

She nodded, and they both sat down. "The hospital did some testing on Mr. Drake's blood. It seems he has some drugs in him which, had he been given more, would probably have killed him," Captain Hafoko said. "He's starting to talk a little, and it looks like he'll be okay. However, there is another problem as it pertains to him. An eyewitness puts him at the crime scene."

He paused while that sank in. Lauren looked helplessly at Donovan. "That can't be. When we left the apartment—"

"Not now, Lauren. Remember, anything you say, whether it's in response to a question or not, can be used against you, even if you think you're saying something harmless," Donovan warned.

"That's right," the captain agreed. "We have also identified the prints on the syringe. They belong to Ms. Vivian Likio."

"Of course—" Lauren began again before Donovan was able to cut her off, this time by grabbing her hand and squeezing sharply.

She looked at Donovan with guilt in her eyes. "I'm sorry. Maybe we should go now."

"Not yet, please," Captain Hafoko said. "Let me just explain a couple of other things. Maybe then you will both see the need to help us. An autopsy on Dr. Mitsui's body has established the cause of death to be an overdose of a drug which is as yet unidentified. Traces of the same drug were found in the syringe, which appears to have been used as the instrument of death. However, that drug is something different from what Mr. Drake ingested."

Donovan spoke up. "Captain, I think we've heard enough for now. Lauren and I would like to have the opportunity to go retrieve some information which we will then be glad to share with you. It will shed a great deal of light on this whole case, and then you can begin to pursue the right people. Dexter and Vivian, as well as Lauren, did not kill anyone. They are innocent. And we can prove that, given a little time."

"That may be the case, Mr. Deru, but for now, we'd like Miss Olcott to remain close by."

"Is Lauren under arrest?" Donovan asked.

"Of course not, but she is an important witness in a murder case."

"Two murder cases," Lauren said sadly before she could stop herself.

The captain's hand came down with a thud on his desk. "What are you talking about?"

"I'm sorry, Donovan," Lauren said. "That just slipped out."

"That's okay. We'll be leaving now."

"Mr. Deru," the captain said sternly. "This is a very serious matter, and if—"

Donovan cut him off. "More serious than you can even imagine," he said sharply. "We need to leave right now."

Just then, the captain's phone buzzed. He picked up the receiver and listened for a moment. Then he said, "I'll let her know." After hanging up he said, "Dexter Drake is apparently doing much better, and he's asking for you to come to the hospital."

A short time later, since the rental car had been towed, Donovan and Lauren were in a taxi on their way to the hospital to visit Dexter.

* * *

Fleming looked at the two bruised men in anger. "I told you where you could probably locate them. And as I predicted, they showed up. But you let them get away. You can't even take care of a very simple and straightforward assignment, and now you've made things very difficult for me. I don't want to have to say this again, but that pair needs to be taken care of immediately. Now get out there and get it done."

One of the hired thugs asked, "Where should we start looking for them this time?"

"Think, you idiots!" he thundered. "Where would they most likely go next?"

"Uh, I don't know. That's why I'm asking you."

"Try the hospital where Dexter Drake was taken in the ambulance this morning. They'll show up there sooner or later," Fleming suggested in disgust.

"Oh yeah, sure," was the response. But it was followed by another question. "Which hospital was that?"

Fleming was on his feet, his jowls shaking and his eyes flashing with anger. "I don't know which hospital he was taken to. Go find out. Now get out of here and do what I'm paying you to do."

CHAPTER 14

"Ned!" Lauren cried as she and Donovan stepped into the hospital lobby and saw the small, white-haired man walking toward them.

Lauren!" he exclaimed in return.

Donovan watched in surprise as the two of them rushed forward and embraced. "What are you doing here?" Lauren asked.

"I just came to check on Vivian," he said. "We've both been so worried about you. Where have you been?"

"Vivian! She's here? What happened to her?" Lauren asked, both relieved and worried at the same time. "Did someone—"

Ned interrupted her. "I thought you must have known. Aren't you here to see her?"

"No. My boyfriend, Dexter, is in here," she said. "Is Vivian going to be okay?"

"Yes, of course she is," Ned said. "She was in a little car accident and got a bump on the head. She's fine now and can't wait to get out of here. The doctor says that he might let her go this evening. I was just going to get some lunch and come back and wait. Oh, Lauren, we were both worried that something had happened to you. I went to your motel this morning after Vivian called me from here, but you were gone. The woman there had no idea where you'd gone to."

Donovan was getting a clear picture of what had happened. His legal mind was working quickly in behalf of Vivian, a woman he'd never met, and yet one Lauren trusted. The time of Vivian's accident was important, as were the location and the direction of travel. Those were all things that could prove her innocence and get the police looking in the right direction for Dr. Mitsui's killer.

Lauren's only concern was Vivian's physical well-being. The relief in her eyes as she turned to Donovan was evident. "Donovan, did you hear that? Vivian's safe. Let's go see her before we talk to Dexter," she said. "I want her to know I'm okay too."

"Of course, and I assume this is Ned Haraguchi," Donovan said.

"Oh, yes. I'm sorry. I should have introduced you two right off. I'm just so . . ." She trailed off as her voice became choked with emotion.

Donovan smiled at her and then said to Ned, "I'm Donovan Deru. I'm a friend of Lauren's."

"Oh, Mr. Deru. Vivian mentioned that Lauren had been in touch with someone from Utah. You are from Utah, aren't you?"

Donovan assured him that he was, and then Ned led them to Vivian's room. While the two women shared a joyous reunion, Donovan stood back. Vivian could be in a lot of danger. Lauren's enemies had no idea how much Vivian knew about their activities at this point, but they were almost bound to assume that she knew too much. He had to find a way to keep her safe. He tapped Ned on the shoulder, and the old man followed him into the hallway. Ned seemed like an intelligent, trustworthy man. Donovan decided to take a chance on him.

"Ned, I don't suppose you know much about what's going on with Lauren," he began.

"I don't, but I'm sure she's in some kind of terrible danger. I'm so worried about her," Ned responded.

"There is good reason to be," Donovan confided in him. "And there is equally good reason to worry about Vivian's safety." He then gave Ned a brief picture of what was happening.

"Oh, my!" Ned said. "We've got to do something. I'd say we should go to the police, but if they think Vivian is a wicked woman, then they might not be much help."

"We can prove that she's innocent of any wrongdoing," Donovan assured him. "But it might take a little while. It might be good if you stayed with her until she can safely be released. Then maybe you could take her someplace safe until I tell you it's okay to contact the police. I hope that can all be accomplished today."

"Whatever you say, Mr. Deru."

"Thank you. Now I need to get Lauren moving so we won't run out of time today," he said, and they stepped back into Vivian's room.

A short time later, Lauren and Donovan made their way to the hospital wing Dexter was in. A police officer was seated outside his door. He stood when the pair approached. "I'm sorry, but visitors to this room are restricted," he said.

"I'm here at his request," Lauren said. "Captain Hafoko knows we're coming."

"Are you Lauren Olcott?" he asked.

"Yes," she said.

"Then you must be Mr. Deru," he said to Donovan.

"That's right. Now if you'll excuse us, we are in a bit of a hurry," Donovan said.

Donovan was surprised at how much better Dexter looked. He was on an IV, but his color was back, and he smiled as they walked in. Lauren leaned down and gave him a quick kiss. "You gave me a scare this morning," she said.

"I'm so glad you're okay. I was coming to help you," he said. "But when I got to your apartment, you were gone." Just then the police officer stepped in.

"Uh, we'd like to have a moment with Mr. Drake," Donovan said.

"Sorry, I have my instructions. I'll be staying in the room with you."

The presence of the officer drastically limited the conversation, and Donovan stepped into the hallway so at least Lauren wouldn't have to be burdened by him listening to her conversation with Dexter.

He thought about Kaelyn and figured it might be good to call her right now before she became even more angry. He dialed Kaelyn's number. She took her time answering, but just before he expected her answering machine to pick up, she finally came on the line.

"Kaelyn," he said, "I'm sorry about earlier. This is a bigger mess here than I expected, and you caught me at a bad time. But I'm sure glad you called."

Kaelyn's tone was both forgiving and understanding when she spoke. "Thanks for calling back," she said. Then she talked about how improved the weather was. She discussed a couple of ideas she'd had for the wedding. From there it was several minutes of small talk.

When Lauren came out of Dexter's room a few minutes later, Donovan realized that Kaelyn hadn't mentioned her at all, nor had she asked anything about Hawaii. He hoped she wouldn't bring up either one. Lauren mouthed Kaelyn's name, and he nodded. She smiled, leaned against the wall, and closed her eyes. Donovan could see that she was both physically and emotionally drained. He wondered how much more she could take, considering what she'd been through the past few days.

"Donovan, are you still there?" Kaelyn asked sharply, and he realized his mind had drifted. He had no idea what she'd just said.

"Yes," he answered. "Of course I'm here."

"Well, so when?" she asked.

When what? he wondered, having no idea what she'd asked. But he didn't want her to know that, so he said, "I'm not sure," hoping that was a safe answer.

Apparently it wasn't, for she said, even more sharply than a moment before, "You don't know when your mother's birthday is? You aren't listening to a word I'm saying. Why bother to call if you don't want to talk to me?"

"Kaelyn," he said, "I'm really tired, and this is a serious matter I'm dealing with here. I've got a lot on my mind. Her birthday is March third."

"Thank you," she said. "And you don't have any idea why I wanted to know that, do you?"

She was right. He had no idea. And he knew there was no point in faking it again. "I'm sorry," he said. "What did you want to know for?"

"Oh, it doesn't matter!" she said. "I'll tell you when you get back. And when, might I ask, will that be? Or aren't you sure of that, either?"

Donovan could see the conversation was deteriorating and hoped it would end soon.

"You're right," Donovan said, apologetically. "I don't know for sure when I'll be back."

Kaelyn had apparently gotten more in control of her emotions, for her voice was much more pleasant when she said, "What kind of trouble is it that you're dealing with there?"

"I really can't talk about it, but it does involve a death," he said, hoping that would be enough to satisfy her.

"Is it murder?" Kaelyn asked, sounding shocked.

"It seems likely," Donovan said.

"Is Lauren a suspect?"

Donovan could feel himself squirming. He had to end this now. "Possibly," he said. Then before she could say something further, he added, "I need to go now. I'll call again."

"Okay, thanks for calling," Kaelyn said. "Call again, soon."

"I will," he promised. "And say hi to Ellen for me."

* * *

Kaelyn was grinning when she hung up the phone. She pounded one fist into the other and said, "Yes!"

Ellen raised an eyebrow. "Is Lauren a suspect in a murder?" she asked.

"It looks like it," Kaelyn said. "I guess I was worried over nothing."

"You usually do that sort of thing," Ellen remarked dryly. "Let this be a lesson to you. And from now on, you treat that guy of yours like you don't ever want to lose him."

* * *

As Lauren and Donovan headed out of the hospital, he asked her how Dexter was. "I think he's going to be okay. We couldn't talk very freely with that officer in the room, so I have no idea how he might have gotten the drugs in him that messed him up. He did tell me that he'd been asleep for a long time and that he didn't hear his phones ringing. When he did finally wake up he was so sick he kept throwing up and getting weaker and weaker. He said he finally tried to call me, but he was so weak by then that he passed out trying to reach the phone in his living room. I guess he was out quite a while that time, and then later the same thing happened when he tried to go to the kitchen to find some food. That's what he'd been doing before we found him. I could tell there was more he wanted to tell me, but he kept looking at that officer and then shaking his head."

"Well, you and I have got to get to the bank and get your documents. That's the only thing I can think of that will get Captain

Hafoko and his officers looking for the real suspects in this case," Donovan said.

Outside, they stood at the doors and looked for the taxi he'd arranged for a little earlier. Donovan wished he had his rental car, but it was damaged enough that he'd need to get another one, and that would take some time, which he didn't have right now. So taxis were the only way they could get around. He hated to be exposed very long out in the open, for he had a feeling that the men who'd shot at him before could easily be around.

As he looked toward the street a second time, hoping to see a taxi, a black van pulled out of a parking area and moved slowly toward them, and he got a sick feeling. "We better get back inside," Donovan said, trying not to alarm Lauren.

They both backed toward the door. "Do you think those guys that shot at us are in that van?" she asked.

"I don't know, but we aren't taking any chances," he said as the black van sped up.

They ducked back inside and hurried around a wall, out of sight. They waited breathlessly for a moment. Then Donovan said, "It's probably just a coincidence, but I'll see if it's gone."

He couldn't see the van, but a taxi was waiting in the loading area. "Let's go," he said. "Our taxi's waiting." They again went outside, hurrying this time, but they were only partway to the taxi when Donovan spotted the black van again. It was coming from the opposite direction.

"Hurry," Donovan shouted, and the two of them ran to the waiting taxi. Donovan opened the door and they jumped in. "Lose that black van," Donovan said to the driver even as the van approached rapidly from the rear.

The driver gave Donovan a look like he couldn't believe what he'd just heard, but Donovan said, "Go, unless you want bullet holes in your cab."

The driver shoved the car in gear and left smoking rubber behind as he pulled into the street and sped off. As Donovan feared, the black van followed, but it did so at a reasonable distance. And Donovan began to feel like he'd made a fool of himself. The driver added to that when he slowed down and said, "Is this some kind of joke? That guy's not chasing anybody."

Sheepishly, Donovan said, "We got shot at this morning. I guess we're kind of jumpy."

The driver didn't act like he believed Donovan. He asked where they wanted to go, and Lauren gave him the address of her bank. As they worked their way through increasingly heavy traffic, both Donovan and Lauren kept looking back. The black van was still behind them, but it was way back there. Gradually, they relaxed. But when the driver turned onto the street the bank was on, Lauren looked back and let out a muffled cry. "It's back there again," she said.

Donovan looked back, and when he also saw the van he said to the driver, "Hey, that van's back there. I don't like this."

The driver looked in his mirror, and Donovan could see his face reflected there. The man's eyes grew wide and he said, "Hang on, folks!"

The cab sped down the street, turned a corner, and raced away. The black van was following. "I can't believe this," Lauren cried.

Donovan couldn't either, but it was happening. The cab driver spoke into his radio and told his dispatcher what was happening. She came right back with the message that the police were being notified and asked for his location. He gave it and sped on, driving like a man possessed. He drove away from the downtown area, heading out past the airport and toward Pearl Harbor. *The farther we go, the more distance there is between us and the evidence we need to steer the police in the right direction in their investigation,* Donovan thought with a sinking heart. Eventually, a police car darted out of a side street and came right up behind them.

Donovan looked back, and to his dismay, the black van turned off and drove down a side street. The cab pulled over, and the driver jumped out to talk to the officers who had stopped behind them. A minute passed as the three men talked. Then the officers approached the car on the passenger side and opened the back door. "Would you two mind getting out?" one of them asked.

They did as instructed and spent the next few minutes explaining what had happened earlier in the day and why they were worried. One of the officers took notes, and then said, "There's nothing more we can do now."

"Call Captain Ray Hafoko," Donovan said. "He'll confirm what we're telling you. Someone could stop that van and have a talk with those hoods."

"We'll do that, but for now, the van seems to have vanished, so why don't you have the cab take you to wherever it is you're headed before the van comes back?"

Seeing no other choice, Donovan opened the taxi door for Lauren. After they were both inside, he said, "Back to the bank?"

Lauren, who'd been looking at her watch, said, "By the time we get back, it'll be too late."

"Take us to the airport," Donovan said.

Lauren gave him a questioning look, and he whispered, "Lots of people there, and maybe we can get another rental car."

* * *

Ned was leading Vivian to his car. They walked slowly, for her head ached terribly. But both of them had no desire to stay at the hospital any longer.

Ned had witnessed the hasty departure of Lauren and Donovan, and he was alarmed. He'd seen the two of them approach the door when he'd gone looking for a rest room. He'd started toward them, but they hadn't seen him and left at a fast walk. When he reached the door, he saw them running to a cab, witnessed the cab race away, and saw a black van speed after them.

He'd practically run back to Vivian's room and explained breathlessly what he'd observed. "We're leaving," she'd announced. "I'll find somewhere to hide."

When they'd announced their intentions to a nurse, she'd protested and called Vivian's doctor. He'd come to their room and explained that it would be better if they waited a few hours. But Vivian was not to be persuaded, so he'd reluctantly released her.

Ned was watchful and relieved when they were finally driving away from the hospital. Vivian told him what she wanted to do, and he didn't argue. He wanted only for her to be safe.

* * *

Kaelyn's phone rang again. She looked at her caller ID, thinking it must be Donovan again, although his last call had been only a couple of hours earlier. The number was listed as being unknown. She decided to take the call anyway.

"Kaelyn Fletcher?" a slightly slurred male voice asked.

"That's me," she said, wondering what this could be about, wondering if she should just hang up. But she didn't.

"Do you know what your boyfriend is up to over here in Hawaii?" the voice asked.

"Yes, I do!" she said defensively, even as her stomach began to churn. "He's working on a case for an old friend."

There was a chuckle at the other end of the line. Then the voice said, "If you care about him, you better call him and tell him to come home right now. If you don't, both him and that good-looking old friend he's getting so chummy with will end up dead."

Kaelyn mechanically hung the phone up, then sank onto the sofa and dropped her head into her hands, her mind whirling, tears running, and her whole body trembling. When the phone began to ring again a few moments later, she just let it ring until the answering machine picked up. She wished Ellen were home right now, for she needed her friend to help her cope with this new and terrifying development.

* * *

When Donovan and Lauren left the airport in a sporty, fast little rental car, Lauren called the hospital and asked for Vivian's room. She just wanted to make sure she was all right. Donovan kept looking over at her face as he drove toward Waikiki. He knew something was wrong when she frowned and said, "What do you mean, she's checked out?"

When she disconnected, she turned to Donovan. "Vivian's gone. She insisted on being checked out."

"We better go to her place right now. If Ned took her home, it won't be safe. Not for long at least. Do you know where she lives?" Donovan asked.

"I'm not exactly sure, but either she or Ned must be listed. We'll just look them up, then ask directions." Thirty minutes later, they'd located Vivian's house out on the Kahekili Highway northwest of Honolulu. It was an older neighborhood full of quaint little houses with flowering plants and vines filling the small yards. Towering green mountains rose close behind the homes, and the constantly rolling ocean was adjacent to the highway in the front. The place had a rural flavor to it, even though the narrow highway that led north to Laie was constantly filled with traffic. The yard was clean and neat. Donovan knocked on the door. When no one answered, he and Lauren went to the back door and knocked. Again there was no answer, but a very large, yellow cat brushed up against their legs, purring loudly. "She's clearly not home," Donovan said. "But I'm sure we have the right place."

Lauren felt a pang of worry. "And I know that's Ned's house right there to the north." They knocked, and both sighed with relief when Ned's door opened and the old man smiled a welcome. "We left the hospital when I saw you two leaving in a taxi with a van following you. It scared me," he told them as he ushered them inside.

"Where is Vivian?" Lauren asked.

"I know this is going to seem a little strange, but I don't know," Ned said. "She took a taxi just a few blocks after we left the hospital. She said it would be better if I didn't know where she was in case the cops tried to get me to tell them. She promised me she'd be safe enough and get rested up from her accident."

Donovan was actually relieved. Lauren was worried, but agreed that since they hadn't been able to get the documents she had stored at the bank, it might be best if Vivian couldn't be located for a few days.

When Lauren and Donovan left a few minutes later, Ned walked over to Vivian's yard and began gently stroking the glistening yellow hair of Vivian's cat.

* * *

Leroy Provost left the hospital in disgust. He was not happy that a police officer was sitting outside Dexter's door. He'd just have to wait until later.

CHAPTER 15

Both Lauren and Donovan were tense but watchful as they drove back to Waikiki. The red sports car not only didn't look like a normal rental car, but it was fast and handled easily. "If we see the black van, we can lose it with this car," Donovan said with more confidence than he actually felt.

"I hope we don't have to," Lauren said. "I just want this nightmare to be over before someone else gets hurt."

"So do I," Donovan agreed as he reached in his pocket to retrieve his vibrating cell phone. "Hello," he said.

"Hi, Donovan, it's Ellen," he heard.

Donovan wondered with a quick twist in his stomach why Kaelyn's roommate would be calling. "Is Kaelyn all right?" he asked quickly.

"She's very upset," Ellen said. "She didn't want to bother you, but I told her you had to know."

"Wait," Donovan said. "What do I need to know? What's she upset about?"

"I'll let her tell you," Ellen said. "Just a moment and I'll get her."

When Kaelyn came on a minute later, Donovan could tell that something was terribly wrong. "Sweetheart, what's the matter?" he asked as a tremor of fear shot through him.

"D . . . Donovan, you might get killed," she said in a very broken voice and so softly that he could barely hear her. "You are in danger over there."

"I know that, honey," he said, "but I'm being real careful. I'll be okay."

"The man said you should come home," she went on, still speaking quietly.

"What are you talking about?" Donovan demanded, aware of Lauren's eyes on him as he spoke. "Who said I should come home?"

"I got a phone call," Kaelyn said. "A man told me that unless you left Hawaii and forgot about whatever it is that you are doing to help Lauren, that you both would end up dead."

The blood froze in Donovan's veins. They not only knew about him and where he was from, but far worse, they'd found Kaelyn. And if they could call her and threaten him through her, then they could go there and threaten her in person—or worse. Now he was afraid in a way he hadn't been just moments before. Whoever was after Lauren didn't like him helping. He'd known that, but apparently they wanted to make sure he knew it so well that he'd leave Hawaii.

"Donovan, that's not all he said," Kaelyn added.

"What else?" he asked, fearing what she might say next.

"He said you and Lauren are getting really chummy," she said, almost in tears.

"That's not true at all," Donovan assured her. "Kaelyn, you can't believe everything you hear, especially from people like the man who called you. Now you've got to quit worrying. I'll be okay, and so will you." But he wondered if that was even close to the truth. He might be in more danger than he thought, and he'd thought he was in a lot. "Kaelyn, let me talk to Ellen for a minute."

When Ellen came back on, she asked sternly, "Are you coming back now, Donovan?"

"As soon as I can, Ellen. But I need your help. You've got to keep Kaelyn safe. Take her somewhere out of town. And take her now, please," he pleaded.

Ellen lowered her voice. "But Donovan, it's you and that other woman who are in danger, not—"

"Ellen, listen to me," Donovan said. "These guys are serious, and believe me, if they went to the trouble of finding out who Kaelyn is and how to get ahold of her, then she is in danger! Please, take care of her."

"Okay, I will," Ellen promised.

"Both of you need to keep your cell phones with you. I'll call again and find out where you are," he said. "And I'll get back there soon, I promise."

Donovan disconnected, his mind whirling furiously.

Lauren was staring at him helplessly. "It's all my fault," she said. "I'm so sorry. I didn't mean to cause you and Kaelyn to be in danger."

"It's not your fault, Lauren, and no one made me come here."

But as he spoke he remembered the prompting he'd received, and he said to Lauren, "Let me tell you something that happened, something that helped in convincing me that I should come over here."

"What was that?" she asked.

"I prayed, Lauren. And I received an impression, a very strong impression, that I should come and help you. I tried for several hours to ignore it, but it was real. It was from the Holy Ghost. A person should never ignore impressions or feelings or thoughts that come from the Holy Ghost. So I came. The Lord wanted me to come. Knowing that, I just have to exercise faith, and when I do, things will work."

Lauren looked at him for a long time. "You really mean that, don't you?"

"I do. So even though there is danger, I know I've done the right thing," he said, "if I just don't get careless and mess things up now. The Lord expects us to help ourselves and make good choices in whatever things we get involved in."

"I've had some experiences sort of like that," she said. "I've learned to pray again."

He smiled at her. "That's great. Keep praying, Lauren. And have faith. If you do, the Lord will answer your prayers."

She nodded, and then her face grew somber again and she looked out the back window, then off to the sides as Donovan steered the little red car into a parking spot at their hotel. Finally, she asked, "Donovan, what exactly happened with your fiancée? Did I hear right? Did someone threaten her?"

"They didn't threaten her exactly, but they told her that if I didn't leave here, that you and I would both . . . well, you know, we'd get what they've already been trying to give us," he explained as he shut the car off and pulled the key from the ignition. He said nothing about the allegation the caller had made that he and Lauren had become chummy, because that wasn't true and he didn't see the point in adding frivolous worries to this woman's already complicated situation.

"Oh, that poor girl," Lauren murmured. "How did they even find her? This whole thing has gotten so completely out of hand." She sat very still in the passenger seat, and the tears began to flow. "I'm sorry," she sobbed. "I'm really, really sorry."

* * *

"Where are we going?" Kaelyn asked. "And why are we going? Donovan didn't tell me that I was in danger. Why would I be in danger? All he has to do is leave Hawaii and that girl over there and everything will be okay. Surely I'm not in any danger."

"You may be right," Ellen said. "But you might also be wrong. All I know is that Donovan said to take you somewhere safe. And he was serious. That means he thinks there's danger. It also means he cares about you and wants you out of any possible danger you may be in. So we are going to do what he asks, and we are going to do it tonight."

"But where will we go?"

"To Rock Springs, to my folks' house. At least for now. Then maybe we'll go someplace else tomorrow. Now get packed."

"But what about my job?" Kaelyn asked. "What about your job? We both have long-term subbing assignments. We can't just leave."

"We'll make a couple of phone calls. Right now, your job isn't very important, nor is mine, when compared to your life. Your life is what matters."

"I wish Donovan hadn't—"

Ellen cut Kaelyn off sharply. "Quit it. He did what he felt he needed to do, and from what little we know, I suspect that he was justified. Trust him, and forget about what's past. What happens next is what's important."

Thirty minutes later, the two women were driving north from Vernal.

* * *

The night was blissfully uneventful. Donovan and Lauren finally had the chance to get to know each other better, to talk a little more about each other's interests and hobbies.

"I know you'll think it's ironic, but I really don't surf that much anymore," Lauren admitted.

"I thought you loved surfing," Donovan said, surprise apparent in his voice.

"Really, I just love the social aspect of going. It was more the friends than the activity for me. I mean, I loved the rush of catching a good wave, but as I got older I realized what a dangerous sport it is, so when my friends started moving away or we started drifting apart, I just stopped going. I still go sometimes, just to stay in form, but it's not my passion."

"So what do you do for fun these days?" Donovan asked.

"Golf, actually. Among my old college friends that became the popular thing, so again I just gave in to peer pressure and learned how. We go weekly."

"Hey, you sound like me! In good weather, I'll sometimes drive for miles just to meet some of my friends and play while we talk. It's very relaxing."

They decided they weren't as different as they might have thought, especially when they were discussing what movie to watch on TV. As they were scanning the listings, they both suddenly exclaimed, "That's my favorite!" then laughed when they discovered it was the same one. The movie did help them get their minds off their dire situation for a couple of hours. Under the circumstances, it was as relaxing and pleasant an evening as they could have hoped for.

The next morning, Saturday, Lauren suggested that they go see Dexter again. Donovan agreed, being unsure what else to do. He was frustrated that they hadn't been able to recover the documents from the bank. Without that, their hands were tied. There was nothing they could do.

So they went to the hospital, being watchful as ever for the black van or anything else that looked remotely suspicious. Lauren was surprised when they found Dexter dressed and ready to leave. "All I need is one more quick check by my doctor and I can get out of here," he explained to them.

"Where's your cop friend?" she asked him. "He didn't seem to want to give you a second of peace yesterday."

"I had a visit from Captain Hafoko, who, it seems, is heading up the investigation into Dr. Mitsui's death. He says I'm no longer a serious suspect. That, he claims, is because I was nearly killed myself, and more importantly because the time of day I was seen at the apartment complex was significantly later than the established time of death."

As Dexter told Lauren that, she wondered if Vivian was also cleared from suspicion. But she chose not to inquire about that. "How did it happen?" she asked instead, glad that there was no unwelcome listening ear that would keep him from speaking freely, as had been the case the previous afternoon. "I mean, how did you get poisoned or drugged or whatever?"

"There were some cherry chocolates at your apartment. I took some before I found Dr. Mitsui dead in your bed," he began.

"So you were at my place?"

"Yes, and it scared me—at first glance I thought it was you that was dead. You can't imagine how I felt," he said. "It was awful."

"Why didn't you report it right then?" Donovan asked.

"I was in shock. I just had to leave. And then I ate some of the chocolates, and first thing I knew I was getting sick," he explained. "It was all I could do to make it home. I'd intended to call as soon as I got there, but instead I passed out."

"Oh, Dexter," Lauren moaned sympathetically. "I got sick after eating just one. Those chocolates were doctored with something."

"Oh, yes, they certainly were. The police had them tested. You and I are both lucky to be alive," he said. "I was told that if I'd eaten one more, I'd be dead now. Three, they told me, might have been fatal for you."

Lauren was feeling faint, realizing that she could have easily downed three of her favorite sweets. For that matter, Dexter could have taken one more. It was a horrible thought.

"Are you all right?" Donovan asked. "You better sit down here while we wait for them to officially release Dexter."

Lauren sat gladly and held her head in her hands for a few moments. She didn't look up until Dexter asked, "Lauren, where did you get those chocolates? We've got to let the police know."

"It was Leroy."

"Leroy Provost gave them to you?" Dexter asked darkly.

"Yes."

Dexter turned to Donovan. "I don't like this at all. Leroy is her old boyfriend. She'd been dating him for quite some time before she and I began going out. He seems like the jealous type. I don't think it was an accident that he gave Lauren drugged candy."

"I fully agree," Donovan said.

The doctor came in, gave Dexter a quick checkup, then said, "You'll be fine now. You've recovered nicely. But I wouldn't take any of whatever that was again." He smiled as he spoke. "You may go now."

"I don't have a car here," Dexter said as they stepped from his room. "Donovan, would you mind giving us a lift to my place?"

"Not at all," he said. "My current rental car is a little on the small side, but we'll manage."

* * *

Leroy Provost watched, seething, as Dexter and Lauren left the hospital. If it had only been the two of them, he would have taken action right then, but that other guy was one too many. He didn't want to take any chances. He could wait, he decided. He'd get another opportunity. And when he did, it wouldn't be with cherry chocolates that he took his revenge.

* * *

On the way to Dexter's house, they discussed strategy. As the discussion went on, mostly between Dexter and Lauren, it appeared to Donovan that he might not be needed anymore. Dexter made that clear when they pulled into his driveway. "Donovan, you've been a great help. Lauren owes her life to you, but I think she and I can handle things from here. We'll stay out of sight for the weekend, and on Monday, we'll get to the bank, pick up the evidence she has there, and get this whole thing taken care of."

Lauren turned to Donovan. "I'll be forever indebted to you for all you've done. But Dexter's right. We'll be okay now. Anyway, I know that Kaelyn needs you."

Donovan knew that too, but for some reason, he hated to leave. "I could stay until Monday night if you could use me," he suggested hopefully.

"No, we'll be careful," Lauren said. "Dexter will take care of me, won't you?" she said to her boyfriend.

"Of course I will, my love. You've been great, Donovan, and you've taken a lot of risks to help us, but you better go take care of things in Utah. I'm sure you have a busy practice there," Dexter said.

Donovan sighed. Unless he wanted to stay and see how things went—and that really didn't make sense—then he might as well catch a plane today. Anyway, it would be hard to explain to Kaelyn why he hadn't come home as soon as he wasn't needed anymore when he'd made her leave Vernal to keep her safe. So he said, "Well, if you two are sure."

"We're sure," Dexter said firmly.

Donovan got back in his car. Lauren lifted a hand in a little wave. He smiled and returned her wave, then pulled away.

* * *

Fleming and Royce were discussing how to wrap up this whole thing and get away. They really needed a few more days, but Royce was worried that they might not have that much time. "We better cut our losses and run," Royce suggested. "We have more than enough already tucked away to keep us comfortable for the rest of our lives."

"But there's that last contract," Fleming shouted in anger. "We almost have it completed, and it's worth millions if it's worth a dime." He was thoughtful for a moment, then he said, "We need to get our group together. Maybe we can still get a little more time. We've cleaned up the computers and the rest of the records, so nobody is going to be able to find anything there. So it will be Lauren's word against ours if it comes to that. Of course, I don't think it will come to that."

"I still say you're premature in ordering killers after her," Royce growled.

"You can think what you like, Royce, but just remember, you'll have it easy the rest of your life because I'm being cautious. Now get over it."

Royce knew from the look in Fleming's eyes that it was time to be quiet. Fleming was greedy, and Royce had pushed as far as he dared. Fleming had already proven that he could be violent. Anyway, they had to stick together or they'd all be in trouble—deep and lasting trouble.

Fleming suddenly smiled. "Hey, we are in the driver's seat, my friend. And I just had an idea. There's something else we could do, just to make double sure we have the time we need to finish up. I don't know why I didn't think of this sooner. It could have saved us some trouble, and it will ensure that Lauren isn't a problem and at the same time possibly keep her alive."

Royce was curious, despite himself. And he really had no desire to see Lauren lose her life. "What can we do that we didn't think of before?" he asked.

"We can temporarily give up a little money in order to gain a lot more. Crank up your computer, you old hacker you. Let's deposit a couple of million into Lauren's account. Then a discreet phone call or two, and she'll be the one in hot water. While she's trying to explain all the money she's accumulated, we can finish up and get on our way out of the country."

Despite himself, Royce was impressed, and he turned on his computer. It might take him an hour or two, but he believed he could accomplish the transfer and make it look like Lauren had done it herself.

Fleming stood. "You get it done, Royce. I'll get ahold of the others. Pretty Lauren Olcott will be more useful to us alive than dead for a little while. And we'll be in much better shape than her when we're done."

Royce looked up at Fleming. He didn't like the sound of that last statement. Fleming was not a man to be trusted. But it was too late now. Royce tried to put his concerns out of his mind and went to work.

* * *

Donovan was feeling empty as he drove his rental car toward the airport. For reasons that he couldn't quite put his finger on, he hated leaving Lauren with Dexter, and yet he had to admit that was foolish. Dexter was, after all, Lauren's boyfriend, and he was clearly a very successful attorney. Besides that, Dexter had experienced a very close brush with death himself, and he was bound to be very careful.

Donovan was tired. He was worried about Kaelyn, and he was worried about Lauren. He had to admit that the sharp edge had been worn off his mind. He needed rest. He'd done what he could, he told himself. And maybe if he left, the thugs would back off and forget about him. He was doing, after all, what someone had told Kaelyn they wanted him to do.

CHAPTER 16

Donovan called his secretary from the airport and informed her that it looked like he'd be home to handle Monday's trial if it was still on.

"It is, and I still don't have anyone to cover for you," Mrs. Olsen told him. Then she asked, "So is everything under control over there?"

"I hope so," he said.

Next, he called Kaelyn's cell phone. She seemed very tense, but when he told her that he was on his way home, he could feel her relief in the very tone of her voice. And he felt guilty for what he'd put her through. "So there's no longer any danger?" she asked. "Ellen and I can turn around and go home right now?"

Donovan again found himself disappointing Kaelyn. "No, I think you better continue to where you're headed. I'll be flying home overnight, but I won't be home until sometime on Sunday. I'll call once I'm home. I want to see you, but I also want to know you're safe."

She said she'd miss him, but agreed it was for the best.

Donovan made it back to Vernal in time to attend church, since his meetings didn't start until one in the afternoon. When he got home, he called Kaelyn. "I'm home," he told her. "I think it's okay for you to come back now."

"Actually, Ellen and I have talked about it. Now that we've come this far, we've decided to make a little trip out of it. I think we'll be back by Wednesday."

Donovan knew there was no point in arguing, so he visited briefly with her and then hung up. First she was angry that he left, but now that he was home, she was taking a vacation. It made no sense to him.

* * *

"Why did you do that?" Ellen asked. "We could have gone back today. We only talked about a trip before we found out Donovan was on his way home."

"Maybe he needs to know how it feels," Kaelyn said. "It'll be good for him to miss me."

"Kaelyn," Ellen said sternly. "Do you really think that's smart?"

Kaelyn didn't answer the question. Instead she said, "Let's hit the road, Ellen. We'd just as well enjoy ourselves."

* * *

Donovan paced around his house for a few minutes, glanced outside at the darkening skies, then walked over to his phone. He lifted it and looked at it as he thought about another call he'd like to make. For a moment he debated with himself, but finally, he dialed the number of Lauren's cell phone.

He let it ring for quite a while and was about to hang up when a voice came on the phone. "Hello." It was Dexter's voice.

Donovan hadn't expected that. "Hello, Dexter, this is Donovan. Could I speak with Lauren for just a moment?"

"I'm sorry, Donovan. She's exhausted and is taking a nap right now," he said. "I'd rather not wake her up."

"Okay, I just wanted to make sure everything's going all right," Donovan said.

"Why wouldn't it be?" Dexter asked sharply. "I'm certainly capable of taking care of my own girlfriend. I'm sorry she had to bother you with her problems, but it won't happen again. I know a place I can hide her away until I can clear this up. You don't need to concern yourself with her anymore."

"Tell her I called," Donovan said.

"Sure," Dexter responded sharply. But Donovan doubted that he would.

Donovan again studied the phone in his hand. Finally, he put it up and paced the floor. There was certainly no reason to believe that Dexter wouldn't take good care of Lauren, but Donovan wasn't sure he liked the man. He had seemed nice enough in person, but that phone conversation showed him in a bad light. *And why shouldn't Dexter be in a bad mood?* he suddenly asked himself. *He couldn't be there when the woman he loved was in trouble, and some stranger just comes in and takes over.* Donovan felt a little better realizing this, but he was still worried. Very worried.

* * *

Dexter thought they should keep a low profile over the weekend, so he checked the two of them into adjoining rooms in a large, upscale hotel away from downtown. Knowing they'd get bored locked up in their rooms, Dexter picked up a couple of magazines and a travel-sized game of Scrabble from a shop in the lobby. Lauren was delighted at his finds.

Sunday afternoon, after a competitive game of Scrabble, Lauren began to tell Dexter about her desire to start going to church regularly.

"What, you?" he said in amazement.

"Yes, me. Why is that so hard to believe?"

"I just think you're too smart to buy into all that religion nonsense."

"In the first place, it's not nonsense, and in the second place, I've told you before that I'm a Mormon," Lauren said indignantly.

"Sure, I knew you were a Mormon, and a Christian, and all that," Dexter agreed. "But there's a difference between believing in a god and spending all your free time talking about rules and how we're all sinners and that. It's just a big guilt trip. It's for the weak, not for intelligent people like you and me."

"That's not true. My parents and many other LDS people I knew growing up were intellectual types. And this isn't just a matter of guilt trips, you know. I think that believing in Christ means living like He would, and part of how I want to do that is to go to church."

Dexter shook his head. "Okay, whatever, baby. Just as long as you don't try to drag me along."

"I'd love it if you'd give it a try too—"

"Don't even go there," Dexter interrupted. "It's a free country, and we've all got the right to think what we want. But I don't want what you think to get in the way of what I think, all right?"

"Of course. I totally agree," Lauren said, sighing. She did agree that they each had a right to their own opinion. But she was not happy thinking that they wouldn't ever agree on this particular subject. And it was becoming increasingly apparent that they would not.

"Hey, I think I have my own religion!" Dexter said with a grin. "It's all about buying Lauren the prettiest jewelry and nicest dinners and having her tell me what a great boyfriend I am."

Lauren didn't think his joke was very funny, but she didn't see the point in saying so. Instead she just made an attempt to smile, and said, "You've been a great boyfriend, Dexter. Now, why don't you find a good movie on TV or something? I'm going to my room to take a nap."

* * *

Monday morning, Donovan walked into court feeling like he had been run over by a truck. He'd gotten a little sleep on the flight home, and he'd even managed a few hours Sunday night at his house, but he was far from rested. Several times he'd been tempted to call Lauren again and ask how things were going, but he'd resisted, thinking that Dexter might answer for her, and he was someone Donovan really didn't care to talk to again.

Surely, he consoled himself, she'd call if she needed him again. She hadn't called and she hadn't e-mailed him, so she must not need him. That thought, which was on his mind even as he entered the courtroom, left him feeling a little empty. They had been through a lot together in the last few days, and he didn't like returning to his "life as usual" knowing hers was likely still in turmoil.

Taking a seat, Donovan shrugged off all thoughts of Lauren and concentrated on the case he had to try that day. His client came in fresh and confident as Donovan sat at the defense table poring over the case file. He envied the young man's energy while resenting the fact that he knew he was guilty of the theft of which he'd been accused. But he had to give him the best defense he could. After all, that was his job.

Despite his present worries, Donovan, who was an excellent attorney, immersed himself fully in the work at hand that morning. Not until the noon recess did he allow himself to wonder once again how things were going in Honolulu. Looking at his watch, he realized it was only nine o'clock there. The bank where Lauren's evidence was secured should just be opening its doors. He wished that he were there, but then reminded himself that, despite all he'd gone through during the short time he was over there, it was no longer his business. He wasn't needed.

With a sigh, Donovan planned to work through the lunch hour, preparing for the presentation of his case to the judge at one o'clock.

* * *

Dexter and Lauren were waiting at the bank when the doors opened. Dexter waited while she went into the vault with her key and opened the box. She was shaking so badly that she spilled its contents before getting it to a table where she could pick out the things that applied to the embezzlement. She scolded herself for having taken those things out of their large envelope prior to placing them in the box two weeks earlier, but she'd wanted to make sure she hadn't left anything out. She'd been interrupted before she'd placed everything back in the envelope. That afternoon she'd been told to hurry, that it was time for the bank to close, so she'd simply placed everything loosely into the box. Now it was all mixed on the floor of the vault with her other records and valuables. Hurriedly, she gathered everything up and sorted through it, trying to put just the things she needed in the envelope, while stuffing everything else back into the safety-deposit box. She hurriedly tucked the envelope beneath her arm, put the metal box back where it belonged, and left the vault. She knew that Dexter would be impatiently pacing the floor outside because it was taking her so long.

When she rejoined him he said, "What took you so long?"

She held out a shaking hand. "I'm scared, Dexter. I dropped everything in there and had to gather it back up. But I've got it now, so let's go."

As they left the bank, Dexter said, "Here, let me have a look."

"You won't be able to tell much until you carefully read it all," she said, "and that will take quite a while."

"Don't you think I should do that before we turn this over to the authorities? I think it would be best if I understood exactly what

Royce and Fleming were doing and how they were doing it. And that way it won't all be on you to explain everything," he said.

"Oh, you're right, that would be great. As long as we can get it to them by this afternoon."

"That isn't a problem. Look, I'll tell you what we'll do. You've gone through enough already. I'll fly you in the firm's plane over to Kauai, where I have a place arranged for you to stay until Fleming and Royce are behind bars. I'll personally take this to the captain. In fact, I think I'll go over it with my boss, Ken Fujimoto, first. We want to make sure we really nail this thing together."

"Sounds good to me," Lauren agreed, even as she wondered what had happened to the e-mail she'd sent to Mr. Fujimoto so many days ago. But it didn't matter now, for he was about to become fully informed. And when he and Dexter presented the material to the captain, she was certain he'd take it very seriously, and maybe the thieves could actually be stopped before it went any further. Maybe the company could still be saved.

The law firm Dexter worked for owned a small jet, and he was one of the men who flew it. Dexter was an excellent pilot. Lauren had flown with him a number of times from island to island. She was tense until they boarded the plane an hour later, and then she relaxed, glad that she would be somewhere safe while Dexter and Ken took care of things for her.

By noon, Lauren was resting in a house in Kauai, and Dexter was flying back to Honolulu. She hoped this whole unbelievable series of events was about over. And when it was, she planned to give Donovan Deru a call and thank him again for all he had so unselfishly done for her. She realized that in spite of the time they spent together, she barely knew him. But she also found that she missed him and thought of him now as a real friend. He was a truly good and generous man.

* * *

By five o'clock, Donovan had lost his case. But he'd worked hard all day and was satisfied that he'd done his best for his client. The judge set a date for sentencing in April. Donovan hurried back to his office, thumbed through a stack of messages there, then drove home. He hoped at least Kaelyn and Ellen were having a good time, because he faced a long, lonely evening.

Donovan heated a frozen dinner, watched a little television, and then spent some time reading the scriptures as a sort of family home evening with himself. He thought often of Lauren and wondered if things were now under control, if the police finally were on track in their investigation. He wanted to call her, but was still not anxious to talk to her boyfriend. However, he finally picked up the phone and punched in the numbers. He mentally calculated the time in Honolulu. It was just before six in the evening there. He really had to know that everything was all right—that she was okay.

He was puzzled when the call was answered, but all he heard was a quick, muttered swearword from a male voice, and then nothing. Whoever it was had hung up. *I guess I dialed a wrong number,* he thought. He dialed again, but was disappointed when the call went to voice mail. He had to know something, so he called Ned Haraguchi.

Ned answered after only a couple of rings. "Mr. Donovan," he said brightly. "It's so good to hear from you. I've been worrying myself sick since you and Miss Lauren left here the other evening. Is she okay?"

"Actually, that was why I was calling you, Ned," Donovan told him. "I'm back in Utah. I spent the day in court here. I tried to—"

Ned broke in and urgently asked, "If you aren't watching out for Miss Lauren, then who is? I didn't think you'd leave until everything was taken care of."

"I'm sorry, Ned," Donovan said. "Dexter Drake is taking care of things now. He and Lauren decided there was no need for me to stay any longer. I was hoping you'd heard something. I tried to call Lauren, but her cellular phone seems to be turned off."

"Dexter Drake," Ned said slowly, as if he were tying to figure out who that was. But it was quickly evident that he knew very well who Dexter was when he said, "Dexter is a very smart man, a successful attorney, and he's certainly got the good looks that turn the ladies' heads, but I don't think . . . well . . ." Ned stopped.

"You don't think what?" Donovan asked.

"I don't think he's everything he seems to be," he said.

"Oh, and why not?"

"Well, I just think he's too self-centered. From even the little I've seen and heard, I think he is more flash than substance."

"I see. But he is basically trustworthy, isn't he?"

"Oh, yes, I suppose so, but it worries me if Lauren's life is entirely in his hands."

"I see." Donovan didn't want to dwell on that thought, so he changed the subject. "Have you heard from Vivian?"

"Oh, yes, a couple of times a day. I don't know where she's staying, but I know she's safe. Like me, she's worried about Miss Lauren. She'll be a lot more worried when she hears that you've gone back to Utah. No, she won't like that at all. She said to me several times that you seemed like such a fine fellow, and one that could be counted on entirely."

"I hated to leave, but, well, I wasn't welcome anymore. Ned, I better let you go," Donovan said, disappointed that he'd been unable to learn anything about what might have happened during the day. He gave his phone numbers to Ned and said, "Call me if you hear anything, will you?"

Ned promised that he would.

After hanging up, Donovan thought about Ned. The old man definitely had his opinions about Dexter, and Donovan had to agree with him. The phone rang a few minutes later, and Donovan wondered if it could be Ned calling back with some information. He looked at the caller ID, and it stated that the number was not available.

Since signing up on the national list to avoid unwanted telephone solicitations, Donovan had received very few such calls. Yet he couldn't help but wonder if that wasn't exactly what he was getting right now. He considered not answering but then changed his mind, thinking that it could have something to do with Lauren and her trouble in Hawaii.

He was surprised but glad when the caller identified himself as Captain Ray Hafoko of the Honolulu Police Department. He hoped that the captain was calling as a courtesy to give him some good news.

"I appreciate your call, Captain," he said. "I hope things are going well in your investigation."

Captain Hafoko cleared his throat and then said, "Actually, I'm afraid I don't have good news."

Donovan's stomach took a hard flip. "Oh, what's happened?" he asked.

"Dexter Drake and his boss, Ken Fujimoto, brought me the evidence that Lauren had in her safety-deposit box," he began. "It's weird stuff. There is some evidence there that some money illegally disappeared from Paradise Pharmaceuticals, but from what I've read, I can't imagine why Miss Olcott wanted me to have the information. I was hoping you could shed some light on things for me. I'm guessing she told you quite a bit. I'm also hoping you don't have an attorney-client relationship with her, for it would be most helpful if you could talk to me about the matter, maybe tell me something that will give the documents meaning."

"Though I tried to advise her as best I could, I was helping her more as a friend than an attorney. Nonetheless, much of my advice to her was legal in nature, so it was best if I treated the situation the same as I would with any other client. It seemed unwise to disclose certain information previously, but I'd be happy to help you as best I can. I don't really know if I have any different information than you, anyway. Surely Dexter told you what Lauren discovered," Donovan said.

"He said she was claiming that two of the top company executives, Royce Cantrell and Fleming Parker, along with some people she claimed to not have been able to identify, were embezzling from the company and altering critical contracts."

"That's right," Donovan agreed. "She told me that the items of proof she was keeping in her safety-deposit box would show that. That's what I told you we needed to get that would make your homicide investigation into the death of Dr. Mitsui go in a different direction."

"Have you seen any of that material yourself?" the captain asked. "Or have you only got Miss Olcott's word on what it contained?"

"I haven't seen it," Donovan admitted with an ever-plummeting heart.

"I thought not," Captain Hafoko said. "The information provided was sketchy at best and doesn't prove much of anything. There's clearly something illegal going on in the company, but there is nothing to indicate that the people she named are the thieves. Their names are in much of the material, but not in the way I would have expected. Frankly, what she gave us doesn't make a lot of sense. It appears to me to be material she made up to try to point fingers. Both Mr. Drake and Mr. Fujimoto were very concerned about Miss Olcott after reviewing everything she gave them. It appears she's been lying to you and to Mr. Drake."

"Oh," Donovan said. His stomach was churning. He didn't know what more to say, so he said nothing; he just listened as the captain continued.

"We've been thinking that maybe she's mentally ill. But then, just an hour ago, we learned that she has two million dollars in her account that was transferred there from one of the banks that Paradise Pharmaceuticals does business with. And it appears that she made the transaction herself."

Donovan was sick. He had come to believe fully in Lauren. Now it seemed she'd been using him all along to further her own selfish interests. She was stealing money from her employer and trying to blame someone else! It was all so unbelievable. But the captain seemed convinced. He was still talking, and Donovan tried to listen as he began to organize his thoughts.

"We've been trying to reach Miss Olcott for the past hour, but we can't seem to locate her," the captain said.

"I'm sure Dexter Drake knows where she is," he said.

"Oh really? He didn't mention that. Maybe he's trying to protect her. I understand he and Lauren have been seeing each other," the captain said. "It sounds like I need to get ahold of him again. He doesn't know about this latest development with the funds transfer, and that might persuade him to bring her in."

"How did you come to learn that she's taken money?" Donovan asked. "You didn't just stumble on it, did you?"

"No, we got an anonymous call. The caller said he didn't want to get involved, but that there were some bad things going on at the company where he worked and that he couldn't let it go on any longer. He told us how to access the information by remote computer, and we did. We found exactly what he told us we'd find," the captain explained.

Donovan's doubts about Lauren began to recede. This sounded to him like something Fleming Parker might attempt in order to buy himself a little more time. But he didn't mention those suspicions to the captain. Instead he asked, "The two million in her bank—is there any way she can get access to it?"

"Not now, because we've got a court order freezing it," Captain Hafoko said. "But we really need to find her. The caller also suggested that she might know a lot more than she's saying about the death of Dr. Mitsui." He paused for a moment, but Donovan said nothing. "Well, I'm sorry to have bothered you, Mr. Deru. I was hoping you could shed some light on all this for me. I guess I'll just have to contact Mr. Drake again. He'll be sick when he hears what we've learned."

After the call to the captain was concluded, Donovan sat back quietly in his chair, put his feet up on his desk, closed his eyes, and began to think. For the next hour he hardly moved as he went over everything he knew about the confusing case in Hawaii. He forced himself to be objective and look at the evidence from every angle. The more he thought, the more wound up and worried he became. He decided to go for a jog out in the cold, clear night air in an attempt to unwind a little. He headed north at a brisk pace, enjoying the cold breeze in his face.

* * *

Kaelyn put down the phone and frowned at Ellen. "Donovan's not home and his cellular phone is apparently turned off," she said. "I can't imagine what he's doing this late."

"Maybe he's eating out tonight. You know he does that a lot," Ellen argued.

"Yes, I know, but not this late at night," Kaelyn said. Suddenly Kaelyn felt very nervous. "I wonder if something's happened to him," she murmured.

Just then the phone rang, and Kaelyn answered without even looking at the incoming number. "It's probably Donovan," she said with relief as she lifted the phone to her ear.

It was not Donovan.

* * *

A small, green rental car cruised the streets of Vernal. The men inside were looking at a map, trying to find a particular address. Finally, they stopped at a service station and asked where Maeser was located. Minutes later they'd found the street they were looking for. They located the house they were interested in, noting that it was dark.

"It's too early to be in bed. He must not be home," one of them said with a grin.

"Then let's get it in place and get out of here," the second man added.

* * *

Donovan thought long and hard as he jogged. Maybe, he decided, he should try again to forget about Lauren and all her problems in Hawaii. Captain Hafoko seemed bright. Surely he and his officers would sort through all the conflicting testimony and evidence and finally reach the truth, whatever that truth was. But what if they got it wrong?

A loud explosion made Donovan look up in alarm. Flames were shooting into the air a couple of miles away. Right in the direction of his neighborhood.

CHAPTER 17

Donovan picked up his pace, literally running toward his house. For some inexplicable reason, the explosion in the area of his neighborhood caused him to worry about Lauren. It also caused him to worry about Kaelyn, although he knew she was a safe distance from Vernal. He reached in his pocket, pulling out his cell phone. He remembered turning it off before he'd left to run. He turned it on and stopped running long enough to call Lauren's number. When there was, as he'd feared, no answer there, he tried Kaelyn's phone next. He'd let it ring five or six times as he began running again before it was finally answered, and then it was Ellen who spoke, and her voice trembled. It was quite evident that things were going badly wherever the two of them were, because Ellen said, "Oh, Donovan, thank goodness it's you. Are you okay? You sound like you're out of breath."

"I'm jogging," he said.

"I see. Well, Kaelyn wants to talk to you. She didn't dare answer the phone after that last call she got."

"What last call?" he asked. "Why didn't Kaelyn dare answer? What's happening?" Donovan was now more concerned about Kaelyn than the explosion he was racing to in the direction of his home.

"Someone called her cell phone a few minutes ago. Oh, maybe it's been a half hour or so. Anyway, he told her that you were about to pay for not staying away from Lauren and from Hawaii. He told her that she'd hear the details soon enough, then he hung up. She's sure it was the same voice that called the other day. Here, she's ready to talk to you now."

Kaelyn came on the line, her voice trembling. "Donovan, be careful. They're still after you. You better get away from there."

"I just wanted to make sure you were okay, Kaelyn. I can't talk any longer, but I'll call you back," he said, finding it hard to run and talk on the phone. And he wasn't about to stop running, for the closer he got to his neighborhood, the more it looked like smoke was rising from very near where his house was. He ended the call against her protestations.

Sirens riddled the night air, and Donovan ran a little faster. When he finally turned onto his street, his fears became reality. A smoldering wreck of a car littered the street in front of his house. The area was lit by floodlights, and people were standing at a distance watching. Something was being pulled from the main part of the shattered car. Something else lay beneath a blanket several feet from the wreckage.

His phone rang and he answered it, out of breath and sick with concern at what had happened. "Donovan, are you all right?" Kaelyn screamed into the phone.

"Uh, yes. Listen, I'll need to call you back," he said, so out of breath he couldn't talk. His heart pounded unmercifully in his chest. A police car pulled behind him, its siren sending an eerie warning into the night. Then it abruptly went silent, as though the warning had come too late.

"Donovan, no, talk to me now!" Kaelyn said. "Was that a siren?"

"Yes, but I'm fine. And I've got to go."

"Please, what's happening?" she cried, anguish in her voice.

Donovan knew she'd learn anyway, so he said, "A car has been blown up in front of my house. I'm okay, and so is the house. I'll call you back. You and Ellen keep going. Don't let anyone know where you're at. I don't want them to find you."

Before she could delay him further, he disconnected and stepped closer to the burning wreckage.

* * *

Lauren was trying to relax, trying to follow Dexter's instructions. He'd left several hours ago, promising to return sometime the following day. "I've got to help them wrap this thing up after Ken and I deliver your evidence to them," he had told her. "I'm sorry to have to leave you alone. Just stay in the house and keep the curtains closed. Don't let anyone see you, not a single person."

"I'll be fine, Donovan," she'd said, not realizing she'd said the wrong name until after it had come out.

"Dexter's my name, in case you've forgotten. Donovan's gone now," he'd barked.

"I'm sorry," she'd said as embarrassment flooded over her.

He'd apologized for his outburst a few minutes later and kissed her. Then he looked deep into her eyes and said, "I keep thinking, what if I'd lost you? When this is over, let's talk about marriage. That sound okay?"

She'd clung to him then, saying nothing, but knowing things would never be the same between them. And even as he released his embrace, looked into her eyes again, smiled, and said, "I'll see you tomorrow," she was thinking of Donovan, wishing he were here. Dexter was doing his best, she was sure, but she no longer knew if that was enough, either for now or for the future. Something about being with Donovan made her feel safe. She missed him terribly.

Lauren rose to her feet and stepped to the sliding glass doors that opened onto a balcony that looked out over rolling, green hills dotted with homes, and beyond that the deep blue of the ocean. She'd never been to this place before, and when Dexter brought her here on Saturday, he'd told her it belonged to a cousin of his who lived in Los Angeles. "He only uses it about one month out of the year," he'd explained. "I called him, and he said to use it for as long as we need to. All he asked is that we keep it clean."

Funny, she thought now, that he hadn't mentioned the house before—or the cousin. Oh well, at least she was safe, and he'd assured her that this whole nightmare would be over soon. She opened the door and stepped outside, then quickly stepped back in, remembering his warning that she not be seen by anyone, even neighbors who didn't know her.

Gazing over the beautiful landscape and seeing her beloved ocean in the distance gave her a degree of peace, but she hated to sit here cut off from the outside world. It wouldn't be nearly as bad, she decided, if she could talk to Donovan for a few minutes. Maybe she could, she decided resolutely.

She picked up the phone. There was no dial tone. *Of course not,* she thought. It would be silly to pay for a phone line year-round when a person only spent a month out of twelve in the house. She'd use her cell phone, she decided. She just needed to let Donovan know she was okay and that all was going well. And she needed to hear his deep, reassuring voice.

Lauren nearly cried when she searched in her purse, then her luggage, and failed to find the little phone. She found only the charger, which was useless to her now. She'd been in a hurry when they left her hotel. She must have left it lying somewhere in the room. She thought hard, trying to recall when she'd last used it. She honestly didn't remember. Maybe she'd left it in the jet Dexter had flown her in from Honolulu to here. That didn't make sense though; she knew she hadn't used it on the plane. She honestly thought it should have been in her purse.

But it wasn't there now, and she felt like her lifeline was gone. The need to communicate with Donovan only flamed brighter with the loss of that ability. Then she thought about her laptop computer. She had just removed it from her luggage as she searched for the phone. She opened it, turned it on, and began searching for a phone jack. Suddenly, she cried openly. That wouldn't work—the phone was dead!

Lauren felt alone, abandoned, and vulnerable.

* * *

The pieces were beginning to fall into place, at least in Donovan's mind, regarding what had caused the explosion in front of his house. The police were a bit skeptical until a neighbor who lived at the far end of his block came forward and said, "I saw the car earlier, not long after Donovan left on his run. I was just taking some garbage out. I watched it drive by, turn around, and then leave. But later, when I went out to walk my dog, it was driving up the street again. This time it stopped in front of Donovan's house," she said. "The man in the passenger side got out, turned around, reached into the backseat, and then came out with a package in his hand. The driver stayed right there behind the wheel. The passenger took a step away from the car, but the man inside called to him. He turned back, seemed to stumble, and then everything just lit up. The noise was deafening. It sounded like a war zone. I'm afraid it might have damaged my poor dog's eardrums. It was horrible."

"A bomb," the sheriff said. He turned to Donovan. "You mentioned a few minutes ago that you'd been threatened. How long ago was that?"

"Actually, it was two or three days ago—the first time, that is. But I was talking on my phone to my fiancée while I was running back here just a few minutes ago, and she said that she'd just received a call a half hour earlier, telling her that something was about to happen to me."

"Didn't she call you then?" a detective asked.

"She tried, but I'd turned my cell phone off before I went running. I didn't want to be disturbed. I guess that didn't work, did it?" he said with a futile attempt at humor.

"You got lucky, Donovan," the sheriff said.

Donovan nodded, for he had truly been blessed and his life preserved. There was no question in his mind that the bomb had been meant for him. Probably all he would have had to do was pick it up, or perhaps open it, and his life would have been over. The only questions remaining in his mind related to the identities of the two men who had died in the explosion and whom they were working for. However, he believed he might know at least partial answers to both questions. He guessed that the two thugs who'd shot at him in Honolulu wouldn't be shooting at anyone again. And he suspected that Fleming and Royce might not have to pay them for any more jobs, botched or otherwise.

The doubts about Lauren that had pushed themselves into his mind when Captain Hafoko had called him earlier were all but gone. He simply couldn't believe that she would try to have him killed, especially considering the fact that the bullets that had been fired at him from the blue Ford could as easily have been meant for her. No, someone else had wanted him dead, and her as well.

The next two hours were spent making statements for the police and talking with friends who came to inquire about his welfare. He also took a few minutes to call Kaelyn. She and Ellen were headed for Chicago that very evening, she told him. She just wanted to go somewhere that no one would even think of looking for them. Donovan had told Kaelyn that he was quite sure the men who had presented a danger to them were no longer going to be a problem. He even explained why—what had happened to them. He'd assured her that he was fine and that she was most likely safe now. Nonetheless, he agreed that it was good that she and Ellen were so far away. That way he didn't have to worry about her.

Now, as the crowd was pretty much gone, the scene mostly cleaned up, and the police satisfied that they'd learned all they could for the night, Donovan started up his steps. The cell phone in his pocket vibrated, and he quickly pulled it out and answered it, hoping that it was Lauren calling to tell him she was okay, that things were going well for her now.

But the voice that spoke to him sounded like it belonged to an old man. He called Donovan by name and said, "You told me to call if I talked to Vivian Likio."

"Is this Ned Haraguchi?" Donovan asked even as a mixture of hope and dread filled him.

"It is, and you said to call if I learned anything. I hope it's okay."

"Of course it's okay, Ned. What have you learned?"

"I talked to Vivian on the phone just a few minutes ago."

"Is she still all right?"

"Oh, yes, but she's scared, especially since I told her you'd gone back to Utah. She says she doesn't dare let anyone know where she is until you say it's okay. She trusts you," he said.

"She's only met me once," Donovan responded. "She doesn't even know me. Not really."

"She knows that Miss Lauren trusts you, and that's good enough for her. It's good enough for me too. I know this is asking a lot, Mr. Deru, but we both wish you'd come back. We don't know who else we can trust," Ned said.

Donovan made a decision. He'd been thinking about it ever since he'd first seen the burning wreckage in front of his house. He was going back to Honolulu as soon as he could. With Kaelyn out of town for at least a few more days, it would be easy to get away. He might not be able to do any good, but he'd always regret it if he didn't try. Anyway, if his life was in danger here as well as over there, he'd just as well go where there was at least a chance of helping. "Tell you what, Ned. I'll come," he said. "Tell Vivian that I'll let you know when I get there, and we can arrange to meet her. If possible, I'll be on my way back in a few hours."

"That'll be wonderful. I'll tell Vivian you're coming," he said. "Do you know where Mr. Drake has taken Lauren? Vivian and I don't have a very good feeling about that man. If he were up to any good, we think we'd have heard from Miss Lauren by now, saying she's okay."

"I'm afraid I don't know where Dexter and Lauren are, but I intend to find out when I get back over there," he promised as he slid his key in the door and turned it.

"She's a sweet girl," Ned said. "She doesn't deserve this mess."

"I agree, Mr. Haraguchi. I want very much to help her out of the trouble she's in."

"Thank you, Mr. Deru," Ned said. "Miss Lauren may not realize it right now, but she'll be awful glad when she knows you've come back. I can just feel it."

Donovan plugged his cell phone in after he'd finished talking to Ned. He needed to have it fully charged for the trip ahead. He picked up the phone in his living room and dialed a now-familiar number. Lauren's phone still wasn't on. Disappointed again, he thought about the attempt on his life so far from Hawaii, and he was rocked by the possible significance of it. Leaving Hawaii had not been enough for Lauren's enemies. They had still considered him a threat. He couldn't help but wonder why.

Someone knocked on the door, and he hurried over and opened it. "Donovan, I'm so glad to see that you're not hurt," Mrs. Olsen said as she grabbed him and gave him a big hug. "My daughter woke me up from a perfectly sound sleep to tell me about the trouble here. I came just as soon as I could."

"Thank you, Barbara," he said. "I'm really just fine though."

She stepped back and eyed him thoughtfully. "I don't think you are. This has something to do with that affair over in Hawaii, doesn't it?"

Donovan smiled at her, trying to make light of things. "Those two thugs I told you about this morning, the ones who shot at me, they won't be doing that again."

"Was it them?" she exclaimed, pointing toward the front of the house.

"I'm not positive, of course, but I have a pretty good idea it was them."

"Donovan, you get yourself right back over there and see that Lauren is okay. I'll take care of things for you here," she said.

Surprised, Donovan said, "I was thinking I better do that, but I sure hate to cause problems here."

"You go. That girl needs you."

"So do my clients. And maybe more importantly, Kaelyn," Donovan said. "What if I don't get back before she does? She'll be upset with me again."

A strange look came across his faithful secretary's face. And she surprised him even more when she said, "I wouldn't worry too much about that. I probably shouldn't meddle but . . . I know you think you love her, Donovan, and I'm sure you do in a way, but the two of you just aren't meant to be."

"Oh really?" he said in shock, as much because she'd say that to him as because she was saying what he'd tried not to admit but had thought increasingly ever since they'd gotten engaged.

"Yes, really. I know it's none of my business, but I think you need someone a bit stronger, someone who doesn't pout and get upset over your every move. Now get packing. I'll use your phone and make flight arrangements for you."

* * *

Patience was not one of Leroy Provost's greater strengths. Lauren and that stranger he'd seen her with had both disappeared since they'd left the hospital with Dexter. He'd seen Dexter, once at Paradise Pharmaceuticals and a couple of times with the old lawyer, Ken Fujimoto. He was getting tired of waiting. But he knew he'd get his chance. He just wanted to get it over with, to even the score as soon as possible.

* * *

Ned Haraguchi didn't have a number to call for Vivian, so he had to wait for her to call him. She wanted it that way, for she said she'd feel safer if no one had any idea how to reach her. So he sat that Monday evening in his house, stroking the long fur of Vivian's yellow cat, hoping she'd soon call.

Ned had lost his wife ten years earlier, and both of their children lived on the mainland. If it hadn't been for his neighbor Vivian, he might have died of loneliness, although his health really was excellent for his age. She'd been almost like a daughter to his wife, but now, after ten years without his faithful companion, Vivian had become Ned's very best friend. Tonight, like so often lately, he thought that if he wasn't so much older than she was, he might ask her to marry him, for he truly loved her. But their relationship seemed to work fine like it was for both of them. He would have to be content to be just her friend and neighbor.

He had a few hobbies, and they occupied a lot of his time. Caring for his yard and helping Vivian with hers was very satisfying to the old man, as were the two or three hours a day he spent caring for the gardens at Paradise Pharmaceuticals. He could sit for hours and put together complicated puzzles, the kind with a thousand pieces. He loved to read, but that was becoming more difficult as he got older. He also collected seashells and had one of the finest collections around, although very few people even knew it existed. But that didn't matter to Ned. He only did it for his own entertainment—and to hear Vivian tell him how nice it was. No matter the weather, he walked for at least a mile every day. He cooked his own simple meals, except when he ate with Vivian, and he washed his own clothes and kept his house neat and clean. He still drove his old Buick to and from work and, once or twice a week, to different beaches to look for shells, and occasionally to the store to get groceries.

Even with all that he did, Ned had some empty time on his hands, and these days he spent that time worrying about Vivian and about Lauren. He knew they were in trouble, and he wanted to help. But what he was contemplating now could be dangerous for a man of any age, and especially for an old man like himself.

"So what if it's dangerous, Tommy?" he said to the cat. "I'm old. I've lived my life. If I could do something to make some young person's life better, then I should do it, even if it brings mine to an end. Miss Lauren doesn't need all the trouble she has. I think she could use my help."

The big cat purred its agreement, and Ned waited impatiently for his next call from Vivian.

It came as he was preparing to go to bed. She was excited when he told her that Donovan was coming back. "Mr. Deru says he intends to find out where Lauren is staying, but I think he might need help," Ned told her.

"But who will help him?" she asked. "Who can he trust?"

"I can help him," Ned announced.

Vivian gasped. "You're too old for that sort of thing. It might involve a lot of running about," she said.

"I can do it," Ned insisted. When he explained what he had in mind, Vivian expressed first concern, then shock, then horror. But he was firm in his resolve. "I've got to do it, Vivian. But I wanted to talk it over with you first."

"Well, I suppose it makes sense, even if it is very dangerous. But you are not going to do it alone."

"I have to," Ned said. "There's no one I would trust to help me right now."

"Shame on you, Ned," Vivian scolded. "Surely you trust me."

"More than anyone in this world, Vivian. But it would be too dangerous for you. You might be recognized."

"I'll just have to take that chance then. I'll use a disguise. I will not let you take all the risk, Mr. Haraguchi. We will do this together."

"Well . . . okay, but you must wear a very good disguise. I would feel just horrible if something were to happen to you. Mrs. Haraguchi would never forgive me."

"You daffy old man," Vivian said affectionately. "Let's get started first thing in the morning."

"I wish we had one of those fancy new phones everyone uses these days," Ned told her. "It would sure be safer for both of us if we did."

"You mean a cellular phone? I think I know where I can borrow one, or even two. It would be better if we both had one," she said. "Oh, Ned, we've got to succeed. That girl doesn't deserve all that she's being put through." She sighed, then asked brightly, "How is my Tommy?"

"Tommy's just fine, Vivian. He's right here on my lap, purring as contentedly as can be."

"That's marvelous, Ned. Tom's a lucky cat to have a friend like you."

CHAPTER 18

From the moment the plane left the ground in Salt Lake City at seven o'clock Tuesday morning until it touched down in Los Angeles for a frustrating layover, Donovan had slept soundly. Exhaustion had finally caught up with him. Despite his many worries, the needs of his tired body overrode the vigorous activity in his brain.

He actually felt refreshed, even though his nap had lasted less than two hours. He turned on his cell phone. It was fully charged, and he hoped he could use some of that stored energy to finally talk with Lauren. But her phone was still off, and he wished he could suddenly be in Hawaii, trying to locate her, instead of in L.A. waiting and worrying.

Donovan dreaded the next call, for he knew that Kaelyn would want to know where he was, and that she would be unhappy when he told her, even though she would be in Chicago and didn't plan to be home for another few days. But he had to call her. He owed her that courtesy. She answered her own cell phone this time. "Are you there yet?" he asked her.

"Actually, we're going to head back home," Kaelyn told him.

"What's the hurry?" he asked. "Why don't you take your time and enjoy the trip? There's lots to see in Chicago," Donovan said.

"We realized we just don't have enough money for the hotel and eating out. Anyway, don't you want us to hurry home?" she asked. "Don't you miss me?"

"Of course I miss you," he said. "But you might just as well enjoy your trip. I'd be happy to pick up the tab. Anyway, I'm not too sure it's safe in Vernal yet," he said. "I think it would be a good idea to give it a few more days if you can. I'm dealing with some dangerous people."

"Not anymore," she told him. "You said yourself that they can't hurt us now."

"That's true of those two, but I'm worried now that there may be others," he told her.

She laughed lightly. "Then you can be my protector," she suggested.

"I don't think that would work," he said, not sure yet how to tell her that he wasn't in Vernal and wouldn't be for a few days.

"Donovan," Kaelyn said, sounding very suspicious, "you are still in Vernal aren't you?"

He'd just as well get it over with, he decided, for she'd given him the opening he needed. "No, and I may not be for a few days."

Her voice was more than suspicious when she spoke again. There was a sharp edge to it. "Donovan, promise me you aren't going back to Hawaii."

"I can't do that," he said. "I'm in Los Angeles right now. I'll be back in Honolulu in a few hours."

"Don't go!" she exclaimed. "I won't let you go."

"I have to, and I need for you to understand," he said.

"It's that girl, isn't it? You're going back to see her! Donovan, I'm warning you, don't you dare go back there. You catch a plane to Salt Lake right now," she practically screamed.

Donovan had never known her to be so angry. He could hear Ellen in the background telling her to calm down, but she didn't. She even yelled at Ellen, saying, "If he wants me, he better go back to Vernal today."

"He'll be back when he's finished with what he's doing. He'll probably even beat us back," Donovan heard Ellen say. "Don't do this to yourself."

"He'll go back today, or he can find someone else to jerk around!" she shouted.

Donovan shook his head. He seemed to have been cut clear out of the conversation. He wondered if he should just disconnect. But he didn't; instead he listened. Ellen, ever calm, ever coolheaded, was saying, "He's the best thing that's ever happened to you, Kaelyn. You treat him like this, and he will find another girl. He might even decide to look at Lauren differently than he has been."

"Then she can have him! If he doesn't call me from Vernal by tonight, I'll throw this ring right through his window when we get home!"

Donovan had heard enough. It sounded to him like he wouldn't be engaged much longer, for he would not be back in Vernal today. He quietly punched a button on his phone, leaving Kaelyn to finish her conversation with Ellen. He choked back tears and just stared at the phone in his hand. He tried to rationalize the situation. He really did care for Kaelyn, but surely it was better that this happen now than after they were married. He may have just avoided the biggest mistake of his life. And maybe she had too. Maybe Mrs. Olsen had been right. They weren't suited for each other.

But those thoughts didn't help the wound that had been opened in his heart. *Where did I go wrong?* he wondered. *I was so sure I could make this work. I was committed to this relationship. What more does it take?* He thought a moment. *I really haven't been very considerate of her lately. Maybe if we could learn to communicate with each other better—*

His phone began to vibrate. He looked at it, discovering it was Kaelyn calling back. He wasn't sure he was prepared to answer it, but he knew he had to. "Hi," he said.

"You hung up on me!"

"Kaelyn, you weren't talking to me anymore. You were shouting at Ellen. I didn't want to hear it," he said calmly, feeling anything but calm inside.

"Well, I don't know when you quit listening, but I'll tell you this," she said, her voice rising again to dangerous levels. "Either you go back to Vernal today, or we're over."

"I can't go back, Kaelyn. I feel very strongly that I need to go to Hawaii right now. Please try to understand. I'll call you every day, twice a day or more until I get home, but don't throw away what we have. We need to talk about it." As he spoke, he suspected they were only words, that he couldn't change anything at this point. But he still felt the need to at least try to save their relationship, even if it meant making a big mistake, if that's what it was.

But Kaelyn had different ideas. "So, you are going to go to Hawaii?" she asked, her voice calmer now, sort of like a lull in a terrible storm.

"Yes, I'm going."

"And she's waiting for you to get there," she said. It was not a question. "She's been begging you to come back, and you finally told her you would."

"I haven't spoken to Lauren since I left her and her boyfriend at his house several days ago. I don't even know where she is," he protested. "But I have spoken to the police and believe she's still in danger, and I hope that I can locate her and help her boyfriend clear up her problems. I feel like it's my duty."

"Okay, fine! Go. And don't think that you're fooling me by talking about her boyfriend. I'm not stupid, Donovan. Don't even call me when you come home. Hold on a second." There was a pause, and she came back on the phone. "There, I just took my ring off. We're officially unengaged."

"Kaelyn," he pleaded, "please don't end it this way." But he was talking to no one now. She'd cut him off.

Forever.

He dropped his head in his hands, and despite himself, he sobbed.

"Here," someone said a few moments later, and a clean, white hankie was dangled in front of him.

He looked up. It was being offered by an elderly woman whose face bore an expression of sympathy. "Take it, young man. There'll be someone else sometime. Believe me, the pain will pass."

* * *

The night had passed. Lauren felt like she'd go crazy. She was not the kind of person to do nothing. She'd tried to watch a little television, but there wasn't a single thing that had caught her interest. She'd finally gone to bed late, slept a little, and awakened early.

She'd climbed out of bed, showered, dressed, and even gone through the house in search of Dexter, hoping he might have come back during the night. But she was alone. The house was silent. She wanted to scream.

She fixed something to eat, forced it down, and once again began to wander through the house. Finally, she ended up back in the bedroom Dexter had assigned to her. There she dropped to her knees.

Never in Lauren's life had she prayed both so earnestly and so unhurriedly as she prayed now. It was good, and she felt a little better there on her knees with her head bowed and her arms folded. Mostly, she just talked to God, telling Him how wayward she'd been, asking Him if there was any way she could ever be forgiven.

She kept praying, explaining the things she hoped to do in the near future. "I'll find my parents and my brother," she promised. "And I'll tell them how sorry I am. I want to have a good relationship with them and learn from them. And I'll go back to church . . . if the people there will have me." Finally, she told the Lord how frightened she was of all the horrifying events of late. She thanked Him for preserving her thus far and asked to be protected from any evil that could still befall her.

She knelt silently for a few minutes, feeling something come over her. She felt like she was being forgiven, which made her spirit feel buoyant. But she didn't feel like her nightmare with the Paradise Pharmaceuticals scandal was even close to being over. Maybe this would be the last thing she ever did in her life, saying this prayer and telling God how sorry she was.

Perhaps her enemies would find her again, and they would take her life this time, and that would be that, she thought. But even then she began to feel something more. Hope was the only word she could find to describe it. She could still hope that things would work out.

Lauren thought about Donovan, and she resumed her prayer. She prayed that the Lord would protect him, that he would continue to have the courage to be the kind of man she had come to admire so much. And she prayed he would be happy, that he would have a good marriage, and that he would be successful.

She wanted to pray that he would come back and help her, but she only thought that; she didn't ask it of God. She felt that would be selfish and unfair to his fiancée. But she certainly wished it would be so.

Finally, she finished her prayer, rose to her feet, and began to putter around the house, determined to keep hope alive in her heart.

* * *

"This is the house, I'm quite sure, but keep driving. We don't want anyone to notice us or get curious." Ned looked over at Vivian in the driver's seat as he spoke to her. Her disguise was not foolproof, but a person would have to take a close second look to recognize her. Her hair, which she usually wore in a tight bun, was hanging loosely over her shoulders. She wore some of her old gardening clothes, which she'd asked Ned to bring when he came to meet her. Very few people outside of some of her neighbors had ever seen her in such grubby, old clothes.

She smiled at him, and he thought how much he was enjoying this little adventure they had embarked on together. "Maybe we can find someplace to park and watch the house without being noticed," Vivian suggested.

Ned agreed, and they chose a place far enough away that it shouldn't seem like they were watching Dexter's house, and yet close enough that they could see when he left, if he left.

There was another occupied car about half a block beyond them, but they didn't pay any attention to it. They were there to watch Dexter's house.

They talked as they waited, discussing again how easy it had been to find where Mr. Drake lived. And once again, they discussed what they should do when he did come out. The only useful thing either of them could think of was to do like they did on TV and in the movies. "We'll tail him," Vivian said.

"But don't stay so close that he figures it out," Ned cautioned.

They again studied the borrowed cell phones. Vivian once more walked Ned through the process of using them. They were confusing to him, even a little bit to her. But after a few more minutes, they felt comfortable that they could use them when needed. In the meantime, they would keep them shut off to save the batteries.

When a shiny car pulled out of the driveway from the back of Dexter's large house, Vivian waited a decent amount of time in the car she'd borrowed from a friend before pulling out and driving after Dexter.

* * *

Who could that be? Leroy asked himself when a car pulled out just a short distance from where he was parked. They looked like they were doing what he'd planned to do—they seemed to be following Dexter. He'd hoped he could tail Dexter this morning and that before Dexter reached his office, he would find an opportunity to pull alongside him when there was no other traffic close by and do what he had to do. He cursed the man's good luck as he started his car and drove in the opposite direction so as not to arouse suspicion. He stopped at a McDonald's and had some breakfast. Even when he'd finished eating, he looked at his watch and realized that he'd be early for work.

So he drove slowly, thinking about how much he hated Dexter and Lauren. Maybe there was an easier way to get even with them, he thought as he drove. Perhaps he could use more of the drugs he'd stolen from work and slip them into something Dexter would be sure to eat or drink. He'd have to give that considerable thought. He slipped his gun beneath his seat after he'd found a parking spot at work.

* * *

With his arms folded across his chest, Dexter stared at the two men he'd been meeting with. "You want me to bring her to you? What if she doesn't want to come?" he asked.

"I don't suppose she'll want to, but it would be in her best interest to cooperate fully at this point," Captain Hafoko said.

"And what happens when I do that? Will she be arrested?"

"All I want now is to be able to ask her some questions. She has some explaining to do. If she can't give us satisfactory answers, then I may have to talk to the district attorney about charging her. But that is premature now."

Dexter unfolded his arms. "All right, I'll see what I can do."

"Have her here at eight in the morning," the captain said.

"It's for the best," Ken Fujimoto agreed.

"Okay, I feel like a traitor, but I'll have her here," he promised. "But you better treat her fairly."

* * *

Vivian did pretty well following Dexter. She was able to follow him first to the police station and then all the way to the Honolulu

Airport—no small feat. She'd had to hustle through a couple of lights that were going from yellow to red. And she'd made some dangerous maneuvers after they'd entered the freeway in order to keep him in sight. Once at the airport, they had to park the car and walk a short distance, but they successfully discovered that he was about to fly away in a sleek private jet. They watched it take off and swing out over the ocean, then wondered what to do next.

"I guess we go in that building there and see if anyone will tell us where he was headed," Ned suggested.

"Let's go then," Vivian agreed.

"No, let me go alone," Ned said sternly. "You wait in the car. I won't be long." This time, she didn't protest.

Ned decided that he was cut out for this sort of work. He learned, without anyone seeming to be unduly suspicious, that Dexter was flying over to Kauai. When Ned got back to the car, the two amateur sleuths decided that they would have to go there as well. Of course, they'd have to fly commercial. They hurried as quickly as they could and got on a plane that arrived at the Lihue Airport shortly after noon.

Then, once again, they had to make some decisions. In spite of having watched many crime dramas on TV, they really were new at this sort of work. They decided that the first thing they needed was a car, so they rented one. Then they were stumped. Nearly sixty thousand people lived on the island, and they were spread through many small towns that ran around the island both south and north of Lihue. They had no idea which direction to go or how they might figure out what Dexter's destination was, although they agreed that if they could find that destination, they'd probably find Lauren. Besides the people that lived there year-round, Kauai also contained about seven thousand hotel and condominium units. Dexter could be headed to any one of them or to a house, they supposed. Dexter could be anywhere on the island by now, and so could Lauren.

They looked at one another in dismay. They had undertaken a truly daunting task.

* * *

It was hard for Lauren to read with so much on her mind, but she had to do something, and that was the only thing left to do. The house had a small library, and she finally selected a novel and sat down near the glass doors where she had a view of the ocean. She'd read the first two pages by the time she realized her mind hadn't been on the book. She had no idea what she'd read. But she did know the conclusion she'd come to while she was reading. She was a prisoner, much like she had been in her own apartment. This time, she was physically able to walk out the door, but she still felt trapped.

That feeling of a lack of freedom wasn't entirely because of the danger that had come into her life. And it wasn't that she didn't trust Dexter to help her as much as he could. *No,* she reasoned, *I feel like a prisoner because I'm completely dependent on Dexter and yet I really want to break up with him. But how could I possibly break up with him now? Everything's just so complicated.* Dexter was no longer the kind of man she was looking for as a husband. She wasn't going to fool herself any longer. Given his views, he wouldn't join the Church anytime soon— if ever—and she had no intention of living the rest of her life without it. She knew he'd just ridicule her if she tried to share spiritual experiences with him. Marriage to him would not even be close to what she now hoped to someday have.

Dexter had all but proposed to her yesterday. A few days ago, that would have made her heart sing, and she would have accepted without hesitation. Now it felt like a cold weight in her chest. She wanted to leave this place behind. She wanted to leave Dexter behind. *Technically,* she thought, *I could leave this house anytime I want to. But where would I go?* she asked herself. Her enemies were out there somewhere. And they could still find her. Dexter was both her captor and her only way out.

That was why she stayed. She didn't dare go anywhere on her own. All she could do was wait for the noose to settle around the necks of Royce, Fleming, and their elusive partners, if any still lived. Then she would be free to go home and resume her life.

A life without Dexter Drake, she vowed, no matter how angry that made him.

But what about Donovan Deru?

Where did that thought come from? she asked herself as she slammed the book down and jumped to her feet. Donovan had done what he could for her. He had reentered and left her life almost as briefly as the first time she'd known him. Only this time, her life was sadder when he left.

Firmly, Lauren grasped reality. Donovan was gone, and there was nothing she could do about that. Now she had to depend on Dexter, Ken Fujimoto, and the police. For now, she needed to be patient, have faith, and get her mind off her troubles. She still had hope.

She picked up the book again and began reading. This time, she forced herself to pay attention to the words her eyes scanned, and by the time she'd read five or six pages, she was interested in the story. She was disappointed when she had to put the book down again as the door opened sometime later.

CHAPTER 19

Dexter walked in. He came straight to her and took her in his arms. "I'm sorry I was gone so long," he said.

For a minute, she instinctively leaned into him, but all she could feel was emptiness. She finally pulled gently away and looked him in the eye. She was certain she saw him flinch. "Okay, Dexter, tell me what's happened. I can tell that it isn't good," she said as fear again stabbed at her heart.

"You're right," he said. "I'm sorry not to be able to bring good news. But we need to talk about something. I want to trust you, and I'll do everything I can to help you, but you've got to be totally honest with me."

"I have been," she protested as she stepped away from him in astonishment. "I haven't lied to you about one single thing."

"I didn't say you had, but you also haven't told me everything," he said pointedly.

"Like what?" she asked, dumbfounded over what could be causing him to act like this, unless, of course, he could somehow sense that she didn't love him the way she had before.

"Like the two million dollars you have in the bank," he said. "Would you like to explain where it came from?"

Lauren was speechless and began to tremble. She had no idea what he was talking about. The last time she'd looked, she had just under twenty thousand dollars in savings and maybe five or six hundred in checking. She had some money invested in the stock market, but it wouldn't amount to a lot.

"You have over two million dollars in your savings account, Lauren. The police are convinced that it came from Paradise

Pharmaceuticals. Now you better get busy and tell me where you got it," he demanded.

For the first time in their relationship, Lauren felt a touch of fear in Dexter's presence. Maybe it was the anger that seemed to be seeping from him as he spoke that made her feel insecure. It seemed clear that he suspected her of stealing money from someone. Of course, she knew she hadn't, and so she said, "Dexter, I don't have that much money. I believe you if you say it's there, but I can't imagine where it came from."

"That's a little weak, don't you think?" he responded sternly. "The captain told me that there is over that amount missing from Paradise, although there's not nearly as much gone from their accounts as you claim Royce and Fleming have taken. They think you must have other bank accounts with the rest of the money in it."

"Dexter, this is insane!" she cried. "I'm telling the truth. There have been several million dollars transferred, besides which, not all the theft was in money. They have secretly been involved in deals that have drained the resources of the company. But I swear to you, I haven't taken a single dollar."

"Then how did that kind of money get into your personal account?" he asked accusingly.

"I don't know, I tell you. Someone must be trying to frame me," she suggested desperately.

"Frame you?" he asked with a mirthless laugh. "By giving you two million dollars or more? That makes no sense at all."

Hearing him say it that way made it seem rather farfetched. *But what else could it be?* she wondered. "Dexter, I didn't put that money in my account, and other than one savings account and my checking, I have no other accounts. I haven't stolen anything from Paradise. You've got to believe me. Why would I try to blame someone else for doing something I did when no one even suspected any kind of embezzlement at the company until I found it? All I can think is that Royce and Fleming must be behind it all. They are involved in a cover-up, and they are trying to get me in trouble to turn suspicion from them while they clean out what's left and leave the country."

Dexter had turned away from her as she spoke. He walked toward the glass doors and stood looking out for a full minute or more while she watched him, her heart racing with fear. She could almost hear the clanging of jail cell doors, hear the taunting of numerous inmates, and feel the mustiness of a tiny cell.

When he finally turned back to her, his features had softened. "Okay, here's what we'll do," he began.

"Dexter," she said desperately, "you do believe me, don't you?"

"I do believe you," he said. "But the police don't. They asked me to have you come back and meet them at Captain Hafoko's office. But I won't do that. I won't turn you over to them. You stay here while I go back and try to figure out what's going on. They can't make me tell them where you are, so you're safe here for now. I hate to lie, but I will if I have to in order to protect you. I'll tell them you fled, that you didn't stay where I asked you to. In the meantime, I'll try to convince them that a cover-up is in progress, and I'll do all I can to help them prove it. And Lauren, if anyone comes to the door, don't answer it. We don't want to take any chances. We don't want anyone to see you here."

He took her in his arms and kissed her with what she was sure was supposed to be warmth and affection, but which felt to her like frigidity and distance. "I love you," he said. "I'll be back as soon as I can. I'll take care of you."

"Oh, before you go . . . Did you happen to see my cell phone last night? Or anytime this weekend? I can't find it in any of my things."

"I'm sorry, sweetheart, but I didn't see it. It must have dropped out of your purse sometime before then. But I'll take another look around, just in case."

"Thank you, Dexter. I feel so lost without it."

"No problem. Anything for you."

After Dexter had left again, Lauren paced the floor and tried to think through her dilemma. She was quite sure that Dexter hadn't believed her. And that distrust on his part must have transformed itself into the coolness that she'd felt from him. She could only trust that he'd do as he promised and look more closely into things, and in doing so would realize that she was being victimized.

Lauren suddenly realized that she wanted and needed her family and the security she used to feel with them, but there was no way to find where they'd moved to while she was staying here without even so much as a phone. And she wanted to talk to . . .

I have to quit thinking of him, she scolded herself. As if that were possible.

* * *

Vivian and Ned watched as Dexter boarded the sleek jet and took off down the runway at the Lihue Airport in Kauai. After the plane was in the air and out of sight, they got back in their car and drove to the rental company his car had come from. Ned approached the desk while Vivian stood back a few feet and watched.

"Hello, sir," Ned said in his smoothest voice.

"How can I help you?" the attendant asked.

"My stepson returned a rental car a little while ago. He just took off in a plane on his way back to Honolulu, and he called me on his cell phone," Ned said, hoping he could make it all the way through the script he and Vivian had hastily prepared. He held up the borrowed cell phone, hoping its presence in his hand would add veracity to his story. "He can't find his watch, a very expensive one. He thinks it might have fallen off in the car. He's been having trouble with the band and was going to get a new one. I wondered if you'd mind if I looked for it."

The attendant looked at Ned suspiciously. "Why did he rent a car if you are here on the island? Not that it's any of my business."

This part hadn't been scripted. Ned squirmed. Then he said, "My stepson and I don't get along real well." He nodded toward where Vivian waited. "He thinks I'm too old for his mother, so when he comes over here, he mostly pretends we don't exist."

"Unless he needs your help," the attendant guessed.

"That's right, unless he's lost a watch he claims is worth nearly a thousand dollars and he's in too much of a hurry to come back and look for it himself," Ned said, trying to inject just the right amount of bitterness into his voice.

"You may have a look if you like, but if I were you, I'd keep the watch if it's there. What right does he have to tell his mother who to marry? Sounds like a snob to me. No offense," he said to Ned.

Ned smiled. "No offense taken. Could my wife and I have a look then? I mean, Dexter's a jerk, but he is her son."

"Sure, just a second and I'll get the keys."

Ned signaled for Vivian to join him. "He's getting the keys," he whispered. "He thinks you're my wife and that Dexter is a jerk of a son—your son, my stepson. This just might work."

Vivian smiled at him. "Let's hope so. We've got to find Lauren."

A minute later, they had the key and the number of the car. They went out and pretended to search just in case anyone was watching them. Finally, hoping enough time had elapsed to make it appear like they'd done a thorough search, they returned to the desk inside and handed the attendant the key.

"Any luck?" he asked.

"No, but if we knew where he'd been, we'd go there and look for it," Ned said sullenly. "Not that he deserves the extra effort on our part, but you know how it is."

The attendant nodded sympathetically. "I don't have any idea where he might have gone," the attendant responded. "If I did, I might go look for the watch myself. I could use a thousand-dollar watch." He was grinning as he spoke, and they knew he wasn't serious. But then he was thoughtful for a moment. Finally he said with a secretive smile, "Actually, there is a way. We track our cars with global positioning satellites. GPS they call it."

"GPS?" Ned said. "I don't see how—"

"Never mind," Vivian said with a gentle pat on his arm. "There's a lot you don't understand about this modern world. Let's let the man explain."

"I shouldn't do this, and if you ever say I did, I'll deny it, but under the circumstances, it seems only fair," the attendant said.

He spent a minute on a computer at the back of the little office. He typed, he studied, and finally, he printed something. When he came back he had a paper in his hand. It was a map, they noted as he handed it to them. "This is where he drove," he told them. "Follow this, and you should be able to find where he was at."

"Look, Ned," Vivian said. "This leads right up to Kapaa. That's where the investment property my late husband left me for my later years is located. We were right. He's trying to sell that property out from under us."

Ned wasn't sure how to respond to this, but it was certainly creative on the part of Vivian. "You must be right," he said very seriously.

The attendant added his disgust at such behavior and said, as he put a finger on the map, "This is the farthest point he went to. That must be where your property is located. That's a beautiful spot there in the hills above the main part of town. It's very valuable property. Again, don't let a soul know that I gave you this information. Please destroy that map after you've searched for his watch."

They assured him that they would, thanked him, and left. Back in their own rental car a few minutes later, Vivian said, "What a nice young man. We're in such luck here. Let's go to Kapaa, and we'll find Lauren. I don't know what we'll do then, but when Donovan gets here, he'll be able to figure something out."

They left Lihue and drove up the east side of the island on the narrow Kuhio Highway, exactly as the map indicated they should. Once in Kapaa, they turned where it indicated Dexter had turned. The map was very specific, and they were quite certain they'd followed it correctly when they finally parked in an attractive neighborhood overlooking the green hills that led down to the main part of Kapaa, the Kuhio Highway, and the broad expanse of ocean beyond. They parked near the end of the street and began walking, admiring the peaceful scenery and the cleanliness of the yards.

"It's got to be one of these houses right here. Let's knock on someone's door," Vivian suggested. "Hopefully, someone will recall seeing either Dexter or Lauren or both."

After several minutes, they'd had no luck. Either there weren't people home at some of the houses, or the occupants didn't answer. People who were home claimed to have never heard of Dexter Drake. They were friendly but of little help. They returned to the car and sat morosely for a few minutes, trying to decide what to do next. Lauren had to be here unless Dexter had stopped somewhere else on the route they'd followed and only drove up here and turned around for some unexplainable reason.

"Ned, how would you feel about praying?" Vivian suddenly asked.

* * *

Lauren parted the drapes and looked down at the street. The car was still parked just a short distance away, and the old couple were sitting in it now. She'd heard them knocking on the door, but remembering Dexter's advice, she'd kept it shut and locked. She'd watched them as they walked away, too far by the time she finally mustered the courage to peek out to be able to identify them. The man appeared to be much older than the woman. From the back he reminded her of Ned with his short-cropped white hair, straight back, and slightly bowed legs. The woman had long, flowing hair, gray, but neatly brushed. Her clothes looked old and worn. Something about her also seemed vaguely familiar. Lauren kept peeking out, partly to break the boredom of the day, and partly because she was curious about them.

Suddenly, both car doors opened and the occupants got out. Once again, they began knocking on doors and ringing doorbells. They first tried the house two doors away, and she could see that they got no answer. They skipped the one to her immediate south, and she wondered why. Then once again, they trudged up the long walk toward her doorway and pressed the bell. Her heart raced upon recognition.

It was Ned! And the woman with him didn't fool her from the front; it was the long hair that had thrown her off. She'd never seen Vivian's hair before when it wasn't neatly tied up in a tight bun. Throwing caution to the wind, Lauren unlocked the door and flung it open. They stared at each other for a moment, then Lauren bounded down the steps and took both of them tearfully in her arms. "What are you two doing here?" she cried. "You are an answer to my prayers."

"And you, my dear girl, are an answer to ours," Ned said, wiping at the tears that had formed in his eyes.

"Does anyone besides Mr. Drake know you're here?" Vivian asked.

"I . . . I'm not sure," Lauren said. "Dexter said no one else knows."

"Lauren," Ned said, "we hate to say this, but we don't trust your Mr. Drake. Do you?"

Lauren was rocked by that question. "Not like I used to," she admitted.

"Who can you trust?" Vivian asked.

"The two of you," Lauren said as she ushered them back into the house. "And I trust Donovan, but Dexter and I sent him away. I wanted to call him, but the phone here is dead. Dexter says he's working to help me, but the police think I've been stealing money from Paradise, and I swear that's not true. I think they are also blaming me for the death of Dr. Mitsui."

"That's outrageous," Vivian said heatedly. "This is the work of that evil Mr. Parker. Get your things, for you're coming with us, if you will. And we have a wonderful surprise for you."

"What could be more wonderful than seeing the two of you here?" she asked as she gathered her few things.

Vivian said, "You'll be surprised, I think."

"I'm already surprised."

"Donovan Deru is on his way back," Vivian then said smugly.

Lauren's hand flew to her mouth and her eyes grew wide. "Oh!" she exclaimed.

"Yes, he should be in Honolulu shortly. He's been so worried about you after what happened to him," Ned said.

"What happened to Donovan? Has he been hurt?" she asked in alarm.

"Oh no, he's fine, but no thanks to a couple of men from here who went over to Utah," Ned said. "Here, let me carry that," he offered as he reached for her suitcase.

"We can explain everything in the car. Right now we need to take you someplace where we can meet Donovan in complete privacy," Vivian said. "He'll know the best thing to do."

Lauren suddenly felt a great weight lift from her shoulders. She could hardly believe Donovan was coming back, but she knew it was true since it came from Ned and Vivian. She offered a silent prayer of gratitude.

Together, they left the house. Dexter would be angry, but she just couldn't stay here anymore. As they drove down the Kuhio Highway toward Lihue, Vivian and Ned told Lauren what they knew about the explosion in front of Donovan's house. She couldn't believe it. "Why would anyone go after Donovan clear over there?" she asked. "It doesn't make any sense. He was no threat to them."

"Somebody clearly doesn't believe that," Ned growled. "And we'll have to trust Donovan to figure out who and why."

CHAPTER 20

Donovan changed the time on his watch while he waited for other passengers to file past, who were pushing in a clumsy mass of humanity toward the exit. It was now just a few minutes after three local time. He was anxious to get off the plane, but he also wondered what to do first when he had a car secured and left the airport. Maybe he should contact Captain Hafoko and see if he could learn just how strong the evidence against Lauren was. He also needed to call Ned Haraguchi and see if he'd learned anything new.

He slipped his wristwatch back on and then turned on his cellular phone. There was still plenty of battery power left in case he needed it. He dropped it in the pocket of his sports jacket and stood up. The main rush of passengers had passed now, and he eased into the aisle and reached into the overhead bin for his carry-on bag. Then he moved forward. As he nodded at the flight attendant at the door, he felt his phone vibrating.

His first thought was that Kaelyn was calling, and he wasn't sure what he felt about that. But when he looked at the number on his phone, it was one he didn't recognize, but it had a local area code. He answered with a tired "Hello."

"Donovan?" asked a familiar voice that made him almost shout in relief.

"Lauren! It's good to hear your voice," he said. "I'm so glad you called. I didn't know how to get ahold of you."

"You wanted to?" she asked.

"Oh, yes, very much. I've been trying over and over again. The first time I called, Dexter answered, and he said you were taking a nap. He wouldn't let me talk to you. Since then, either you've had your phone off or the battery is dead," he explained.

"Dexter answered my phone?" she asked.

"Yes, the first time."

"Donovan, I haven't used my phone since you left. I thought I'd lost it in a hotel room or something," she told him, sounding puzzled.

"I see," he said, but he really didn't see at all.

"If Dexter had my phone, he's lied to me," she said. "He told me he hadn't seen my phone all weekend. Why would he do that?"

Donovan didn't have an answer to that question, so he asked, "Where are you?"

"I'm with Vivian and Ned," she said.

"What!" he exclaimed. "How did that happen?"

Lauren explained quickly, then she said, "I'm so worried, Donovan. The police think I've stolen millions from Paradise and that I had something to do with the death of Dr. Mitsui. I would never do either of those things."

"I know that, Lauren," he told her. "I know you're honest. You and I need to talk, but not on the phone," he said. "I need to meet you and we can figure out what to do next."

"Oh, thank you, Donovan," she said. "You don't know what a relief it is to have you here again. I'm sorry I told you to go home. I guess I shouldn't have listened to Dexter, but I thought he'd get things taken care of."

"He may have tried, and that's what I'll do too. We can't underestimate Fleming and Royce. I'm becoming more convinced all the time that they are very smart men. So, tell me where you are."

"I'm in Kauai," she said. "If you can come here, Ned says he'll meet you at the airport."

"I'll do that. I was going to go talk to Captain Hafoko and find out exactly what he's thinking and what he knows, but that can wait."

"Oh, thank you," Lauren said. "And Donovan, I heard about the bomb. I had no idea they'd go after you over there."

"It turned out okay, actually. The bomb got my attention. I should never have left here. It woke me up and sent me back to finish what I'd started. Anyway, I'll be there as soon as I can get a flight arranged. I have the number of the phone you're calling from. Can I reach you there to let you know when I'll be getting to Kauai?" he asked.

"Perfect. I've missed you, Donovan. I was afraid I'd never see you again."

* * *

Dexter walked into a meeting at Paradise Pharmaceuticals. He was late, and for that reason, he was greeted with a glare by Milo Thurman. "We've been waiting," Milo said. "Where have you been? I'm paying good money to your firm for the work you do for us, and I think I deserve timeliness on your part."

"Sorry, sir. I'm sure it won't happen again," he said.

"I'd appreciate it," Milo responded. "Now we need to discuss this unfortunate development. I'm told that one of my most trusted employees, your girlfriend, has been taking money from my company and doctoring our records to cover it up. Mr. Fujimoto assured me that your loyalties are with your client—that's me and my company—not with my employee, Miss Olcott. Is that a fair representation?"

"It is, sir. Lauren—Miss Olcott—and I have dated, but we're not at all serious in our relationship," Dexter said. "You know how rumors go. Things get blown all out of proportion."

"I hope that's true, because I expect you to do whatever it takes to see that the proper action is taken against her in my behalf. Mr. Cantrell and Mr. Parker, my two most loyal men, tell me that two million dollars of the missing funds they've identified are sitting in an account of Miss Olcott's."

Dexter nodded at Royce and Fleming, his lips curling just slightly as he did so. "Apparently that's the case. At least, that's what the police told me."

"That's not all that's missing," Milo informed him. "There is another three million. I suspect she knows where it is. Fleming and Royce have been working on finding what she did with that money, but they are also spending a huge amount of time working on company records. They need help, and I want you to help them. When you locate the accounts she's put those funds in, I expect you to take whatever legal action is necessary to secure that money."

"That's what I'll do," Dexter said.

"You fellows work closely with Mr. Drake," Milo said to Royce and Fleming. "He can do much of the running for you."

"We'll do that," Royce promised. "We're glad for the help."

"You know that our entire concern is the solvency of this company," Fleming agreed. "We'll take care of you and your assets."

"Thank you, gentlemen. Now, I understand that Miss Olcott has disappeared," Milo continued. "She was last seen with you, Dexter."

"That's right. I left her at a hotel," Dexter said with a straight face. "When I went back to pick her up, she'd gone. But I believe I know who can help me locate her. I'm sure she isn't far away."

"Good, you work on that too then. In fact, if we could get her in here with the three of us, I have a feeling she'd break down and tell us everything she knows," Milo said confidently.

"I'm sure you're right about that," Royce agreed.

"Good, then I'll let you gentlemen get to work." That was a dismissal, and all three of them filed from the office.

"Hey, Dexter," a voice called from behind him just as he reached the elevator.

Dexter turned and scowled. "What do you want, Leroy?"

"I know something I think you'd like to hear," Leroy said. "Maybe we could have dinner somewhere tonight and I could fill you in."

"I don't think we have anything to talk about," Dexter said to him.

"Oh, but we do," he said. "I've been hearing things down in the accounting department. I think you better give me an hour of your time."

Dexter's stomach twisted. He wasn't sure what Leroy might have heard, but he decided he better listen to him. He glanced at his watch. "Why don't we eat at, say, six thirty? But it will need to be fast. I have a lot to do."

They agreed on a location, and Dexter left, fuming that he had to take time for such people as Leroy Provost.

* * *

When Donovan stepped into the hotel room in Lihue, Lauren's heart nearly stopped. More than anything, she wanted to run to him and throw her arms around him, but she couldn't do that. So she just said, "Aloha. Thanks for coming back."

"I should never have left," he said.

"But you had to," she replied softly. "I know that. I can't believe you came back—that she let you come back."

"You mean Kaelyn?" he asked.

"You know I mean her. Your fiancée."

"My former fiancée," he said.

"Oh, Donovan, I'm sorry. I hope it wasn't my fault," she exclaimed.

"It wasn't your fault," he said. "It would never have worked anyway. We just weren't getting along very well."

"So you told her it was over?" she asked.

"No, she told me it was, right before I came back here."

"Then it was my fault," she cried. "I'm so sorry. If you hadn't come to Hawaii, it would never have happened to you."

"Actually, it was something that was bound to happen—I just hadn't realized it. So please don't worry about it." He was thoughtful for a moment, and she wondered what he was thinking. When he spoke again, there was pain in his voice. "It hurt, Lauren, having her tell me she didn't want to marry me. But I've had a few hours to reflect, and I know she did us both a favor. I need to move on now, and so does she."

"I'm sorry," Lauren said again. She didn't know what else to say. She couldn't say, "I'm so glad," even though that was the truth, for she knew that deep in her heart she was beginning to have feelings for this man that no one else, Dexter included, had ever come close to instilling in her. Not that it meant he would ever return those feelings, but now there was at least the possibility.

Donovan smiled, then said, "I didn't come to talk about me. I came to see how I could help you. We have work to do, all four of us." He picked up a bag Lauren assumed held his laptop computer, opened a side pocket, and pulled out a legal pad, which he dropped on the small hotel table. "Let's begin with you, Lauren. Tell me everything you can about what's happened to you since I left."

Ned said, "I've had a rather active day, and I'm tired. Do you young people mind if I go into the adjoining room and lie down for a while?"

"Of course not," Vivian said solicitously, and she ushered him to the next room. Shortly thereafter she poked her head through the door and said, "There's a second bed in here, and I could use a little rest myself."

"Go right ahead," Lauren said. "We'll fill you in later."

Lauren related recent events, answered Donovan's questions, and asked a few of her own. He took a lot of notes. When they got to the part about the retrieval of the evidence she'd left at the bank, he asked, "Did Dexter go with you into the vault to open your box?"

"No, they said only one person could go in there at a time. So I went alone."

"Was everything like you left it when you put things in there?"

"I don't know, but I think so," she said as she recalled the way she had so clumsily dropped the box and mixed things up in it.

Donovan looked at her for a long moment, and she squirmed under his gaze. "You don't know? Weren't the things you'd taken from your office in an envelope or a manila folder or something? And wouldn't that have been on top of everything else?" he asked.

Lauren explained why the things from the office were not in the envelope. "The bank was hurrying me when I was putting things away," she said. "I had taken everything out of the big envelope to make sure I hadn't left anything at home. They told me to hurry, that they needed to close the bank. So I just dropped everything in there without putting it back in the envelope."

"Okay, but do you have some recollection of the order things were in?"

"Not really, and I know this sounds stupid, but I was shaking so badly when I pulled the box out that I dropped it. Everything scattered all over the floor. So I had to gather it up, and I mixed things up when I did that."

Donovan sat back and smiled reassuringly at her. "Hey, there's nothing stupid about that, Lauren. You've been through more than anyone should have to go through. I just wanted to make sure no one else could possibly have tampered with things."

"The bank is really careful about that, and anyway, it takes two keys to open the safety-deposit box. The bank has one, which they only let me take when I show my identification. I have the other one," she explained.

"Good. Now, when you gathered things up, how did you go about it?"

"There's a table in there. I put everything on it and then sorted through it. I put the stuff I needed for the police in the envelope and put everything else back in the box."

"Okay, but you're sure you took everything that pertained to the embezzlement?" he asked.

"Well . . ." Lauren said as she reconsidered the box's contents. "Oh!" she exclaimed.

"What?"

"I did leave one disc, but it doesn't matter," she said.

"Are you sure?" Donovan asked urgently. "This could be important. There might be something missing that Captain Hafoko needs."

"No, he has everything. The one I left was a duplicate of the other one. I backed everything up twice from my hard drive," she explained. "I have some other discs in there that are of other work I've done that I didn't want to lose. I guess I'm just overly careful. Some might call it paranoia," she added with a small smile.

"Well, I'm glad you have another copy, and I hope it's still there." He smiled back at her. "That way maybe you can go over it with me and explain what you found."

"Yeah, that would be great."

"Does anyone else know about your extra copy?"

"No. Even I had forgotten it until now."

"Okay, so you put everything in the envelope and joined Dexter in the lobby?"

"Yes."

"Did he look at anything before you took the envelope to Captain Hafoko?" Donovan asked.

"He took everything, and my understanding is that he went over it all with his boss, Ken Fujimoto, before taking it to Captain Hafoko."

"So you didn't personally take the material to the captain?" Donovan asked. "I do recall the captain saying Dexter and Ken brought it in. Why didn't you go too?"

"Dexter wanted time to go over it, and he felt it would be best for me to stay hidden for a while longer. So he flew me over here and took me to the house where Vivian and Ned found me."

"So it was Dexter's idea that he go to the captain without you, not yours?"

"That's right," she agreed. "He did it because he felt like I'd been through too much already. But I'm sure he didn't go alone. He said he would take Ken with him."

"Where was your documentation while Dexter was taking you to Kauai?"

"We stopped at his office briefly before going to the airport. Of course, I stayed in the car, but Dexter said he put the things in his office and locked it."

Donovan rose from his seat and paced the room for a moment. He seemed deep in thought, and Lauren wondered what he was thinking. Finally, he stopped pacing and looked right at her. "If we were in a courtroom, you wouldn't be allowed to tell me what you just did. It's known as hearsay. That means that you wouldn't be allowed to tell the court or jury what someone else told you. Dexter would have to testify about what he did with the documents himself."

"Yes, I know that," she said. "But he's not here, and we're not in court."

Donovan sat down again. "That's true, but how do I know Dexter told you the truth? How do you know he didn't lie to you?"

Lauren didn't love Dexter like she thought she had, but she also didn't have any reason to think that he'd intentionally do anything to hurt her. "I don't know that, Donovan, but I'm sure he did as he said."

"But you don't know that Dexter or Ken didn't remove or add anything or make changes of any kind before delivering it to the captain?" he asked.

"I don't," she admitted, "but I can't imagine why he'd do something like that. I'm sure he didn't."

"I'd like to see that backup disc you think you may have left in your safety-deposit box," Donovan said. "Where is the key to that box?"

"It's in my purse," she said. *Where my phone should be and isn't,* she thought with irritation.

"Will you get it for me?" he asked.

Lauren stood up and crossed the room. Her purse was on one of the beds beside her suitcase. She began to rummage through it. She began to worry when she couldn't find it. She wondered if she'd misplaced the key the way she'd misplaced her phone. Or, she thought with a sinking feeling deep inside her, had Dexter taken them both? The fact that he'd used her phone and then told her he hadn't seen it was disturbing, and it made her think more seriously about Donovan's questions.

There wasn't much left in her purse, and she was worried now, wondering what she'd do if she couldn't find it. Finally, in desperation, she tipped the purse upside down and dumped all of its remaining contents onto the bed. To her relief, the key appeared, landing on top of everything else. It had simply worked its way to the bottom of her purse.

"Is that it?" Donovan asked from right behind her. She hadn't heard him walk over, and it startled her.

"Yeah, I was afraid I'd lost it," she admitted. "In fact, why don't you take this, Donovan?" She held out the key to him.

"I hope we can use it soon," he said as he put it in his pocket. "Okay, let's get back to work here."

Lauren was relieved an hour later when Donovan ran out of questions. She hoped she didn't have to go through this again with someone else, separated from him, for until this ordeal was ended, she wanted Donovan at her side every waking moment.

CHAPTER 21

Captain Hafoko was just ready to leave for the night when a call came in. He picked up the phone. "This is Captain Hafoko," he said.

"Captain, this Donovan Deru calling. Are you aware of Lauren's location?"

"No, but Dexter promised he'd have her here by morning," he said. "I really need to talk to her."

"Dexter said he'd bring her in? I take it that he knows where she is," Donovan said.

"He says he does, and he promised to bring her in tomorrow morning."

"I see. Well, I sure hope she's okay," Donovan said. "I'm not sure how much I trust that Drake fellow."

That made the captain think for a moment, and he had to agree that he didn't much like Dexter himself, but there was nothing concrete he could base those feelings on. "I'm sure she's safe," he said. "But it isn't looking very good for her legally."

"I'm sorry to hear that," Donovan said. "I've tried to call her several times, but I guess there's a problem with her cell phone. If you do hear from her, or if Dexter brings her in, would you mind letting me know?"

"I'd be glad to," the captain said.

After hanging up, he was thoughtful for a moment. Was Donovan trying to tell him something? he wondered. Or was he just worried about the young woman? He had no idea, but he did begin to wonder a bit more about how trustworthy Dexter Drake was.

* * *

"He told the captain that he was going to turn me in?" Lauren asked, as much in shock as in anger.

"That he did."

"That lowlife!" she said. "I *knew* he thought I was guilty. I wonder what he'll do when he finds out I'm no longer where he thinks I am."

* * *

Leroy was already at the restaurant when Dexter arrived. He was waiting outside, near the entrance. "Glad you could make it," he said to Dexter.

"I haven't much time. Unlike some people, I'm a very busy man," Dexter said snidely.

"What I have to tell you won't take long, but we are going to take time to eat. And you are buying," Leroy informed him.

"I suppose that will depend on what you have to say," Dexter said. "It better be good."

"Oh, it's good, all right."

They said very little until the food had come. Dexter was angry that he even had to waste time on the man. He would have liked to turn him in to the police over the poisoned cherry chocolates, but that wouldn't have been wise. At least not yet. He knew why Lauren hadn't reported him either, because they'd talked about it. She was almost certain that Leroy was part of the embezzlement ring, and she hadn't wanted to name anyone until she'd given her proof to the police.

Now she was a suspect, and maybe when he turned her in tomorrow morning she'd tell about the chocolates, though he didn't think anyone would believe her at that point because of all the holes in her story.

Dexter took a couple of bites of his salad, then said, "So, Leroy. What have you been hearing that is of such concern to me?"

Leroy leaned over very secretively and said, "There is something very crooked going on at Paradise Pharmaceuticals, and your little girlfriend is right in the middle of it."

Dexter could have laughed. But he didn't, and he asked very seriously, "Do you believe she's actually involved in something illegal?"

"I'm surprised, but yes, I've learned she can be very treacherous."

"You mean because she left you for me?" Dexter asked. He was ready to leave but thought better of it.

"That's part of it, I suppose. But there are those who believe that if she's involved, then you must be too. I just thought you might like to protect yourself," Leroy said. "Because she will turn on you just like she turned on me. Only you have a lot to lose."

Dexter had heard about enough. "And you don't?" he asked. "Maybe it's time someone official learns about who gave Lauren the drugged chocolate cherries."

The color drained from Leroy's face. For a moment, he stammered, then he said, "I don't know what you're talking about."

Dexter pushed back his chair. "I'm not hungry. You can pay for this meal. And I don't want to hear that you've said another word about Lauren to anyone. Understand? Poisoned candy given to someone is considered attempted murder. So you keep your mouth shut, or that's what you'll be facing."

* * *

Long after Dexter had left, Leroy sat nibbling at the meals he was going to have to pay for. The deadly powder was still in his pocket, and Dexter had gone off laughing at him. He'd rubbed salt in an open wound. The hatred Leroy had felt before was nothing compared to what he felt now. He didn't care what it took—he'd see Dexter Drake and Lauren Olcott in their graves.

* * *

"I shouldn't have left her here alone!" Dexter hissed to the walls of the empty house. "She could be anywhere by now. I thought she trusted me."

It hadn't even occurred to him that she might decide to strike out on her own. She was probably looking for a phone so she could call Donovan, he decided. As if Donovan could do anything for her. If she wanted to live, she had to trust him, Dexter Drake, and no one else. He could keep her alive, and that was something. She might go to jail, but she would at least live.

He didn't really love her, but he also didn't hate her. They'd had some good times together. He didn't mind using her to achieve his own ambitions, but the thought of her dying at the hands of her enemies was unthinkable. He had to find her, and he had to either keep her hidden or do as he'd told the captain he'd do and turn her in.

In a few days, whatever was going to happen would happen, and surely then she'd be safe without him having to watch out for her, for he couldn't and didn't want to be her guardian forever. If only she'd stayed put like he'd told her to.

He had no idea where to look for her. Then he had a thought. Maybe she'd found a phone and succeeded in calling Donovan. Dexter went out to his rental car, grabbed his briefcase, and returned to the house. He pulled out Lauren's cell phone and turned it on. As he'd suspected, she had the data on a number of calls stored from before he'd turned it off. And two of them had a 435 area code. That would be Donovan Deru. Using his own phone, he called one of them, and it rang several times before an answering machine picked up. He listened, then left a short message, telling Donovan it was an emergency, to please call. And he gave him his own cellular number.

Then he dialed the second number with a 435 area code and listened while it rang. Finally, he heard it click.

* * *

"Hello, this is Donovan Deru," Donovan said, his eyes on Lauren. She'd already confirmed that the number being displayed was Dexter's cell phone.

"Donovan, I'm glad I reached you," Dexter said. "I've been calling all over."

Donovan nodded at Lauren and spoke to Dexter. "Is everything okay? I've tried to call Lauren, but her phone doesn't seem to be working."

"Actually, it's not okay. That's why I'm calling. I had her staying at a secure and secret location, and I thought she'd stay there while I made sure she was safe. But when I got back a few minutes ago, she was gone," Dexter said. "I'm hoping you might have heard from her."

"Why would she call me?" Donovan asked while watching the anxious face of the woman they were talking about. He stepped over beside her and signaled for her to listen, pressing the volume button to its max. He tipped the phone slightly away from his ear, and she moved her head so close to Donovan that their faces were almost touching.

"Maybe she wouldn't, but if she does contact you, you've got to convince her to come back. I think her life's in danger, and the very thought of someone hurting her is more than I can stand," Dexter said.

Donovan had the urge to tell Dexter what a liar he thought he was, but he restrained himself. "Captain Hafoko told me on the phone that the evidence she turned over wasn't exactly what she claimed it was," Donovan said.

"Unfortunately, that's true, but I'm sure that if she would talk to the captain and his people, they could work something out. Milo Thurman himself told me that all he wants is his money back. I'm afraid she may be mentally ill, Donovan, and we are all committed to getting her some help."

Donovan was aware of Lauren clenching her fists in anger. With his free hand, he took hold of one of hers and gently squeezed it while shaking his head to remind her to stay calm. "You say she's in danger. I'm confused. If she's in danger, who's it from? If she's the one stealing from the company, then it wouldn't be Royce or Fleming, would it?"

"No, it's not them," Dexter agreed. "They're angry, and I can't say I blame them, because she accused them of embezzling when it was apparently her that was doing it all along. But they understand that she's ill, and they only want to get her some help, just like the rest of us do."

This time it was Lauren squeezing Donovan's hand, and she was doing so with all her strength, expressing her frustrations in the only way she could at the moment.

"Then who would want to hurt her?" Donovan repeated.

"I hate to have to tell you this, Donovan, because I know she's your friend. And she's more than just a friend to me. I was hoping to marry her, but I have got to face up to reality here, even though it's almost killing me. And you must face that same reality."

"What are you trying to say?" Donovan asked sharply.

"She had someone helping her. I haven't been able to figure out who, but the cops tell me that the word on the street is that she double-crossed someone, and they've put a contract out on her life."

"Really!" Donovan exclaimed. "Does she know this?"

"Unfortunately, she doesn't. I just learned about it today. That's one of the things I was going to tell her when I came back and found her missing. I was hoping to be able to convince her that she had to turn herself in for her own safety."

"Do you think she'd do that if you explained it to her?"

"I think so. Even though she's ill, she'll listen to me. She knows I love her and that I only want what's best for her," he said. "And she loves me."

He wasn't sure what Dexter's motives were, but something was motivating him, and he intended to find out what it was as soon as he could.

"I wonder if she might try to e-mail me," Donovan said suddenly, curious to see if he could trick Dexter, without his knowing it, into telling another lie.

"She might. She couldn't do it from here, because there are no phone lines that work. But she might be trying it from wherever she's run off to," Dexter said.

"Does she have her laptop?" Donovan asked slyly.

"Yes, I'm sure she does. I'm glad you thought of that. Watch for a message from her, if you will."

"I'll do that," Donovan said. "I wonder what happened to her cell phone? I can't imagine her not having it with her."

There was a brief pause. Then Dexter said, "She always carries it. And I'm sure she'd have noticed by now if it were turned off. It must be broken."

Another lie, Donovan thought. Dexter knew that Lauren didn't have her phone with her. He asked one more question, "Where are you calling from? Are you in Honolulu?"

"No, I'm not, but I'd rather not say exactly where I am right now. Not that I don't trust you," Dexter said smoothly, "but I'm not taking any chances that whoever has the contract on her won't trace her here if she comes back. And she's got to do that for her own well-being."

"If she calls or e-mails me, I'll tell her," Donovan said. "She probably doesn't realize that she's not safe if she isn't with you. Maybe I better check my e-mail in case she is trying to contact me. Give me some numbers where I can reach you if I hear from her."

Dexter did that, then he said, "Tell her I'll be right here where she was staying. I'll wait for her to return."

"Okay, thanks for calling," Donovan said, and he disconnected. "Lauren, are these numbers legitimate?" he asked as stuffed the phone in his pocket.

"They are. One's to his home. One's to his office, and the third one is his cell phone, the phone he just called us on," she said. Then almost without taking a breath, she added angrily, "He's such a liar. What's in it for him? Have they offered him a reward to get me to turn myself in?"

"Could be," Donovan agreed. "That makes more sense than anything I can think of."

* * *

Dexter called another number. "Captain Hafoko, I'm sorry to report this, but Lauren's disappeared. When I got back where I'd left her, she was gone. You might want to have some officers come here and wait in case she comes back. I'd wait myself, but I have some other ideas where she may be now. My time might be best spent looking in those places."

"What makes you think she might come back?" the captain asked.

"I don't know what she'll do, but I spoke on the phone to Donovan Deru a few moments ago. He promised to tell her to return here if she calls or e-mails him. And I think she'll do what he says."

The captain agreed with that and promised to arrange for an officer to relieve Dexter there as soon as possible. Dexter smiled to himself. He had a feeling that she'd call Donovan and that Donovan would have her come here. When she did, she'd be safe, for they would arrest her. And then he could claim that he knew nothing about it when he saw her next.

In the meantime, there was something else he needed to do.

* * *

All four of them agreed that, even though two men had died when their own bomb had prematurely exploded in front of Donovan's home in Utah, they were still not safe. Donovan told the other three that he was certain Fleming and Royce would stop at nothing to ensure the success of their illegal venture. Donovan said to Vivian, "Would you be willing to talk with Captain Hafoko if he could meet you someplace safe, someplace other than at his office, and if he would give his word that he won't arrest you?"

"If you think that's a good idea, then I'll certainly do it," Vivian responded.

"After he's heard your story, then maybe he'll look deeper into this thing again. And if we can find a way to get that other disc, if it's in the bank still, then we'll be back in the driver's seat," he said confidently. "But that can all wait until tomorrow. We need some sleep tonight."

The women took one room, the men the other, but they kept the door cracked between the rooms when they all retired for the night. Donovan didn't want to take any chances. He didn't sleep well, as he kept listening for anyone who might try to break in on them. While he tossed and turned, he thought about what should be done next. And he made some decisions.

The next morning, Donovan laid his plan of action out to his three companions. They all agreed that it sounded like a reasonable plan. So Donovan called Captain Hafoko again. This time he started out by telling him that he was in Hawaii. He just didn't say exactly where in the state he was.

"What are you doing back here?" the captain asked. "Just because those two men died who tried to blow up your home doesn't mean there aren't others who might try to do the same thing."

"I'm glad you realize that," Donovan said. "I decided that if they'd try it there once, they could try it there again. So maybe I'm not in any more danger here than I am there. Anyway, I'd like to know who's behind it. If Lauren is the one who is embezzling, then why did someone try to kill her? And why would I be in danger if she's guilty? Have you thought about that? I'll tell you why they're after the two of us, Captain. It's because she's innocent and because I believe her. That gives both of us the ability to cause them great trouble."

"Please, Donovan," Captain Hafoko said, "don't think that I haven't thought long and hard about all that. But the evidence, even that which Lauren gave me, points to her as the one who was taking funds from the company."

"I wasn't aware that *she* gave you anything," Donovan said. "Didn't you say that it was Dexter and Mr. Fujimoto who brought *her* evidence to you?"

"Yes," the captain said slowly. "Oh, I see what you're thinking. But I need proof, Donovan."

"Would it help if you could talk to Ms. Vivian Likio?" Donovan asked.

"It would help a great deal, but we can't find her. Frankly, I'm expecting her body to turn up one of these days."

"You don't think Lauren killed her, do you?"

"I don't know what to think. All I know is that she's disappeared. And so has Lauren. Dexter promised he'd have her here this morning, but he doesn't have any more idea where she is than I do. He even had me put an officer in a house over in Kauai where he discovered that she'd been staying. But she hasn't shown up there."

"Maybe she's heard about the contract that's out on her," Donovan said.

"Contract? What are you talking about?" the captain demanded.

"Dexter called me on my cell phone, wondering if Lauren had called me. He said she needed to be warned that there was a contract on her and that he'd wait for her in that house you just mentioned so he could protect her from the paid killer or killers. But it sounds like he had you arrange for that protection while he went off doing who knows what," Donovan said with disgust.

"Donovan, I haven't heard anything about a contract. Dexter certainly hasn't mentioned it to me."

"Oh really? He told me he learned of that information from the cops."

"Why would he say that?" the captain asked.

"You tell me, but again, if you would talk to Ms. Likio, I think it would be helpful," Donovan said.

"I'd love to, but I'm afraid that if we find her at all, all we'll have is a dead body," the captain reiterated.

"No, you won't find a body," Donovan told him.

"How do you know that?" the captain asked sharply. "Is there something you're not telling me?"

"Yes, as a matter of fact, there is. That's why I called. Ms. Likio is very much alive. I had assumed Dexter Drake gave you this information, but clearly he did not. Ms. Likio was in a car accident the night of Dr. Mitsui's death. She was hospitalized for several days. When you verify the details with the hospital and the precinct that covered the wreck, you'll see that she can't be a suspect in the doctor's murder. But she does have firsthand information relevant to Lauren's case. And she'd like to talk to you, but she's scared, and has a right to be."

Donovan smiled as he heard the captain take a deep breath. "Okay, Deru, tell me where to meet her. You know where she's at, I presume."

"You presume correctly. And I've gotten her to agree to meet with you if you promise she'll be kept safe and not arrested," Donovan said.

"All right. You have my word."

"Good. Then fly to Kauai. An old fellow by the name of Ned Haraguchi will meet you at the airport. Go with him. And make sure you aren't followed. I don't want any harm to come to Vivian."

"Don't worry, Deru. She'll be safe. I'll arrange for a department plane. I'll call you back as soon as I know when I'll be there. You'll make sure this Ned fellow is there when I arrive?"

"You can count on it, Captain. Talk to you later," Donovan said.

"He's coming?" Lauren asked.

"He is," Donovan answered. "So we need to have Ned and Vivian find another hotel, preferably on the other side of town. You and I will stay right here at the Marriott."

After the captain called back, telling Donovan what time to have Ned at the airport in Lihue, Vivian let her hair down, put on her dark glasses, and left with Ned in search of another hotel.

After they were alone, Donovan turned to Lauren and said, "We'll get through this. You know that, don't you?"

"I believe you," she said. "Let me tell you about something that happened to me." And she proceeded to share with him the prayer she'd offered while in the house up the coast.

When she described the feeling of peace she'd felt, he said, "Now you know why the Holy Ghost is often called the Comforter."

* * *

Vivian was nervous as she waited for Ned to return with the captain. And when there finally came a knock on the door, her legs were shaking as she walked over and peered through the peephole. The person she saw was not who she had expected, which caused her legs to give way, and she collapsed to the floor. A minute later the door opened, and Dexter Drake walked in.

CHAPTER 22

Vivian opened her eyes to find Dexter Drake, along with someone she didn't recognize, leaning over her. She struggled to get up, unable to find her voice.

"Thanks for your help," Dexter said to the other man. "I think she'll be fine now. She hasn't been feeling well and must have just passed out."

"Call the front desk if you need any further assistance," the man said. He shut the door behind him as he left.

"I'm looking for Lauren Olcott, and I believe you know where she is," Dexter said firmly. Vivian tried to speak but her voice was weak, and she was so frightened she thought she'd faint again. "Here, drink this. I'm not going to hurt you," Dexter said.

She sipped at the water, and after a minute or two, she was able to speak. "How did you find me?" she asked fearfully. All she could think of was Lauren. She was determined to protect her at any cost.

"I have a friend at the police department here. I had him on the lookout for you and the car you rented," he said. "He recently saw the car leaving here, but with only one occupant. I followed a hunch and came here."

"But how did you—" she began again as her mind raced to find a way she could keep this resourceful man from finding Lauren.

"Ms. Likio," he said, "let me help you to a chair. Then I'll explain."

Unable to find a better alternative, she accepted his help. Once she was seated, he pulled up a chair and sat facing her. "Lauren was staying at a house I arranged for her in Kapaa," he said. "She was safe there, but a neighbor said she left with someone who met your description. I figured it must be you and Ned."

"Oh," Vivian moaned.

"You should leave these sleuthing matters to the professionals," he said as he shook his head. "It could be dangerous, you know. Now, I must find Lauren immediately. She's in grave danger."

Vivian was confused. Dexter seemed sincere, and he didn't act like he was in any hurry to leave. But she still wasn't about to lead him to Lauren, even though Donovan was with her and was quite capable, she felt, of dealing with Dexter. "I know she's in danger," Vivian said. "But she's safe enough now."

"Ah, so you do know where she is," he said triumphantly.

"I didn't say that," Vivian said, knowing she'd made a grievous error. "I think you should leave," she added. "Captain Hafoko will be here shortly."

She'd thought that would rattle him, but all Dexter said was, "Good, because he and I are working together to keep Lauren alive. There is a contract out on her life, and we have got to catch the hit men before they get to Lauren."

Vivian's mind was working better with each passing moment. She almost made another slipup, but stopped herself just in time. It wouldn't be a good idea, she decided, to tell Dexter that Captain Hafoko didn't know anything about a contract, for then he would know that she knew he was lying to her.

"We'll wait for the captain," Dexter said when Vivian made it clear that she wasn't going to budge in her resolve. So he spent the next twenty minutes trying to make the older lady feel at ease with him—at least that's the way she interpreted it. And she had to admit, despite herself, that she was beginning to warm up to him. He seemed to be genuinely concerned about Lauren, and he spoke very kindly of the young woman. Vivian began to understand why Lauren had been drawn to him.

When Captain Hafoko and Ned finally arrived, Vivian was feeling fairly comfortable with Dexter, and she felt even better when the captain said, "Looks like you're on the right track here, Dexter. I assume you're still trying to find Lauren. And I appreciate it. I just learned a little while ago that there is a contract on her life."

"Yes, I know," Dexter said. "One of your officers told me that yesterday." He paused for just a moment, and then he added, "I just wish I knew who was behind it."

"So do I," the captain said. "I now have men looking into that, but so far without success. I was hoping you had located her. But I take it you still don't know where Lauren's at."

"I haven't a clue, but I think these two know," Dexter said.

"I came to question Ms. Likio," the captain said. "And that's what I intend to do. If I find Lauren, I'll let you know."

"Thanks," Dexter said, but Vivian could see that wasn't the answer he wanted, and he was clearly unhappy with the captain. Dexter turned to her once more and said, "Please, Ms. Likio, she's in danger. If you won't tell me, then tell the captain where she's hiding."

Dexter had softened her up, but not to the point of giving up any information about Lauren. So she smiled and said, "Lauren's a very good person. It sounds like we're all interested in her well-being. I'm sure she'd be glad to know of our concern, poor girl. It's been nice meeting with you, Dexter."

After the captain had dismissed Dexter and he had finally left, the captain asked, "Did you tell him you were here?"

"No, he found us," she said, then hastily added, "quite by accident."

Over the next hour, Vivian told the captain her story, all but the part about knowing where Lauren was presently staying. She told him of Fleming's visits and of his attempt to inject Lauren. He seemed quite impressed when she told him how they managed to fight him off with the vases the roses had come in. She told him about binding Fleming with tape and leaving him there when she and Lauren went to find a motel. Finally, she admitted that she'd tried to return to get the poisoned cherry chocolates. Then she told him that she never made it because of the car wreck that left her unconscious, and next thing she knew, she woke up in the hospital.

"So where have you been the past few days?" the captain asked.

"I've been with friends," she said truthfully. "I was afraid for my life, and I still am. The only reason I'm even talking to you is that I am appalled Lauren is being accused of being a criminal, and I think you should know the truth."

"Can you tell me where Miss Olcott is now?" Captain Hafoko suddenly asked.

"No, I can't," she said with a straight face.

"Or you won't," the captain said with an equal lack of expression. Then he added, "You've been a great deal of help. But please remember this, if you do happen to hear from Miss Olcott and fail to let me know, you could be charged with obstructing justice."

Vivian felt just a twinge of guilt and worry, but she knew that she'd go to jail before she'd ever let that dear girl be placed in the path of danger again.

"Mr. Haraguchi, if you'd be so kind, I'd like to return to the airport now," Captain Hafoko said. "My pilot will be getting anxious to get back. I pulled him from another assignment."

As soon as Ned and the captain left, Vivian called Donovan and recounted the morning's events in some detail. The confirmation from Captain Hafoko that there was indeed a contract out on Lauren's life brought an exclamation of extreme concern from Donovan. He gave Vivian some instructions, and then she disconnected and settled in to wait for Ned's return.

* * *

After watching Ned drive away from the airport, Captain Hafoko called the local police department. Then he told the pilot to wait for him. "I have some unfinished business here. I might have to return to Honolulu at a moment's notice. And I could have another passenger or two."

"I'll be here," the pilot said with a yawn.

A few minutes later, a detective in an unmarked car picked up the captain. Together, the two officers drove back through Lihue.

* * *

Royce and Fleming were meeting again in Fleming's office. The door was closed and they spoke in low voices.

"Time is of the essence," Fleming said. "Unless our men find Lauren and silence her before the cops arrest her, things could get messy for us. We've done a good job of turning the tables on her, but I'm afraid now that it's not going to be enough. Someone smart enough could still figure out what we've done. And Lauren is smart enough."

"But surely she couldn't do it very quickly," Royce said.

"Maybe a couple of days," Fleming guessed. "And that's only if the cops let her dig into the company's affairs, which I doubt they would, but we can't take the chance."

"Maybe when those two we sent to Utah get back, we can put them on the job as well," Royce suggested. "By the way, what's taking them so long?"

"I told them not to rush it, to make sure they do it right this time," Fleming told him. "And I told them not to check back with us until Saturday." He smiled wickedly. "That way they won't get the rest of the amount we agreed upon."

"You old devil," Royce said with a grin. "We'll be gone by then."

"That's right, and who will they complain to when they can't find us to get their money?" As he spoke, Fleming had turned to his computer. "Just to be sure, let's check the Internet and see if there's anything about Donovan Deru meeting an untimely end in Vernal, Utah."

Royce sat back with his arms folded across his chest, thinking about the easy life that lay ahead of him in Argentina. Already, a new identity had been prepared, a passport obtained under his soon-to-be name, and airline tickets purchased. He would be leaving Friday evening, on a different flight and to a different destination than his collaborators.

He was jarred from his daydreaming by Fleming. "Royce, it says here that two unidentified men died in the explosion of a homemade bomb in Vernal on Monday night. However, both men were believed to be from Hawaii. They hope to have them identified soon."

"What!" Royce said in alarm. "Did they fail to kill Deru?"

"Looks like it. Apparently the explosion was in the street in front of his house. He wasn't home at the time."

"The bumbling fools," Royce growled.

"It gets worse," Fleming said. "The writer of this article says he attempted to contact Mr. Deru, but that he'd apparently left the area. He even said that his secretary refused to comment on his whereabouts, but it appears she has arranged for other attorneys to cover his work for several days."

"It's possible that he's running scared, but from what we've seen of him so far, he's probably over here," Royce said. "He could be trouble."

"Unless our new men can find him first. I'll find our guys and give them new instructions," Fleming said angrily as he shut down his computer. "And they better perform."

"It'll cost us more," Royce complained.

"What's a measly ten or fifteen thousand?" Fleming reminded him. "We're about to become very wealthy men. I'll talk to you tonight. Usual place, usual time. We'll go over the final arrangements then."

Royce asked if any of the others would be there.

"No, I didn't tell them we were meeting," Fleming said.

"Why didn't you tell them?" Royce asked.

Fleming shared another mirthless smile. "You and I have done most of the work. We've taken all the risks. I was thinking that perhaps this would be a good time to cut them out. We can finish up without them, and they won't know until it's too late," Fleming said smugly.

"But we've already purchased their airline tickets, and we've already got money banked overseas using their new identities."

"You and I have ours. I took the liberty of changing a few things. They have nothing, Royce. We each have a bigger split. And believe me, they won't know what we're doing."

"Why didn't you mention this before?" Royce asked, wondering what other changes Fleming might have made that he didn't know about.

* * *

Fleming was a believer in the principle of only giving out the exact amount of information someone needed to do the job they were hired for and nothing more. He had confidence in the two men he'd hired recently. He hadn't told them that they were not the first to be given this assignment, nor, when he contacted them in a few minutes to add Donovan to their contract, would he tell them what had happened to that first unfortunate pair.

Fleming contacted the men who'd been searching for Lauren. He told them they would now be looking for two people. He gave them the details they needed and then said, "You know what to do when you find them."

* * *

Donovan answered the phone as soon as he felt it vibrate. "Donovan, this is Captain Hafoko. The interview with Ms. Likio went well."

"Does that mean that Lauren is no longer a suspect?" he asked.

There was a pause, long enough for Donovan to feel like his stomach did a somersault. "It means that it looks much better for her. Unfortunately, there is still the matter of an illegal transfer of two million dollars from a company account to her personal account."

"What will it take to convince you?" Donovan asked angrily. "She's been framed. That should be obvious to you. It certainly is to me."

"If there was something that dated back to before that money transfer showing that the men she accused did in fact radically alter the company's records and make unauthorized contracts like she said they'd done, that would probably do it."

"You don't ask for much, do you? That's what Lauren's records were supposed to show, but apparently they didn't," Donovan said. "Any sign of Lauren yet?"

"I'm getting close, I think. I found out after I talked to you this morning that there is a contract out on her, according to an informant. But I suppose Ms. Likio already told you that."

"Yes, she did," Donovan said. "Ms. Likio also told me about Dexter finding her. I told you before, I don't trust that man."

"I don't think he's dangerous, Donovan. Now, if you learn anything more, let me know," the captain said.

"Sure thing," Donovan agreed, debating if he should tell him that Lauren was right here with him. But he was still afraid that she might end up in jail, and he wasn't about to let that happen. He decided to say nothing about her location yet.

"Was that Captain Hafoko?" Lauren asked a moment later.

"It was, and I have a gut suspicion that he's watching Vivian and Ned, hoping they'll lead him to you," Donovan said. "It's good we told them to stay put for now."

"What are we going to do?" Lauren asked. "We've got to get to my bank. If we don't stop them now, Fleming and Royce will have maneuvered things to the point that the company can't be saved even if they were to be arrested. I've been thinking the past few minutes, and if I remember right, there was something in what I found that indicated that Friday is the day that the company will essentially collapse. Paradise should be receiving money on the cosmetics deal, but the money will be diverted. And contracts with suppliers and the advertising company that Fleming keeps putting off will become past due, and on top of all that, there's payroll. Fleming and Royce will disappear, and Milo will find that there is nothing to pay with. After that, Paradise Pharmaceuticals will be essentially bankrupt."

"And today is Wednesday. Lauren, I hate to even suggest what I'm thinking, because it will place you at risk," Donovan said.

"I know what you're thinking, and I'm ready to do it," she said solemnly. "Let's go back to Honolulu and see if I really did leave a disc in the bank like I think I did."

"But there's a known contract on your life," he reminded her. "This frightens me for you, more than ever."

"They've tried before and failed," she said. "We've got to take the chance. Let's go before I chicken out. Together, you and I can do this."

* * *

"It's Donovan," Vivian said to Ned as she looked at the digital readout on the borrowed cell phone.

"Then answer it," he said.

She did, and for over a minute she listened. Then she said, "I'll do whatever you say. If Lauren trusts you, so do we."

"What did he want?" Ned asked. "Is there something else we can do?"

"There is. He wants us to go back to the other hotel. He and Lauren have already left. He checked out of room 405. Your things are in my room. He thinks we'll be followed, but it'll probably only be the captain. He wants us to admit that Lauren was there when we left but that we don't know where she went. We're not to mention that Donovan was also there."

Ned raised an eyebrow. "Why does he want us to do that?"

"To give him time to take Lauren someplace else is all he would tell me," Vivian explained.

"Did he tell you where they were going?"

"No, so that way we don't have to lie about her. We don't know where Lauren's at anymore."

* * *

It seemed like forever before they landed in Honolulu. "We'll rent a cab," Donovan suggested. "Safer and faster that way." He didn't want Lauren exposed to the public any longer than was absolutely necessary. With the death of the two thugs in Vernal, Fleming and Royce might have turned to more professional killers. That thought gave him something more to worry about. He'd have to be more alert than ever.

Lauren clung to his arm as they hurried to find a cab, carrying only her purse and his laptop computer. "What about our luggage?" she asked.

"They'll keep it when we don't pick it up. We can get it later, when it's safer."

He breathed a sigh of relief when they were tucked safely inside a cab. He gave the driver the name of the bank and sat back next to Lauren.

* * *

Two men in dark suits with slight bulges beneath their coats ran into the airport. They checked the monitors. "Their plane's already landed," one of them said.

"They had luggage," the second one remarked. "We'll locate them at the luggage carousels and follow them out of the airport."

"That works. But if they happen to split up, you take the man," the older of the pair said. "I'll take care of the woman. Just make sure it isn't near the airport. There are too many cop types around here."

The second nodded an acknowledgment. They had worked together for several years. They never argued when on a job, and they understood one another very well.

They stood back for a minute and watched as luggage rolled onto the carousel. "There were only forty passengers on that flight," the younger man whispered. "The luggage is going fast, and I don't see anyone here that fits their descriptions."

In a couple of minutes, all but two suitcases were gone. The older man stepped up to the carousel and grabbed one of the two remaining bags. He examined it for just a moment and dropped it. Then he grabbed the second one. He also dropped it and turned to his partner. "Looks like they don't want their luggage. Let's split up and start checking car rental agencies. We can't afford to lose them. Our contact said the final payment would be double if we got them today."

* * *

The cab delivered Donovan and Lauren to the bank. Donovan felt like a sitting duck as he paid the cab driver. Then, holding tightly to Lauren's hand, he led her inside at a fast walk. She was trembling ever so slightly as she presented her ID and made her request. A moment later, she was told, "This way, ma'am."

"I'll need to come too," Donovan said. "I'm her lawyer."

"Sorry—bank policy—you'll have to wait."

"I'll hurry," Lauren said.

"I'll be right here," Donovan promised.

She'd been gone only a couple of minutes, but it seemed like an hour. Donovan kept glancing around nervously, then he'd watch the door she disappeared through. There was a disturbance at the front doors. Donovan glanced that way and saw someone he didn't want to see, and who he hoped wouldn't see Lauren. He hurried that way, trying to think of something to say.

Few words were exchanged before a shot rang out.

CHAPTER 23

Lauren had offered a silent prayer of thanks. She'd found the backup disc mixed in with several documents and several other discs in the safety-deposit box. She'd placed it carefully in her purse, making sure it was secure. She had just locked the safety-deposit box and returned it to its place when she heard what she was almost certain was a gunshot in the main lobby. Her heart jumped into her throat, and she ran from the vault and into the lobby. Donovan wasn't standing where he'd promised to wait, and a cold chill settled over her. Though most people were scurrying toward the exits, a crowd had gathered across the lobby. She could see a pair of feet lying on the floor and she knew someone had been shot. She rushed to the crowd, determined to find out who was on the floor and at the same time not wanting to know. She shoved her way to the prostrate body on the floor and nearly fainted. Donovan, who was covered with blood, was struggling to sit up, shaking his head. He looked up when she called to him.

When he saw her, he shouted, "Run, Lauren. Get away from here!"

She was only vaguely aware of a second man. He was also on the floor, flat on his back, but a half-dozen crouching men hid that second man from her full view. Anyway, it was only Donovan that mattered.

"Go, Lauren, go!" Donovan continued to shout.

But she couldn't leave him. "Not without you," she said, totally ignoring any danger to herself. He struggled to get up, reaching for her hand. "Then pull," he urged.

There was blood on his jacket, on his face, even a little on his hands. But she grabbed hold and helped him to his feet. He looked around and then shouted, "Get down!" He lunged at her and literally dragged her to the floor as another bullet flew through the lobby.

There was an instant mass of confusion as the remaining people scattered everywhere. The security guards, who had previously been trying to determine the source of the shot, now gave chase. She started to get up, but Donovan tugged at her. "Stay down," he ordered as he sat up and glanced at the scattering crowd. "They've got him," he said a second later, and the two of them got to their feet. "Let's go. Fleeing the scene has become a very bad habit of mine, but I don't dare stick around."

The wail of a siren cut through the humid air and the shouting, screaming, and cursing of the crowd. Donovan swayed on his feet, and Lauren put an arm around him.

"Hey, buddy, there's an ambulance coming," a bystander shouted with concern.

"I'm okay; save it for him," Donovan replied, pointing to the prostrate man almost hidden by those who were again swarming around to give him aid. Donovan reached down and picked up the case containing his laptop computer.

"They've got the shooter," the bystander said again. "There's help—"

"I'm fine. They can help him!" Donovan interrupted, and he and Lauren hurried away from the growing crowd, across the lobby, and out the other side.

* * *

Ellen had gone alone to visit some of the sights. Kaelyn sat in her hotel in Chicago and thought about Donovan. Kaelyn knew that she'd made the breakup with him very final. She hadn't given him a chance to explain himself, or even to argue with her over why she should keep his ring.

She'd been so angry that as soon as she and Ellen had finished breakfast on Tuesday morning, she'd mailed Donovan's ring back to him. She didn't even bother to insure it, not caring if it got lost in the mail. That was his problem, she'd thought. But now, whenever she looked at her hand, the absence of the ring was sobering.

Kaelyn was on the phone when Ellen came in a few minutes later after her most recent foray into the city. When she hung up, Ellen asked, "Did you call Donovan?"

"No, I was talking to my mother," she said.

"Did you tell her that you broke up with Donovan?"

"Yes, and she cried. She likes Donovan. I was so stupid, Ellen. I should have listened to you then, but I was so angry that all I could think of was hurting Donovan. Well, I'm the one that's hurt," she admitted. "In spite of everything I said before, I've decided I'm going to marry him after all."

"Kaelyn, you are my best friend, and I don't want to hurt you, but I think you better back up and think about this," Ellen cautioned.

"What's there to think about?" Kaelyn asked. "I was wrong for getting so mad at him. As soon as I see him, I'll apologize and tell him the wedding's still on."

"You were pretty final with him, Kaelyn. He might have accepted what you said and moved on," she said.

"Moved on? What do you mean by that? There isn't time enough for him to have moved on," Kaelyn argued. "It was only yesterday morning that I talked to him."

"And you told him it was over," Ellen reminded her. "He might not want to risk taking you back for fear you would do something like that again."

"I wouldn't do that, Ellen. I've learned my lesson."

"Maybe, but he doesn't know that."

"But I just told you, I'll tell him I'm sorry, that it will never happen again, and that I love him. He loves me, Ellen. He'll understand."

"Kaelyn," Ellen said firmly, "I think you might be wrong. You let him know that you don't trust him. You hurt him. And you let him know in no uncertain terms that you were through with him."

"But you're the one who kept telling me what a great catch he was and to not let him get away," Kaelyn whined.

"Yes, but you didn't listen. You're the one who broke it off. I have a feeling it's too late now."

"No it isn't," Kaelyn argued. "It'll still work out for the two of us. You'll see."

"I hope you're right, that you aren't setting yourself up to get hurt all over again, and to hurt him all over again."

Kaelyn said, "Well, I'll show him I love him. I'll convince him I've changed."

Ellen shook her head sadly.

"Oh, I get it. You think he likes that other girl."

"I don't know if he does or not, but you certainly opened the door for him," Ellen told her.

"You're wrong. You'll see," Kaelyn said. "I'll let him know I still care in a way that will impress him."

"Oh? So what are you going to do?" Ellen asked suspiciously.

"I'm going to Hawaii," Kaelyn announced. "I'm sorry to do this to you, but you'll have to drive home alone."

"Kaelyn, are you nuts? You can't afford a trip to Hawaii," Ellen argued.

"I'll use my credit card," she said stubbornly. "I'm going."

* * *

At Captain Hafoko's insistence, Vivian and Ned had been sent back to Honolulu with a young detective by the name of Jason Salter. He took them to their homes, with orders to get them into a safe house.

"I hate to leave Tommy alone again," Vivian said.

"He won't be alone. I'm staying here," Ned announced.

"But the captain said you both needed protection," Jason argued.

"I'm fine here. It's Vivian they're after," Ned insisted.

"Ned, I don't want you to be here alone," Vivian said sadly.

"I'll be fine," Ned said. "Anyway, someone has to take care of Tommy, and they won't let him live at the safe house."

They moved around to the back of the house, where the thick trees and shrubbery hid them from the highway and the neighboring yards. Vivian stuck the key in her door and let out a little squeal. "What's the matter?" Detective Salter asked as he rushed toward her.

"It's been forced open," she said, leaning against the door frame as her legs became weak. "Someone's been in my house." Tommy immediately rushed to Vivian, purring loudly.

"Stand back," the officer said as he pulled his gun and stepped inside.

He was gone for only a minute or two. When he came back outside, he said, "There's no one in there, but they've made kind of a mess of your house, ma'am. I don't know what they were looking for or if they found it, but I'm afraid they've done some damage. They've broken some furniture, tipped a few things over, that sort of thing. Looks more like the damage someone might do who was angry than someone who was searching for something, but I could be wrong."

Vivian's heart sank, but when she went in, it wasn't as bad as she'd feared. Her furniture was old anyway, and she'd been thinking about buying a few new pieces. She automatically began to straighten things up, but Ned interrupted and said, "Vivian, my dear, I'll clean things up here a little bit. You need to hurry along."

"Actually, I'll need to ask you both to leave things as they are. We'll need to do an investigation before you can move things," Detective Salter said.

She knew he was right. Anyway, there was time to take care of her house later. She went into her bedroom and shut the door just as the officer's phone rang. When she came out a minute later, she could see from the frown on Ned's face that something she wouldn't like was going on. Detective Salter spoke quickly. "It's probably not related, but there's been a shooting in the bank where Miss Olcott has her account. The captain wants me to deliver you to the safe house immediately and head over there."

Vivian had to bite her tongue to keep from asking if Lauren or Donovan were involved. She didn't know where they'd gone, but it seemed likely that the bank could be a destination. Instead she asked, "Was anyone hurt?"

"Witnesses said that two men were injured," Jason said. "I don't know who either one of them is. One is on his way to a hospital. The other one fled the scene with a young woman. Both men may have been shot. The shooter is in custody. Are you ready to go?"

Vivian was, but she was trembling when she bade Ned good-bye and left the house. "Everything will be okay," he promised as she climbed into the unmarked car.

* * *

"I'm not hurt, Lauren," Donovan insisted again. "I don't know if the first bullet was meant for me or him—me probably, but he caught it. The second bullet might have even been meant for you. There's no way of knowing. Anyway, none of this is my blood except for the little bit on the back of my head where I hit the floor when I fell."

They were in a public rest room several blocks from the bank, trying to get as much blood off themselves as they could. But Donovan's jacket was ruined. He finally emptied the jacket's pockets into a pocket of his computer case and stuffed the jacket in a trash can. The small scalp wound had stopped bleeding, and Lauren cleaned it with cold water.

She'd gotten some blood on her blouse, but it had washed out fairly well. Finally, having done all they could do, they stepped cautiously out and checked around them. They couldn't help but be nervous, despite the fact that Donovan had seen some men drag the shooter to the ground. Seeing no imminent threat, they walked quickly to the street and hailed a taxi. "Are you two okay?" the driver asked, obviously noting the stains they couldn't get rid of.

"I got a really bad bloody nose," Donovan said quickly. "I got it all over both of us. Now we need a change of clothes. We flew in today and our luggage is lost. Would you take us to a clothing store and wait while we pick up a few things? Then you can take us to our hotel."

They didn't have a hotel at the moment, but Donovan thought it would be better if they didn't mention that until they were back in the car. Less than an hour later, they were safely locked into a pair of adjoining hotel rooms, booked under fictitious names. Both of them let out a sigh of relief before going to their respective bathrooms to clean up. Donovan was the first one to finish dressing in the newly purchased clothing. He plopped down on the bed in his room and waited. Five minutes later, Lauren knocked on the door that joined their rooms, and Donovan invited her in.

"So, will you finally tell me what exactly happened at the bank?" she asked. He still hadn't told her who the man was who had been shot.

"First things first," Donovan said.

She wanted to know the details but knew she'd have to trust him on this. "Okay, so what's first?" she asked.

"The disc. Let's pop it in my laptop and have a look," he said.

With Lauren explaining what they were looking at on the screen, he felt a thrill of hope wash over him. What she had previously described was all there. Dexter had definitely delivered something other than her disc to the captain. Donovan's biggest question now was why. It was Lauren's biggest question too, and she said, "Why did Dexter take something different to the captain? Is he in on the scam? Or is it his boss?"

"I don't know. For right now, let's get this to the captain."

"Oh, Donovan, I don't think we better. I don't dare go downtown again," she said.

He smiled at her. "There is another way."

"Oh no, I don't want anyone else but us to deliver it," she said. "I trusted Dexter and look where it got me."

"Actually, I was thinking about e-mailing it," Donovan said.

Lauren began to laugh. "It never occurred to me to do it the easy way."

"You have rather a lot on your mind, and after your first attempt to e-mail this, I can't blame you for not thinking of it now," Donovan said gently as he began to connect to the Internet.

"Let me," Lauren said. "I'll send it. We don't want the captain to know I'm with you right now, do we?"

"You're right," he agreed.

So while Donovan called the police station to get the e-mail address, Lauren typed a lengthy message to Captain Hafoko, explaining to him what to look for in the information she was sending. Then she attached the files from the disc and sent them to him from a newly created e-mail address.

"Now, just to be on the safe side, let's also send it to my office in Vernal. The more copies of this there are around, the better it will be," Donovan suggested. So he sat down and sent it off with a note to Mrs. Olsen to back it up on their hard drive and another disc when she opened her e-mail the next morning.

"What about Milo Thurman and Ken Fujimoto?" Lauren asked.

"Can't hurt to send it to them as well," he agreed.

So once more, Lauren sat down at the computer. She looked up Milo's e-mail address on the company Web site, then she sent the information to the president of Paradise Pharmaceuticals and the head of the law firm Dexter worked for. That done, Lauren and Donovan ordered room service and relaxed the best they could while waiting for replies to the e-mails they'd sent.

The first to respond to Lauren's e-mail was Milo Thurman. He'd written a short message asking Lauren to please call him. He also wrote, *I'm sorry I ever doubted you. I need your help. Please don't let me down.*

She was so hopeful that she reached for the phone beside her bed. Donovan, who was lying down in the adjoining room, heard her dial. "No, don't!" he called out in alarm as he scrambled from the bed.

Lauren slammed the phone down, and a moment later Donovan rushed in. "Who were you calling?" he asked, trying to be gentle after having shouted so loudly.

"Milo Thurman. Look, he e-mailed me. He wants me to call," she said.

"That's great, but you can't do it from here. It might give away our location," Donovan said.

"Oh, Donovan, I'm sorry," she said. "It was just so nice seeing that someone believes me. I guess I'm still not thinking very clearly. What should we do? I really think it would help if I could talk to him now."

"There's a pay phone in the lobby. Let's slip down and call from there," he suggested. "And let's take your purse and the computer with us," he added as an afterthought.

"Why? We'll only be a minute," she said.

"I don't know why," he said. "I just think we should." He knew it sounded absurd, but he also knew the feeling, and he wasn't about to ignore it.

They rode the elevator from the tenth to the first floor, where they located the pay phone. It was in a hallway off the main lobby. While Lauren made her call, Donovan kept checking the lobby. The feeling he'd had as they'd left the room intensified. He ducked out of sight when two men in dark business suits entered the lobby. They spent a few minutes at the registration desk. He was too far away to hear what they were saying and only dared peek around the corner occasionally for fear of being seen. But one of the times he looked, he saw one of the men pass some cash to one of the hotel attendants, who stuffed the money in a shirt pocket before saying something to the men.

Donovan ducked out of sight again. When he looked a moment later, the two men had entered the elevator. He watched the lights as it went up. When it stopped at the tenth floor, he was almost positive that they were looking for either him or Lauren—or both.

He stepped back to the phone booth. "Hurry," he whispered. "We've got to get out of here."

Lauren reacted to the urgency in his voice. "Thank you, Mr. Thurman," she said. She listened for a moment more, then she added, "No, I don't think I better tell anyone where I'm at right now. I believe my life is in danger. I've got to run. Talk to Captain Hafoko, will you please?" After that she hung the receiver up and stepped close to Donovan, taking hold of his hand. "What is it?" she asked.

He told her, and her face lost its color. "How did they find us so fast?"

"I could be wrong," he said. "It might be a coincidence."

"You don't believe that," she said, "and neither do I. Let's go."

They hurried toward the front exit. But Donovan stopped briefly at the registration desk. He spoke to the young fellow who had taken money from the two men. "How much did they give you to tell them what rooms we were in?" he asked, his deep voice reverberating with anger.

The look of guilt that crossed the attendant's face before he denied that he'd done any such thing was all Donovan needed. He then turned to the other desk attendant and said, "We'll be going now. This young man will pay for our rooms since he just sent two men up there to kill us. He can use the money they gave him. It's in his shirt pocket."

He looked back as he and Lauren hurried through the front doors. There was quite a scene going on at the desk. He'd have liked to have seen how it ended, but there wasn't time. Another taxi took them north to a rental car company. They had to wait there for what seemed like an eternity. But finally they were on their way to Laie, which was almost at the far end of the island from Honolulu. On the way, Lauren told Donovan that Milo Thurman was desperate. "He needs my help to see if he can save the company, he told me. He wants me to meet with him."

"As soon as we're sure you're totally cleared and safe," Donovan said, "it'll be okay to do that. But right now, your life is far more important to me than Milo Thurman's company. After all, he chose to believe the word of a couple of thieves over yours. And who knows, he could be part of it."

"What!" Lauren said.

"You heard me. Until this is all over, you aren't meeting with anyone in the company, including Milo."

She was thoughtful for a moment, and then she said, "I guess anything's possible, but I really hope he's not involved."

They drove for nearly an hour, going north up the coast. They found a room at the Laie Inn near the Church-owned Polynesian Cultural Center, and once again they got Donovan's laptop computer out and accessed the e-mail. This time there was a message from Captain Hafoko. He'd written,

> Please contact me right away. This is the information I've been after. My computer specialists say that the stuff the lawyers brought me was bogus. We need to meet. We can't let those men get away. I need your help tonight, Miss Olcott. And tell Mr. Deru that I'd like him there as well. I know that he's with you.

"I guess it's time to take another risk," Donovan said. Using his cellular phone, he called the captain.

"Donovan, I'll meet wherever you and Lauren would like. This information is dynamite."

But Donovan wasn't ready to take that chance yet. He named the hotel they'd been in just an hour ago. "I left there in a hurry. Two men were on the way to our rooms on the tenth floor. I watched them pay off a man at the registration desk. I was in room 1055, Lauren in 1053. You won't recognize the names. Anyway, these men are clearly still tracking us. When I know it's safe, then we'll talk."

"Hold on," Captain Hafoko said. "I'll send people there right now."

When he came back on the line, he said, "We'll see that you're safe. Name the place."

"Catch those men, then we'll talk. In the meantime, you could be looking for Royce and Fleming," Donovan suggested.

"We already are. But we don't have a clue who those paid assassins are, if that's what they are."

"Get Fleming and Royce in. Ask them who they hired." Quietly he put the phone down and looked at Lauren. She looked tired and nervous.

"Hey, we're making progress," he said cheerfully.

A half hour later it turned dark outside. Lauren quit pacing the floor and said, "Let's take a walk. I'm going crazy in here."

"It could be dangerous out there," Donovan said.

"What would have happened if we'd stayed in our rooms earlier?"

Donovan saw her point and said, "Should we walk over to the temple grounds?"

CHAPTER 24

The scent of sweet blossoms drifted through Ned Haraguchi's open bedroom window. He'd gone to bed early but had been unable to sleep as he worried about Vivian, Lauren, and Donovan. Finally, he climbed out of bed, pulled on a pair of slippers, and called to Tommy. The big cat stirred at the foot of his bed.

"Come on, old fellow, let's go out and sit on the back porch," he said softly. He got to his feet and left the bedroom. He could feel Tommy brushing his leg as he stepped slowly through the darkness toward his back door. There was just enough moon outside to give a little light in the house, so he didn't disturb the night with unneeded artificial light. "Whenever I get restless, it does me good just to go outside and smell the blossoms in my yard, listen to the sound of the ocean, and enjoy the cool peace of the night," he explained to Tommy.

Once on the porch, he closed his door and sat down in an old armchair he kept there for just this purpose. He hadn't been there long before an unnatural sound came from next door, Vivian's house. It sounded like the opening of a door. Suddenly alert and slightly worried, he rose to his feet and stepped down from his porch and into his garden.

He moved slowly and silently toward Vivian's yard, stepping into the shrubs and avoiding the sidewalk. He listened for more unusual sounds as he crept forward, carefully parting the branches in an attempt to avoid making any noise and to keep from dislodging the highly scented blossoms as he passed through his plants. He heard another sound, and this time he was certain it was the closing of Vivian's back door.

The hair began to rise on the back of his neck, and a prickle of fear ran all the way down his spine. At every slow and deliberate step, Ned experienced growing—but what he tried to tell himself was unreasonable—fear. What had for years been a pleasant sanctuary to Ned became a garden of terror as he heard the soft noise of what could only be the shuffling of feet near Vivian's back door.

A wave of affection washed over him as he thought about her being safely tucked away under the protection of the police. He was glad she wasn't home, but he couldn't help but wonder what kind of further damage might have been inflicted to her home or what might be about to occur. He began to back out of the dense shrubbery, intent on returning to his house and dialing 9-1-1.

But he stopped short, and a shiver of fear ran through him as he realized that the intruder at Vivian's was coming slowly across her lawn to the little, private gate that separated their two yards. Silently, Ned dropped to his knees and moved deeper into the dense vegetation that occupied much of his well-tended backyard. It was a fairly good hiding place, but only if no one decided to search it. Then he'd be trapped. But there was no place else to go on such short notice, so he crawled a little farther, then stopped and listened again to the progress of the invader.

Ned couldn't see anything from where he now lay, but he knew when the person had entered his yard, for he heard the gate latch as it was first opened and then clicked shut. And he knew when the person had arrived at his porch, for his wind chimes began to clang. It was not a gentle, soothing sound, but evidence that they'd been struck—evidence that Ned's home was about to be invaded.

So attuned to the progress of the intruder were Ned's ears that every other sound was shut out. He listened as the door was opened, and then as it was closed. Because his windows were open, Ned could hear the intruder moving through the house. Then he began to hear drawers opening and closing.

Ned decided that he'd never been a man of cowardice and this was not a good time to become one. He crawled from his hiding place and worked his way quickly to his porch, grabbing a shovel he'd left stuck in the dirt beside his sidewalk. Then he stood in the dark shadow beside the door.

Soon he heard the invader coming back to the door. He gripped the shovel tightly when the door opened, hiding him behind it. And he cringed when a voice spoke into his backyard. It was not a shout, not something meant to be heard by neighbors, but it was loud enough that Ned could hear it clearly.

"Mr. Haraguchi," the speaker said, "I know you're out here. Your door was open. If the nurse is with you, have her come out where I can see her. It's not you I need to talk to, just her. I don't intend to do harm to anyone."

Ned scarcely breathed, prepared to use the shovel when the man stepped a little farther onto the porch, almost to the point that he was beyond the open door that separated him from Ned. The invader spoke again, but not to Ned this time. "Vivian Likio, I'm not here to hurt you, but we need to talk about some things," he said. "I need to find Lauren before someone else does. I don't want her to be killed, and unless I find her, she will be."

There was no sound for a few moments except the slight rustle of leaves as a gentle breeze disturbed the stillness of the night and caused the vivid scents of his yard to tease his keen sense of smell. Under ordinary circumstances, Ned would have savored the pleasant aroma and breathed deeply of the scented air, but this night he ignored it, concentrating instead on the man who was standing to his right. That man spoke again. "I know you're out there," he said. "And I'm not leaving until we talk. I'll come root you out if I have to, both of you!"

There was another moment of silence. Then the old wood of the porch creaked and Ned raised the shovel, afraid that the invader was about to carry out his threat. In the dim light, Ned saw the man raise his foot to step just as Tommy moved in front of him. When his foot came down, it accidentally struck the cat, who let out a shrill shriek of protest. The man stumbled forward in surprise, the cat shot away, and the wind chimes sang out when the man's head struck them. The invader cursed, a vile, threatening sound that carried through the night, and then Ned brought the shovel down firmly on the back of his head.

There was a loud crash as the man tumbled forward and off the porch, crushing some of Ned's beautiful flowers. The trespasser's head and outstretched arms landed on the unforgiving concrete of the sidewalk. Ned turned on his porch light, and while still holding his shovel threateningly in his hands, he stepped off the porch and took a closer look at the injured man. His head was bleeding profusely, dark blood pooling on the gray cement, some of it fertilizing the desecrated flowers. Ned also saw the shattered remnants of his pride and joy, a porcelain statue of a ship's captain that had stood overlooking his yard from a perch just in front of the porch.

"Ned, are you all right?" came the voice of a neighbor. "I've never heard such a noise at this time of night."

"Someone broke into my house," Ned said. "Would you mind calling the police before he regains consciousness?"

Instead, the neighbor came running over and saw for himself that the burglar was indeed out cold and that Mr. Haraguchi was no longer in danger. "Ned," he said, "you go call the police. I'll tie this man up so he can't go anywhere except with the cops."

"Thank you, Bentley," Ned said, and he hurried to a phone.

As soon as the call was completed, he went back outside. "Have I hurt him too badly?" he asked his neighbor, whose wife had joined him by that time.

It was the woman who answered, "Not as bad as you had a right to, Ned. I can't imagine why anyone would break into your house like this. Did he do any damage?"

Ned shook his head. "Not that I know of."

Soon Ned was kneeling beside the unconscious intruder. He finally took a close look at the bloody face and then groaned in recognition.

* * *

Donovan and Lauren had been walking for close to an hour. They'd passed through the BYU–Hawaii campus and had just come to the locked gates in front of the temple. There they both stood gazing at the magnificent structure, glowing in its blanket of artificial lighting. Not a word passed between them for a couple of minutes.

Lauren was the first to speak. "It's beautiful, but it's also something more," she said in hushed, reverent tones.

"It's a spiritual place, a house of God."

She turned her face toward him. "To think that my stubbornness made me almost miss experiencing this kind of feeling in my life," she said quietly.

"What are you feeling?" he asked.

"Peace. Even with all that's happened these past days, and all the evil that's been pursuing me—both of us, I mean. Even with all that, I feel good right now. It's like this is where I belong."

"In Laie?" he asked.

"With God," she said. "Oh, Donovan, I miss the Church."

"You'll have the Church in your life again, Lauren," he said. "And someday, you'll have the blessings of the temple."

The phone in the pocket of Donovan's new jacket began to vibrate. "I hope this is good news," he said. "I think we've both had about enough bad." He put the phone to his ear. "Hello," he said and then tensed as he listened to Ned's voice. "Ned, are you sure you're okay?" he asked, provoking a look of alarm from Lauren.

"I'm fine. The cops are here now. And Royce is conscious again. He says he was only trying to protect Lauren, that he came looking for Vivian, hoping she could help him find Lauren so he could warn her that someone is after her."

"You're not serious," Donovan said.

"Yes, quite," Ned responded.

"Did he say who's after her?"

"No, but he only wanted to warn her is what he claims."

"What did he do at your house, Ned?"

"He shuffled through all my papers and messed up some drawers, but at least he didn't find Vivian. I am so glad she's somewhere safe. I can clean up my house," Ned said quite calmly. "Will you tell Lauren?"

"I will," he promised, looking at Lauren as he spoke. She had questions in her eyes, but he mouthed, "I'll explain in a minute."

"Hey, Donovan, the captain just arrived here. He wants to talk to you," Ned said.

"Put him on."

"Donovan, are you two as tired as me?" Captain Hafoko asked.

"Or more so," Donovan said.

"Well, are you ready to meet with me yet? Mr. Cantrell is under arrest, and I think that if Lauren were to be with us when we begin to question him, he'd be more likely to talk."

"Maybe," Donovan said. "Or he'll just lawyer up and say nothing."

"He might, but we've got enough to hold him for a while, and when confronted with Lauren's evidence, I think he just might be willing to start throwing blame toward his partners. There is an assistant DA on the way over here. I think that between me and him we can convince a judge to set Cantrell's bail out of his immediate reach," the captain said. "What do you say—can I send someone to pick both of you up and give you a ride in?"

"Give me your number," Donovan said. "I'll talk it over with Lauren and call you right back."

Donovan explained everything that he'd just learned to Lauren. Then he asked, "What do you want to do?"

She nodded and said with a quivering voice, "I think it's time to meet with the captain. They may have Royce, but we've still got to stop Fleming. I think he's the brains behind the whole scam."

Donovan called Captain Hafoko back and said, "Okay, Captain, we'll meet if I have your word that you will not arrest Lauren for anything," Donovan said into the phone. "If you'll just listen and let her explain everything she knows."

"You have my word, Mr. Deru," he said formally. "This breaking and entering act of Mr. Cantrell's is the real clincher. Where do you want to meet?"

"I'm not coming back there until we have a police escort. So you'll need to come to the Mormon temple in Laie," Donovan said. "We'll watch for you. Or will it be one of your men?"

"I tell you what. Things can wait here. Your lives are more important. I'll come personally," the captain promised. "That'll give us a chance to go over some strategy before we visit with Mr. Cantrell. It'll also give my men a little time to get Royce patched up before they take him to the station. But why don't I just pick you up at your room? You do have rooms somewhere, don't you?"

"At the Laie Inn, but I think we'll let you pick us up near the temple. Then you can accompany us back to the motel. We've had enough surprises for one day. There's no point in taking more chances now."

"That's not too likely, is it?" the captain asked. "You seem to have picked a spot far enough away."

"Vernal's farther," Donovan reminded him. "They found me there."

Captain Hafoko chuckled. "Sorry. You have a good point. I'll leave right away and meet you there in a little less than an hour."

"You can't imagine the relief I feel in knowing that one of them has been caught," Lauren said to Donovan after the phone call had been completed. "Now if they can just get the others."

Donovan said, "Let's get out of sight where we can see without being seen. We've left ourselves exposed too long as it is."

Lauren nodded and followed him back into the shadows of the trees in the neighborhood of the temple. When they were finally where Donovan was convinced they wouldn't be easily seen and yet where they could watch for Captain Hafoko, he said, "I think I know who one of the others is. If I'm right, he will soon be in custody as well. For now, he's not going anywhere."

"What are you talking about?" she asked. "You can't mean Dr. Mitsui. She's dead, but I'm no longer convinced that she was ever part of it anyway."

"I have no idea about that yet, and I guess it doesn't matter too much now," Donovan said. "But I was talking about someone else, a man I believe is a co-conspirator."

"Donovan," she said sternly, "how do you know about another person? And why haven't you told me about him before now?"

"Well," he said awkwardly, "I guess I didn't think it was wise, because you would have insisted on talking to him, and that would have been risky."

Lauren showed a little temper then. "Donovan, be straight with me. Who are you talking about?"

"Are you sure you want to know?"

"Of course I'm sure," she snapped. "Why wouldn't I want to know?" Then she suddenly said, "Oh, are you thinking of Leroy? But I've suspected him all along. After all, he was the one who gave me the candy laced with drugs."

"Leroy may be involved with the scam," he said, "but I don't think so. I think he's just an insecure and excessively jealous ex-boyfriend."

"Maybe that too, but surely he wouldn't try to kill me or anyone else just because I broke up with him," she said. "That's just too much to believe."

"Maybe, but it could be an even harder stretch when you realize who the other one is," he said. "Think back to the bank."

"Was it the man who was shot that you suspect?" she asked. "Or was it the man who was shooting?" She looked puzzled for a moment, then said, "You never did tell me who was shot."

"Well, I know the man, and I can guess who the shooter was. If I'm right, then you know both of them very well. I hate to have to tell you this, but—"

"It was Dexter. One of the men was Dexter."

"Yes. I'm really sorry."

"Was he shot or was he the shooter?" she asked.

"He was shot, but I think he'll recover," Donovan told her.

"If he was the one who got shot, then that means he's not involved, right?" Lauren said hopefully.

"That's what I would have thought too, but we did speak briefly before the shooting. He told me I should go back to Utah or I'd end up with a contract on my life too. So I asked him why he wasn't worried about his own life, since he was also supposedly trying to help you. And he said, 'Oh, I'm safe. No worries there.' It was his confidence that gave him away. I could tell it wasn't just bravado. He didn't feel in danger because he is in league with Fleming. Ironically, he was shot moments later."

It was one thing to decide she wasn't in love with Dexter, but it was another thing entirely to find out he was part of a murderous embezzlement ring. She didn't want to accept it, but her doubts about Dexter's honesty and goodness had been adding up. She struggled to remain in control of her emotions as she acknowledged that Donovan was right. "It makes sense," she said, her voice trembling. "It fits. Was he there to take the other disc too?"

"I really think he was just looking for you, but that's possible," Donovan said. "Did you mention it to him sometime?"

"No, I don't think so. I didn't remember myself until you made me think harder."

"He may have considered the possibility. He probably knew you'd be thorough," Donovan said.

Lauren slowly nodded her head. "Speaking of the disc, as much as I've tried to deny it, Dexter must have given something entirely different to Captain Hafoko. And if so, then Ken Fujimoto, his boss, is also probably involved, since they took it together."

"Until we learn differently, we'll have to assume that he is," Donovan agreed.

"He must be. That would explain why nothing was done when I sent that anonymous e-mail to him," she said. "He wouldn't do anything about it if he was helping Fleming and Royce."

"That makes sense," Donovan agreed.

Lauren was quiet for a minute or two. Donovan knew she was thinking, letting things fall into place. He stood quietly beside her, watching the street from the shadows, praying that it would all soon be over and that they would be safe.

When Lauren spoke, her voice as much as her words conveyed little doubt. "Dexter was always greedy. I've known that and purposely overlooked it," she said.

Donovan turned toward her, but she wasn't looking at him. She was staring into the darkness. He looked away from her, shared that stare, and listened, knowing there was more she wanted to say.

"He used me. He never intended to marry me. He was going to take his money and run," she said.

"Maybe not. Maybe he thought he could keep his cut, act innocent, and go on with his life, and with yours," Donovan said.

"Why do you say that? Are you trying to defend him?" she said a little angrily.

"I don't know," he answered honestly. "It's just a thought I had. Do you really believe he would have ever hurt you?"

Their eyes drew themselves from darkness and met there in the shadows. "Would he have hurt me? If you mean physically, then the answer is no," she said firmly. "But I do believe that he was planning to hurt me in other ways. Dexter is not a man who loves deeply. He's too self-centered for that. I've always known that, I guess, but I just overlooked it. But he's also not a violent man."

"Consider this, then. He must have known what his partners were planning, and maybe he wanted you out of their way. Maybe that was why he was hiding you there in Kauai, because he knew they would harm you if they found you. And maybe that was why he came to the bank, to see that you were safe."

Slowly she nodded her head. "You could be right. I hope you're right," she said. "I'd like to think he wasn't as terrible as Fleming."

"I think he was out of his league plotting with Fleming," Donovan said. "Maybe he really did want the money, but also wanted to protect you."

"And maybe Fleming knew that. What if Fleming decided he was no longer useful to them?" she asked.

Donovan nodded slowly as understanding dawned. "Then they might have wanted Dexter out of the way the same way they wanted me and you out of the way," he said.

"Yes," Lauren agreed. "That's what I'm thinking. The shooter may have been hired by Fleming. How badly was Dexter injured?" she asked.

"Like I said a moment ago, I'm sure he'll live. But if that's how things were arranged, then I'm puzzled over the shooter."

"You saw him, but you only think you know who it was?"

"That's right, but he wasn't someone I'd seen before. If our theory about Fleming hiring him is right, then it doesn't make as much sense to me. Otherwise, I can see why he'd want all three of us dead, I guess. I could be wrong. I figured the man who tried to kill him was Leroy," he said. "And I'm sure he also tried to shoot you. That's why I pulled you down. Remember how the bullet went flying by?"

"Yes, I remember. Leroy . . ." she said thoughtfully. "What did he look like?"

"I didn't see him well, but he was wearing a yellow flowered shirt and tan shorts. His hair was light brown, and he would be about my height."

Slowly Lauren nodded. "That is Leroy," she said. "His favorite color is yellow. He and Dexter will both go to jail," she said, and there was sadness in her voice.

"Probably, but if Dexter will cooperate with the authorities, I'd be willing to bet that he'll get a lighter sentence. I'll even put that idea in the captain's head if you'd like."

"Please do," Lauren said. "I'd like that."

"I will. I wonder what time it is," Donovan said as he pressed the light on his watch. "The captain will be here soon. We better pay close attention. We don't want to miss him."

CHAPTER 25

The caller ID indicated that Fleming Parker was calling from his cell phone. Denise Cantrell had taken about all she could stand of the man. It seemed like all Royce did anymore was work, and she blamed it on Fleming. Royce was gone in the evenings, and he was gone on weekends. He occasionally made it home to eat with her, but then he generally seemed to have somewhere he had to be after that. If he didn't, then more often than not, Fleming would call, and off he'd go again. He always made it home to sleep at night, but it was often so late that she didn't even wake up.

She was reaching the point that she wished he'd just sleep somewhere else if that was all the interest he had in her anymore. Even the kids, when they called home, had quit asking about their father. Since they'd both graduated and moved out on their own, Royce seemed to have forgotten they existed. All that mattered was his job and the chief financial officer of Paradise Pharmaceuticals, Fleming Parker.

The phone continued to ring. Denise had the impulse to fling it across the room. But finally she did what she always did and pushed the talk button. "What do you want tonight, Fleming?" she asked.

"I need to talk to Royce. He seems to have forgotten a rather important meeting," Fleming said.

"He doesn't forget meetings," Denise argued. "Especially these after-hours ones."

"Well, he has this time. Get him on the phone."

That was what bugged Denise the most about Fleming. He always shot orders at her, like she worked for him or something. Nothing could be further from the truth. For that matter, Royce didn't work for Fleming. As rank in the company went, Royce was a rung higher as a senior vice president than Fleming was as chief financial officer. And yet it seemed like Royce was always bowing to Fleming's bidding. It made her sick. "I'd get him on the phone," she said to Fleming, "if he was here to get."

"What do you mean by that?" Fleming demanded.

"I mean he's not home," she said crisply. "What did you think I meant?" But then she added, "I'll tell him to call you when he comes in." She hung the phone up with some sense of satisfaction before the pompous man could say another word.

When the phone rang a moment later, she almost didn't pick it up, thinking it was probably just Fleming again. But when she saw a different number on the caller ID, she changed her mind. It could be one of the kids, and she'd hate to miss a call from them. Right now they were the only bright spots in her life. She picked up the phone and answered.

"Mrs. Cantrell?" the voice on the other end asked.

"I'm Mrs. Cantrell," she said.

"My name is Detective Salter. Your husband said you might be worrying about him, and he asked me to call and tell you he's all right," she was told.

That was strange, she thought. Royce hadn't been that thoughtful in years. It was more with curiosity than concern that she asked, "Why would he ask you to call? Surely he's not gotten himself into some kind of trouble, has he, Detective?"

She nearly choked when the young detective said, "Actually, I'm afraid he has. He's been arrested for two counts of burglary, two more of criminal mischief, and other much more serious charges are pending."

"Oh," she moaned. "Are you sure you have the right man?"

"Yes, we have Royce Cantrell."

"What did he break into?" she asked, rattled. "Or what did he burglarize? What I'm trying to say is, what exactly did he do?"

"He broke into a couple of homes and caused some other damage."

"I see," she said, very confused. "How did he come to be arrested?" This was all so absurd.

It got more absurd. "An old man knocked him out," the caller said. "Your husband's not here at the station yet. He suffered a mild concussion and got a couple of rather nasty cuts on his head. But as soon as the doctors are finished patching him up, he'll be brought down to be booked."

"I see," she said again. She was sure she'd never understand, and suddenly she didn't care. He was hurt, but he probably deserved it, she decided coldly. He'd certainly hurt her enough these past months.

"Bond hasn't been set yet, but when it is, he'll be allowed to call you," the detective said.

"Please tell him not to bother," Denise said bitterly. "If he's gotten himself in trouble, he can rot in jail for all I care."

"I'm sorry you feel that way," Detective Salter said.

"Please don't be," she said. "Is there anything else?"

"No, I guess not," the detective answered.

"Fine, then. Good-bye," Denise told him and cut the connection.

More puzzled than she'd ever been in her life, Denise tried to make sense of the phone call. But that couldn't be done. One thing did occur to her, however. Fleming Parker was somehow involved in this. It was probably largely his fault that Royce had done whatever stupid thing it was that had gotten him in trouble, she concluded. With that thought, she dialed Fleming's cellular phone number.

When the chief financial officer answered, he said, "About time you got home, Royce."

"I'm not Royce, and he's not home," Denise said. "And he's not coming home. He can rot in jail for all I care." And before Fleming could respond she again slammed the phone down. It gave her even more satisfaction than the first time. Now maybe she could spend the rest of the evening in peace.

* * *

Fleming flew into a rage. Here they were, just hours from wrapping up this deal, and Royce gets himself arrested, he thought bitterly. "What an idiot!" he shouted to the walls, wondering what Royce had done. He knew that Royce hadn't liked the idea of people dying, but it had seemed like he'd finally come to understand the necessity.

Fleming wondered if Royce had been drinking to drown his guilt and then had gotten himself arrested for drunk driving. Slowly, he calmed himself down. Finally, he made another call.

The phone was answered. "What do you need?"

"I need to know if you've gotten the job done," Fleming growled, "because I have another one for you if you do."

"We're trying."

"I take it that means no," Fleming said. "Can't you two get anything right? I want those two wasted before daybreak, is that clear?"

"Clear, sir. We're getting close."

"Getting close? That's what you said two hours ago, Snake. Don't get close, get done! And call me the moment they're both dead," he ordered.

"Yes, sir," the man called Snake said. "That tracking device we told you about worked to perfection. They went north. We followed them at a safe distance. They checked into the Laie Inn. They parked the car a little ways away. Thought they'd fool us, I suppose. We found where they're staying, and we got into the room without any problems, but they weren't there. We did take a laptop computer and a disc I think you're interested in."

"Smash both the computer and the disc. I don't need them, I just want them destroyed. Now, about the car—it's time to put that other device on it, if you've got it ready yet."

"It's ready now. I just had to make a few adjustments before we could use it," Snake told him.

"Then use it. Make sure they don't get away again."

"What if they don't come back?"

"They will. They don't know you're on to them, do they?"

"I don't think so."

"Keep an eye on the motel. And watch their car if you can. Maybe one of you could check around the area a little. They might just be out for an evening stroll," Fleming said sarcastically. "Whatever you do, don't you leave there until you've finished the job. Is that understood?"

"Yes, sir, it is. And what other job do you need done? It better be a quick one, because me and Luis need to split for a while when this one's finished," Snake told him.

"The next one's a piece of cake, as you would say," Fleming told him. "The target's sitting in jail at the moment. When I figure a way to spring him, I'll let you know. He needs to finish one matter for me, then I'll give you the word. He'll be a sitting duck."

"It won't be cheap," Snake said. "One job right on the heels of another is risky."

"I'll make it worth your time," Fleming promised as he began to plan how he'd get all of Royce's share of the profits, as well as that of the other conspirators. But first he needed Royce to get on the computer and finish a couple more things. That should only take a little while. Then the hired guns could have him. He wouldn't need Royce's help any further.

"Call me when you've finished," Fleming said.

Fleming was sitting in a hotel room. The last thing he had wanted tonight was to see his wife, Polly. He was tired of all her questions. He knew she suspected that he was up to something, and he wasn't about to give her the satisfaction of knowing she was right until he was far beyond her reach. The last thing he wanted was for her and the kids to come along and tell him how to spend his new wealth.

He turned on the TV even as he was wondering what he'd need to do to get Royce out of jail long enough to finish his work and give the hired men a crack at him. He watched the end of some cop show, his mind entirely absorbed by the tasks he had to complete before he could leave for Brazil on Friday. The news came on, and even then he didn't focus on it until he heard the name Dexter. That caught his attention.

He'd completely missed the first part of the report, but now the newscaster was saying, "The victim, who was shot in the head, has been identified as Dexter Drake, a well-known lawyer from a highly esteemed firm here in Honolulu."

Fleming shut the TV off and began dialing his phone again. This changed everything. He hadn't even had to offer money to get the attorney out of the way, but he wondered why his man hadn't reported in like he'd been told to do. A moment later, he had that man on the line. "Good job," he said.

"Thanks," he was told.

"Are you ready for a little more action?"

"It's been a rather busy day. I guess it depends what it is."
Fleming told him.

"I'm heading north," he said.

Fleming put down the phone and smiled in satisfaction. He'd always believed in insurance. The man he'd just sent north was insurance. Fleming couldn't have been more pleased.

* * *

Lauren was perspiring, not from heat, not from the humidity, but from nervousness. The black Ford that had just stopped a mere hundred feet from where she and Donovan were partially secluded was not what she'd been expecting to see Captain Hafoko arrive in. She'd automatically assumed that it would be a clearly marked patrol car, which it wasn't. She hesitated when Donovan whispered, "That might be the captain, although I didn't expect him quite this soon."

"It probably isn't him," Lauren answered. "Surely he'd come in a marked police car, not that."

"Either way, we'll step out there only when we know it's the captain, not before." So the two of them watched the car after slipping deeper into the darkness and pressing themselves behind the trunk of a large palm. "It looks like there's only one person in the car," Donovan observed. After a moment, the Ford moved slowly forward, then stopped again. No one got out, and Lauren became increasingly nervous.

The car started up again and continued to move at a very slow pace. Eventually it turned a corner about a block past the temple and disappeared. "That's strange," Donovan said. "I should have asked Captain Hafoko what he'd be driving. We'll wait. Maybe if it was him, he'll call my cell phone in a minute. Or maybe even if it wasn't, he will."

A minute passed, then two, then three, and eventually five. There was no call, and no more cars came by. "Donovan, I wonder who that was," Lauren said, unable to keep fear from her voice. "Surely no one would know where we're waiting for the captain."

"I hope not," he agreed. "Then again, I don't mean to scare you, but I suppose they could be listening to the police radio or they might have even somehow found the frequency of my cell phone and listened to me talk to the captain."

Lauren shivered. "Then they could know we're waiting for him near the temple," she said softly. "Let's move from here."

"Okay, but we need to hurry," Donovan said. They walked several blocks toward the north edge of town, pausing each time they had to cross a street, and when they were sure it was clear, darting across quickly. They finally stopped in a large grove of trees in a sparsely populated neighborhood. It was too dark to tell what kind of trees they were, but they had large, flowering branches that hung close to the ground.

"Let's wait. I don't think anyone can see us here," Donovan said.

They waited in relative silence for a few minutes, speaking very little. The only sounds came from the ocean, only a few blocks away, and the breeze that blew lightly through the trees. There had been no traffic, but eventually a set of headlights came up the street, and the vehicle was going very slowly. Lauren let out a little gasp when she recognized the black Ford they'd seen earlier. It passed by, the lone occupant looking this way and that as he drove. After the car disappeared, Lauren could hear the beating of her heart as it competed with the sound of the surf and the constantly rustling leaves and blossoms.

Another car passed, and Lauren was relieved to see it was a patrol car, but her relief vanished when she saw a second car come by, driving with its headlights out. It looked like a light blue Grand Am, but it was hard to be sure in the darkness and with the overhanging branches. She knew someone with that kind of car, but also knew he couldn't be here.

After it disappeared, Donovan whispered, "That was strange for that car to have its lights off. I suppose it's too much to hope that they weren't looking for us."

Lauren didn't bother to mention whose car she'd thought it looked like. There was no way *he'd* be in Laie.

Suddenly Donovan reached inside his coat. "It's my phone vibrating," he said to Lauren. "Hello," he said softly, after recognizing the captain's cell phone number.

"I'm sorry I'm so slow," Captain Hafoko said. "There was an escape from the jail, and I had to run back there. It happened a couple of hours ago, but when I learned who it was, I decided that I needed to talk to the officers there. Again, I'm sorry, but I'm on my way now. You guys stay put, and I'll call you when I get there. I'm driving a silver Expedition, and I have two other officers following me."

"Do you have any cars in the area now?" Donovan asked.

"Yes, there are a couple of patrol units cruising the area. They're in marked cars," Captain Hafoko said.

"One of them passed a couple of minutes ago. But you don't have anyone in a black Ford Crown Victoria or something very similar?" Donovan asked.

"No, why do you ask?"

"Someone drove by a few minutes ago in a car of that description. We couldn't really see the driver, the only occupant, but he kept stopping and looking around. He never did get out," Donovan explained. "He spooked us, so we walked several blocks from where we were."

"Okay, if you see it again—" the captain started.

Donovan interrupted. "It went by our current location a little while ago. Same car, I'm positive. And it was going very slow."

"Be careful. Tell me where you are, and I'll have the patrol cars keep a closer eye on that neighborhood."

A few minutes later, a patrol car again cruised by. It was followed a minute later by the Grand Am with its lights off. Lauren glanced at Donovan in the darkness beside her. She could barely see his profile, but she knew that he was watching the Grand Am as it slowly drove out of their sight. She felt the hair standing up on the back of her neck. She almost mentioned the coincidence to Donovan, but resisted, feeling that she was letting fear get the best of her. She just had to be brave and wait. They would soon be with the captain, and then she'd confront Royce, and maybe this whole nightmare would come to an end.

The next time a patrol unit came past, it was driving in the opposite direction. And this time no one followed it. Lauren felt better and forced herself to relax. But her calm was short-lived. A third time, the Grand Am appeared. Twice more the marked units passed, but when the Grand Am didn't appear again, Lauren tried to tell herself she was working herself up over nothing.

The captain called again. "Everything okay?" he asked.

"Yes, we're fine," Donovan said. "Except we've seen a light blue Grand Am three times now. Each time it was following one of your patrol cars at quite some distance."

"That doesn't sound good," the captain said.

"And he had his lights off," Donovan said. "All three times he had his lights off."

"That's bad. We're hurrying. We won't be long now. I'll alert our patrol units about the Grand Am," Captain Hafoko said. "I'll have them stay close too. But I don't want you trying to flag one of them down. I'll explain why later."

Lauren had her head close to Donovan's in order to hear what the captain had to say. She leaned away when she heard him say he'd explain why later, and again she wondered if she did in fact know who was driving the Grand Am. She shivered as she tried to listen to Donovan's conversation with the captain. He was just saying good-bye when Lauren suddenly tensed at the sound of a breaking branch behind them in the darkness.

"Donovan," she whispered. "I think there's someone back there."

Donovan had just shut his phone and was returning it to his pocket. They listened together for a moment. Lauren was sure she heard something shuffling and that it was moving in their direction. Donovan grabbed her hand and tugged. "Come on," he whispered urgently, and she knew that he'd heard it too.

They moved together as silently as they could. Every few steps, they would stop and listen. Finally, Donovan whispered into Lauren's ear, "I don't hear it now."

"Me either," she whispered back.

"Okay," he said. "Let's stop here." They were in another dark clump of trees. They dropped to the ground near some thick shrubs and silently waited.

A set of headlights approached, and they both stood up in order to see over the bushes. They sighed in collective relief when they recognized a patrol car followed by a silver Expedition. Another car followed that, and Lauren assumed it was an unmarked police unit. All three of the vehicles stopped over a half block from where Lauren and Donovan were standing. The driver of the Expedition got out. The marked unit parked just in front of the Expedition, and the unmarked car parked behind. The rest of the officers got out and conversed for a minute. Then Donovan's phone vibrated. He was already holding it in his hand and answered quickly.

"Donovan," the captain said as Donovan turned the phone slightly from his ear and leaned close to Lauren so she could hear. "I'm in the area where you said you were earlier. There are two other units with me. I'll need to have you give me closer directions now."

"We can see you. You passed us. We are about a half block back."

"Great," the captain said, sounding relieved. "Stay put until we are as close as we can get before you come out of the darkness. The officers haven't seen the Grand Am, but we don't want to take any unnecessary chances."

"Nor do we," Donovan whispered.

"I don't want to alarm you, but the man who escaped from jail earlier may be in a Grand Am."

Lauren felt her knees go weak. *Surely it couldn't be . . .* she thought frantically. Donovan turned toward her. "Lauren, are you okay?" he asked urgently as he put an arm around her waist for support.

"I'll be fine," she said, trying to be brave, sure they were safe now with the police right there.

"Lauren isn't feeling well," he said into the phone. "Back up about a half block. And hurry."

The men got back in their cars and began backing. "You say when," Captain Hafoko said on the phone.

"Stop right there," Donovan said a moment later.

"Okay, what side of the street are you on?"

"We're to your right," Donovan answered.

"Wait a minute," the captain said. He then maneuvered the big Expedition to the edge of the street nearest to where Donovan and Lauren waited. The patrol car parked parallel to the Expedition in the middle of the street. The unmarked car parked behind them. The officers all got out, two watching the far side of the street, their guns drawn, the others facing Donovan and Lauren. "Okay, when I say to come, do it fast," the captain instructed. "Come together, and keep low. Go past the rear of my car and get between it and the patrol car."

For a moment, the captain looked up and down the street. He looked toward the neighboring yards, where a few lights had now come on in the houses. Lauren knew that they were attracting attention. She just wanted this to be over with. Captain Hafoko spoke again. "Okay, you can come now. Keep low and run fast. Don't slow down until you're between our cars."

Lauren hesitated, offering a silent prayer. Donovan took hold of her hand and pulled. "Let's go," he whispered. They moved slowly to the edge of the trees and shrubs. Lauren hesitated as she looked at the fifty feet they'd have to go in the open. Again, Donovan tugged. "Fast now," he said. Together, they ran, their heads down, bending forward at the waist.

They were within ten feet of the back of the Expedition when Lauren felt something strike her leg about the same time she heard the sharp report of a gun. She felt herself going down as officers began firing all around her.

"Lauren!" Donovan cried.

She felt him slip his arms beneath her legs and back and pick her up. He carried her the last few steps, dropping to his knees with her beside the rear tire of the car. She heard a bullet strike the body of the Expedition, and a scream rose in her throat, but she suppressed it when she heard Donovan shouting, "Lauren, are you okay?"

As suddenly as it had begun, the shooting was over. "I think I'm shot," she said as tears blinded her eyes and pain shot up her leg. "Did they get him?" she asked faintly, for she was almost certain now who had been following them in the darkness, and who had driven the Grand Am earlier.

"I don't think so. I don't think the officers could see anything but his muzzle flashes. At least that's what I heard one of them shout after I'd picked you up," Donovan said. "Where did it hit you?"

CHAPTER 26

Fleming received a call from the man he thought of as his insurance. "I got her," he said.

"You're sure?" Fleming asked.

"Of course I'm sure. Do you think I'm an idiot?" he said.

Fleming didn't comment on that. He still needed this young man to do his bidding. "What about Deru?"

"Didn't have time. There were six of them shooting at me. I'm lucky I got away without getting shot," he said.

"You let them see you?" Fleming asked, unable to keep his disgust from his voice.

"Nope. I stayed in the dark."

"Good. If you get another chance, take it," Fleming ordered, relieved.

"He's with the cops now. I don't think I can. Anyway, I'm tired. I've had a hard day. I'll try again tomorrow."

"Tomorrow may be too late. I need Deru taken care of now," Fleming fumed.

"We'll see," the young man said, and the phone went silent. Fleming had just been hung up on.

He was still fuming when he called Snake a minute or two later.

"Are you finished yet?" Fleming demanded.

"Still waiting," Snake drawled lazily.

"You wait too much. I need action."

"You said to wait."

"Never mind what I said before. The girl's taken care of. Find the guy," Fleming ordered.

"Hey, you got someone else up here we don't know about?" Snake asked. "I don't take no double-crossing."

"Calm down. You'll get paid the same. This other guy, it's personal with him. He's on his own. Is the device in Deru's car?"

"It is now. He starts the ignition—boom!"

"Fine, but don't wait for that. He might not come back to his car with the gal out of the picture. Find him." Fleming disconnected.

* * *

"That's the car, the black Ford," Donovan said.

They were on foot now, he and Captain Hafoko, two detectives, and two uniformed officers. They were looking toward the parking lot of the Laie Inn. Lauren, whose wound turned out to be superficial, had been taken to the nearest hospital for treatment. Donovan was still reeling from the emotions that had washed over him when he'd felt Lauren stumble in unison with the first gunshot. As frightening as recent events had been, he'd never experienced such terror in his life. And it hadn't been for him, but for her.

Fortunately, now he knew she'd be fine, just sore for a few days. But he still worried about her. And he wanted more than ever to help her out of this mess she was in.

"There are two guys in the car," the captain said. He was looking through a pair of binoculars. "One of them has been talking on a phone."

Donovan shook his head, determined to concentrate. Lauren was safe with those officers, he kept telling himself. And they had two men here, just waiting to be captured. But he couldn't help but think about the third, about the man who drove a Grand Am. He was certain who it was now. It was the man who'd shot Dexter and escaped from jail and who had tried to kill Lauren. He was still out there somewhere. But they needed to finish up here—then they could look for him, he reminded himself.

"We'll arrest them where they sit if you're sure it's them," the captain was saying.

"I'm sure of the car," Donovan said. "I'd have to get a closer look at the men to be able to tell you if they're the ones from the hotel last evening."

The captain turned to his men. "We've got enough to make an arrest. Let's pick them up."

The car was parked in the lot of the Laie Inn, but the engine started up and the car pulled toward the entrance of the parking lot.

"Take them!" Captain Hafoko yelled. "Donovan, you wait by your car."

The officers scrambled for their cars. Donovan, whose car was just a few feet away in the parking area of McDonald's, hurried over to it. He couldn't see what was happening, and he held his breath as he listened to the screeching of tires, then a single, very loud gunshot from maybe half a block away, followed by the distinct sound of metal striking metal and the breaking of glass. In spite of the commotion, Donovan's attention was attracted to a set of headlights that was turning off the highway toward him. He instinctively moved down on the far side of his small rental car, shielding himself from the lights. The car kept coming, and when Donovan took another quick look, he almost panicked. The car was the same light blue Grand Am that he'd seen earlier.

Leroy Provost.

The Grand Am's lights went off, and it stopped just short of the McDonald's parking lot. Donovan grabbed his cell phone and punched in the captain's number. He heard a door of the Grand Am open. The captain's voice came on the phone. "Leroy's here," Donovan whispered.

He didn't even dare look in the direction of the highway now. The only thing he could think of doing was keeping his car between himself and Leroy. He stayed low, his ears tuned to the steps he could now hear beside the Grand Am. They moved toward him for a moment. Then they stopped. Suddenly a siren began to wail, and he heard running footsteps. The door of the Grand Am slammed shut, tires shrieked, and Leroy was gone.

A moment later, the captain and one of the detectives, a Detective Kono, raced up. "That was him," Donovan said as he pointed in the direction he'd last seen the Grand Am.

The captain nodded and began speaking rapidly into his portable radio. Donovan asked Detective Kono, "Where is the hospital? I think I'll drive over and make sure Lauren's okay."

The officer gave him directions, and Donovan pulled his keys from his pocket.

He'd just unlocked the door when the captain said, "Wait a minute, Donovan. We've got those other two in custody. They aren't hurt, so a couple of my officers can take them to Honolulu. Let's leave your car for the moment and you can ride with me to check on Miss Olcott. I'd appreciate the company."

Donovan shut the door and locked the car, sticking his keys back in his pocket. They drove back to where the black Ford, a front tire shredded from the blast of a shotgun, rested against a truck that had been parked on the side of the highway. Two men in dark suits were shackled tightly in the backseat of the marked patrol unit. "Captain, a tow truck is coming for the Ford, but look what we found in it. A tracking unit."

Captain Hafoko turned to Donovan. "That's how they've been following you so easily. They must have planted a bug on your car sometime. I guess we can be grateful it was only a bug, not a bomb."

Lauren was bandaged and ready to go when they met up with her a few minutes later. "I'll be fine," she said. "Mostly what I got was a scare," she told Donovan. "The bullet didn't do anything more than open up a little bit of flesh. They disinfected it, stitched it up, bandaged me, and I'm fine, other than a little blood on my pants and a sore leg."

The captain drove them back to the motel. "We don't have much here, but we do want my laptop and Lauren's purse," Donovan said. "We left them in our rooms. Our luggage, what little we have, is still in the hotel in Waikiki. The rest of it is at the airport."

Lauren's purse was beneath the bed where she'd shoved it before they left the motel. The laptop was gone. "It wasn't in the Ford," the captain said.

"Then it must be outside somewhere. I hope they didn't ruin it," Donovan said.

They found it in a nearby alley, smashed. "I'm sorry," Lauren said. "I'll buy you a new one."

Donovan just shook his head. "It's nothing, Lauren. Don't worry about it. I'm just glad we sent the information you had on the disc to the captain and a few other places."

"Donovan," Captain Hafoko said, "with Leroy still on the loose, I think we better leave your rental here and you two can ride back with me to Honolulu. We'll worry about your car later."

On the way back, the captain told them what he planned to do next. "If it works, we'll have the proof we need to shut down the embezzlers, and maybe even save Paradise Pharmaceuticals before the day is over," he told them.

* * *

It was nearly two in the morning when the phone woke Fleming up. "What's going on?" he asked groggily.

"Just wanted you to know, we got the lawyer cornered," Snake said.

"Where are you now?" Fleming demanded.

"Tell you later, boss," Snake said, glowering at Captain Hafoko. "I'll call when the hit's gone down."

"Snake, I demand to know where you are." He listened for the reply, then looked at his phone. Snake had disconnected. He could only hope his men really were about to get Donovan this time. He couldn't wait any longer. He had to get Royce's wife to get Royce out of jail even if he had to force her to do it, Fleming decided in desperation. After Royce had things wrapped up on the computer, he'd take care of him without the help of anyone else, he promised himself as he caressed the little pistol he now carried in his pocket. He put his coat on and left, intending to pay a late-night visit to the Cantrell residence.

* * *

It was another ten minutes before Captain Hafoko's trap was fully set. After being quickly told what Royce and Fleming had been doing, Denise Cantrell proved to be not only willing to help the police, but quite eager. From the Cantrell residence, Denise called Fleming's cell phone. He answered on the second ring. "Hello, Denise," he said. "I was just coming over. I thought maybe we could go ahead and get Royce out of jail now."

Denise looked in alarm at Captain Hafoko, who whispered, "Keep to the plan."

She nodded. "Fleming, I'm going down to the jail myself to put up the bond to get Royce out," she said as smoothly as a professional. "I don't need your help."

"Decided not to let him rot in there, did you?" he said with the smugness that so infuriated her.

But she kept her cool. "I was angry. But you know I can't do that to Royce. He's my husband. I haven't been able to sleep, so I'm headed down there now. I have the bond worked out and they're expecting me."

"That's a good girl," Fleming said to Mrs. Cantrell, to Captain Hafoko, who was listening on another line, and to a sophisticated tape-recording device. "Wait up and I'll go with you."

"No, I can handle it," she said. "I'm ready to leave now."

"I can be there in fifteen or twenty minutes," Fleming insisted.

"No, I'll take care of it."

"Okay, if you insist, but when he gets home, have him call me. There's a critical matter at the office that he's got to help me with, and it can't wait."

Denise looked at Captain Hafoko, who nodded. "That might be kind of difficult," Denise said. "It's the middle of the night, but I suppose if you really need him . . ."

"I really need him," Fleming said, trying to control his anger. "All he has to do is meet me at the office like he should have done a few hours ago. It won't take more than an hour, and you can have him back. Then you can both get some beauty rest."

"I don't know, Fleming," she said, following her script as closely as she could. "The people at the jail said I have to keep him at home after I make his bail."

"Oh, phooey," Fleming scoffed. "Bail doesn't work that way. They're just giving you a hard time. Anyway, they won't have to know, now will they?"

"I guess not," she said. "But when you're finished, he's going to need some rest."

"I'm sure he will," Fleming said, thinking how surprised she'd be when Royce didn't come home. She'd think he'd decided to run from the law. "Okay, Denise," he said. "As soon as he's home, get him on the phone."

* * *

Despite the lateness of the hour and their lack of sleep, both Lauren and Donovan were reasonably alert. Lauren's leg hurt, but it only helped keep her awake. They were sitting together on the sofa in the Cantrell living room when Royce was ushered into his own home by a couple of officers. He had a large bandage on his forehead and one on the back of his head. His face was swollen and his eyes were red. When he spotted Lauren, his face lost all its color. She rose to her feet, and with Donovan at her side, she limped over to him. "Hello, Royce," she said kindly. "How are you doing?"

He didn't look her in the eye, but he responded. "I'm sorry, Lauren. I didn't mean for you to get hurt. I'm just a greedy fool, I guess."

Donovan and Lauren already knew that he'd made a full confession an hour earlier, and he'd done it without Lauren even needing to be present. Lauren looked at him, her face sad, as the officers led him into the kitchen, where he was about to make a phone call. "He's wasn't such a bad man, Donovan. He was a good boss. He's just a sucker for Fleming's promises. Now his life is ruined."

"And so are a lot of others," Donovan said coldly.

Lauren nodded. "I know that. It's just so unbelievable that he could turn so evil so fast," she said sadly.

Five minutes later, Denise Cantrell dialed the phone. When Fleming Parker answered, she said, "I've posted his bond. Royce is home now. But he's awfully tired."

"I don't care how tired he is. He has work to do. Put him on," Fleming snapped.

Royce took the phone, his hands shaking. "Sorry, Fleming. I didn't know you needed me at the office last night," he said.

"Say what you want for Denise's sake," Fleming growled. "I couldn't care less. But we are too close to finishing this thing for you to mess it all up now. You fool! Getting yourself locked up was stupid."

"Sorry," Royce said.

"You should be," Fleming snarled. "Be at the office in twenty minutes. And don't bring your wife."

"I'll be there in a few minutes," Royce promised.

Royce put the phone down, and Captain Hafoko turned off his little recording device and stood up. "Let's go make another arrest," he said to Detectives Kono and Salter.

* * *

Lauren and Donovan were sitting in the police station lobby when the detectives brought Fleming in nearly an hour later. His fat hands were cuffed uncomfortably behind his back, and his face radiated pure hatred. He didn't even acknowledge Lauren when he passed her. She looked up at Donovan. Despite herself, she couldn't keep from crying as she faced the man who had repeatedly tried to kill her. "I never did anything to him," she said.

Donovan shrugged his shoulders. "Neither did anyone else," he said.

"You two need some sleep," Captain Hafoko said as he walked up to them.

Donovan stood up. "And you don't?" he asked.

"I do," the captain admitted. "But I need to talk with Fleming first, if he'll talk. Would you two consent to getting some rest in a safe house here in town if I had someone take you over?"

"A hotel would be fine for me," Donovan said. "But I think Lauren should be in a safe house, with Leroy still running around out there. They haven't caught him yet, have they?"

The captain shook his head. "They found his car a little while ago. It's parked near the beach just outside of Laie. So either he's on foot somewhere or he's in a stolen car. Either way, we can't take a chance on you being anywhere but where we can keep you safe, Lauren," the captain said. "We'll take you to the same place where Ms. Likio is staying."

Lauren agreed, and then Donovan said, "I'll get a taxi and find a place to stay for a few hours. Then, if you don't mind, Captain, maybe one of your men could take me to Laie to get my rental car."

"I suppose we can do that," the captain said. "Or, like I told you earlier, I can have someone pick it up for you."

"No, I'll do it, but I could use a few hours of sleep first," Donovan said. "Then I suppose I should probably be getting back to Utah."

"Can't you wait a day or two?" Lauren asked, her eyes pleading. "Please don't go yet. Help us make sure everything is taken care of here."

"That'll be done with or without my help," he said. Then he smiled at her. "But I'll try to see you again before I fly out."

CHAPTER 27

Donovan's cell phone awoke him at eight o'clock that morning. He was groggy but in better shape after having received a few hours of sleep. He plucked the phone off the bedside stand, looked at the number, and moaned. He was too tired for another argument.

Donovan spoke into the phone. "Hi," he said, unable to put any cheer into his voice.

"Donovan, we have to talk," Kaelyn said.

"I'm not up to that at the moment."

"But I need to talk now," she insisted.

"I'm sorry, but I really think it would be better if we waited to talk in person. I'll be back in Vernal by tomorrow night at the latest. We can talk after that," he suggested, hoping that when they did they could end up still being friends to some extent, even though he was sure that was the most that would survive their shattered relationship.

"No, it has to be this morning," she said firmly. "I'll meet you at the airport."

Donovan was suddenly very suspicious. "What airport?" he asked.

"Honolulu—where do you think?" she said with a small giggle. "Surprise!"

Donovan was stunned. "You're here in Hawaii?"

"That's what I just said. I need to have you come pick me up."

"It'll take me about an hour to get there," Donovan told her. "I have to shower and shave—"

"You mean you weren't up yet?" she interrupted. "You never sleep this late."

"That's right," he said. "But I didn't get to bed until three hours ago. I've had a very long, very difficult night. Anyway, I'll need to catch a taxi because my rental car is up near the Polynesian Cultural Center. I had to leave it there yesterday."

"I don't get it, but that's okay. I can hardly wait to see you, Donovan," she said.

He didn't get it either. This was the girl who had broken off their engagement, and he'd quickly come to accept the fact that it was best for both of them. Seeing her now was going to be very awkward, but, he asked himself, what else could he do?

"Where will I find you?" he asked Kaelyn with a clear lack of enthusiasm.

She told him which terminal she was in. "I'll be by the luggage carousels. And please do hurry. I don't care if you don't take time to shower first."

"You don't understand. I've got to shower. And I've got to go somewhere and get some clothes. The ones I have are a little bloody, and my suitcase is still at the airport," he said. "So you'll just have to wait until I can get there."

"Well, okay," she responded. "I don't understand why your luggage is here and why you have blood on your clothes, but I'll be waiting since I don't have any other choice."

Even though he hurried, it took Donovan over an hour to accomplish all he needed to do and then ride to the airport. When he located Kaelyn, at first she looked grumpy. But her expression quickly changed into a smile, and she practically skipped toward him. She threw her arms wide, like she expected an embrace, but he didn't give her one. He tried to be polite, but he was also direct. "Hi. These yours?" he asked as he reached for her suitcase and carry-on bag.

"Yes," she said, a hurt look appearing in her eyes.

Donovan picked them up and said, "I hope my rental car's okay. We'll have to take a taxi to get it."

"What are you talking about?" she asked.

"I came in a taxi. I told you that earlier. I left my rental car in Laie early this morning."

"Why did you do that?" she asked.

"It's a long story, and I don't think it would interest you," he told her. "Oh, and I guess I should get my luggage while I'm here."

She gave him that puzzled look again, which he ignored. "Let's put your luggage on a cart," he suggested. "My stuff is in a different terminal. Come on, we need to hurry."

When they finally found Donovan's luggage, he realized that he should pick up Lauren's too. So he said to the attendant who was helping him, "There should also be a suitcase for Lauren Olcott. Here's her claim ticket."

"A suitcase for Lauren?" Kaelyn said snippily. "Where have you two been traveling?"

"Kaelyn, please," Donovan said as patiently as he could. "I have been very busy. Lauren and I are both lucky to be alive. You wouldn't believe it if I told you everything that has happened. You also wouldn't be interested."

"This is all about you and her, isn't it? I should have known," Kaelyn said, her eyes flashing with indignation.

"Actually no, it's not about me and her," he said. "She's someone who asked for help and I came to see if I could give some. I'm about done and will be going home soon. I told you that before."

"Have you kissed her?" Kaelyn asked stubbornly.

"Good grief, Kaelyn, you haven't listened to a thing I've said. No, I have not kissed her."

"But you've wanted to," she said.

"I haven't thought about it," he told her.

"But she's really pretty, isn't she?"

"Yes, as a matter of fact she is, but my relationship with Lauren is not a romantic one," he said.

"But you like her, don't you?" Kaelyn asked, and Donovan could see her eyes were getting misty. He hoped there wasn't going to be a scene. "Donovan," she said as her anger dissolved into tears, "I'm sorry. I shouldn't have come."

"But you did, and as you'll soon see, Hawaii is a beautiful place," he responded with a smile.

"Donovan, I'll see if I can get a flight home. You go ahead and finish whatever you have to do."

"Sir, here is the missing luggage," the attendant interrupted.

"Thank you," Donovan said, and he loaded the suitcases onto the cart. They walked a few steps, then he turned to Kaelyn. "Kaelyn," he said gently, "I was really hurt when you called off our engagement. But I've thought about it a lot, and you were right, you know. It would never have worked between you and me. I'm sorry I didn't realize that a long time ago."

"I didn't want to face up to that either. I didn't want to pass up a chance to marry such a great guy. You know, it's hard to admit," she said tearfully, "but when I prayed about whether or not I should marry you, I never got a confirmation. I've been fighting it and fighting it. I think I've made myself a little crazy over it. I wanted to marry you, and still do, but I know I shouldn't, and now that I'm with you again, I can tell that you know we shouldn't," she said. She wiped her eyes, then put on a brave smile. "You can go now. I'll be fine."

"Kaelyn," he said with the caring smile she'd grown accustomed to, "you're here now. You'd just as well make a vacation of it."

But she shook her head. "No, I couldn't enjoy it. I have just one more question, Donovan. Did you really only come over because Lauren needed help?"

"Yes," he said. "That's the only reason."

"I misjudged you, didn't I?"

"That's two questions," he said.

"But I did, didn't I?" she insisted.

"You did us both a favor. Think about it. I have a way of irritating you. I don't mean to, but I do, don't I?"

"Yes," she said with lowered eyes. "You can be so infuriating."

"Marriage isn't going to work if there's a lot of anger, is it?"

"No," she agreed. Then she said, "Sorry to beat the issue to death, but even the last time, when I got so mad at you on the phone, were you only coming to help again?"

"That's right."

"But if you come again, it'll be because you want to see her, won't it?" she asked.

Donovan said lightly, "I've lost count of the number of questions. No more, okay?"

"Okay."

"Come on. I really do need to get back."

She shook her head. "No, you go finish what you were doing," she said. "I need to see about arranging a flight."

"Hey, we can still be friends," he said. "Come on, let me show you around. My car is at the Cultural Center. Maybe we could get tickets and let you see it while you're here. We could go to Pearl Harbor and maybe a few other sights too. Then we can go home together in a day or two."

Kaelyn didn't know if she could enjoy herself with Donovan right now, but she thought maybe the sights of Hawaii would at least be less depressing than returning to Vernal's snow and fog. "Are you sure?" she asked.

"I'm sure," he responded.

Over an hour later, the taxi pulled into Laie. A police car raced by, its lights flashing and its sirens blaring. Donovan got a sick feeling in the pit of his stomach, but he told himself that it had nothing to do with him or with Lauren, that he could just pick up his car and he and Kaelyn could drive back to Honolulu, deliver Lauren her luggage, and then spend the day sightseeing.

When they approached the Cultural Center, there were more sirens, and smoke was rising from beyond the parking lot—at about the location of the McDonald's restaurant. The taxi driver said, "Did you say your car was at McDonald's?"

"That's right."

"It looks like there's trouble there."

"It sure does," Donovan said. He glanced at Kaelyn, whose eyes were wide with fear.

"Hey, it's okay. It can't be anything to do with me," he assured her.

But it had a lot to do with him. An officer stopped the taxi. "There's been a car blown up," he said. "I'm afraid this road is closed."

Donovan couldn't see past the police cars, the fire trucks, and an ambulance. So he asked, "Was it a little red car that blew up?"

"Yes, as a matter of fact," the officer said suspiciously. "Sir, do you know something about this? Maybe you better come with me."

"I think it's my car," Donovan said. "And I'm sure the bomb was meant for me."

Donovan's cell phone rang, and he pulled it from his pocket as he climbed from the taxi. "Hello," he said as he took Kaelyn's hand and helped her out as well.

"Donovan, I'm glad I reached you. I don't think you'll want to go to Laie. There was a bomb planted in your car," Captain Hafoko told him.

"Yes, so I see," Donovan said.

"Are you already up there?"

"I am. What happened, or do you know yet?"

"I'm on my way from Honolulu right now. But I understand that someone tried to hot-wire your car," the captain said. "Had that not happened, it would have been you."

"And Kaelyn," he said, looking at his former fiancée, who looked like she was about to be sick.

"Who?" Captain Hafoko asked.

"Never mind. I'll explain when you arrive. Or do you even need me here? My taxi hasn't left yet, so we could go back to Honolulu," Donovan said.

"Lauren told me you were planning on flying home today or tomorrow," the captain said. "But it might be helpful if you waited. If you want to go back to Honolulu, go ahead. I'll call you later and we can meet at my office. I'll have them bring Lauren there too. There are a few things you both should know."

"Thanks, that'll be fine," Donovan said.

After hanging up, he said to Kaelyn, "I'm sorry. Now you can see what I've been going through over here."

"Somebody tried to kill you," she said. Her face was very pale, and she appeared to be dazed.

"Again," he said. "Hey, we don't have to go to Honolulu yet. We can still go to the Cultural Center."

Kaelyn shook her head. "I don't think so. I'm not feeling too well."

She was quiet most of the way back to Honolulu, but finally began to come out of it a little and said, "You've been involved in something really dangerous, haven't you."

He smiled tiredly and said, "That's an understatement. The bomb in that car was meant for me, or more likely for Lauren and me."

"But the danger's over now?" she asked.

"I sure hope so," he said lightly, but he wasn't positive, although he wasn't about to tell Kaelyn that. He couldn't help but wonder where Leroy was now, and he also wondered who else might still be on the loose that had been involved in the plot, who else might still have evil designs toward him for his interference.

"I'm sorry I've been so awful," Kaelyn said. "Where are we going now?"

"To the airport," he said.

"But I thought the police decided they didn't want you to leave yet," she said. "Or are you thinking that maybe I better go now after all?"

Donovan forced a chuckle. "No, I told you we'd go see a few places, and I meant it. The least I can do is show you a good time. But we can't keep running around in a taxi, so I thought I'd rent another car at the airport," he said, thinking how unlikely it would be that anyone would rent him one if they knew what a bad history he had with rental cars.

He got one all right, but he used a different agency. When he and Kaelyn were finally on their way from the airport, Donovan called the captain and asked him when they needed to meet. "Give me an hour and a half or so," Captain Hafoko said. "And oh, I suppose you guessed, but the man who tried to steal your car died. He never stood a chance. What's left of him has been shipped to the medical examiner. We hope to be able to get an identity. He'll be someone's son, and they'll want to know what happened to him."

After clicking off, Donovan thought that whoever it was had received swift and rather harsh justice. But he was grateful it wasn't him and Kaelyn. He looked at his watch. "Hey, we have a little over an hour. That would be just enough time to see one of the sights," he told Kaelyn.

"Pearl Harbor?" she asked.

"No, we don't have enough time to go there," he said. "We'll do that tomorrow. But we do have time to visit Kali Lookout. That's a unique place, one you'll enjoy, and it's close by."

The drive to the lookout was stunning. "It's hard to believe there can be a place so pretty so close to such a big city," Kaelyn said in awe as they drove beneath the sprawling branches of huge trees and wound their way up the mountain. When they pulled into the parking area, they parked the car and walked up to the scenic lookout. Dozens of people milled about, their hair blowing in their faces, the children shouting and laughing.

"It's windy all of a sudden," Kaelyn said. "Is it going to storm?"

"No, the wind somehow funnels off the mountain here. In fact, after we take a look over the edge, we'll walk down to where the wind blows the hardest. It is unbelievable," he told her.

Kaelyn squealed in delight when they stepped to the fence. Before them lay one of the most spectacular views on the island of Oahu. The drop-off at the lookout was straight down and fell into dense jungle hundreds of feet below. The green foliage fanned out for miles, at places giving way to stretches of city bordered by stately green mountains. In the distance, the ocean met the sandy beaches where the surf rolled in, just tiny strips of white from their vantage point.

"Legend has it that warring armies would throw people over the edge here and that the wind was so strong blowing up the face of the cliffs that the bodies couldn't fall—they'd just bounce around," Donovan told Kaelyn.

She gave him a skeptical look, but she also grabbed at her hair, which looked like it was being snatched right off her head. She laughed, and he said, "Let's go down there," pointing to a trail that looked like it had once been a narrow road. "Then you'll discover the real force of the wind."

Kaelyn grabbed Donovan's hand as they stepped past the point of the mountain that rose sharply above them. The wind was so strong it was difficult to stand up, and it was so loud that it was impossible to speak to each other. She clung tightly to him, as if in fear of being swept away. For the next fifteen minutes or so they strolled down the trail where the wind wasn't so bad, then they returned and felt again the savage power of the wind.

After they'd returned to the lookout, Kaelyn asked, "Does it ever quit blowing?"

"They say it never does," he said as he looked back toward the parking area. A small gray car was just rounding the upper end. It was too old to be something a tourist would drive. And when Donovan saw that it had no license plates, he felt an all-too-familiar twist in his gut.

Kaelyn didn't notice his distraction and said, "Oh, it couldn't blow all the time. Not like this."

But he didn't hear her, for he was watching the car as it started to approach the exit of the parking lot. It was going way too fast, he was thinking. A child who darted away from a parent could get hit.

Kaelyn grabbed his hand. "Hey, are you still with me?" she asked.

"Oh, yes, did you say something?" he asked, even as he wondered what the gray car might have been up to.

"We were talking about the wind."

"Oh, yeah," he said. "They say it not only never stops, but that it is much harder at certain times of the year."

"We don't have to leave already, do we?" she asked.

Before Donovan could answer, a woman shouted from a hundred feet beyond them. "Joe, the horn's honking. I think our car's been broken into!"

A man Donovan assumed was her husband broke into a run from just behind him. Donovan shouted, "Hurry, Kaelyn, let's see what's going on down there."

As they neared their car, which was parked near the farthest point in the lot, he could hear the blaring of two horns. It only took a minute to figure out that one of the cars was his newly rented Pontiac. The other one was next to it, and a distraught lady was standing there as Donovan and her husband ran up.

"Don't touch anything," Donovan said as he dug in his pocket for his phone.

"But someone has been in my car," the man protested.

"Yes, and mine too," Donovan said as he began punching in a number. "I'll have the police on the phone in just a moment."

The man's horn quit honking, and a moment later, Donovan's did the same. "Captain," Donovan said as soon as the phone was answered, "I'm at Kali Lookout and my car has been broken into. So has the one next to it."

"Don't touch a thing," the captain said. "I'm on my way, and I'll have a patrol car dispatched at once. Move the people way back. We don't want to take any chances."

Donovan disconnected and said to the couple who were standing next to him, "The cops are on the way."

"I'd just as well see what's been taken," the man said, clearly upset by the intrusion into his vacation.

"You can't do that," Donovan said.

Before he could finish explaining why, Kaelyn said, "Donovan, could it be another bomb? Are they still trying to kill you?"

Those words and the look of terror on her face were all it took to convince the tourists to move far back and leave their car untouched. Donovan took charge and kept everyone away. He could still visualize the damage that bombs had caused to both his red rental car and the one that had blown up in front of his house in Vernal.

Ten minutes later a patrol car drove in, followed shortly by an unmarked police car. He recognized the driver as Detective Kono, someone else who must have had very little sleep. He didn't remember having seen his partner. But Donovan was both pleased and worried when he realized that there was a passenger in the backseat. Lauren's face had a look of fear etched on it. Their eyes met briefly, then Detective Kono spoke to him.

"Hello, Donovan," he said. "Trouble seems to follow you and the cars you rent. Lucky you weren't in the red car when it blew."

"Real lucky, Detective Kono," he agreed. "Were you just headed to headquarters with her?" He nodded toward the detective's car.

"Yes, but the captain called and said to get up here," he said. "We have a bomb unit on the way too."

"Thanks," he said as he watched Lauren get out of the car.

She moved around it and walked over to Donovan. "Was Leroy up here?" she asked, voicing his own dark suspicions.

"I don't know. I think whoever did this was driving an old gray car."

"He was," said the lady whose car had been broken into. "In fact, there were two men, and the car didn't have license plates."

"Oh, Donovan, will it never end?" Lauren asked hopelessly.

"It will," he assured her.

"I'm just so sorry I got you into all this," she went on.

"Are you Lauren?" a voice asked from over Donovan's shoulder.

Donovan moaned inwardly and turned. "I guess it's time you two met," he said, trying to put some cheer into his voice, and failing miserably. He told each who the other was.

Kaelyn was stiff as she said, "It's nice to meet you. I'd love to get to know you better."

Lauren was close to shock and seemed at a loss for words for a moment. "You came all the way over here?" she asked at last.

Kaelyn nodded. "I was worried about Donovan," she said.

"With good cause," Lauren responded. Suddenly—and without another word—she returned to the patrol car and climbed in.

"She's even prettier than in the picture," Kaelyn remarked as Donovan watched Lauren wipe her eyes and then lay her head back against the seat.

* * *

Lauren was in a hurricane of emotions as she walked into the police station with Detective Kono and his partner thirty minutes later. Ahead of them, Captain Hafoko accompanied Donovan and Kaelyn, who was walking so close to Donovan that their arms kept brushing. Lauren had noticed the absence of a ring on her finger, but surely the woman wouldn't be in Hawaii if she hadn't reconsidered her breakup.

She was angry with herself that she felt more preoccupied with Donovan than with all the terrible things that had happened the past few days. People had died, the company she loved was near collapse, deceit and greed had consumed colleagues she'd known and trusted—but what hurt the most was that another woman was with the man she couldn't stop thinking about.

The captain ushered everyone into a small conference room. Lauren and Donovan exchanged smiles of relief when they were joined by Milo Thurman, CEO of Paradise Pharmaceuticals, and Ken Fujimoto, the senior partner of Dexter's law firm, as well as a couple of men who were introduced as prosecutors. Kaelyn reluctantly agreed to wait in another room, since the proceedings would be confidential.

After everyone was seated, the captain took charge. "We think, with the help of Mr. Royce Cantrell and Mr. Dexter Drake, who have been very cooperative, that Paradise Pharmaceuticals can be saved from ruin. However, not without a great deal of cost. Already we've identified staggering losses in money, contracts, and, most tragically, human life." He then briefly recounted the chain of events as they had been pieced together, not much of which was new to Lauren.

"So who exactly was involved?" Donovan asked. "Have Royce and Dexter identified all of them?"

"We think so, and we have reason to believe they are telling the truth," the captain said. "Of course, there are Fleming, Royce, and Dexter. Mr. Drake's involvement was a little unusual in that he had originally planned to help keep the crime under cover and help the other group members leave the country, but he himself intended to stay here. You see, there was nothing to implicate him in the crime if everything went smoothly. Recently, however, he revised his plan in that he would assist in the cover-up, and then gain some glory in the covert trial. He thought he had everything perfectly planned, but being shot blew his plans out of the water."

Ken Fujimoto spoke up. "Lauren, I'm so sorry. If I'd only known. I got the e-mail you sent, and I asked Dexter to look into it immediately. He told me, after a couple of days, that there was nothing to it, that it was a hoax. I trusted him."

"So did I," Lauren said. "Is he going to be all right?"

"He'll live," Ken said darkly.

Lauren turned to Captain Hafoko. "Were Dr. Mitsui and Billie Maio involved?"

"Dr. Mitsui was the most tragic victim of all," the captain said. "She was totally innocent. She died because she got in Fleming's way. However, her assistant, Dr. Rhoades, a seemingly quiet and intelligent man, was very much a part of it. He's the one who substituted the drugs for Dr. Mitsui's sedative. Billie, I'm afraid, was also involved. It turns out that her job was to make sure Mr. Thurman here didn't get wind of anything, and if he did, to steer him away."

"But she was killed," Lauren protested.

"She got cold feet," the captain said. "Dr. Rhoades used the same drug on her as he did on you, only it was a stronger dose. Dexter claims it wasn't meant to kill her. Royce said he had protested their using it at all. But Fleming didn't tolerate people who were not loyal."

Milo Thurman snorted. "Who's he to expect loyalty?"

"There was another man involved, but he came in later," the captain said. "And only Royce and Fleming knew of his involvement."

Just then the door opened. It was Detective Kono, and he said, "Captain, the information you wanted just came in."

"Excuse me for just a moment," Captain Hafoko said.

He stepped out, talked very briefly with the detective, then stepped back into the room. "Donovan, you'll be relieved to know that there were no bombs in the cars at Kali Lookout."

Donovan sighed. Lauren caught his eye and gave him a weak smile, which he returned.

"Common car burglary was all it was. That particular spot is notorious for that," the captain explained. "Did you have any bags or valuables in the car?"

"There were suitcases," Donovan stated.

"If there were any suitcases in the car, they were taken," the captain said. "One of my officers is bringing the car down, Donovan. We'll make a complete inventory later and give you a report. I'm assuming your friend from Utah had something in there as well."

He nodded, thinking how upset Kaelyn would be about the theft, then said, "Sorry, Lauren, so did you. I'd picked up the luggage we left at the airport."

"Well, it was nice of you to get it for me. It's the thought that counts, right?" She shrugged then said, "Captain, you were about to tell us who the other party was."

"Yes, so I was. He wasn't part of it at first, but like you, Lauren, he discovered some irregularities. But unlike you, he decided to nose in on the action," Captain Hafoko said. Then he turned toward Donovan. "He was the one who was blown up in your car, according to the report Detective Kono just delivered. The final conspirator was Leroy Provost.

"He was the wild card in it all. His motives were both money and revenge. Only Royce and Fleming knew of his involvement. According to Royce, Fleming would have had him killed, except that he could see a use for him. As you know, it was his chocolates, Lauren, that made you sick in the first place. His anger was directed at both you and Dexter, though Dexter had no idea about the hatred he fostered. He was the one who shot Dexter at the bank, as I'm sure you and Donovan already figured out. I'm sorry."

Ken Fujimoto stood. "I've got another appointment and will need to be excused," he said. He walked around the table and held his hand out to Donovan. "Obviously I have a vacancy in my firm. I could use an honest and bright attorney to fill the slot. There will be others applying, I'm sure. But call if you're interested. If you're anywhere near as good as you seem, you'd have a good shot at getting on."

The meeting broke up shortly thereafter, but Lauren managed to catch Donovan before he'd left the room to go find Kaelyn. "So, is the wedding on again?" she asked him, trying to smile.

"Oh, Kaelyn? No. She came here to try to patch things up, but it didn't take long for us to come to an understanding that it's better for us to go our separate ways."

Relief washed over Lauren, rejuvenating her in a way that the little sleep she'd gotten the previous night hadn't been able to.

"Will she be flying home today, then? And will you be staying a little longer?"

"I feel I need to take her to a couple of sights, just to make her trip worthwhile, but then both of us will need to get back to Utah." Donovan could see Lauren's disappointment, so he quickly added, "I would love to stay longer, but since I can't, I promise to call you as soon as I get home."

"That will be nice. And will you call me again?"

"Sure. I'll call you again."

"And again after that?" Lauren persisted, a smile tugging at the corners of her mouth.

"Again and again and again," Donovan said, grinning broadly.

EPILOGUE

Three Months Later

As the plane touched down, Donovan wondered again what his decision would be. After corresponding and completing a couple of phone interviews, he'd agreed to meet with Ken Fujimoto and his partners for a final interview. The money that was being talked about was several times what he was making in Vernal, but he honestly didn't know what he wanted to do. He enjoyed his independence working as a one-man law firm. Would he like the pressure of working for other people, of worrying about whether he was producing enough billable hours to please them? He wasn't at all sure.

He loved Vernal, except for the extreme cold and that terrible fog that came every winter. He also liked Hawaii. It was always warm. It was exotic, aromatic, and exciting. But it was far from his family and friends. And it was also small. You could only go so far in any direction before you met the ocean. Would that become too confining for a country boy like himself? he wondered.

Again he thought about the salary Ken had hinted at. It was staggering, even adjusting for the higher cost of living. And when he'd mentioned it to a couple of his colleagues in Vernal, they'd both said, "What's to decide?" They each wished it could be them, they'd informed him. They made it clear that they'd be gone the next day if they had such an opportunity. Donovan just didn't know. There were so many things to consider. Anyway, the firm could decide he wasn't the best choice.

At least he wasn't worried about leaving a girlfriend behind in Utah. The split with Kaelyn had been final, and he hadn't dated anyone since returning to Vernal. He felt ready to date, but the woman who was constantly on his mind was in Hawaii. *And if I moved to Honolulu we could see each other. But what if it doesn't work out?* he thought. *Well, so what? Is it so bad to live in Hawaii? Of course not! And I could always move back. I could reopen my practice there. It's not like I'd be stuck with my job decision for the rest of my life. Besides, isn't Lauren worth taking the chance?*

In the last three months, Donovan and Lauren had talked on the phone and e-mailed regularly. He knew she'd found her family and was trying to strengthen her connection with them. She had become involved in the Church, and she was working hard at helping rebuild the company two of her former boyfriends had helped tear down. Even long distance, he knew he had begun to fall in love with her, but he needed more in-person interactions to really know where the relationship might lead. Up to now they had kept their relationship very light, on a "just friends" level. And after what he'd experienced with Kaelyn, he didn't want to rush into anything without being sure they were truly right for each other. He felt good about pursuing the relationship further, but hadn't had any spiritual confirmations regarding anything as serious as marriage yet.

He grabbed his carry-on bag and started up the aisle. *So, is this home?* he wondered as he entered the airport terminal and looked out the windows.

When he left the secure area, he spotted Lauren and his heart quickened. She was even more beautiful than he'd remembered. He'd told her when he'd be arriving, but he hadn't asked her to pick him up when he flew in. Their eyes met, and she surged forward, her long, dark hair bouncing, her face lit up in a welcoming grin. They shared a quick embrace, and then stood back and gazed at one another.

"Three months is a long time," she said. "You saved my life and then left. I've missed you, Donovan Deru."

"And I've missed you," he replied.

"I've got two days off, so I can chauffeur you while you're here."

"What? Don't you trust me to rent a car?" Donovan protested.

Lauren laughed. "I might, but I doubt the rental companies will."

"Okay, okay. So I guess we should get my bags and head to my hotel."

"But only long enough for you to check in. And then, since your appointment with Mr. Fujimoto is at two, we have just enough time to go someplace nice for lunch. Does that sound good to you?"

"Oh yes, I'm starved," Donovan said.

"And just think, we can eat without worrying about getting shot at or blown up."

"Won't that be nice." He chuckled. "Those were frightening days."

"They were," Lauren agreed. "But you made them bearable for me. Speaking of frightening, are you nervous about the interview?"

"Of course I am," he said.

"Well, I've got a surprise for you that should help get your mind off it."

"A surprise? What is it?"

"You'll see. But you'll have to be patient. It's waiting at the restaurant."

Not much later, Lauren and Donovan pulled up at an impressive-looking Japanese restaurant. As a hostess walked them to their table, Donovan suddenly shouted, "Ned! Vivian!" making all the other patrons stare. Their stares turned to smiles, however, as they saw the tall, dark-haired man warmly embrace an older Hawaiian woman and shake hands vigorously with an even older Japanese man.

"This is a good surprise," Donovan said to Lauren.

"I thought you'd like it," Lauren replied smugly.

Over lunch the four friends happily chatted about their recent activities. Vivian had recently acquired a kitten. Her tomcat had at first been wary of the newcomer, but Vivian insisted that now the two were like littermates. Ned agreed that the two got along nicely and admitted that he was very fond of the new little fluff ball himself.

Mostly it was just nice to be able to talk together without worrying about plots and intrigue. Every once in a while Lauren realized she had no idea what the conversation topic was; she was too engrossed in watching Donovan as he smiled, laughed, and talked. She knew that she cared deeply for him, but was still trying to make sense of her feelings.

As well as frequently talking to her bishop, Lauren had been to a counselor recently to help her deal with the grief and inner turmoil of the Paradise Pharmaceuticals scandal. One of the things that had come up was her feelings for Donovan. She had realized that some of her affection might have been caused by how he had played the part of the knight in shining armor for her. But now, as she watched him across the table from her, she knew that there was more to her feelings than that. This was a man who had proven himself. This was a man worth getting to know better.

All too soon, lunch was over and Donovan had to get to his interview. Vivian and Ned wished him luck and invited him to visit them later. He promised he would, then got into the car with Lauren.

"Hey, I think that did the trick!" he said.

"What?" Lauren asked, confused.

"I'm not nervous anymore!"

And if any of his nervousness came back, it certainly didn't show itself during the interview that afternoon. He answered all the law firm partners' questions with confidence, and asked them a few well-thought-out questions himself. When it was over, the partners asked him to give them just a few minutes.

"How did it go?" Lauren asked when he came out of the conference room.

"Seems like it went well," Donovan said. "But you never know."

Only five minutes had passed when he was invited back in and offered the job at an even greater salary than had been discussed before. "You're just the man we're looking for," Ken said. "So what do you say? How soon can you start?"

"May I have a little time?" Donovan said.

"Take what time you need," Ken said confidently. "And feel free to talk it over with the young lady. I think I know what she'd like you to do." He smiled as Donovan felt his face flush.

When Donovan again left the room, Lauren was still standing nervously where he'd left her. "Did they offer you the job?" she asked.

"They did."

"What are you going to do?"

"What do you think I should do?" he countered.

For a moment she was quiet, and she studied his face. "Can we talk about this outside?" she finally asked.

"Sure, but I do want your thoughts," he said.

As soon as they'd left the building, Lauren turned to him. "I'm going to be frank with you. I would like very much for you to move here. I think it's only fair that you know that when making your decision. That being said, I think you should do whatever you want to do. I will still be your friend, no matter what you decide."

He nodded his head thoughtfully. "Well, it is cold in Vernal in the winter, and there's a lot of fog," he said, watching her closely. He could see the corners of her mouth moving upward just slightly. "But there's one problem with the idea of living near all these warm, sunny beaches."

Her brow wrinkled. "What's that?"

"I don't know how to surf."

She smiled openly now. "Oh, I know just the person to help you overcome that. As long as you don't want to go on Sundays!"

ABOUT THE AUTHOR

Clair M. Poulson was born and raised in Duchesne, Utah; he spent many years patrolling the highways and enforcing the law in Duchesne County as a highway patrolman and deputy sheriff, followed by two years of service in the U.S. Army Military Police Corps. He completed his twenty-year law enforcement career with eight years as Duchesne County Sheriff. For the past fifteen years, Clair has served as a justice court judge in Duchesne County.

Clair also does a little farming. His main interest is horses, although he has raised a variety of other livestock, including cattle, pigs, and sheep. Both Clair and his wife currently help their oldest son run Al's Foodtown, the grocery store in Duchesne.

He met his wife, Ruth, while they were both attending Snow College. They are the parents of five married children and grand-parents of twelve. Ruth has been a great support to Clair in all of his endeavors and now assists him with his writing by proof-reading and making suggestions.

Clair has always been an avid reader, but his interest in creating fiction found its beginning many years ago when he told bedtime stories to his small children. They would beg for just one more story before going to sleep. He still practices that hobby with his grandchildren. He uses his life's experiences in law enforcement and the judicial arena to help him develop plots for his novels.